THE FROZEN RIVER

CLARE FLYNN

CRANBROOK PRESS

CRANBROOK PRESS

THE FROZEN RIVER

Copyright © 2018 by Clare Flynn

This is a work of fiction.

Cover design JD Smith Designs

ISBN 978-0-9933324-9-4

1

*S*he could hear the doctor's footsteps on the linoleum floor of the bedroom above. He'd come to certify that her mother was dead, and Ethel didn't want to be in the room with him when he did it. Not that there was any doubt. She'd held the mirror from her powder compact against her mother's lips. She'd seen them do that in films, but it felt strange, disrespectful, doing it herself. They also pulled the lids down and put coins on dead people's eyes to keep them shut, but she hadn't needed to do that, as her mother's eyes had been closed anyway for many hours. Ethel was grateful for that – she would have hated to see her mother's dead eyes when they had always been so very alive and ready with a smile.

She got up and went to fill the kettle, in case the doctor wanted a cup of tea before he left. She didn't want one herself. A glass of something stronger than her occasional port and lemon would be welcome, but there was no alcohol in the house.

Glancing at the clock on the kitchen wall, she saw it was ten o'clock. Too late to go down the road to tell Aunty Chris that her sister had passed away. Ethel dreaded doing that. Dreaded also that her aunt might blame her for encouraging her to go home earlier that evening, saying that Vi would surely last the night out. But when the end came, it came quickly – a sudden change in breathing that, within a few minutes, faded to a flutter and then stopped altogether. Ethel had sat by the bed, uncomprehending at first. Unprepared.

When she was able to move, she had combed out her mother's hair, straightened the bed clothes and went next door to telephone the doctor. She should have gone for Aunty Chris at the same time, but she didn't want to leave her mother's body alone in the house. 'Her body'.

Strange how quickly she had become a body rather than Mum.

She heard the doctor's heavy tread on the stairs. He came into the kitchen and refused her offer of tea. Ethel looked at him, taking in his tired features, his overweight body and the worn tweed suit he wore every day.

Handing her a piece of paper, he said, 'Heart failure. I'm sorry, Miss Underwood.'

Ethel took the paper. 'I thought you said she'd last through Christmas.' As soon as the words were out, she realised she was being unfair.

'I know. I really believed she would, but it's hard to predict these things.' He drew his lips into a narrow line. 'You'll need to take that to register the death. Is there anyone to help you?' He looked at her with concern.

'I'll be fine.' She gave him a tight smile. 'I'm an old hand at this now.'

He shook his head. 'I'm so sorry, Miss Underwood. Both your parents and your brother. You've had more than your fair share of grief. Is there anyone you can stay with tonight?'

'My Aunty Chris. She's just down the street.' Ethel handed him his hat. 'Goodnight, Dr Farrell. And thank you for coming out in this weather.'

After he'd gone, she sat at the kitchen table and lit a cigarette. No way was she staying at Aunty Chris's. The smoke curled upwards and the kitchen clock ticked in the silent house. She didn't want to go to bed though. Didn't want to go upstairs and climb into her bed in the room next to where her dead mother lay.

The realisation that she was now completely alone in the world struck her like a blow. Even though she'd known her mum was dying – known it for some time – she hadn't confronted the implications.

Her father died before the war. His heart had let him down too – in his case not the slow chronic erosion Violet had experienced, but a coronary that felled him in one explosive moment as he was enjoying a pint of best bitter in the public bar of his local pub.

Her brother, Mark, had survived the war, but died in a car accident last year. And here she was now, about to plan another funeral.

Ethel looked around the kitchen, at the old enamel stove, the sink with a crack in it, the glass-panelled back door that looked out onto a grim little yard that housed the privy. When the other houses in the street began putting in bathrooms, Vi said they'd better things to do with their money. 'That privy's seen me through two wars. If we could manage to get to it in the blackout, we can manage to use it now.'

Ethel hadn't bothered to argue with her. They were dependent on her mother's small widow's pension and the money Ethel earned in the hairdressing salon. But at least the house was paid for.

What was she going to do? She was more alone and lonely than she'd ever felt. Even after Greg, her fiancé, had died from a brain haemorrhage. He'd been defending his best friend, Jim. Their corporal, the man who'd started a brawl and struck him down, had been court-martialled and sent home to Canada in disgrace. Ethel had gone from being enveloped in happiness and love, to a grief-stricken woman who, at only twenty-two, felt her life was over.

Her mum had been the one who'd kept her going. Given her a reason to keep 'buggering on' as Mr Churchill used to say. Cousin Joan had helped too. But Joan had gone to Canada six years ago as a war bride in the middle of 1946, leaving Ethel behind in Aldershot.

Ethel got up and lit the burner under the kettle. If she was going to sit here brooding all night, she might as well fuel herself with tea.

Would it have been easier if Greg had been killed by enemy action? The pain might have been greater. No, how could it have been any greater? And she'd at least have had more time with him. Possibly children. A lasting legacy of him. Now, all she had was the fading memory of his face, those kind, laughing eyes, those long lanky legs. Legs that had earned him the nickname 'Grass' from his pals – short for grasshopper. How different her life might have been. Living in Regina, Saskatchewan, married to Greg, with a mother-in-law and three sisters-in-law. She'd have been in the same country as Joan – even if thousands of miles away.

What if? What if? What was the point?

She moved back to the cooker and decided to make herself a mug of cocoa instead of tea. It might help her sleep. She mixed the drink and carried it with her into the front room. After drawing the curtains, she curled up in an armchair and wrapped her mum's crocheted shawl around herself. Tomorrow she'd have to fetch Aunty Chris and break the news. The two of them could lay her mum out together.

The rain lashed against the windows, whipped up by a strong wind. Ethel drank her cocoa and then slipped into an exhausted sleep.

2

HOLLOWTREE, ONTARIO, CANADA

Joan was in the kitchen washing the breakfast dishes when the telegraph boy arrived. She wiped her hands on her apron and waited until the lad had mounted his bicycle and set off down the track, before opening the envelope. She guessed what the contents would be. Her Aunty Vi was dead.

Sitting down at the big table in the kitchen, Joan thought about the woman who had been a second mother to her – at times more of a mother than her own. A kind-hearted woman, Aunty Vi had extended an invitation every Sunday afternoon in the early years of the war to Canadian soldiers, serving tea and scraping together her rations to make sugarless cakes when possible – so they'd experience a homely atmosphere and feel appreciated.

In the corner of the room, Harry stirred. Joan pulled herself out of the chair and went to look at him. Fast asleep, his little face puckered, the baby was only eleven months old and Joan was already heavily pregnant with another child. So much for breast feeding preventing conception. She pulled the covers over the sleeping child and went to sit down again, her hands placed protectively over her swelling belly.

If only she could go back to England for the funeral. But Aunty Vi would be long in the ground before Joan could complete an Atlantic crossing – even if there was money to spare for the trip, which there was not. Every penny Jim earned on the farm was ploughed back into it. They'd acquired another thirty acres last year and Jim had put in a new silo for the bean crop. There was a new roof needed on the Hollowtree barn, they wanted to install a new bigger sugar shack for maple syrup and he'd said something just that morning about needing to paint the fencing. It went on and on. One expense after another.

Joan knew he was investing in their future, building up the farm to be successful and thriving, capable of providing a livelihood and inheritance for their three children, Jimmy, Sam and Harry and their future brother or sister. But sometimes Joan wished he'd ease up a bit, spend a little on themselves – a holiday or the occasional treat. How many times had she tried to tell him that there was no point in building a future if it was at the expense of the present? But he always flashed a grin at her and kissed her, until she was distracted into dropping the subject.

There was a sound outside and the kitchen door opened. Jim pulled off his boots and came in.

'Saw the telegraph boy. What's happened? Bad news?' His face was full of concern.

She handed him the telegram. 'Aunty Vi's gone. Her heart gave out.'

Jim bent over Joan, wrapped his arms around her and kissed the top of her head. 'I'm so sorry. She was a lovely lady.' He kissed her again.

Tears pricked her eyes. 'She was far away, and I'd probably never have seen her again, but just knowing she was there. And Ethel. Poor Ethel. She has nobody now.'

'She has you. And your mum just down the street.'

'What good am I thousands of miles away? And Mum, God bless her, has never had a lot of time for anyone other than herself. Ethel will be so lonely.'

'Get her to come out here for a break. You've always wanted her to visit. A change of scene will be good for her. And a chance to meet Sam and Harry. She could stay and help you when the baby comes. We've plenty of room. And Jimmy would be thrilled to see his Aunty Ethel again.'

Joan looked at him gratefully. 'Really? You wouldn't mind?'

'Ethel's my friend too. If it weren't for her, you and I would never have happened. And she was my best pal's girl.'

Joan stretched her lips tight, thinking of Greg and how his sudden death had shattered her cousin's life. It didn't seem right that Ethel should be denied the happiness she and Jim had, especially when she had brought them together.

'I'll write to her this afternoon. Six years' worth of tips must be enough to cover her ticket.'

'What about the funeral? There'll be expenses for that.'

'Aunty Vi had a funeral plan. A couple of insurance policies too. Same fellow Mum used. From the Co-op. A bob a week on each. She'd been saving for years. That'll be a little nest egg for Ethel now.'

Jim slipped into the seat opposite. 'Since I'm here now, I wouldn't say no to a cup of tea.'

Joan put the kettle on.

'What about the house? Did Vi own it?'

Joan nodded. 'Yes. It was all paid off before Uncle Kevin died.'

'She could take in a lodger. That'd be company for her as well as some additional income. Don't like to think of her alone in that house.'

'I doubt she'll want to do that. I don't think our Ethel would like a stranger living there with her.' Joan sat down and poured the tea. 'It will be so sad for her though. All those memories. That house was always lively. Before the war, when Uncle Kevin and Mark were alive, there were always parties. People would come round and listen to the wireless and sing along. Uncle Kevin used to play the banjo.' She gave a wistful smile. 'And then in the war. All you lot crammed into the front room every Sunday afternoon.'

Jim put his hand on hers. 'I remember the first time I went to one of Vi's tea parties. It was so crowded and smoky I went through to the kitchen to escape.'

She knew what was coming next.

'Thought I'd be on my own back there, away from the smoky atmosphere, but instead there was a beautiful, aloof woman, smoking her head off and delighting in giving me the runaround.'

'I didn't give you the runaround.'

'Yes, you did. I never knew where I was with you.'

She grinned. 'I was just terrified you'd see how crazy I was about you and run a mile.'

Jim stroked her hand. 'So, instead, you gave me the impression you weren't interested in me at all and left me standing there.'

'I didn't know then what I know now.'

'And what might that be?'

'That you'd end up loving me like I already loved you.'

'So, what did you know?'

'That you were a great kisser.' She laughed.

He leaned towards her and kissed her slowly on the mouth. 'Still am?'

'Still are.'

'I'd like to stay here all day kissing you, Mrs Armstrong, but I have a wagonload of beans to get in the ground.' He glugged down his tea, pulled back his chair and moved towards the door. 'Make sure you tell Ethel to get herself over here. And send her my condolences for Vi.'

Joan walked over to the window so she could watch him walking back down to the fields. She never tired of looking at her husband, never stopped being thankful that she'd been so cold that night in a London hotel that she'd crawled under the blankets with him. One night. A half asleep, early-morning, semi-conscious attempt at love-making – the first time for both of them. A glorious accident that had led to their son Jimmy and to the transformation of Joan's life from a small English garrison town to the farmlands of south Ontario.

3

The hand bell jangled insistently. Alice Armstrong looked up at the clock. It was only six but her great-aunt ought to be well on the way to inebriation, given how much whisky she'd consumed. Alice walked into the room, where the old lady was sitting upright and alert in her chair. She must have an iron constitution.

'Get me another drink, my dear. And don't even think about diluting it this time. I know what you're up to, Alice.'

'Aunty Miriam, don't you think–'

'Yes, I do think. And what I think is that I want another drink. Straight up. No ice. Chop-chop.' The old lady winked at her.

Alice shook her head but went off to the kitchen to refill the glass with her aunt's favourite scotch whisky. Not much of a drinker herself, Alice hated being complicit in Aunty Miriam's alcoholic tendencies. No, not tendencies. She had to be a full-blown alcoholic, as not a day passed when she didn't get through almost half a bottle of whisky. As her aunt's companion, Alice was dependent on her for bed and board for herself and her two young daughters. She walked a fine line between a sense of responsibility for the elderly lady and respecting her independence and autonomy.

Alice had asked her own doctor in confidence about her aunt's drinking.

'How old is the lady in question?' he'd asked. When Alice told him she was eighty-seven, he laughed and said, 'If it hasn't killed her yet and she gets pleasure from it, she's not likely to stop now. A little scotch before bedtime never did anyone any harm.'

'Half a bottle?' Alice was incredulous.

'Mm, that does seem excessive. The older one gets, the harder it becomes for the body to process alcohol. Does she have falls?'

'No. She only moves between her bed and the armchair with the aid of a walking stick and uses a commode in the bedroom. She never goes out of the house. Doesn't even come downstairs.' Alice hesitated. It felt like a betrayal to be telling the doctor all this. Although he was not her aunt's doctor, he must surely guess that it was Miss Cooke to whom she was referring.

'What about bathing?'

'I give her a bed bath every day. She can't get in and out of the bathtub anymore.'

The doctor nodded. 'As I say, Mrs Armstrong. It's not a good idea to drink such a quantity of strong alcohol but if, as I imagine, she's a stubborn woman, you're unlikely to get her to cut back on her consumption now. She's not incontinent?'

Alice said she was not.

'Is she unhappy? Does the drinking make her morose?'

She shook her head. 'She's always very cheerful and appears to have the constitution of an ox.'

'If she's not a risk to herself and has you to care for her, why not leave her be?'

Alice had been hoping for some kind of medical intervention. While her aunt showed little evidence of her extraordinary intake, never slurring her words, never stumbling, it couldn't be right, could it? But then they said Winston Churchill had drunk all day long starting at breakfast and it hadn't inhibited his ability to vanquish Hitler.

She went back into the bedroom and handed over the glass to her great-aunt.

'Sit down, I want to talk to you, Alice.'

Alice pulled up a chair.

'I wish you'd join me in a drink. It's not natural never to touch a drop.'

'I have Rose and Catherine to think about.'

The old lady nodded. 'Of course you do. I shouldn't be criticising you. I've never been a mother, so I can't imagine what it entails.' She sipped her scotch, running the liquid around her tongue. 'That's better. No water this time. Just how I like it. Pass me my shawl, will you, dear.'

Alice folded the mohair wrap around the old lady's bony shoulders.

'Too selfish, that's me. I'd never have been willing to make sacrifices to put a child first. Even nice well-behaved ones like your Rose and Catherine. I wasn't even prepared to put a husband first. That's probably why I never took one.' She gave a dry laugh and winked at Alice again. 'Not that I lacked for offers. Where *are* the girls?'

'Rose has a school friend here. They're doing their homework together. Or trying to, but Catherine seems determined to stop them.'

'She's a holy terror, that Catherine. She's going to be a

handful. Mark my words. Don't forget to send them up to say goodnight before they go to bed.'

Alice adjusted the shawl around her aunt's shoulders where it had slipped. Her aunt's words bothered her. Was being 'a holy terror' a stepping stone on the way to Catherine turning bad like her father? Tip Howardson, the man who had fathered Catherine, was definitely bad – a man responsible for the death of another Canadian soldier from a brain haemorrhage and for the attempted rape of Alice's sister-in-law, Joan.

'Do you ever get lonely, Alice?' Miss Cooke leaned forward, fixing her with a stare.

'I miss Joan, my sister-in-law, in particular – she's been a good friend to me.' Alice looked down at her hands, feeling her aunt's penetrating gaze on her. 'And Walt all the time. It doesn't get any better. Even after ten years.'

'I hate to pry, dear, but haven't you ever thought of marrying again? A lovely girl like you? I would hate that, of course, as it would mean losing you, but I won't be around for much longer and I would like to think of you settled and happy.'

'But you've just said you never wanted that for yourself, Aunty. Why should you want it for me?'

'Because, my dear, you always look so sad. There are some women who get by splendidly without a husband and there are others who can't – or don't want to. You appear to be one who doesn't want to. But you haven't answered my question.'

Alice breathed slowly. It was uncomfortable being asked about her personal life. She had intended to marry Catherine's father, but it had come to nothing when he told her he was already married. Knowing what she now knew about him, she bitterly regretted her liaison with him.

'Getting involved with Catherine's father was a terrible mistake. He was a bad man. It put me off marriage.' Alice examined her fingernails, bit her lip. 'I can't imagine why I was with a man like that. Why I didn't see though him.' She turned her head and stared into the fireplace.

'Maybe it was because you were lonely. You probably missed the sex thing or whatever you young people call it these days.' She chuckled. 'Never tried it myself – I had a feeling I'd have liked it rather too much for my own good. And in my day, it was only supposed to happen after the gold band was on your finger.'

Alice felt herself blushing.

'But I can imagine you might miss it if you'd had it and then it stopped.'

Alice squirmed in her chair, then nodded, avoiding her aunt's eyes. 'I wanted to marry when I found out Catherine was on the way. Hollowtree's a small town. Children need a father. And Walt's pension was barely enough for Rose and me. Certainly not enough for me to live anywhere but on the Armstrongs' farm. But Walt's mother wasn't exactly happy about me expecting another man's child.'

'Well I'm very happy you chose to come to me.'

Alice reddened again. 'You've been incredibly kind to me, Aunty. You've taken me in, given me and the girls a new home.'

What Alice didn't say was that no one in Ottawa knew about her past and she was able to pass as a widow with two children.

'I'm so grateful to you, Aunty.'

'Grateful? Nonsense! How many times have I told you, it's me who should be grateful to you. Having you and the girls here has brought light into my dreary old life. If you hadn't come to live with me they'd have carted me off to some old folks' home long ago. And you know how I'd feel about that?' She pulled a face and took another sip of scotch.

'Let's say we have a mutually beneficial partnership then, Aunty.'

'A partnership indeed! But alas, one that is drawing to a close.'

Alice's throat constricted. 'You want us to leave?'

'No, my dear girl.' The old lady stretched out a hand and patted Alice's. 'I'm the one who must leave.'

'Where are you going?' Alice was confused.

'To meet my Maker. I've outlasted my three score years and ten by a long way. What was it they used to call it in England? A good innings. Comes from cricket I think.' She pulled her shawl tighter round her shoulders. 'I'm not as hale as I appear and I know my time is coming so I wanted to speak to you before the good Lord comes and bowls me out!'

'Please, Aunty Miriam, don't talk like that.'

'I'm being realistic. I'm living on borrowed time. I have a strong sense it will be any day now. I can't delay talking things over with you any longer. I want you to know that all my affairs are in order. My lawyer has the will. Apart from a small legacy to your mother, everything goes to you, Alice. This house. The money in the bank. At the last statement it was around five thousand dollars. And there's a portfolio of stocks and shares. The most recent valuation put it at sixty-nine thousand dollars. You will be financially secure.'

Alice gasped.

'And some investment properties. Commercial premises. Let to reliable tenants. That, plus the dividends, brings in a regular income that should be more than sufficient for your needs.'

Sixty-nine thousand dollars – more money than Alice could imagine. It was too much to take in. Surely her aunt wasn't serious? 'I can't believe it.'

'Well, it's true.' The old woman smiled. 'You won't have to settle for second best now. If you marry again, do it for love, not because you're worried about those girls. And if you can't find love, it's better to be on your own. Believe me.'

Alice was shocked. Did her aunt know she was seeing someone? How was that possible when she never left her room?

Aunty Miriam grinned at her. 'Now, how about fetching me another glass of that single malt before I change my mind and leave the money to the cats' home or the foreign missionaries.'

Alice kissed her on the cheek. 'Thank you, Aunty. I still can't believe it.' She moved towards the door and paused. 'But please don't die yet. Not for a long time.'

It was ten o'clock before Alice had cleared up after supper, put the girls to bed and checked on her aunt, now in a whisky-induced slumber. She went downstairs, sat in front of the fire and finished off a pot of tea.

How had Aunty Miriam known about her seeing some-one? What was it she'd said? *You won't have to settle for second best.* And that was what Alice had been about to do. Well, not right now. Bob Hardcastle hadn't even told his elderly mother he was engaged to be married yet. Everything he did happened at a snail's pace.

Bob was an insurance clerk. Alice had met him in the post office, when she was buying postage stamps and he was dispatching a parcel. In the long queue they'd got chatting and a courtship by default resulted. A half-hearted affair that Alice hadn't even mentioned to her aunt, let alone her daughters.

Alice glanced down at the ring he had given her. That must be how Aunty Miriam knew. And perhaps she had seen Bob through the window – even though he only visited late at night and never rang the doorbell. Her aunt was a wise old bird and evidently knew more than she let on. And she was right about Bob. He was definitely second best. Alice had a feeling that she was second best for him too – after his precious mother, who ruled him like a despot. When Aunty Miriam eventually passed away, Alice would have no more financial difficulties. No reason to marry a man for whom she felt no attraction. Bob Hardcastle had a reliable job but, apart from a pleasant face, a kind heart and a friendly disposition, he had little to recommend him. He dressed badly; he was awkward and unromantic. Sometimes Alice wondered if he had any sexual drive at all. So far, he had never tried to move beyond kisses. And, instead of setting Alice on fire, as had been the case with her husband, Walt, Bob's kisses left her feeling flat.

She would end it. Now that she knew she would have the means of bringing up her girls, there was no point in stringing Bob along any longer.

She cleared away the tea things and went upstairs to look in on the two girls, fast asleep in the bedroom they shared. Rose was curled up on her side, the book she'd been reading discarded on the quilt. Alice picked up the book-mark from the floor, put it inside the book and placed it on the chair.

Moving to the other bed, she looked down at Catherine who, as usual, was lying with the bedclothes in complete disarray. She drew them into place and looked at her daughter's chubby face, the strands of dark brown hair and the cupid's bow mouth. Every day she examined the five-year-old's features, looking for signs of the child's father and praying she would never find them. So far, Catherine still had the rounded face of a small child and soft downy skin. Much like Rose at that age. There was no sign of the cold eyes, narrow-lipped mouth and bull neck of Tip Howardson. Alice loved her daughter but lived in fear that might change, if, one day, she recognised Tip in her face.

Her relationship with Tip had been disastrous. She had allowed herself to be seduced and flattered by him, a former classmate back in Hollowtree after years away. Lonely, after the death of Walt in the early years of the war, Alice had been easy prey. Refusing to listen to the warnings of her brother-in-law, Jim, she had embarked on a brief clandestine affair. The relationship had cost her her home, her family and caused her to flee here to Ottawa, where nobody except Aunty Miriam knew her.

But to admit that Tip had been a mistake was tantamount to admitting that Catherine was too. There was also Rose to worry about. Now ten years old, the little girl one day was bound to ask questions about the sister who was born five years after their father had died.

But tonight she had something else to think about. When Aunty Miriam died, Alice would become a wealthy woman. Free to do whatever she wished, live wherever she wished. Money was power. Money bought respect and protected you from gossip. Alice craved respect. If she were ever to return to Hollowtree, she wanted to go back with her head held high and dare those people to cast aspersions on her character. She'd show the lot of them.

4

ALDERSHOT, OCTOBER 1952

*T*he letter lay on the table in front of Ethel. She picked it up and read it for the umpteenth time. Joan was very persuasive. Ethel remembered only too well sitting at this same kitchen table with Joan when their situations were reversed. Her cousin had been agonising over whether to take up the offer by the Canadian military to transport her and four-year-old Jimmy over to Canada to join her husband Jim. Ethel had been incredulous at Joan's indecision. Yet now here she was, in a quandary herself – and only over whether to go out to Canada for a holiday.

How many times had Joan written to Ethel, begging her to come and stay with them? Ethel had always used her mother as an excuse for not making the journey. If she were honest though, it was because she couldn't bear to see what her own life might have become if Greg hadn't died.

The sound of the front door opening made her jump.

'Only me, Ethel. Made your mind up yet?' Aunty Chris asked as she swept into the back kitchen. 'I'll stick the kettle on for a brew.'

'It seems such a big step.'

'Don't be daft. It's not as if it's for ever. Just 'til the new baby's born. A couple of months or so. I wish it were me, but I can't leave Ron and I'm too old to be gallivanting half-way round the world.'

Ethel was ashamed at her own reluctance. Aunty Chris had never met her two younger grandchildren and, with a fourth on the way, all she had were the snaps that Joan sent over.

'Is it the cost that's worrying you, love? Or are you worried the salon won't be happy?'

Ethel shook her head. 'Vera's told me I can have as much time off as I need. It's not the money. With Mum's insurance policies I've got nearly two hundred pounds, even after the costs of the funeral. And I've been saving my tips up for years for a ticket to see Joan.' She fidgeted with the letter. 'I'd want to pay my way while I'm out there. I'd hate for Jim to think I was sponging. But there should be enough to see me through until it's time to come home.'

'If you run low on money and want to stay out there longer just let me know. I can sort out a tenant for this place and keep an eye on things here for you.'

Ethel stiffened. Aunty Chris was clearly thinking that once she got out there she might not want to come back.

Life here in post-war England was grim, to put it mildly. Even now, seven years after the war had ended, there was still rationing – apart from tea which came off the rations only a matter of days ago. There were bomb sites in major cities that were still not redeveloped. Money was tight, and people were getting fed up with the continuing need to pinch and save every last penny.

Ethel was no economist, but she could tell from Joan's letters that it was a different story in Canada. There seemed to be a post-war boom over there. Yes, Joan complained that

Jim worked too hard and money was tight, but it was all relative. Hadn't they recently got a brand-new car? Here, in this little street of shabby terraced houses, Ethel was still using an outside privy, doing the washing with an ancient boiler in the wash-house in the back yard, and getting down on her knees to scrub the front doorstep. No one in the street had a television yet. And certainly, no cars. Whichever way you looked at it, the country was grim, grey, tired and run-down.

Ethel put the letter down and cupped her chin in her hands. She decided to voice her concerns. 'What if going out there puts me off Aldershot and makes me discontented with my life here? Now that Mum's gone, and you know how much I miss Joan.'

'Well, love, what will be will be. Must say I wouldn't fancy living anywhere but here. Too late for me to adapt to foreign ways. But you? Your life's ahead of you.'

Ethel looked away, twisting her hands together. She hated the idea of becoming a dotty ageing spinster, an object of pity. 'Hardly, Aunty. I'm thirty-three.'

Christine shrugged. 'I was twenty-six when Joan's father walked out on me and I thought it was the end of the world. Didn't expect to meet anyone else but Ron came along and I was married again at thirty-eight. We've never been Romeo and Juliet, but we muddle along fine and I can't imagine life without the old fool now.

'You'll find someone else, Ethel, love. A lovely looking girl like you. Can't believe no one's snapped you up already.'

'No.' Ethel's voice was sharp. 'I'll never marry now.'

Her aunt shook her head. 'Can't grieve for ever. How long now since that fellow of yours died?'

'Eleven years.'

Christine snorted. 'Enough's enough, girl. Single or

married, your future will be rosier if you get yourself out there and have a good time. See another part of the world. Get to know my grandchildren – I'll expect detailed reports and lots of snaps. Our Joan doesn't send enough of them.'

Ethel nodded.

'Think about it. But not too much!' Christine got up from the table. 'Now I need to get down the butcher's. I promised the old man I'd do lamb chops if I can get some.'

When she'd gone, Ethel washed the teacups, still agonising about whether to make such a big trip or not. She shuddered at the possibility of Joan and Jim feeling sorry for her. Of discussing what should be done about 'poor Ethel'.

She dried her hands and went into the front room. *The Daily Herald*, unread, lay on the arm of the chair where she'd left it, automatically, for her mother to read. Ethel closed her eyes. Better nip down to the newsagents later and cancel the delivery.

Picking the newspaper up, she sank into an armchair. The front page was full of the horrors of a triple train crash at Harrow the day before. The headline read 'Death Toll Nears 100' and there were two photographs, almost filling the whole page, of twisted wreckage and people desperately trying to rescue any survivors. A sub-heading read 'Disaster in Pictures on Back Page'.

Why did the papers take such delight in the misfortunes of others? Hadn't everyone had enough of death and destruction during the war, without wanting to look at pictures like that? Tears threatened. Since her mum died, they appeared at the slightest provocation.

Putting down the newspaper, Ethel made up her mind. A change would do her good and give her something else to think about. Her mum would have approved. Hadn't she always said Ethel should take a trip to see Joan?

Joan was whooping for joy and dancing round the kitchen with Harry when Jimmy and Sam got home from school.

'What's going on?'

'Aunty Ethel's coming!' Harry was in her arms and she was waltzing him around to his great delight.

'Oh,' said Jimmy, as if to say, is that all? 'That's nice.'

'She'll be here next month. In time for your birthdays. And Christmas, of course.'

'My birthday? Will she bring me a present?' Sam piped up.

'Aunty Ethel always remembers both your birthdays, whether she's here or not.'

Jimmy pulled a face. 'Yes, but it's usually money and you put it in my stupid savings. That's not like having a proper present.'

'You'll thank me one day, young man, when you're old enough to spend it.'

Jimmy slouched into a chair. 'I'd rather have something to play with. Not a load of stupid money I'm not allowed to spend. A bow and arrow set or a gun. Bobby Sheldon has a Red Ryder BB gun. I'm sick of pretending.' He pointed two fingers at his mother. 'It's stupid.' Jimmy had a tendency to adopt a favourite word and employ it at every available opportunity until he moved onto another one. 'Stupid' was evidently today's.

'It's called using your imagination.'

'No. It's called using your stupid fingers.'

Joan was about to respond but decided it was pointless. She wasn't about to get into a long debate with a ten-year-old about the merits and demerits of toy weaponry. She didn't want to dampen her excitement about Ethel's visit.

She put Harry down and moved to the stove to check on the casserole in the oven.

The door opened, and Jim came in. He ruffled the two boys' hair in turn, kissed the baby, then bent over his wife's neck and planted a kiss there. Slipping his arms around her he rested his palms on her swollen stomach. 'How's your afternoon been?'

'I've been across helping Ma pickle up a batch of cabbages.' She put her hand against her back, tired.

'I told you, Joan, I don't like you trudging over there now the winter's coming. It's muddy on the track and you could slip and have a nasty accident.'

'I'm not an old lady, just pregnant. It doesn't make me an invalid. Anyway, I took the car and went round the long way. Harry's too heavy for me to carry now and it was too muddy for the pram.' She turned to face him, unable to conceal her excitement any longer. 'Guess what was waiting for me when I got back here.' She pulled the letter from the pocket of her apron.

Jim took it and went over to the table, reading. He looked up. 'That's great. So, Ethel will be here for Christmas – and in time for the baby.'

'And my birthday,' said Jimmy.

'My birthday too.' Sam's voice was indignant.

'Of course,' said Joan. 'I'll have to run up some new curtains for the guest room.'

'The guest room?' said Jim, eyebrows raised.

'Sam doesn't need a room of his own. He'll be fine sharing Jimmy's room for a while.'

'Oh no!' Jimmy shook his head violently. 'No babies allowed.'

'I'm not a baby! I'm five.'

Joan stroked her middle son's head.' Take no notice,

Sam. Jimmy's only teasing. The two of you will be fine in that room together.'

Jimmy huffed and folded his arms, his face screwed up in an exaggerated grimace.

'I shared a room with my brother until I left to join the army. And it was half the size of your room. Now, I don't want to hear any more from you, squirt!' Jim jabbed a fist playfully in his son's direction.

Joan turned to the sink and began to peel potatoes. With Ethel coming, she couldn't imagine a more perfect end to the year.

5

*A*lice stood at the graveside, Rose and Catherine each clutching one of her hands. She'd been uncertain whether to bring them to the funeral but Aunt Miriam, or Tanty Mimi as they'd called her, had been the only relative the girls had seen over the past five years, or in Catherine's case, ever. They should have the chance to say a final goodbye. Alice believed that children shouldn't be cocooned from the concept of death.

How easily a life could be snuffed out. She thought of Walt. Lost to her only months after their marriage and his departure for the war. That loss had cast a shadow over every day since. The pain would never wholly leave her. It was as much a part of her as the heart pumping inside her chest.

It was a bitterly cold day. If Aunty Miriam had died a month later the ground would have frozen and they would have had to wait until spring to bury her.

The old lady had died three days after their talk. Alice had gone into the bedroom with her morning cup of tea and found Aunt Miriam had expired during the night. As she smoothed away the hair from the old lady's forehead, Alice shivered at the marble cold of her face. But rather than being upset, she was glad for her aunt – it was a perfect death, a quiet slipping into sleep after a long and happy life.

The wind cut into Alice's neck between her hat and the collar of her coat. She'd left her woollen scarf off as it had seemed too casual, disrespectful, being bright scarlet. The girls were well wrapped-up, but Catherine was starting to shiver.

When the priest intoned the final blessing, Alice threw her clod of ice-cold earth into the grave and nodded to the girls to do the same, clinging onto Catherine's gloved hand as the child approached the edge of the hole.

'Is Tanty Mimi really down there?' The little girl's lip quivered. 'She'll be cold.' She looked up at Alice with teary eyes.

'Tanty Mimi is already up in heaven. With Daddy.' Why did the lie come so easily? At some point Catherine would find out that Walt was not her father. There was no name under father on her birth certificate. Perhaps Alice could say it had been left blank because he was already dead? But Rose knew her father had been killed at Dieppe when she was a baby and once Catherine was a bit older the lie would be apparent. It was simple mathematics. Rose might have already worked it out. Alice pushed that alarming thought to the back of her head.

She squeezed her daughters' hands and turned to lead the girls away from the graveside. Maybe it wasn't a lie. Tip Howardson could well be dead.

But if he was, he certainly wouldn't be in heaven.

There was no wake. Alice didn't see the point. All Aunty Miriam's friends were long dead, and Alice had none of her own in Ottawa. The few attendees at the church service had been business acquaintances such as the bank manager and Aunt Miriam's lawyer and accountant. Alice had decided against inviting Bob Hardcastle to the funeral and he hadn't tried to argue with her about it.

That evening, after the girls were fast asleep, Alice sat in the front parlour waiting, tapping her foot in irritation against the fender. Just before nine o'clock, there was a rap on the window.

She went to the front door to let Bob in. 'You're late,' she said, her voice accusatory.

'I'm sorry. Mother wanted me to listen with her to Don Messer on the radio.' He had the grace to look embarrassed. 'It's her favourite show.'

Alice held the door open for him. He took off his overcoat and hat to reveal a check sports jacket and wool flannel pants that were slightly too short, skimming greying white socks. He wasn't a handsome man: at forty-three, his skin was pale, as though he spent too much time indoors, his eyebrows had the appearance of corn silk – growing with wild abandon in different directions – and he had the beginnings of a paunch. His best asset was his eyes, which twinkled when he smiled and were the reason she'd first struck up a conversation with him.

She went into the kitchen and brought him a beer from the refrigerator. He took it, looking up at her, his expression still sheepish.

'You're cross with me, Alice?'

Saying nothing, she stared at him, wondering how they had got to this point and debating how best to break the news to him.

'Only, Mother's old and gets lonely.'

'Did you tell her about me?'

Bob turned his head and stared into the fire.

Alice was relieved. She had her excuse now. 'I thought not. You're never going to tell her, are you?'

He opened his mouth, struggling to form words, his lips moving like a goldfish.

'Very well.' Fiddling with her finger, she pulled off the solitaire ring he had given her and held it out to him.

He drew back, horrified. 'No, Alice, please. Give me another chance. I just need a bit more time. I'm working on her. Getting her used to the idea that I have a young lady.'

Alice cringed at his words.

'Please, I promise you, I'll tell her before Christmas. It's just... you know... she's elderly and doesn't understand these things. She's used to having me around all the time. You know she depends on me. It will be a big shock for her. And then there's your daughters. I have to think about how to tell her about them. It requires a lot of careful thought.' He smoothed his hands over the legs of his grey flannel pants.

'I buried my aunt today,' she said at last. 'My circumstances have changed. I no longer want to marry you, Bob. And it's clear to me that you don't want to marry me either. Marriage would upset the comfortable life you share with your mother. If you cared for me you'd have found a way to tell her about me by now.' She met his eyes. 'Please don't make a fuss. My mind is made up. It's for the best.'

She moved across the room and held the door open. 'I'd like you to leave now.'

Bob Hardcastle struggled to his feet, looking wretched. She handed him his hat and coat.

'Alice... just one more chance. I beg you.'

She pursed her lips. 'Goodbye, Bob. I think it's better if you don't call here again.'

When she closed the front door behind him, Alice leaned her back against it. She was shaking, and her palms were clammy.

How could she have contemplated marrying him? But before she knew of her great-aunt's inheritance, Bob had been her only route to financial security. She'd had to think of the girls.

She went back into the parlour and sat down in front of the fire. What was it her aunt had said about her? That she was someone who couldn't get by without a man? No – that she didn't *want* to be without one. Well, now she'd made her choice. If Aunty Mimi had been happy as a wealthy, unattached woman, then so could she.

After damping down the fire, Alice went up to bed. Lying in the cold cotton sheets, relief washed over her that she didn't have to see Bob Hardcastle any more. Kissing him had been like kissing a relative. No passion. No emotion at all. The idea of sharing a bed with such a mother's boy was abhorrent.

Rolling on her side, Alice did what she did most nights now. Picturing the grinning face of Walt Armstrong, his tousled blond hair and tanned skin, she imagined his arms encircling her and his mouth on hers. Her hand slipped between her legs and she gave a deep sigh and tried to pretend it was Walt touching her.

*J*oan put the telephone back in its cradle. She had intended to get on with washing the curtains for what was going to be Ethel's room, but her mother-in-law had sounded distressed. It was rare for anything to disturb Helga Armstrong's stoicism, so Joan didn't want to ignore what was clearly a poorly-disguised need to unburden herself. Helga rarely used the telephone and had taken a lot of persuading before agreeing to its installation. The clinching argument had been Jim's – that emergency help might be required at some point for his father, who had been suffering from chronic emphysema for several years.

Harry was asleep in his bassinet, so Joan lugged it across the yard and put it on the rear seat of the car. With a bit of luck, he'd sleep on for another hour or so. She climbed into the front seat, squeezing herself behind the steering wheel. It was getting harder to reach the pedals as she needed to move the seat back to accommodate her stomach. All three of her sons had been born in November but this baby wasn't due until January, as though she were defying the convention established by her brothers. Joan couldn't help thinking of the baby as a girl. She wasn't sure why – she just had a strong sense that this time she was going to have a daughter.

If it weren't for having Harry with her, Joan would have walked across the fields to her in-laws' home, the original Hollowtree farmhouse. When Jim had bought the adjacent Rivercreek Farm, it was to provide a spacious home for their growing family – and more privacy than living in the old farmhouse, cheek by jowl with Jim's parents. The two properties now formed part of one much larger acreage, farmed by Jim.

At least the snow hadn't come yet. With a bit of luck, it would hold off until after Ethel got here. Joan wanted her cousin to experience the magic of its sudden arrival, an event that still enchanted Joan.

It was a fifteen-minute walk between the two houses, but the road route was more circuitous. Joan pulled into the yard, chickens scattering at the motor car's approach.

Helga appeared in the doorway but went back inside as Joan got out of the car. Too cold to stand around with open doors. When Joan entered she was greeted by a delicious scent of baking. A tray of Helga's renowned butter tarts was waiting on the table.

'You can take a dozen of those home with you, Joan. I promised Jimmy I'd make some for him.'

'You're determined to make my children fat.' Joan softened her words with a smile.

'No chance of that, the way those two boys run around like little dervishes. More energy than a pair of young colts.'

Helga poured coffee for them both and they sat down at the kitchen table, the basket, with Harry still asleep inside, beside them. Helga didn't spend time today on her customary grandmotherly inspection of her youngest grandson. Her face was worried.

'What did the doctor say?' Joan asked.

'Reckons Don doesn't have much longer.' Helga jerked her head back, as if gravity might hold the threatened tears in check.

Joan's mouth tightened. She loved her father-in-law and had never stopped being grateful to him for his kindness and friendship when she first arrived as a war bride in Canada. Helga, at the time, had subjected her to extensive hostilities.

'We knew the emphysema would get him in the end, but the medicine seemed to be keeping it at bay. Specially the inhaler. It was a godsend when he got breathless.' Helga gripped the edge of the table, her knuckles white.

'So, what's changed?'

'He's started turning blue. Round the mouth and the fingertips.' Helga leaned across the table and picked up a scrap of paper and looked at what was written there. 'Cyanosis. I got Doc Robinson to write it down as I knew I wouldn't remember it.'

Joan thought for a moment then said, 'I've never heard of that. What does it mean?'

'Means it's getting worse. The doc wanted to move him to the hospital.'

Joan stretched a hand out and took her mother-in-law's.

'I told him no. Don won't have it. He says he'll die here or he won't die at all.'

'Isn't that rather the point?' Joan said. 'Moving him to hospital to prevent him dying?'

'They can't prevent it. It'll happen sooner or later, and he doesn't mind if it's sooner as long as it's in his own home.

He's never trusted hospitals since the war.' She looked up at Joan. 'The other war. His war.'

'What does the doctor say about that?'

'Says he's going to get an oxygen tank over here. That's all they'd give Don in hospital anyway. He may as well have it in his own home. Just takes a bit of arranging. Knocking a few heads together. I told the doctor that's what he must do.'

'And?'

'That's what I hope he's busy doing now.'

Joan hesitated, uncertain how to frame her next question, but Helga anticipated it.

'You're going to ask how long he's got?'

Joan nodded.

'Maybe he'll see Christmas. But probably not long enough to see that babe you've got in there.' She nodded at Joan's spherical belly.

'So soon? Oh, Ma, I'm so sorry.' She squeezed Helga's hand. 'Can I go up and see him?'

Helga nodded. 'He's probably sleeping. Just tap him on the shoulder. He won't want to miss seeing you.'

After a last check on her sleeping baby, Joan went out of the kitchen. The door to the Armstrongs' bedroom was open and she could hear Don's rasping breaths as she climbed the steep stairs.

His eyes were open when she entered the room and they lit up when he saw her.

'Don't try to talk, Don. Ma's filled me in on what the doctor said.' She bent over the bed and kissed his whiskery cheek. Sitting on a wooden stool by the bedside, she took his hand in hers and began to stroke it, noticing the dark blue tinge to his fingertips.

'I'm done for... girl. Did she tell... you?' He struggled for breath. She saw how barrel-chested he had become as a result of the pressure his overinflated lungs put on his chest.

'I told you, Don, don't try to talk. It'll make the breathing harder.' She tried to swallow a welling up of emotion. Once the doctor gets an oxygen tank rigged up it's going to make a big difference.'

His eyes were rheumy. She had to remind herself that he was not an old man. Early sixties.

'It was the gas... slow death... years later.' He began coughing again.

'Is that what the doctor told you?'

'Doc knows... nothing... Never went to... war.'

'Maybe he wasn't a soldier, but he knows more about medicine than you do.' She grinned at him, hoping he wouldn't notice she was trying not to cry. 'I'm sure the oxygen will make a huge difference. We've got to have you well for Christmas. And then in the New Year you have to meet your new granddaughter.'

He raised an eyebrow.

'I know,' she said. 'But I feel sure it's a girl this time.'

Her father-in-law smiled. 'I'll stick... around... for that.'

His hand fumbled, looking for something on the night-stand, so she handed him his inhaler. He put it into his mouth and pressed. Exhausted from the effort, he closed his eyes.

Joan kissed him on the forehead. 'I'll let you try to get some sleep now. I have to get home before the boys are back from school and I've curtains to wash. My cousin will be arriving soon. She's going to stop off at Alice's on the way.'

'She knows Alice?'

'Not yet. But I wanted her to break the journey. And Alice has some photographs of her girls for us. Ethel can pick them up. Did Ma tell you, Alice's great-aunt died?'

Don shook his head. 'She coming... home... then?'

'I doubt it. She's come into her aunt's money. The house too. Our Alice is a wealthy woman now. Can't see her moving back to Hollowtree.'

But Don had already closed his eyes. Joan slipped out of the room and down the stairs, followed by the sound of his laboured breathing.

7

NOVEMBER 1952

*E*thel stood on the deck of the RMS *Scythia* at Southampton, looking back at the port as the liner eased away from the dock, leaving a churning wake behind it. Her trepidation about the trip had turned to excitement as soon as she'd written her name on the Cunard luggage labels, with their illustration of a bright red funnel, and now here she was, looking up at that same red funnel as it towered above her.

Ethel hadn't thought about who else would be making the voyage across the Atlantic to Halifax. If anything, she'd imagined it would be only a small number of people. After all, who could afford to make such a trip? The war brides, like Joan, had all been shipped across years ago. But to her surprise, the boat was packed with families, from every country in Europe as well as Britain. Not impoverished refugees, but prosperous people, bursting with excitement about emigrating. Their exuberance was contagious, and Ethel found herself caught up in the party-like atmosphere. Everyone in tourist class was friendly – a camaraderie arising from them all being prospective settlers, looking forward to a new life in the Promised Land of Canada.

The ship proved a revelation over the coming days. Delicious and plentiful food, orchestral concerts relayed live from London, a fancy-dress party – which Ethel decided to give a miss – and a different film show every night. Even her fears about seasickness proved unfounded. She relished being at sea and, if it weren't for the cold November weather, she would have happily stayed up on deck as much as possible, watching the grey water merge into the grey sky.

Over dinner one night, Ethel talked with a Belgian family. They spoke perfect English which made her ashamed of her own lack of any other language. The husband was an accountant, but they planned a change in direction, having purchased a parcel of land in Saskatchewan. The mention of Greg's home province sparked a twinge of familiar grief. She would never be able to forget what might have been, the life that had been stolen from her.

The man proceeded to talk at length about his plans for large-scale grain production, while also rearing chickens. 'I've won prizes for my chickens in Belgium. It was only a hobby there, but I know what I'm doing and we'll have some income to tide us over while my sons and I learn about growing wheat.'

Ethel looked at the two sons – big, silent men in their early twenties. She couldn't help wondering how much of this grand plan was theirs and how much had been dictated by their father.

'What about you, Mademoiselle? What will you be doing in Canada? Joining your family?'

'I'm only going for a holiday. To visit my cousin. I'll be returning home before spring.'

The husband looked at his wife. They shared a knowing smile. 'If everything we have heard about Canada is true, you will not go back to England. North America is the land of growth and opportunity. The countries of Europe are tired and battered, crushed by debt and will take decades to recover.' He shook his head and waved a hand expansively around the dining room. 'All these people can't be wrong.'

Ethel wondered what he had witnessed and experienced during the long war years when Belgium was occupied. She refused to admit, even to herself, that there was any possibility she would be staying in Canada.

One of the stewards told her the ship had been a troop carrier during the war. She couldn't help wondering if this might have been the ship that Greg had sailed on to England, with Jim. She remembered him telling her how it was so overcrowded they'd had to sleep in the empty swimming pool. It was too cold now for swimming, but she walked past the pool and imagined her fiancé lying with his buddies on the bottom, crammed together like sardines. For how many of them would it have been a one-way journey?

Joan had explained in her letters that it was impossible for her and Jim to travel the 1200-mile journey to Halifax to meet her from the ship. It was only when she'd read the distance, that Ethel grasped the enormity of Canada. The train journey would take more than twenty hours and she had originally intended to take the trans-Canada train straight to Toronto. But Joan had made arrangements for her to break her journey by travelling via Ottawa, where Alice, Joan's sister-in-law, would put her up for the night.

Ethel would have preferred the anonymity of a hotel; although that too made her nervous, having only stayed in one once before. Joan assured her that Alice was friendly. It was hard, though, not to remember that it had not always been so – Joan's letters, when first in Canada, had given Ethel the distinct impression that Alice had been less than welcoming.

Inside the cavernous Union Station in Ottawa, Ethel felt strange, disorientated, foreign. French was being spoken as well as English. Canada was not like a day-trip to London – exotic as that might have been to her until now. She stood on the platform, looking around as people hurried past. What if Alice had got the time wrong? How would she recognise her?

She felt a tap on her shoulder. 'You must be Ethel?' A pretty blonde woman, with two little girls, stood behind her. 'I recognise you from a photograph Joan once showed me. You look more beautiful in real life.' Alice held out a hand, then changed her mind and drew Ethel into an awkward hug. 'You're family. No need for us to be formal.'

Ethel was relieved on several counts. 'Pleased to meet you, Alice.' She turned to greet the two girls. 'Now don't tell me... You must be Rose and you're Catherine?'

Rose smiled shyly while Catherine ignored Ethel and concentrated on sucking her thumb.

'That all the luggage you've got?' Alice pointed at the suitcase and small holdall.

'I'm only here for a couple of months. And, to be honest, I don't have a lot of clothes anyway.'

Alice led them outside the station towards a line of waiting taxicabs. 'I've given up on buses. I thought we'd travel in style. I'm coming into some money soon and have to keep reminding myself that it's there to be spent.'

Ethel, embarrassed, rummaged in her handbag. 'No, I must pay...' Her hostess brushed her protest aside.

Fifteen minutes later they pulled up outside an imposing suburban villa. 'It was my great-aunt's house,' said Alice. 'She passed away a few weeks ago. Not long after you lost your mum. I was sorry to hear that, Ethel.'

Ethel thanked her and reciprocated the condolences.

'I haven't decided yet whether to carry on living here or move somewhere else. The house is in need of modernisation. Not been touched for fifty or sixty years, but it's comfortable enough. And after the place Rose and I were living in before—'

'I thought you used to live at the farm?'

'We did. But in a lean-to tacked onto the end of the barn. My late husband built it before he went to England. Did you ever meet Walt?'

Ethel told her she hadn't.

'I loved it because it was our special place and because Walt built it. But, I must admit, it was a bit a primitive. This house is a palace in comparison.'

Ethel looked around the spacious entrance hall with its grand staircase, elaborate corniced ceiling and elegant chandelier. 'It's beautiful. And enormous.'

'The kitchen's in the basement. Our rooms are upstairs. There's another floor above that with five more bedrooms. Never used. The housekeeper's quarters are also in the basement and my aunt didn't have any other servants. Apart from me – I was her companion. In exchange for our bed and board.' Alice raised her arms in a sweeping gesture. 'I never expected to inherit anything. Least of all this place. I have to do a big clear-out. Aunty Miriam had all kind of papers and junk stored upstairs.'

She took Ethel's coat. 'There's a fire in the front parlour.

And Mrs Browning should have supper ready in half an hour. Let me show you your room. Do you need the case bringing up or are you all right with just the holdall? If so, the suitcase can stay in the vestibule.'

Alice's manner was an odd mixture of breeziness and organisation. Ethel felt slightly overwhelmed.

After a supper of roast chicken followed by apple pie, Alice left Ethel in the front parlour, while she took the girls upstairs to supervise their bedtime and to read Catherine a story. Left alone, Ethel looked around the room. It was filled with rather grand, dark wood Victorian furniture. Hanging over the fireplace was a portrait in oil of a young woman wearing a pale blue ballgown, her neck encircled by a string of over-sized pearls. The late Miss Miriam Cooke, she supposed, in her prime. There was a slight resemblance to Alice – Miss Cooke was a handsome woman, but the set of her brow indicated she was not someone to be trifled with.

Ethel picked up a magazine and flipped through the pages, nervously, without reading. All she really wanted was to go to bed, but now she faced the prospect of an evening of conversation with Alice Armstrong. She told herself it was just the same as chatting to customers in the hairdressing salon.

Alice returned, bearing a tea tray. 'Should I have offered you something stronger? Only I don't drink. Aunty drank like a fish – but only whisky. There's enough left to stock a bar if you'd like one.'

Ethel declined, though she'd give anything for a lemonade shandy or a port and lemon. Instead she sipped her tea. 'It's very kind of you to put me up.'

'Not at all. I've been dying to meet you. Joan talked about you so much. And we have a lot in common, Ethel.

Both of us lost the men we loved.' Straight in. No preliminaries.

Ethel swallowed. She didn't want to talk about Greg with someone she barely knew. It was too personal. Too painful.

She nodded but said nothing.

'Of course, I do have Walt's child, Rose. Even though he never got to see her. I found out I was expecting soon after he left for Europe. He was killed less than a year after she was born. If it hadn't been for her I don't know how I'd have coped. It was only because she needed me that I was able to crawl out of bed each day.' She looked directly at Ethel. 'It must be so sad for you that you never had children.'

The teacup rattled in Ethel's hand. She wanted to be home in Aldershot. Why had she agreed to come? Why had she let Joan push her into staying with this woman whom she didn't know and wasn't sure she was even going to like? She forced words into her mouth. 'Rose must be a great comfort to you. Is she very like her father?'

'The spitting image. It takes me by surprise sometimes. Little gestures. The way she lifts one eyebrow and squints when she's thinking.' Alice stared at the fire.

Ethel swallowed and said, 'My life ended when Greg died.'

Alice's mouth formed a smile, but her eyes were expressionless. 'You've just put your life on hold. But you're far too pretty for it to be over. Some handsome fellow will come along and snap you up. I'm surprised it hasn't happened already.'

Ethel felt herself blushing. 'I don't think so. I'm perfectly happy on my own.'

Alice leaned forward to stir the fire with a poker. 'I was going to remarry, until Aunty died. I was engaged to a fellow called Bob. Broke it off.'

Ethel looked up, surprised but interested.

'I was only marrying him to give the girls some security for the future. And he was half-hearted at best. There was only one woman in his life.'

'He was a widower?'

Alice laughed. 'No. I meant his mother. He was a mummy's boy. No spine.'

'How long were you engaged?' She wondered if this man was Catherine's father, but was reluctant to pry.

'Two years. All that time and he never plucked up the courage to tell the old bat about me. Once I knew I was inheriting my aunt's money I gave him his marching orders.' Another little laugh.

Ethel was starting to find her archness annoying.

'Do you mind awfully if I have an early night, Alice? I don't mean to be rude but I'm very tired after the train journey.'

'Not at all. I should have realised. I talk too much. It's because I miss having female company.' Alice jumped up. 'I'll make up a hot water bottle for you. It's cold tonight. You get ready and I'll bring it in to you.'

Before Ethel could protest, she had disappeared downstairs to the basement.

When Alice knocked at Ethel's door with the hot water bottle, Ethel was sitting up in bed. Alice handed her the bottle then sat down uninvited on the edge of the bed.

'Do you know about Catherine's father?' she asked.

Ethel hesitated, puzzled, cautious. 'No.'

'I wondered whether perhaps Joan told you?'

'No. Joan wouldn't betray a confidence. Why would she tell me? It's none of my business.'

'Well, it is in a way. I'd rather get it out in the open than have it festering between us.'

Ethel said. 'I'm sorry, Alice. I'm completely confused.'

'Catherine's father is Tip Howardson. The man who was responsible for your fiancé's death. The corporal who knocked him down in a fight.'

Ethel was dumbstruck. She drew her knees up under the covers to her chin.

'Did you know him? Tip, I mean?' Alice tilted her head on one side.

Ethel shook her head. Her body was shaking and she felt sick.

'Jim warned me about him, but I didn't believe him. I'm sorry. If I'd known, I'd never have had anything to do with him.' Alice scrunched the coverlet under her fingers. 'I was lonely. I suppose I was flattered by the attention. I didn't want to believe what Jim said.'

Ethel watched Alice's face, scarcely believing what she was hearing.

'I don't know why you've told me this, Alice. I can't begin to imagine what your motive is.'

'Well, you know... you'd be bound to hear some time. Even if Joan wouldn't say anything, Helga surely would. She's never forgiven me for going with another man. Seems to think I should stay a widow forever, true to Walt's memory.' Alice got up. 'But she doesn't understand what it's like. Being without a man. I was only twenty-two when Walt died.'

Ethel thought Alice's voice was beginning to sound whiny.

Alice moved to the door. 'Anyway, I've got it off my chest now. But I'd rather you don't mention it in front of the girls. Catherine doesn't know who her father was. I've never talked about it. Rose may have worked it out by now but if so she's keeping quiet. One day I'm going to have to find a way to tell them. Goodnight, Ethel. Sleep well.'

Alice shut the door behind her, leaving Ethel trembling with rage. She couldn't wait for morning to come so she could get out of this house. How could she trust a woman who made a habit of jilting her fiancés? For hadn't Alice been engaged to marry Jim, until he'd found her in the arms of his younger brother?

8

*T*hroughout the train journey from Ottawa to Toronto and then onward to Kitchener, Ethel stared blindly out of the window. She was oblivious to the passing scenery, as all she could think about was her strange encounter with Alice Armstrong. Why had Alice told her about the Howardson man? Or more to the point, why hadn't Joan?

Ethel's stomach churned whenever she remembered that terrible time, eleven years ago. She had been on a cloud of happiness when Greg Hooper asked her to marry him – even though she had known that it was inevitable the first time they met in the Snug bar of the Stag Inn. Until that night she'd thought love at first sight was a tired cliché. Something that only happened in the pictures. But the long-legged Canadian soldier had melted her heart.

That same night, Joan and Jim also met for the first time. While Greg and Ethel immediately hit it off, Joan and Jim were thrown together, obliged to make conversation with each other. Jim had appeared bored. Poor Joan pretended to feel nothing for him, but Ethel knew her cousin too well not to see through the pretence. Ethel had never imagined that one day she would be making this visit, alone, to join the married Joan and Jim, while Greg remained back in England, in the Canadian war graves section of Brookwood Cemetery.

Her pain over Greg's death had softened into a dull ache, an abiding sense of loss. But Alice telling her about the man who had brought about his untimely death had torn open the wound again. Over breakfast that morning, Ethel had been unable to take her eyes off five-year-old Catherine, the innocent progeny of that terrible man.

Why had Alice brought up the subject of Howardson? What good could she have possibly thought would come of mentioning it? Ethel didn't believe the excuse that she'd have found out anyway. It seemed unlikely that Jim's mother would raise it and, if Joan hadn't done so already, why would she now? Even if she did, it would have been easier to swallow than hearing it from Alice, when they'd only just met for the first and – she now hoped – only time.

The train ploughed on, through farmlands, past woods, lakes and towns. It swung south, then followed the shore of Lake Ontario until it reached Toronto. Instead of absorbing the view and being excited about what lay ahead, Ethel had a mounting sense of anxiety. Her stomach hadn't stopped churning since she'd left Ottawa. Perhaps she was being unfair at casting Alice in a consciously hostile role, but in her turmoil she could see her no other way.

By the time the train pulled into Toronto and she had to get off, drag her cases to another platform and change trains, Ethel was cursing Alice Armstrong to the darkest corner of hell. Why had she gone via Ottawa? Montreal would have been a much better place to break her journey. Ottawa had added time to an already exhausting trip, and what had been the point of having a bed for the night when she had been unable to sleep?

That morning as she was leaving, Alice told her she had put the photographs for Joan and birthday gifts for the boys into Ethel's suitcase. Too shocked to say anything at the time, Ethel had been in an increasing rage about the liberties the woman had taken. It was hard not to imagine Alice having a good rummage inside the suitcase.

Once settled into the smaller local train for the last leg to Kitchener, Ethel tried to calm herself. She looked out of the window at the monotonous scenery and decided she hated Canada. The weeks ahead loomed in front of her and seemed an interminable prospect. She wished her mum were still alive. Nothing would be nicer than being drawn into Violet Underwood's ample bosom for a hug and a good cry.

As the train drew into the station she saw Jim immediately. He was holding the hand of a tousle-haired boy of around five while a much-grown Jimmy stood slightly apart, watching the train and the disembarking passengers.

Momentarily forgetting her anger at Alice, Ethel allowed herself to be caught up in a bear hug from Jim. Knowing how small boys hated to be kissed by 'aged' aunties, she had planned to show some respectful deference to Jimmy but seeing the little boy so grown-up after five years, she couldn't help planting a kiss on his soft cheek. Evidently a polite little boy, he didn't attempt to rub it away afterwards. Little Sam was shy, clinging to his father's trouser legs.

'Harry's teething at the moment so Joan has stayed home with him. Mind you, the size she is now, you'd probably not have fitted in the car if she'd come along too. It would have been you or your luggage.'

Ethel smiled and gave his arm a squeeze.

'I can't tell you how excited Joan is,' he said. 'I don't think she's slept for days. Keeps beating carpets and cleaning windows. Anyone would think the new queen was coming to visit.' He grinned at her.

They piled into the car, where a small scruffy dog was waiting for them on the back seat. 'This is Olive,' said Jimmy, solemnly. 'Short for Olive Oyl. She's my dog.' The word 'my' was emphasised.

Ethel reached over the back of the seat and patted the dog. 'Pleased to meet you, Olive. I hope we can be friends?'

'Yes, I think she likes you.' Jimmy looked at her with a serious expression. 'She doesn't like strangers usually.'

'You're honoured.' Jim manoeuvred the car out of the station onto the road. 'Now sit back and enjoy the trip. It'll take us about an hour.'

They drove for a while in silence, punctuated by the chatter and intermittent squabbling between the boys in the back.

Eventually Jim asked, 'How did you find Alice?'

'She was well.'

'The girls?'

'Very sweet.'

'We've never met Catherine. Alice doesn't seem to want to come back to Hollowtree. And with the farm and everything, we've never had the chance to visit her in Ottawa. Although there's talk between Alice and Joan about Jimmy going for a visit in the school break. And Rose has been to stay with Ma and Pa every once in a while, and with Mrs Ducroix, Alice's mother. But Alice and her mother haven't spoken in years. Poor Joan has to play go-between to sort out the arrangements.'

Ethel turned and looked out of the window. She didn't want to hear any more about Alice. She was surprised Jim was so affable about her, given that she'd jilted him for his brother and then had a child with the man responsible for his best friend's death.

'You all right, Ethel? Tired? How was the trip?'

Grateful for the change in subject she said, 'I loved the sea crossing. I'd no idea so many people emigrate to Canada. They were all so excited.'

'It's a great country. As long as you're prepared to work hard. Many people aren't. A family from England bought up the old Howardson place a few years ago. Only lasted there ten months. One winter was all it took, and they were on the next ship back to Britain.' He grinned at her. 'No spine. You've got to be prepared to live with snow for four or five months every year.'

Howardson again. There was no escaping the man. Ethel refused to let her curiosity get the better of her by asking if this was the same Howardson.

'You'll see the snow soon enough, Ethel. Won't she, boys?'

'Coming in a week or so.' Jimmy nodded his head sagely.

'It's usually here until late March.'

'How do you manage to get around?'

'Snow tyres. Horses. Snow shoes. A good pair of water-proof boots. You adapt to it. Trains and buses still run. We have snow ploughs. Nothing grinds to a halt.' Jim brushed his hair out of his eyes and grinned at her again.

'So, did Alice look after you well?'

'Yes.'

Jim seemed to be waiting for her to elaborate and when she didn't, he glanced at her and seemed about to say something else but must have decided against it. How could he be so casual about that woman? How could he forgive Alice for ignoring his warning about Tip Howardson after what he'd done to Greg?

The forest and farmland gave way to houses on the side of the road and these turned into a small town.

'Welcome to Hollowtree. Not sure which came first, our farm or the town, but we like to claim it was the farm.'

Jimmy, and a now more vocal Sam, pointed out the places of interest, including their schools and the local library. It made sleepy old Aldershot seem like a buzzing metropolis in comparison. How on earth could Joan stand living here?

*J*oan was standing at the window watching out for them.

The boys and Olive, the dog, barrelled into the house first, with Ethel close behind them and Jim bringing up the rear with the luggage. Joan rushed over to Ethel, wrapping her arms around her and squeezing her as tightly as her bump would allow. Over Ethel's shoulder she could see Jim pulling a face. He raised his hands as if to indicate caution. Joan realised that Ethel was standing stiffly, rather than returning her embrace with matching enthusiasm.

Jim called to the boys and suggested they come with him into the next room and leave their mother and Aunty Ethel to catch up.

'The kettle's boiled. I'm sure you'll be ready for a cup of tea after the journey,' said Joan, suddenly nervous. What was wrong with Ethel?

She didn't have to wait long to find out. As soon as the door closed behind Jim and the boys, Ethel said, 'Why didn't you tell me the man who killed Greg had turned up here in

Hollowtree? Why didn't you tell me he'd had a child with your sister-in-law?'

Joan twisted her head to the closed door to the family room – what the hell had Jim said? 'Ethel, I'm so sorry. It wasn't the kind of thing I wanted to put in a letter. I knew it would upset you.'

'Did you know your sister-in-law was going to tell me?'

'Alice? *Alice* told you about Tip?' Joan was incredulous.

'Oh, yes. Sat on the end of my bed and told me he was the father of her little girl. Why on earth would she tell me that? And why the hell didn't you warn me?'

'Oh, Ethel. I'm so sorry. I had no idea. I can't think what possessed her.'

'She said if she hadn't told me, your mother-in-law would.'

'What?' Joan gasped. 'Ma would never dream of it. I don't understand what's got into Alice. It was cruel and unnecessary. Look, sit down. Have some tea.'

Ethel sat, still angry, but unable to resist a cup of restorative tea.

As they drank the tea, Joan wrestled with herself. There was more Ethel should probably know about Tip Howardson. She was reluctant to dredge up the unpleasant details, but Ethel would be furious if she kept it from her. It was only since coming to Hollowtree herself that Joan had found out that Tip Howardson was the man who had attacked her on the way home from her job in a fish and chip shop in Aldershot, early in the war. Gulping down her tea and refilling her cup she swallowed and told Ethel.

Gasping, Ethel asked, 'You mean the man who killed my Greg was the same Canadian soldier who assaulted you in the bus shelter?'

The memory of that night was something Joan didn't

want to dwell on. The attack had terrified her so much that, despite the fact she had escaped before the man raped her, she had given up her job in the chippy and joined the ATS.

'My God, Joan. How on earth did you find out?'

Joan shivered, remembering the afternoon when Tip Howardson had materialised in front of her in the local Hollowtree café. 'He came up to me when I was having a coffee in town and tried to grope me under the table.'

Ethel gasped, hand over her mouth.

'He made it clear it wasn't the last I was going to see of him. I was too scared to go into town on my own again. I still had no idea he was Tip. The man in the bus shelter said he was called Bill. I didn't realise he was the same chap Jim was warning Alice to keep away from.'

Ethel reached for her cousin's hand. 'Did he hurt you again, Joanie?'

Joan closed her eyes for a moment. The memory was painful. 'He tried. One night at a barn dance. I'd gone outside for a few moments and he appeared from nowhere and tried to ... you know. I don't have to spell it out. Jim got there just in time.'

'Why didn't you tell me all this?'

'I didn't want to put it in a letter. Then when I came back to Aldershot I had other things on my mind.'

Ethel nodded and squeezed Joan's hand. 'Is Howardson still around?'

'No. He was practically run out of Hollowtree. Half the town saw what happened at the barn dance. He has no friends here as a result.' She gave her head a little shake as if trying to dismiss the memory. 'There were rumours about him being chased by some hoodlums from the United States. Must have owed them money. He's bad to the bone, that man.'

Joan sipped her tea and looked at Ethel, her face still anxious. 'Once he'd gone we all wanted to forget about him as quickly as possible. Including Alice. That's why she went to Ottawa to start a new life. So, you can see why I never dreamt she'd tell you all that.'

Ethel took a deep breath. 'I'm sorry, Joan. I didn't mean to question your loyalty. You've always been there for me.'

Joan got up from her seat and came around to Ethel's side of the table and hugged her cousin again. 'Oh, Ethel, love, I can't tell you how much I miss you and how happy I am you're here. I'm sorry about what happened with Alice. Don't let it come between us.'

'As long as you don't expect me to like her.'

'In view of what's happened, how could I? I can only think she's upset by her Aunt Miriam dying.' She paused. 'And oh, I haven't even said how terribly sad I am about Aunty Vi. Was it awful? I so wish I could have been there for you.'

Ethel put her cup down. 'Oh, Joan, it was horrible. Her breathing getting weaker and fainter all the time, slowly slipping away. For hours and hours.'

'You poor thing. All on your own.' Joan's eyes filled with tears.

'Your mum was with me a lot of the time. Not right at the end. That came quicker than I thought, and I'd told her to go home. I had no idea it was going to happen when it did.'

Ethel wiped her eyes with her handkerchief then passed it to Joan who did the same. 'Look at us. A right pair of weepies. Enough of sadness. Stand up and let me get a proper look at you. I want to see if Jim was right when he said you were as big as a house.'

'He said what?' Joan put her hands on the table and

pulled herself upright, thrusting her belly out in front of her.

Ethel grinned. 'He wasn't wrong either. You look as if you're already about to pop, girl.'

Joan groaned. 'I know. And I've another six weeks to go. I won't be able to walk soon – I'm already waddling like a duck.'

'Are you excited?'

'Yes, I am, actually. Even though it's number four. I should be quite blasé about it, shouldn't I? But I'm absolutely certain it's going to be a girl. And much as I adore all my boys I do feel a bit outnumbered at times!'

'Do you have a name in mind?'

'Not yet.' She grinned. 'Maybe Ethel?'

'I'll kill you, Joan Armstrong, if you dare to inflict my terrible old-fashioned name on a poor innocent child.'

Joan laughed. 'You're going to be her godmother, though.'

'Oh, how can I refuse that? I'll be thrilled and honoured.'

'What do you think of my boys?' Joan's eyes lit up with pride.

'Jimmy's grown to quite the young man. I don't think he remembers me though.' She pulled a sad face. 'And Sam's the cutest little fellow. So shy.'

'Shy?' Joan chuckled. 'Wait 'til you hear him and Jimmy having one of their regular fights. Or have to listen to him chattering on and on about every single thing that happened in school. He just needs to get used to you. You'll soon be wondering where that shy little chap disappeared to.'

'And I'm dying to see the little one.'

'Harry's having his afternoon nap. He'll be awake soon and you can meet him.'

As Joan spoke, a high-pitched wail came from upstairs and the two women laughed.

~

Later on, after supper, Joan sat at the table feeding Harry, while Ethel washed the dishes.

'You shouldn't be doing that. You're the guest.'

'If you treat me like a guest I'll be on the next ship home. Besides, I like being useful.

'Tell me all about the journey. How was the ship? Did you get seasick?

Ethel told her about the *Scythia* and how much she'd enjoyed the crossing. Joan listened, unable to stop smiling that at last her beloved cousin was standing here, doing the dishes, as if they were in Aunty Vi's back kitchen in Aldershot.

Eventually, and probably inevitably, the conversation found its way back to Alice.

'Do you really like Alice, Joan? Don't you find her a bit, you know, mean?'

'Mean? No. Well, maybe at first. 'Til I got to know her better. She can be a bit wary, untrusting. Brittle even. She's never got over Walt dying. They'd only been married a few weeks when he joined up.'

'You don't need to tell me what that feels like.'

'I know, love.'

'I can't imagine wanting to marry anyone else after losing Greg. Yet there's Alice, having a child with a man she claims she didn't even like. Then getting engaged to another one and jilting him.' She looked at Joan. 'She seems to make a habit of jilting her fiancés. First Jim and now this other chap.'

'Alice was engaged?' Joan gasped.

'You didn't know?'

'No. She never mentioned a thing.'

'Told me it was some fellow she met a couple of years ago in the post office. As soon as she heard she was inheriting her aunt's money she gave him the push.'

'Goodness me. I knew about her inheritance. But I knew nothing of an engagement. She's a dark horse, is Alice.'

Ethel sucked her lips inwards. 'She said she was only marrying him because of her girls. She'd expected to be homeless when her aunt passed away. I think she was astonished to find she's been left the house.'

'More than the house. Miss Cooke was a wealthy woman. Alice won't have to worry any more about money. Did she give you the snaps for me?'

'Upstairs in my suitcase. You want them now? I can go and unpack.' Ethel started to get up.

Joan laid a hand on her arm. 'Tomorrow will do. Stay where you are.'

'There's birthday gifts for the boys from Alice and the girls.'

'That's good of her.'

Ethel snorted. 'That's the other thing that made me dislike her. She opened my suitcase, without asking, and packed the photographs and presents inside.'

Joan laughed. 'That's because she sees you as family. She will have been trying to make things easy for you.'

'Hmm, I'm glad you see it that way.'

Joan reached for her cousin's hand. 'Look, I'm sorry you and Alice have got off on the wrong foot. And if it's any consolation, I did too. But she's got a good heart. She's just different from us.'

'I hope your Jim thanks his lucky stars every night that she dumped him for his brother and he ended up with you.'

Jim's voice came from the doorway. 'You don't have to worry on that score. He does.' He walked into the kitchen and dropped a kiss on his wife's head. 'Every day of my life I say a little prayer of thanks that I have Joan.' He smiled at Ethel then turned back to Joan. 'Boys are both in bed. You going up to kiss them goodnight, Joan?'

He reached for Harry, who was now fast asleep in her arms. 'Come on, little 'un. Come to Daddy.'

10

*T*he lawyer had warned Alice it could take up to six months for probate to be granted and her aunt's assets transferred to her. During the waiting period, Alice and her daughters would remain in the house, in accordance with Miss Cooke's wishes.

Alice was able to get by on the small cash sum the old lady had the foresight to give to her before her death, in order to tide her over until her estate was settled. Alice was not extravagant and managed to make ends meet without difficulty, her only indulgence being to get each of the girls a pair of new winter shoes and a warm coat. She sent up a silent prayer of thanks to her late aunt. The children grew so fast it was hard to keep up.

She hadn't yet made up her mind what to do once the money came through: remain in Ottawa or return home to Hollowtree? If they were going to move, now would be the logical time, as Catherine was due to begin school soon and Rose would be starting at high school the following year. But it would still be a big disruption for them. Rose had made friends in Ottawa. Catherine had known no other home.

And as for Alice's parents? They had disowned her when she left Hollowtree and Walt's mother, Helga, had made her disapproval clear too. Perhaps it would be better to stay put for a while? A year maybe? Long enough to get used to her new circumstances. But there was a yearning inside Alice to go back to Hollowtree. She missed the small-town life, the familiar countryside. Rose loved visiting her grandparents and Alice wanted both girls to grow up among her extended family. She counted Joan as her only friend and it would be good for the girls to be able to play with their cousins, just as Rose had done with Jimmy when they had lived on the farm.

Once she had control of her inheritance she would be able to return home with head held high. She could buy a house in town, do as she pleased, immune to the tittle-tattle that would have dogged her before. With money in the bank she wouldn't be dependent on her old job at the library. Not that she wanted to go back there anyway. The chief librarian had been an old dragon and doubtless would be horrified at Alice being the mother of an illegitimate child.

There had been substantial obituaries for Miriam Cooke in all the leading newspapers when she died. Alice was surprised to learn that her great-aunt had been active in the women's suffrage movement in her youth, as well as campaigning for improvements in public health. Why had she had been so incurious about the old lady's past? It was hard to imagine that Aunty Miriam had once been a young woman, in spite of the oil painting in the drawing room.

To have established and run her own business as a single woman, in the late nineteenth century and the turn of the twentieth, must have been an unusual and notable achievement. No wonder her aunt had never got around to marrying. Inspired by her example, Alice would prove Aunt Miriam wrong. She neither needed nor wanted to have a husband in her life.

Alice spent hours sorting through old photographs and newspaper cuttings, piecing together her great-aunt's story. One day she would pass all this on to her daughters. They had reason to be proud of their great-great-aunt and Alice wanted to be sure they wouldn't forget her – or the way she had secured their future wellbeing.

Not long after Miriam Cooke's demise, her lawyer, Mr Freeman, summoned Alice for a meeting at his firm's imposing downtown offices to update her on progress with the resolution of the estate. He took her through balance sheets and bank statements until her head was spinning.

'Once probate is granted, I strongly recommend you keep the funds under the management of a broker. While Miss Cooke liked to oversee her stock portfolio herself, she had a property management firm look after the commercial properties. You would be well-advised to appoint a stockbroker and continue to use the same property management company. Just sit back and enjoy the profits.' He gave her a patronising smile.

'I would like to have a more active involvement,' she said. 'I don't mean in managing what's there already. Unlike my aunt, I know nothing of the stock market and I can't see how I would add anything in the collection of rents for the properties. Those are specialist fields. But I would like to set aside some money to invest in something that would provide me with employment as well as income.'

Mr Freeman raised his eyebrows. 'But you will have no need of employment, Mrs Armstrong. You will never need to work again.'

'I am not ready to retire. I'm only thirty-two. I want to have something to do.'

'You are a mother to two lovely daughters. Isn't that employment enough?'

'My daughters are at school. What do you expect me to do all day?'

'I suppose you could get involved in charitable works.'

'Possibly. But I'm not a woman who would fit in well on a committee. I have no interest in organising fundraising events. I'm not used to mixing with the kind of people who do that sort of thing.' She twisted her hands together, suddenly nervous. 'And I have no wish to do so. After all, my aunt worked hard to make the money in the first place. I know so little of her history, Mr Freeman.' She turned her smile on him. 'Can you tell me something about her?'

He appeared surprised and not a little impatient. 'Your late aunt benefited from a small legacy on the early death of her parents, soon after the family arrived here from England. Miss Cooke invested it wisely and was able to build a sizeable amount of capital.'

'But how?'

'Gradually, over the years, she built a commercial property portfolio of over twenty shops and offices. It all started with one small haberdashery store which she expanded and eventually sold off in the late twenties to Ogilvy's department stores.'

Alice nodded. 'She was quite a woman, my Aunty Miriam.'

'A formidable lady. She was also an active patron of the arts.'

'When my aunt inherited her money from her father, what was it worth?'

The lawyer took his glasses off, polished the lenses, replaced them, then pressed a bell on his desk. A woman came into the room.

'Bring me the Cooke files, Miss Jenkins.'

The woman disappeared for a few minutes then returned, bearing a box file which she placed on the desk.

He waved her away and opened the file, shuffling through papers and sighing occasionally. Alice sat with her hands in her lap, refusing to be intimidated. After all, she was the client. She was paying for his services.

At last he looked up. 'Miss Cooke, and her brother, your maternal grandfather, Martin Cooke, were each left one hundred and fifty dollars upon the death of their parents in 1885. Before my time of course.' He coughed and adjusted his glasses. 'The parents died within days of each other. Influenza.'

Alice nodded. 'When my grandfather died, he was worth little more than the clothes he stood up in. My mother was his only child and she inherited nothing. My great-aunt must have worked extremely hard to turn that one hundred and fifty dollars into the amount she has left to me.'

The lawyer nodded. 'That is undeniable. A woman to be reckoned with, was Miss Cooke.'

'So, if she could do that in the days when women didn't even have a vote, then I should be able to work just as hard today.'

'You want *more* money?'

Alice tried not to sound exasperated. 'No. I have more than enough. It's not about the money itself. I want to prove to myself that I can be successful. That I can be independent.'

Mr Freeman shook his head. 'But you *are* independent. That's what Miss Cooke's money has done for you.'

Alice was never going to convince the man. And she didn't need to. It was her money. All she had to do was decide what she was going to do with it.

*D*espite Jimmy's prediction that snow was on the way, the boy was proved wrong. By the time the week of his birthday arrived in late November there had not even been a flurry.

'This time last year we'd already had eighteen inches,' said Jim over breakfast. 'Looks as though this year's going to be a mild winter.'

He was trying to diffuse the tension at the table caused by Joan breaking the news to their eldest son that his birthday celebrations this year were going to have to be very low key, spent over at his grandparents' place, and shared with Sam. This had provoked an outburst of protests. Sam, for his part, had taken the news happily, unconcerned about sharing the limelight with his older brother.

'For goodness' sake, Jimmy. I've explained to you about Pop being ill. You can have a party with your friends next year, but this year is going to be a quiet celebration with the family only.' Joan wiped her hands on a dish towel and rolled her eyes heavenwards.

'It's not fair. I don't want to have my birthday with a baby.'

'How many times have I told you? Stop calling your brother a baby. You know very well he's not a baby. Harry's a baby. Sam's a boy and will be going to big school with you after Christmas.'

'But he goes to baby school now.'

Sam looked up. 'Not baby school and I'm not a baby,' he stated mildly.

Jim got up from the table. 'Come on now, both of you, or you'll miss the school bus. I don't want to hear any more about it.' He kissed Joan, waved to Ethel and ushered the boys out of the house.

Joan sat down at the table. 'Sometimes I'd like to knock Jimmy's block off. He knows how ill his grandfather is. He can be a little devil. It's just one year for heaven's sake. He can have a proper party with all his classmates next year.'

'I suppose a year is a long time when you're only ten.' Ethel got up and began to clear away the dishes. 'You stay sitting. Keep the weight off your feet. You work too hard, Joanie. You look done in.'

'I'm fine – apart from a bit of backache, lumbering this giant football of a baby around.

Ethel finished the washing-up and came to sit down opposite her cousin. 'I must admit, I'm a bit nervous about meeting your in-laws.'

Joan laughed. 'Don's a pet. An absolute sweetie, poor soul. I'm going to miss him so much.' She swallowed. 'And Helga's like a friend to me now. Hard to believe she was such a cow when I first arrived here.'

'Bad as that? You were always so chirpy in your letters.'

'Putting a brave face on it.' She winced and stretched her back. 'It wasn't personal. I don't think anyone would have been good enough for Jim in Ma's eyes. And, of course, she'd been nursing this private fantasy that Jim and Alice would end up together.'

Ethel's eyes widened. 'You're kidding.'

'Nope. She honestly thought that Jim would come back from the war and he and Alice would fall gratefully into each other's arms.'

'After what she did to Jim? Dumping him for his brother?'

'Yup! When Ma gets an idea in her head it takes a ton of dynamite to shift it.'

'And did she make it obvious? Even after you got here?'

'Every bloody day! Pardon my French. She acted like the sun shone out of Alice's backside and I was nothing but a cheap tart.'

Ethel stretched out her hand and took her cousin's. 'You poor love. I don't know how you stuck it out.'

'Yes, well. She came round in the end. And once Ma's in your corner, she's a formidable ally. I love her to bits now.'

'You're a very forgiving woman, Joan. But I'm terrified at the prospect of meeting her.'

'Don't be. She'll love you. What's not to love? And you're not a threat to her masterplan.'

'What's that?'

Joan laughed. 'I don't think there is one now. Not since I thwarted her last one!' She turned serious. 'I suppose it's to make Don's last days as good as they can be. She'll be a mess when he's gone. He's the only person who's ever been able to stand up to her. She worships the ground he walks on.' Joan gave a little sob. 'Oh, Ethel. I'm going to miss him so much. He's been a father to me. I never had one before, with my own father running off when I was little.'

Ethel squeezed her hand and said, 'I'm here for you now, Joanie.'

The day of the boys' joint birthday party dawned bright and sunny, with still no sign of snow in the sky. The Armstrongs and Ethel walked along the dirt track that linked their home with Hollowtree Farm, Jim carrying Harry, Ethel carrying a bag with the boys' presents, and Joan holding a tin with the birthday cake inside. Despite the sunshine, there was a chill in the air. Ethel looked around at the farm, its rows of cabbages, potatoes and beets, neatly regimented.

'You just grow vegetables?' Ethel asked Jim.

Jim laughed. 'No. Just at this end of the farm. Over that rise in the ground there, there's beans, some winter wheat, then in summer we grow sweetcorn and we've put in a couple of acres of apple orchards.' He pointed. 'Down there, past the new silo.'

'Don't forget the maples,' Joan chipped in.

'Yes, there's a stand of maples behind the house and another smaller one over near the creek at Hollowtree. We make our own maple syrup. Right now, Ma is in charge of production, with Joan helping when the kids permit, but next winter I'm planning on putting in some equipment and building a proper sugar-house so we can produce on a larger scale. Maybe buy in sap from outside to process into syrup.'

'You haven't tried our maple syrup yet,' said Joan. 'We'll have to sort that. I'll fix up some pancakes for breakfast tomorrow.'

Jimmy looked up at Ethel. 'It's made from trees. The sap

comes out of the tree trunks and Grandma and Mum turn it into syrup. I help.'

Ethel's expression was dubious.

Jim, always happy to talk about the farm, said, 'Right now it's just a small-scale operation, but if we install some proper kit we can increase production. There's more profit in selling finished products than raw produce. I went to a talk a couple of months ago in Kitchener. They called it "adding value".'

Joan put her hands up. 'Don't get him started. You'll feel like you're a student at agricultural college by the time he's finished.'

As they approached the farmhouse, Joan turned to the two boys. 'Remember what I said, boys. Pop's not well, so no shouting and horsing around. Best behaviour.'

Jimmy gave an exaggerated sigh and headed across the yard, Olive Oyl at his heels, with Sam scampering along behind them.

Joan turned to Ethel. 'He's behaving badly because he's upset. It's his way of covering it. He adores Don.'

They followed the boys into the house. The kitchen table was laid for tea with plates of sandwiches and jam tarts, and another awaiting the birthday cake Joan had brought with her. On the sideboard was an over-sized jelly, which the boys were already eyeing.

'I told you not to go to any trouble, Ma. You've enough on your plate without doing all this baking too,' said Joan.

'If I can't bake for my grandsons' birthdays then that would be a sorry state of affairs.' She raised her arms to Jimmy and Sam, squatting low and drawing them into a hug.

Helga looked up and noticed Ethel standing back by the kitchen door. 'You must be Ethel. Welcome to Hollowtree.'

She moved across the space and wrapped her arms around Ethel in an effusive welcome. 'I've heard a lot about you, young lady. All of it good.' She beamed as she released Ethel from her embrace.

'I'm sorry to hear about your husband being so poorly, Mrs Armstrong.'

The smile faded from Helga's face. 'It's Helga and Don. And thank you, dear. The doc's upstairs with him now.' She turned to her son. 'Your pa wants to see the boys. We have to bring them up as soon as the doctor's done with him. He's fitting him up to the oxygen machine.'

'It's arrived then?' said Joan.

'Came this morning. A big metal cylinder. Two spares in the barn. Doc says he had quite a battle convincing them to allow it for home use. It's normally strictly hospital only. They're scared we might blow the place up.' She shook her head. 'Had to go through all sorts of safety instructions. And he has to come out every day to make sure we're using it right. At least for the first couple of weeks.' Helga turned back to her son. 'When we're on the last one, we'll need to run the empties over to Kitchener and swap them for filled ones. Doc says your pa's going to need these pretty much all the time since his breathing's so bad. He's shown me how to change them over, but I'll need you to haul them upstairs, Jim.'

Jim nodded, his face grim.

Helga turned to the two boys. 'Your grandpop needs a bit of help with his breathing. He has to use a mask and oxygen. When you see him, I don't want you to be scared.'

The boys stared at her and nodded, both subdued.

The door into the kitchen opened and Dr Robinson came into the room. 'I understand it's a special birthday celebration today. Happy birthday, boys! Your grandfather is waiting to see you. But no shouting. No climbing on the bed. And try not to tire him.' He nodded at Helga. 'Maybe you should go up too, Mrs Armstrong.'

Helga took the two boys by the hands and went upstairs.

Joan had already put the kettle on to boil. 'You must stay for some tea and birthday cake, Dr Robinson.'

The doctor glanced at his watch. 'I guess it is Saturday and I've finished my rounds. This was my last call.'

Jim made his excuses and went upstairs too.

'I can't imagine how they'll all fit in that bedroom.' Joan carried the pot of tea to the table. 'Sorry, Doc, I didn't even ask. Is tea all right or would you like me to fix you some coffee?'

'Tea is perfect.' The doctor sat at the table.

Dr Robinson was probably in his early forties, Ethel guessed. He had a nice face. Warm, friendly, with brown eyes. His hair was thick with a slight wave in the front. A bit like Greg's. Ethel became aware of Joan watching her, blushed and looked away.

Joan made the introductions and Ethel squirmed as she felt the doctor's eyes upon her, conscious of the heat in her face.

Jimmy burst through the door. 'I need some cake for Pop.'

Joan smiled at him. 'I'm making him a cup of tea. I'll bring them both up in a minute.'

'No.' Jimmy looked fierce. 'Pop doesn't want tea. Just cake. I want to take it up to him. It's my birthday. It's my cake.'

'But you haven't blown out the candles yet.'

Jimmy scowled. 'I don't want to blow out the stupid candles. Just give me the piece of cake.' His lip was trembling.

Joan opened her mouth to reprimand him, then thought better of it. She cut the piece of cake and handed it, wordlessly, to her son, who pushed the door open and scuttled back up the stairs.

Joan shook her head. 'I know he's upset about Don, but he's behaving like a little monster at the moment.'

'It's understandable, Mrs Armstrong. Cut him some slack. He probably senses his grandfather is dying and he's struggling to come to terms with it. It's hard for a child to understand death.' The doctor's words were addressed to Joan, but his eyes were fixed on Ethel, as though seeking her endorsement.

Ethel looked away from his gaze, face burning. Tongue-tied.

12

*E*thel awoke early from a troubled sleep. The bedroom was dark, and she lay listening to rain falling outside the window, wondering whether it was night or morning. Her head was full of the dream she'd woken from. Usually she struggled to hold onto a dream, but this one was stubbornly concrete. Maybe not the finer details, but its central premise. She had been dreaming about Dr Robinson.

She rolled over, trying to push away the image of him imprinted inside her eyelids. But he wouldn't budge. Instead, Ethel found herself looking into his eyes, those kind eyes, that seemed to see right inside her. Go away, she told him. Get out of my head. I've no room for you.

She turned onto her back, adjusting her vision to the still dark room, hoping that normality would return, that she could expunge this man from her head, block out his unwanted intrusion. But the dark shapes of the furniture were not enough to make him recede into her subconsciousness. So she told herself to think about Greg.

Usually, Greg appeared on command, his features blurrier over the years, but his voice still imprinted on her memory, wrapping her in a cocoon where only the two of them could exist. But this morning Greg wouldn't oblige. The more she tried to summon him, picture him, shape him in her head, the less he was Greg, morphing instead into Dr Robinson. It was like seeing a reflection in a pond, throwing a stone in to make it disappear, only for it to form again as the ripples faded.

Ethel dragged herself up into a sitting position, then swung her legs out of the bed. Telling the recalcitrant doctor to leave her alone, she pushed her feet into her slippers.

The room was cold. She shivered and pulled the counterpane around her shoulders and moved towards the window. Drawing open the curtain, to her disappointment she saw it was still dark. The sky was clouded and black with no sign of moon or stars and heavy rain was beating a tattoo on the porch roof below her bedroom window. Ethel shivered, pulled the curtain back into place and returned to bed.

Still no snow. She'd been looking forward to finding out what a real Canadian winter was like. But all this rain? She could have that back in England.

Think of Christmas, she told herself. She lay on her back, imagining a tree decked with baubles, holly and ivy draped over the mantelpiece. Did they have holly and ivy in Canada? She must ask Joan. She pictured the little boys' faces full of excitement, eager to find out what Father Christmas had brought them. And there was Santa Claus, grinning though his fluffy white beard. He was moving towards her holding up a sprig of mistletoe. Dr Robinson! No! Go away!

Ethel thumped the pillow. Pull yourself together, woman! You can't blame the poor chap. He has no idea he's haunting your dreams and stalking you as you wake. It's all in your own head. Stop it. Right now. You saw the wedding ring on his left hand. And anyway, there's no one else in this world for you but Greg. Even thinking about anyone else is betraying his memory.

But Greg wasn't in this world. Not anymore. Tears rose, and Ethel didn't try to stop them. It was so unfair. Every day observing how happy Jim and Joan were. Seeing the joy they got from their family. Witnessing love that had been denied to her.

Ethel wiped her tears away. She despised self-pity and she wasn't going to indulge in it now. She was only here for a couple of months then she'd be going back to Aldershot, back to the salon and her regular customers. Back to her everyday routine and the life she knew, in the place that had always been home...Yes, and back to an empty house and another grave to tend. Back to putting on a bright face while her heart ached with loneliness.

Ethel closed her eyes, breathed slowly and let herself drift back to sleep. It was pointless fighting it. And what harm was a dream?

Across the landing, Joan was also lying awake. It was hard to get comfortable enough to sleep for long. She'd be glad when the baby was here. This one made her more tired than the boys had – often waking her in the middle of the night by sudden movements – and she was convinced the bump she was carting around in front of her was bigger at this stage than the others had been. This baby certainly put more strain on her back.

She felt Jim stir beside her. He had to be up early, and sleep was precious. She leaned over his body, reaching for his wristwatch, and looked at the luminous dial on its face. Four o'clock. He'd have to be up in an hour. Better lie still and try not to disturb him.

As she was thinking this, Jim's arm reached out and pulled her closer to him. 'Can't you sleep, hon?'

'Sorry, I didn't mean to wake you.'

He put his hand against her stomach. 'Is she kicking you again?'

'No, just fluttering about.'

Joan could feel his soft breath against the back of her neck. She loved moments like this, lying here together, warm and close, listening to each other's breathing. No children making demands, no food to get on the table, no fields to plough or machinery to clean. Just each other.

'Jim?'

'Yes?' His voice was drowsy.

'Do you think Dr Robinson likes Ethel?'

'Go to sleep.'

'Just tell me first.'

Jim grunted. 'Course he likes Ethel. Everyone likes Ethel. Now go to sleep.'

'I don't mean like. I mean _like_.'

No answer.

Joan propped herself on her elbow, but he was already sleeping again.

∾

Ninety minutes later they were both awake and in the kitchen. Joan always got up with him to fix his breakfast, enjoying the precious time they were alone, before the boys had to be roused and readied for school.

She cracked two eggs into the frying pan. 'You didn't answer my question about Dr Robinson.'

'What question?' Jim rubbed his eyes and sipped his coffee.

Joan set a plate of bacon and eggs in front of him and sat down opposite, nursing a cup of tea. 'Whether he really likes Ethel.'

'You mean does he find her attractive? He must do. Ethel's a beautiful woman.'

Joan was persistent. 'I know that, but did you notice anything special between them? Because I did. They kept looking at each other, pretending they weren't.'

'Can't say I did. But then I'm not the most observant of guys, am I? Took me forever to realise you were interested in me. And women notice these things more than men do anyway.'

'Well, I'm certain of it.'

'In that case, why are you–'

'I think they'd make a lovely couple.'

Jim paused, his fork halfway towards his mouth. 'What plot are you hatching now, Joanie? You know she's only here for a couple of months.'

'A couple of months is plenty of time to fall in love. It only took her a couple of minutes with poor Greg.' Whether he wanted this conversation or not, Joan was going to make sure they had it. Jim suppressed a sigh and resigned himself to talking. 'I don't think she's ever got over Greg. Must be more than ten years now.'

'Eleven.'

'But you can't just shove her and the doc together. And what's the point if she has to go back to England?'

'That's the whole point! Why should she go back? She's nothing there to go back to. All her family's dead. Just her job in that crummy hairdressing salon, where she does all the work and the owner gets all the money. Exploitation, it is. I don't think she's had a pay rise since she started there after the war.'

'Times are tough in England.'

'Not that tough. Anyway, never mind all that. Wouldn't you like Ethel to be happy again? Don't you think she deserves it?'

'Course I do. But you can't force these things. If they like each other they like each other. Give it time. Don't interfere. Anyway, isn't he married? I thought he had a daughter who works as the receptionist in his surgery.'

'Wife's been dead for years. Ma thinks she died in childbirth. They came from up north during the war and no one knows much about them.'

'He's older than Ethel.'

'So? Not much. Maybe ten years. What's wrong with that?'

Jim shrugged. 'Nothing, I suppose. But as I said, Joanie, let things take their course.'

'I think I might just give them a little nudge. In fact, I have a brilliant idea.'

'Oh yes?' Jim's tone was sceptical.

'We could invite him and the daughter to Hollowtree for Christmas dinner. We can squeeze a couple more round the table. Ma won't mind. It'll be a chance for him and Ethel to get to know each other better.'

'What if he and his daughter have other plans?'

'I bet they haven't. And what's the harm in asking?'

'You mentioned this to Ethel yet?'

'No. I thought we'd ask the doctor first. Don't want to get her hopes up if he has other arrangements.'

'Sometimes I'm in awe of your devious mind, Mrs Armstrong.'

'Only sometimes?'

13

*L*ater that morning, a Sunday, after Jim had headed out with the two boys to church, Joan and Ethel remained in the kitchen. Ethel washed the dishes, while Joan was feeding Harry. Joan hadn't felt up to going into town to church and Ethel was only too happy to stay behind with her and the baby.

When she'd finished the washing-up, Ethel moved over to the window and looked out at the rain-soaked farm. It was still pouring.

'I thought you told me it snowed in December.'

'It usually does. But I don't control the weather. Once it comes you'll long for days like this.' Joan gave a dry laugh. 'I'm certainly glad to delay tramping or driving through drifting snow for another month.'

'How will the midwife get here if there's thick snow?'

'We're used to snow. Anyway, Ma delivered Sam and Harry.' Joan sighed. 'I had hoped she'd help bring this one into the world too. But if Don's still with us, and please God he will be, she won't be able to leave him. I'll have to have someone from town.'

Ethel took her hand. 'I'm no use to you in delivering the baby, but I can always go and sit with your father-in-law. He seemed such a lovely old chap when I saw him yesterday, even though it was only for a few minutes.'

'He's not even old.' Joan grimaced. 'Though he looks it. But I can't expect you to do that when you barely know him.'

'It's only to sit with him if he needs company, make the odd cup of tea. I can always telephone here and ask Jim to come over if the need arises.'

Joan thought for a moment. 'I'll ask Ma. Maybe it's not such a bad idea. And my labours have thankfully been fairly short so, with a bit of luck, you won't be over there for long. When Jim's finished work he can take over and you can come back here and keep an eye on the boys.' Then she grinned. 'Even better idea. Once I know it's started, Jim can take Sam and Jimmy to the Carlsons' place to stay overnight. I had their kids here when Betty Carlson was in labour back in June.'

'Right. That's settled then.'

'As long as Ma's happy. She may decide she'd rather be with Don than put up with me yelling and cursing her. Apparently, I came up with some choice expressions last time.'

'You're so brave,' said Ethel. 'It must be awful giving birth.' She shuddered.

'Yes, it's bloody awful. If men had to do it, babies would all be born under general anaesthetic.' She laughed. 'But as soon as you hold your baby in your arms, you forget all about the pain.' She shifted Harry in her arms. 'Talking of medical matters, what did you think of Dr Robinson?'

The blood rushed to Ethel's cheeks. She turned away and went back to the window. 'Why do you ask? He seemed pleasant enough.'

'Oh, just wondering... Actually, I did think he seemed rather taken with you.'

'Don't be silly, Joan. We barely spoke. You read all kinds of things in where they don't exist.' She kept her head turned away from Joan's gaze.

Jim poked his head around the door. 'Is it women only in here or can I come in too?'

Joan went to stand up. 'Stick the kettle on, Jim, and I'll make us all a coffee.

'I'll make it,' he said.

'No, you won't.' She turned to Ethel. 'Last time he offered to make the coffee it tasted like dishwater.'

'I'll do it,' said Ethel. 'But don't you want tea?'

'We always have a coffee on Sunday morning. You can have tea though if you want.'

'No. I'll have a coffee,' said Ethel, doubtfully.

'It's not that horrible Camp muck we have to drink at home. It's proper coffee, made with beans not chicory.'

'Well, in that case, I'll give it a try.'

Five minutes later the three of them were settled around the kitchen table.

'Did you ask the doc?' Joan threw a meaningful look at Jim.

'Ask him what?'

'About Christmas, dopey!'

'Yes.'

'And?'

'He said he needs to check with Sandra. But he reckons it'll be all right.' He glanced towards Ethel then back to Joan.

'Well done. I'll let Ma know,' said Joan.

Ethel twitched, sensing a plot afoot. She hoped they were referring to some aspect of Don's medical care but feared they weren't.

'It will be nice for them to enjoy a proper family Christmas. It must be a quiet affair for them, usually.' Joan was looking straight at Ethel.

Ethel squirmed, uncomfortable. Why would Joan want to include the doctor and his wife in the Armstrong Christmas? She prayed she wasn't blushing again.

As though reading her thoughts, Joan said, 'Dr Robinson is a widower. Sandra's his daughter. His wife died during childbirth years ago – before he moved to Hollowtree.'

Jim interrupted. 'We don't know that for sure. It's just what Ma's heard in town. It might not be true. I don't think we should be speculating.'

Joan ignored him. 'Anyway, however she died, she's dead. It's just him and the daughter. Sandra must be about eighteen.' She grinned at Ethel. 'It will be nice to have a couple more adults to talk to. I'm sure Ma's going to be up and down those stairs all day. In fact, she'll probably have her dinner upstairs on a tray with Don.'

Ethel sipped her coffee, trying to suppress the feeling that she was being set up.

14

Two weeks later, Ethel, wanting to buy Christmas presents, set off alone into the small town of Hollowtree. It was a bitterly cold day, barely above freezing, and the light smattering of snow that had fallen a couple of days ago was lingering, even though there had been no fresh falls. Joan had offered her the use of a bicycle but fearing icy patches and an unfamiliar road, Ethel decided to walk. A good, long, bracing walk would give her plenty of time on her own to think. Much as she loved her cousin, Jim and the boys, Ethel was used to spending time alone and craved a little silence and solitude.

She set off walking briskly, enjoying the crispness of the day, breathing in lungfuls of fresh cold air. The first part of the road into town was an unmade track but it was level, broad and straight. It passed through fields and woods and Ethel relished being out in the countryside. After she had covered a couple of miles, the road converged with another and the surface turned to concrete. Her feet became numb with cold inside the heavy boots Joan had lent her, despite two pairs of socks. She picked up her pace. The faster she walked, the warmer she'd be.

Her nose was so cold she pulled her woollen scarf up over half her face, but the dampness of her breath created was clammy against her skin, and she pulled it down again. She went on like this, jerking the woollen scarf up and down. By the time she got to town, she'd be too cold to do any shopping – and as for walking back again – she dreaded the thought of it.

A car came round the corner, overtook her and, braking suddenly, screeched to a halt, waiting for her to catch up. It was a smart-looking saloon car. Normally, she would never accept a lift from a stranger but today she decided she would willingly make an exception. The prospect of a hot drink in the little café Joan had told her about floated into her head. As she reached the car, the door opened, and a voice called out, 'Hop in, Miss Underwood. I'll give you a ride.'

Only as she clambered into the passenger seat did she realise her Good Samaritan was Dr Robinson. Gulping, she murmured her thanks.

'It's a long walk into town,' he said.

'I hadn't realised it was quite so far. Or quite so cold.'

'This is mild yet.' His lips twitched in amusement.

Uncertain how to respond, Ethel said nothing. It was hard being in such close proximity to the doctor, aware of his presence next to her within the confined space of the car, his ungloved hands on the steering wheel. Nice hands. Pushing her unease aside, she stretched her legs out, luxuriating in the heat inside the car.

After several minutes' silence, the doctor spoke. 'I've just come from Hollowtree Farm. Mr Armstrong is responding well to the oxygen.'

'Oh, that's marvellous!'

'It may buy him a little more time. Long enough to meet his next grandchild if we're lucky, but the prognosis isn't good, I'm afraid.'

'It's so sad. He's only in his early sixties.'

The doctor nodded. 'He's very weak now. Too weak to get out of bed. Mrs Armstrong was hoping he might make it downstairs for Christmas dinner, but he can't manage the stairs.'

'What a pity.'

'Hauling the oxygen tanks up and down those stairs is not a satisfactory solution, so we've decided to move a bed downstairs. He'll be warmer down there near the stove and it's easier for Mrs Armstrong to manage if he's right there where she is most of the day.'

'A bed, in the kitchen?'

'Yes. I've promised to go round after surgery tomorrow and give Jim a hand to move it. It's the least I can do to thank him for his kind invitation to my daughter and me to join you all on Christmas Day.'

Ethel said nothing, hoping her face wasn't giving away her discomfort.

'Christmas is going to be at Rivercreek Farm.'

'Not at Hollowtree? What about Mr and Mrs Armstrong?'

Dr Robinson turned his head to glance at her. 'To be honest, I think Mrs Armstrong is keen to spend her husband's last Christmas alone with him.'

She hesitated, 'I'm sure it will be lovely – and I'm looking forward to meeting your daughter.'

By now they were drawing into the centre of Hollowtree. 'Where are you headed?' he asked.

'I've some Christmas shopping to do at the general

stores, but thought I'd have a warm drink first. Joan says there's a café.'

'Here it is.' He pulled up outside. 'They do a very good hot chocolate and the store's right opposite. I have a few things to deal with at the surgery, but how about I meet you back here in an hour or so and I'll run you home.'

'I couldn't possibly let you do that.'

'I have to drive right past Rivercreek on the way to see a patient. It's not out of my way.'

'If you're sure?'

He turned his smile on her again and Ethel knew she was blushing. What was wrong with her?

The doctor drove off and Ethel went into the café. It was warm inside and had a big window with a view onto the street. She slipped off her coat and laid it on the banquette at one of the window tables.

The man behind the counter looked up and called out a cheery greeting when she approached. 'You must be Joan Armstrong's cousin from England.' He stretched out a hand. 'I'm Freddo. Pleased to meet you.'

'Hello,' she said tentatively. 'I'm Ethel.'

'Right, Ethel. The first drink for a first-timer in Freddo's café is on the house. It's tradition.'

'Doesn't that prove expensive for you?'

Freddo snorted. 'Last time was more than three years ago. We don't get many strangers round here.' He pushed the menu towards her. 'A family from England, renting a farm outside town. They only lasted one winter. Not a great return on my investment.' He laughed.

'I'm afraid I won't be very profitable for you either. I'm only staying a couple of months.'

He tilted his head, eyebrows raised. 'We'll see about that, we'll see. Now what will it be?'

Ethel ordered a hot chocolate and went to sit by the window, watching the comings and goings at the general store opposite. Why did everyone assume she was going to stay on in Canada? What had Joan been telling people?

Her thoughts turned to the doctor. It wasn't as if he was incredibly handsome – although she had to admit he was a good-looking man. But so what? She wasn't staying. Besides, she wasn't looking for a relationship. Not now. Not ever. No one could ever replace Greg.

Ethel firmly believed that the stars dictated only one person for each of us. Not everyone found that person. She and Greg had been lucky to do so. They had enjoyed a glorious magical time together, even though it had been cruelly cut short. What was the likelihood of finding another person to love in that way? It was impossible. She needed to stop daydreaming and be practical. Anyway – why would the doctor even be interested in her? He was probably only being friendly.

She sipped the hot chocolate. The doctor was right about that at least – it was delicious: thick and creamy and quite unlike her distant memories of pre-war cocoa. Her drink finished, she said goodbye to her new friend and headed over to the store to make her purchases. She had brought gifts for all the Armstrongs from England, but she hadn't planned on spending Christmas Day with the doctor and his daughter. It felt wrong not to include them, but she hadn't even met the daughter and barely knew the doctor. She needed to find something small and inconsequential, just a token gesture.

The storekeeper also knew who she was. Joan had evidently told the whole town her cousin was coming to stay. He was more taciturn than Freddo, and Ethel was relieved that he didn't try to engage her in conversation.

After much deliberation, limited by the narrow range in the general store, she settled on some lily of the valley bath cubes for Sandra Robinson but was still undecided what to get for the doctor. Any gift could be subject to misinterpretation. The present for Sandra would have to suffice as an acknowledgement of their joint presence – no need to buy something separate for the father. After paying the store-keeper, she had enough time for a short walk around the centre of the town.

Hollowtree was little more than a village, but it did boast a few amenities. As well as the café and the general store, she passed a library, an office housing the local news-paper, a small hotel with a licensed bar, a garage repair shop cum blacksmith, a park, two schools and a barber shop.

Ethel glanced at her watch and walked back to the café. The dark blue saloon car pulled up alongside and the doctor stepped out.

'Get what you needed?' he asked. He took her by the elbow and steered her towards Freddo's café. 'I've been looking forward to one of Freddo's hot chocolates all after-noon. My treat.'

'I couldn't possibly. You've been kind enough already – and I've already had one.'

'Don't deprive me of the pleasure of buying you a drink, Miss Underwood.' He looked hurt.

Ethel said nothing, slipping into the same seat she had vacated an hour earlier. The place was still deserted. It couldn't be much of a living for Freddo.

Dr Robinson slid into the seat opposite, leaning back against the banquette. As if reading her mind, he said, 'It's quiet in the afternoons, apart from Wednesdays and Fridays when people come in to pick up provisions. Weekends are busy too. And most mornings you can't move in here. You met Freddo then?'

She nodded as the owner placed the tall mugs in front of them. Two in one day! She couldn't get anything like that back home, with sweets and chocolate still rationed, so it was a reasonable indulgence.

She felt the doctor looking at her. Telling herself to stop being behaving like a shy schoolgirl, she raised her eyes to meet his. Her stomach flipped. She choked on her chocolate and began to cough. He jumped up and went to the counter to get a glass of water for her.

Mortified, Ethel sipped the water, her appetite for the chocolate gone. 'I'm sorry,' she muttered.

He said nothing.

Come on, Ethel. Fill the silence. 'Do you have a lot of patients?'

The doctor looked puzzled, then laughed. 'Ah, you mean patients? I thought you meant patience! I have about four hundred patients on my books but if you ask my daughter, Sandra, who looks after the surgery for me, she'd probably tell you I don't have a lot of the other sort of patience.'

'I'm sure that's not true.'

He continued to study her face. Ethel breathed slowly, telling herself to calm down. He couldn't possibly have any interest in her. And she certainly didn't have any interest in him. But she knew she was lying to herself.

Picking up her mug, she forced herself to drink some more. This time the warmth and sweetness had a soothing effect. She glanced up and decided Dr Robinson had the most beautiful eyes she had ever seen in a man. And his thick, lustrous hair with the little kink in the front was so like Greg's.

Greg, Greg, Greg. What was she doing? How could she

even think this way when she knew perfectly well that the only man she could ever want was gone? Anyone else would be a poor substitute.

Even the doctor with the warm brown eyes.

She swallowed again, hoping he wouldn't be able to detect her nerves. 'Have you always lived in Hollowtree, Doctor?'

'Since '42. My wife had died ten years earlier.'

'I'm sorry,' Ethel muttered, feeling awkward.

'It's a long time ago.' He looked away out of the window.

There was a protracted silence, then Dr Robinson said, 'How about you, Miss Underwood. How come you're not married?'

'I was engaged, but he died.' Her voice was barely more than a whisper.

The doctor reached across the table and brushed his fingers across her hand. It was only a momentary touch, but it was a bolt of electricity.

'He...he was a C... Canadian soldier, a friend of Jim's. We met the same night Joan and Jim did. Only Greg and I hit it off immediately and they took a bit longer.'

As she spoke, she was conscious of him watching her, his eyes fixed on her face. She lowered her own and stared at the tabletop. 'We'd only just got engaged when he died.

'When was that?'

'In 1941.' She paused. 'He's buried in a war grave in England. He hadn't even left the base. Never saw any enemy action. A brain haemorrhage. He was from Saskatchewan. Have you ever been there?' Ethel was conscious of speaking too quickly.

He shook his head.

'Where are you from then, Doctor?'

'A place called Sioux Lookout in Northwest Ontario. It's

about eighteen hundred miles from here. Much further north.'

'Gosh. All that distance and it's still in Ontario.'

'Canada's a big country. Ontario's a big province. And we're right down near the bottom of it here.'

'What's it like there?'

'Cold. You think it's cold here now. You can't imagine how much colder it is up there. Snow for nine months of the year. And temperatures way below freezing. The summers are warm though. Sometimes hot. But they're short. Blink and they're over.' He flicked his fingers. 'It takes a certain type to cope with living up there.'

'You were born there?'

'No, in Nova Scotia. Near Halifax. I moved to Sioux Lookout when I qualified.'

'Did you meet your wife there?'

He shook his head. 'She was from Nova Scotia too.' He looked at his watch. 'I'd better get you back to the farm.'

'Are you sure I'm not taking you out of your way?'

'I told you it's on the way to my house call.'

She glanced at him. His jaw was set firm and they drove back to the farm in silence.

15

*A*lice still had no idea where to invest her money. She was determined to find something that would occupy her and give her a chance to prove to herself that she was not one of those women who could only exist in the shadow of a man. Her aunt had done it. She would do it too.

Imagining Aunty Miriam looking down on her from heaven, she wanted to make her proud. She also wanted to make Walt proud. Although she was less sure Walt would approve of her working. On the other hand, Helga had worked day and night all her life. As well as running the household and raising two sons, she had done all the milking, looked after the livestock, churned butter, pickled vegetables, tended the vegetable garden that covered the household's needs and prepared and bottled Hollowtree Farm's maple syrup. She'd always had time for others, offering help to anyone in the district who needed it, and was renowned for making the best butter pies in the county. Helga Armstrong and Miriam Cooke were very different personalities, with very different interests, but both were worthy role models as far as Alice was concerned. Walt's death had deprived her of the chance to emulate Helga as a farmer's wife, but she would take Aunty Miriam – outspoken suffragette and businesswoman – as her exemplar. Yes, surely Walt would approve – he'd want her to do all she could for their girls. Though *Catherine* wasn't *his* girl. A stab of pain went through Alice, the recurring guilt that she'd betrayed Walt by going with Tip Howardson, by having another man's child.

One afternoon, while her daughters were at school, Alice was walking around the centre of Ottawa, mulling over her dilemma, when she came upon a movie theatre. She had never been inside one. There wasn't one in Hollowtree. She remembered how much Joan claimed to have loved her visits to 'the pictures' in England, frequently lamenting the lack of a cinema in Hollowtree. Looking up at the signage above the entrance, she saw that a film called *High Noon* was playing. On impulse, she bought a ticket for the matinée, which was about to start. There was just time to see it before the girls finished at school.

Inside the almost empty theatre Alice took a seat in the middle of a row, with an uninterrupted view of the screen, and waited for the performance to begin. The lights dimmed, she was swallowed up by the dark, waiting impatiently through the news reels and advertisements. At last, the titles rolled, and the film began.

As she listened to the words of the theme song, tears coursed down her cheeks. It could have been Walt singing it to her, with its talk of being torn between love and duty and his plea for his new wife to understand the difficult choice he had made. Alice was transported back to the day he told her he was leaving Hollowtree to follow his brother into the army and fight for his country.

By the time Kane cast his marshal's badge of office into

the dirt and, with his new wife, climbed up on their wagon and drove out of town, Alice was in love. Not with Gary Cooper, but with the world of cinema even though the marshal and his bride had a happier ending than she and Walt. No wonder Joan loved it so much.

Alice left the movie house, with the refrain of 'Do Not Forsake Me, Oh My Darling' ringing in her ears. The image of Grace Kelly shooting one of the villains in the back, to save her husband, was burnt onto her brain.

Every afternoon from then on, she went to a matinée. She watched dozens of films; from *The Snows of Kilimanjaro* to *The Quiet Man*. How had Joan survived without this? Once you had experienced the joy of moving pictures, how could you possibly be without it? It became like a drug to Alice. On Saturdays she returned with her daughters in tow, the three of them sitting side-by-side, watched Danny Kaye in *Hans Christian Anderson* and Abbot and Costello having adventures in Alaska.

One afternoon during the Christmas break, while Catherine and Rose were playing at a friend's house, Alice took herself along to the movie house she liked best, the Royal, allowing plenty of time before the start of the picture. Marching up to the box office, she asked to see the manager. A puzzled assistant told her to wait in the foyer and went in search of her boss.

The manager was a short stout man, wearing a bow tie. Alice gave him a beaming smile and asked if he could spare her a few minutes to seek his advice.

She came straight to the point. 'I want to open a movie theatre in a small town that doesn't have one. Can you tell me how I go about doing that, please?'

The chap was taken aback. He gave a little snorting

laugh. 'If there was demand for a movie theatre they'd have already opened one. How big's the town?'

'Population's about nine hundred, last I heard.' Seeing the scepticism on his face, she added, 'But there's nowhere for miles around. Nearest cinema is in Kitchener and that's an hour's drive away.'

'If the place has got by without one 'til now, it'll get by in the future.' The man folded his arms.

'It's got by because everyone there is the same as I used to be. They don't know what they've been missing.'

'So, you're going to show them, are you?' He sniggered and glanced at his watch. 'Look, lady, I'm just an employee but I can assure you one of the big exhibitors would have opened one already if there was any money to be made. Television's the next thing now. In places like your town that's what people will be buying soon. Then there'll be no need to go to the pictures. I'm glad I'm retiring in three years. Reckon most of the picture palaces will be closed down before long – and there's you wanting to open a new one.' He shook his head and snorted again.

'I'm not talking about a big fancy picture palace. Just a small space to show films.'

He sneered. 'No distributor is going to take a woman on her own seriously. The Canadian market's all sewn up by two big exhibitors. Famous Players and Odeon. You think you can compete with them, lady?'

'Distributor? What's a distributor?'

'A company that controls the release of films. They rent out the movies from the studios to the theatres. They pick the films they reckon will draw the biggest crowds. It's all about how big the box office is.'

'How big?' She looked across the foyer to the booth where the tickets were sold.

'Not the box office itself, but the number of people who buy tickets through it for each film.' The man spoke with disdain.

Alice gritted her teeth, determined to plough on. 'How do they know if it will be a success? You know, when it's a new film?'

'They don't. It's all a big guessing game. How big's the star? What was the take on opening night? How did the preview audiences like it? We get the films later than New York and the big American cities, so we only get to pick the ones that are already hits.'

'Hits?'

The manager was looking increasingly impatient. 'Successes. Look, lady, I've got work to do. If there's nowhere in that town of yours, you go and live somewhere else.' He turned on his heel and disappeared through a door, leaving Alice standing in the now-filling foyer. She gritted her teeth and went to join the queue to buy a ticket for Charlie Chaplin's *Limelight*.

She didn't give up. The following day, she returned to the Royal. This time, she was ready for the man. His name was Hall, according to the badge on his lapel.

'Mr Hall. I need to ask you more questions.'

As he was about to turn away, Alice revealed a twenty-dollar bill. 'I'll pay for your time.'

He looked around to see if anyone was watching. Muttering to her to follow him, he led her into a small, windowless office into which were crammed a desk, two chairs, a filing cabinet and a cardboard box stuffed with rolled up film posters. An overflowing ashtray, a writing pad and a stack of unopened mail sat on the desk.

Hall moved round to sit behind the desk. 'You have ten minutes. What do you want to know, lady?'

Alice stretched out a gloved hand to him. 'Alice Armstrong.' She indicated the writing pad. 'I'd like you to write down the equipment you need in a cinema. Everything you can think of.'

Hall leaned back in his chair, studying her. 'You're one crazy lady, ma'am. You don't give up, do you?'

'No, I don't.'

He gave his head a little shake, then picked up a pencil and began to write. 'Biggest expense is projection equipment and screen. That's assuming you've already got the building, the seating, the box office, the ticket machine, the cash register, the washrooms, the lighting system, the loudspeakers for the sound.' He looked up from the page. 'You want me to go on?'

Alice nodded. 'Yes. You're doing fine. Put it all down there. And the names of the places where I can buy the projection equipment.'

Shaking his head again, Hall opened the drawer of his desk and consulted a book inside, transcribing information from there to the paper in front of him. He looked up at her. 'You need to be accepted by a distributor. That'll cost you. They'll want to know you can pay their bills, whether you manage to bring in an audience or not. You'll need a line of credit. And they'll want to know that you have the right kit to show their pictures to the best advantage. Otherwise it reflects badly on them. On the studios too.'

'How do I contact these distributors?'

He shrugged and wrote again on the pad. Tearing off the sheet of paper he handed it to her. 'Here you are. That's everything I know.'

Nodding her thanks, Alice said, 'Any other advice for me?'

'Yeah. Make sure you're married to a rich man. One daft

enough to pay the hefty bills you're going to run up and who doesn't mind taking a pile of money and setting fire to it. Is Mr Armstrong ready for that?'

'There is no Mr Armstrong,' she said, getting to her feet. 'You've been very helpful, Mr Hall.'

He shrugged and called out as she left the cramped office, 'Good luck!'

If Mr Hall at the Royal had been sceptical about Alice's venture, it was nothing to the reaction of Mr Freeman, the lawyer.

'Mrs Armstrong, forgive me, but as your legal representative I'm duty bound to tell you that this is a fool's venture.'

'You're calling me a fool, Mr Freeman?'

'Of course not, but you know nothing of... business. Nothing of the running of an enterprise such as you propose.'

'Nobody knows these things automatically. You have to learn them. I intend to learn.'

Before he could reply, she spoke again. 'I don't suppose Miss Cooke knew as much about millinery before she opened her store as she did by the time she sold it. And I think it unlikely you were born with a full understanding of the law. With all due respect, I think you'll admit it was something you had to learn.'

Mr Freeman took off his spectacles and polished them on a white linen handkerchief, before replacing them. 'But why this? Why there? Hollowtree is a small community. Are you sure it can support a venture like this?'

'Nothing is certain, but I intend to find out. I think a movie theatre is exactly what the town needs, so I intend to give it one. Whether it makes me a fortune is beside the point.'

'But whether it loses you one is not.' He picked up a pencil and tapped it against the surface of his expansive oak desk.

'How much can I afford to lose? I want to protect most of Miss Cooke's money. I'm thinking of my daughters.'

'Are you suggesting we set aside a sum for the cinema venture and you don't exceed that amount?'

'That's exactly what I'm suggesting.'

'It would still be a substantial sum to put at risk.'

'It will be my money though, won't it?' She spoke pointedly. 'Mine to risk.'

The man nodded. 'Very well. But I intend to put on record that it was against my professional advice.'

'Do as you see fit.'

'And you can't spend a cent until probate is granted.'

'I was coming to that. When will that be?'

He raised his hands, palms open. 'The proverbial piece of string.'

She kept her gaze steady on his face.

Another big sigh. 'Don't hold me to it, as it depends on the Probate Office, but as there is a will and this firm has always managed Miss Cooke's affairs I am optimistic it will be granted quickly. It will take rather longer for the funds to be transferred – I'd say sometime between the end of January and Easter. And it will not all happen at once. We have to register the grant with each institution.'

'Thank you. I'm grateful for your help, Mr Freeman.' She turned one of her winning smiles upon him. 'As always.'

*W*hen Ethel walked into the house, Joan had evidently been watching at the window.

'Was that Dr Robinson I saw dropping you off just now?' There was a sly grin on her face.

Ethel pulled off her hat and gloves and went to hang her coat up, anxious that Joan shouldn't see her face. She called back, airily, over her shoulder. 'He rescued me from a long walk in the cold – he was on his way to see another patient.'

'Another patient?'

'Yes. He said he was passing right by here.'

'Did he now?' Joan's grin was wide. 'Can't think who that might be as the road leads down to the creek and then it's just open fields.'

'Really?'

Joan nodded, still grinning. 'This is the end of the line, baby!' She laughed.

'So, he was telling fibs?'

'I told you you'd made a conquest. Where did you run into him then? In town?'

Ethel confessed that the doctor had picked her up on the

way into town, bought her a drink and offered the lift home. 'He did say he was passing the farm anyway. To be honest, Joan, I was so cold I probably would have said yes even if I'd known.'

'So?' Joan filled the kettle.

'So, what?'

'What do you think of him? Do you like him now you've had more time to get to know him?'

'Stop it, Joan. He's a perfectly nice man but that's that. Neither of us have any interest in the other in the way you'd like. He was just doing a good deed.'

Joan plonked herself down in a chair while the kettle boiled, rubbing her back. 'A good deed? My Aunt Fanny!' She winked at Ethel.

'I'll make the tea,' said Ethel, ignoring Joan's teasing. 'You relax for a few minutes.'

'So, tell me. What did you talk about?'

Ethel groaned. 'Stop it right away, Joanie. I've had enough. There is not and never will be anything romantic between me and Dr Robinson.'

'In that case you can tell me what you talked about.'

Ethel narrowed her eyes. She carried the teapot and cups over to the table. 'He told me there's a change of plan and we're having Christmas lunch here rather than at Hollowtree. Did you plan to tell me that at some point?' She raised an eyebrow.

'Only found out myself about an hour ago when Jim told me.'

Ethel sipped her tea, feeling guilty. 'Are you sure you can cope with a houseful, with your time being so near?'

'It'll take my mind off things. You'll help me with the cooking, won't you? And to be perfectly honest, I'd rather be in my own kitchen than mucking-in over at Hollowtree and taking Ma's instructions. There's more space here too and the boys can play in the other room. Over there we'd all be crammed into the kitchen. I'll have to think of some ways to throw you and Duncan Robinson together. It's a pity you can't get mistletoe in Canada.'

'Stop it!'

'Come on, Ethel. Where's your sense of fun? You have to admit he's a very attractive man.'

'No, I don't admit anything. He's a perfectly nice, but perfectly ordinary, man and I can assure you my heart isn't the slightest bit aflutter.'

Joan looked at her pointedly. 'Seriously, a bit of a flirtation would do you good, Ethel. Where's the harm?'

Ethel slammed her cup down on the table, slopping tea onto the cloth. 'I've told you. I'm only here for a couple of months. There's no point. Even if I did find him attractive – which I don't – what's the point, when I'll be going home soon anyway?' She scraped her chair back. 'I have a headache. I'm going to lie down for a while. I'll see you at supper.'

Joan reached a hand out to stay her, but Ethel was already on her feet and leaving the room, banging the door behind her. The baby started to cry.

When Jim came in later, there was still no sign of Ethel. Joan told him she'd been teasing her cousin about the doctor and may have gone too far.

'Give it a rest then, Joan. Best not mention it. Just let things take their course.'

'I know he likes her. And I can tell Ethel likes him too. She's just too proud to admit it.'

Jim tilted his head on one side. 'Why does she have to admit it? Why do you have to force a confession out of her? Let the poor woman be. If they like each other they don't need us to help them on their way. I don't remember Ethel needing a shove when she met Greg Hooper.'

'That's exactly the problem. She's turned Greg into a saint and thinks she'll be betraying his memory if she so much as looks at another man. It isn't natural.'

Jim put an arm round her. 'I know you want her to be happy but let her find happiness her own way and in her own time. And if she chooses to be alone for the rest of her life surely that's up to her.'

'But she doesn't. I know Ethel. She's not cut out to be on her own. And she's lonely. Surely you can see that. And so's Duncan Robinson.'

'You're probably right. You usually are. But if you carry on like this you'll drive her away. I bet she's dreading Christmas, thinking we've both got our eyes on her and Duncan. Give her a break, Joanie.'

Joan tutted. 'Allow me to know my own cousin better than you do. She says there's no point in getting to know him when she'll be going back to England soon.'

'Well, she's right about that.'

'Not if I get my way she isn't. Don't you see? If she and the doctor fall in love, then she won't have to go home at all. What does she have to go back to? She'll have a much better life here than mooning around Aldershot with a pile of sad memories.'

Jim put a finger to his lips. The door opened, and Ethel came in. 'Sorry. I fell asleep. What can I do to help with supper?'

'All done. It's been in the oven since early afternoon. Jimmy! Come and lay the table.'

'I'll do that,' said Ethel.

'No, you won't, my love. Sit down. That's what ten-year-old boys are for. Jimmy!' Joan screeched in the direction of the adjoining room. 'Get yourself in here right away.'

Jimmy, trailing untied laces from his shoes, slouched into the room, and dutifully, if slowly, laid out the cutlery.

'Hear you went into town today, Ethel. What did you think of it?' asked Jim.

'It's a nice little place. And I fell in love with the hot chocolate drinks in the café. I got to meet Freddo – he gave me the first one on the house.'

'The first one?'

'I went back for another after I'd been to the store and had a walk around.'

Joan and Jim exchanged glances but neither commented.

'I saw there was a barber shop but no hair salon. What do the women do around here to get their hair done?'

'We do it ourselves. Or do each other's. That's why I keep mine in a bob – haven't had a proper shampoo and set since I left Aldershot.'

'Then I'll give you one after supper.'

'You will?' Joan's face broke into a smile. 'But you're meant to be on holiday from all that.'

'I don't need a holiday from hairdressing – just from Vera and the salon. You know I've always loved doing your hair.' She nodded at the baby who had fallen asleep in Joan's arms. 'Settle him down and we can get on with it.'

Joan grinned. 'Jim, can you keep the boys out of the way until their bedtime?'

'Come on, fellas, we can have a go at that jigsaw Aunty Alice sent for your birthdays.'

Forty minutes later, Ethel was dabbing setting lotion

onto Joan's hair, the last roller ready in her hand, when the boys careened back into the kitchen.

Joan dispatched them upstairs to bed. 'I'll be up in a minute to say goodnight and read Sam his story.'

'What on earth are you doing to my wife, Ethel?' Jim was leaning against the doorframe, watching them.

'You won't recognise her when I'm done. She's going to look drop-dead gorgeous.'

'She always looks drop-dead gorgeous.' He winked. 'Though maybe not so gorgeous right now.'

Joan poked her tongue out at him.

17

*C*hristmas morning arrived without snow. There had been flurries earlier that month and about three or four inches had fallen since Ethel had arrived, but warmer temperatures had followed, and the snow had completely melted away. More like England. Ethel was beginning to believe that Joan had exaggerated the snowy Canadian winters and was disappointed not to see the farm transformed.

Ethel stood at her bedroom window, watching a bright red-crested bird pecking at the wooden fence, the only splash of colour in a gloomy landscape. The mantle of swirling mist covering the fields summed up how Ethel felt. Miserable.

Why had she come? Why had she blown her life savings to travel all this way? She loved her cousin, but it was hardly the holiday of a lifetime.

But her restlessness and gloom had little to do with staying with the Armstrongs – it came from being cast adrift on a vast ocean with no horizon in sight, floating endlessly and alone though a monotonous sea.

If she were in Aldershot she'd feel the same. In truth, she'd probably feel worse. Back home, she'd have only Aunty Chris and the taciturn Ron as company, and miserable Vera in the salon. On the news on the wireless in Joan's kitchen, she'd heard that Britain had been besieged by impenetrable fog. London's notorious pea-soupers had turned into the worst smog in living memory, with thousands dead in the capital. A national emergency.

No, if she was feeling melancholy here, she'd be even more lonely and morose back in England.

Picking up a book she'd left on the chest of drawers, she opened it to where she'd placed the photograph she used as a bookmark. The photo was falling apart – taped across the back and dog-eared around the much-fingered edges. Greg's face smiled up at her. He'd taken a series of photographs of her that day and Ethel had persuaded him to yield the Box Brownie to her. He'd shown her how to use it and allowed her to take this one precious photograph of him, standing on the Embankment in London, under a lamp post, with St Paul's cathedral in the background and sandbags heaped up against the embankment walls.

It was one of the happiest days of her life, wandering aimlessly, hand-in-hand, through the bomb-blasted streets of London with the man she had intended to be with for the rest of her life. Tears pressed at the corners of her eyes and she brushed them away with the back of her hand. Since she'd been in Canada, Greg had stopped appearing in her dreams and she was finding it harder to remember all the little details about him. It was as if she were losing him all over again. Every day he moved further and further away from her, his features blurring, his voice harder to summon up; even the words he had said to her were drifting away like dandelion clocks in a breeze.

She opened the top drawer of the chest and ran her fingers over the soft silk of a headscarf that lay there, folded, unworn. Greg gave it to her when he asked her to marry him. He promised the ring would come later – but it had never come at all. She would never wear the scarf. She didn't want it to suffer the fate of the photograph, its vibrant colours growing paler with every washing, or slipping from her neck to lie abandoned on a bus seat. Lifting it out of the drawer, she laid it on the bed, opening it out and smoothing it flat so she could admire the riot of tulips against a cream background with a deep green border. When he bought it for her, in a little shop in Bond Street, he had unwrapped it on the crowded train back to Aldershot from London and placed it round her neck, adjusting it and standing back to assess his handiwork. They had both laughed. Then he moved close to her, bent over and kissed her slowly, oblivious to the catcalls of the other soldiers on the train. Ethel tried to remember the feel of his lips on hers, the way his arms encircled her, the look in his eyes as he moved in for that kiss – but it was impossible. All she could see were the deep brown eyes of Dr Robinson, looking at her intently across the table in Freddo's café. She gathered up the scarf, folded it and put it back in the drawer.

Angry with herself, she quickly dressed and went downstairs.

'Merry Christmas, Ethel! Sorry we couldn't manage a white one for you,' said Jim, who was sitting at the table, bouncing Harry on his knee while Joan was at the stove waiting for the kettle to boil. 'The boys have been awake since five and they've already opened Santa's stockings.'

Sam bounded over to Ethel. 'Look, Aunty. See what Santa brought me.' He held out a colouring book and a set of crayons.

He tugged at her hand. 'Come and look.' He led her across the room to where he had laid out the treasures from his Christmas stocking on a chair. 'A chocolate dollar, and candies, and a little orange.'

Jimmy, who was sitting on the floor, playing with pick-up sticks, looked up. 'There's always an orange in the toe. Every year.'

'Not back in England there wasn't.' Remembering not to shatter the children's belief in Father Christmas, she added, 'During the war, Santa had to cut back on the oranges, but he's got a good supply now.'

Little Sam asked, 'What's the war?'

'Before you were born.' Jimmy's voice was smug, exercising the superiority his age afforded him.

After breakfast, it was time for the exchanging of the family presents which were stacked under the Christmas tree. The delight on the children's faces made Ethel forget her personal misery. She busied herself with the preparations for the Christmas meal, the little paste brooch, her gift from Joan and Jim, proudly pinned to her sweater.

'We need to do mash as well as roasties,' said Joan. 'In Canada they always have mashed potatoes, but you and I are not going to be deprived of our roasties on Christmas Day, are we, Ethel?'

'Not blooming likely.'

'If we were at Helga's we'd have sauerkraut and pickles as well,' Joan whispered conspiratorially. 'Not my idea of the perfect accompaniment to roast turkey.' She pulled a face.

'What are you two whispering about?' Jim called across the room.

'None of your business!'

The boys were surrounded on the floor by their

Christmas booty – a hockey stick and fountain pen for
Jimmy, a chalkboard and a toboggan for Sam.

'Take your presents into the other room now, boys. We
need plenty of space in here. The Robinsons will be
arriving soon. Hurry up!' Joan was starting to look slightly
frazzled. She stood by the stove, one hand on the small of
her back, watching as Ethel inspected the progress of the
turkey.

'Another half hour then we can let it rest.'

There was the crunch of a vehicle on the gravel outside.

'All set, girls?' Jim moved towards the door. 'Guests are
here.'

Dr Robinson came into the house, his daughter a couple
of paces behind him, looking wary. Jim offered him a beer,
leaving Joan to hand a glass of hot apple cider to Sandra and
do the introductions.

Ethel wiped her hands on her apron and came towards
the guests, praying that her tell-tale blushing would be put
down to the heat of the stove.

Sandra was a stern-looking young woman. Her hair was
scraped back from her face in an old-fashioned style and
she wore no make-up. Ethel longed to give her a makeover.
A shampoo and set, lipstick and a touch of mascara would
make a big difference in softening Sandra's appearance –
not to mention some more feminine clothes. She was
wearing a pair of baggy trousers and an oversized white
shirt, which emphasised rather than disguised how skinny
she was. Her clothes gave the impression she'd made no
effort at all – unless it was to choose something to deliberately make her appear austere.

Duncan Robinson produced a bottle of wine and
another of rye whisky. He handed a bag to Joan. 'There's
candies for the boys in there but I imagine you'll want to

take care of them until after we've eaten.' As he was speaking, his eyes were on Ethel rather than Joan.

Ethel moved towards Sandra, hand outstretched. The young woman's hand was cold and bony and was withdrawn after a very perfunctory shake.

'Hello, Sandra, I'm Ethel, Joan's cousin.'

'I know who you are.'

When her father gave her a pointed look, Sandra added, 'Hollowtree's a small place. Everyone knows everything and everyone.'

Ethel couldn't help feeling a touch of frost in the air around Sandra Robinson. She wondered whether she and her father had been arguing.

Joan moved forward and ushered everyone into the adjacent room. 'Now you all go and sit down and have a drink. I need an empty kitchen while I do the final touches to the meal.' Looking meaningfully at Ethel, she said, 'You too, Ethel. You've done quite enough already. Go and help Jim entertain our guests.' She gave her a little shove towards the doorway.

Once settled in the sitting room, Jim and Duncan Robinson began talking about the stalemate in the Korean War. Ethel turned her attention to Sandra, conscious that the doctor's eyes kept glancing in her direction as he talked.

'Hollowtree is a very pretty little town,' she said, desperately scrambling for a topic of conversation.

'It's all right, I suppose.'

'Do you go to Kitchener or Toronto often?'

'Not really.'

'Not even for shopping? Or to see a film?'

'I don't like shopping.'

She tried to ask Sandra about her job but met a similar brick wall. Ethel breathed in slowly. It was an ordeal. The men were now talking about ice hockey. She glanced towards the open door to the kitchen. 'Maybe I should go and help Joan.'

Jim heard. 'I was just saying to Duncan, we should all go and see an ice hockey game some time – introduce you to our national sport, Ethel.'

'There's a big game in Kitchener next week.' Dr Robinson looked at Ethel. 'Would you like to go?'

Panic closed her throat. Everyone was looking at her. 'I don't know... I've never seen an ice hockey game.'

'That's the point.' Jim grinned at her. 'You can't come to Canada and not experience one.'

Ethel turned to look at Sandra. 'What do you think?'

'I don't like any sports.'

The doctor rubbed his hands together. 'You can babysit the boys then, Sandra.'

The young woman opened her mouth to protest, but evidently catching a look from her father, closed it again. 'Yes, of course.'

Joan stuck her head round the door. 'Jim, I need you to carve the turkey and Sandra, can I borrow you for a moment?'

Sandra followed her into the kitchen, a sour expression on her face. Ethel was sure she was the cause of it.

The two of them left alone, Dr Robinson moved to sit in the chair his daughter had vacated, next to Ethel's. 'I'm sorry if Sandra's a bit cranky today. She finds Christmas hard.'

'Oh?'

'Her mother died when she was just a baby, but she's always very conscious of her absence at this time.'

Ethel met his gaze. 'It must be even harder for you, then.'

He shrugged. 'Not my favourite time, but as the years go

by it gets easier. And it's good of the Armstrongs to invite us here. Otherwise we'd have been a pretty miserable pair.'

Their visit didn't seem to be doing much to lessen Sandra's misery though.

Ethel looked away. 'It's not a great time for me either. Christmas is special when there are children around. When you're on your own it just reminds you of everyone who isn't there.'

'Your fiancé?'

'Yes, but not just him. My dad, my brother and this Christmas, my mum too. She died in October.'

He reached his hand out and took hers. 'I'm sorry, Ethel. You must feel very lonely.'

Ethel drew her hand away, afraid she was about to cry. She rose from the chair, desperate to get away.

'Don't go.' His voice was quiet, sad almost.

She let herself sink back into the chair.

He leaned towards her. 'I know you're only here for a short visit, Ethel, but I'd like to get to know you better. I was–'

Before he could finish his sentence, Sandra returned. 'Dinner's ready.' She looked as though she were sucking a lemon. Ethel wondered if she'd overheard what her father had just said.

To her relief, Ethel was next to the doctor, rather than opposite him. She didn't think she could have coped with feeling his eyes upon her across the table, knowing that every time she glanced up he would be gazing at her. Sitting next to him she was able to pivot towards Jimmy, who was on her other side. Across the table from her was Jim. She hoped he would occupy the doctor in conversation.

Sandra, next to Jim, ate in silence. Was she always like

this? Was her mood really due to her sadness at Christmas?
Or was it, as Ethel suspected, hostility towards Ethel?

'After we've finished, who's up for a walk?' asked Jim.

The proposal was greeted with enthusiasm. Even Sandra
nodded.

'Not me,' said Joan. 'I can barely move with this bump.
I'll stay and clear up and Harry can have his sleep.'

'I'll help you.' Ethel jumped up.

'Oh no, you won't, Miss. I want a bit of quiet time and I
actually like clearing up. I do my best thinking when I'm
restoring order.'

'Don't argue with her, Ethel. She's got that look on her
face!' Jim laughed.

They set off as a group, walking along a footpath that led
to open pastureland, sloping down to meet the creek and
the bathing pond that was part of the main Hollowtree
Farm acreage. Since he had acquired Rivercreek Farm, Jim
had removed some of the dividing fences, so it was now
impossible to see where one farm ended and the other
began.

After a while, the boys, Olive the dog, and Sandra moved
ahead, leaving Ethel to walk with Jim and Duncan Robinson. The two men talked about Jim's plans for the land, and
how he had planted two acres of apple trees on Rivercreek.
If they did well, he was thinking of adding more fruit.

'Margins are higher. Of course, we're too far north for
peaches and cherries here. You need to be down by Lake
Ontario, where it's warmer, to grow them successfully. But
apples, and maybe pears, should do well here.'

There was a high-pitched wail from ahead of them. Jim

rolled his eyes and ran off, leaving Ethel and Duncan to walk on together.

'Jim's a good man,' said the doctor.

'The best.'

'He and Joan are very happy together. Anyone can see that.'

'It's such a relief.'

'What do you mean?' he looked at her curiously.

'At one time it looked as if they might split up. Jim went through a lot during the war. It was hard for him. And hard for Joan adjusting to life here in Canada.' She stopped. 'I shouldn't be telling you this.'

'Don't worry. It will go no further.'

'They sorted it out in the end – once he'd opened up to her about what he'd experienced in the war. My mum used to say, "A trouble shared is a trouble halved".'

He nodded. 'I didn't serve in the war. It's hard to imagine what some of the men went through. Lots of people round here were critical that I didn't join up. Some still are, I think.' He kicked a pebble out his path. 'I was accused of being a pacifist at best and a coward by some. But I had Sandra to think of. How could I head off to Europe or the Pacific and leave an eight-year-old motherless child behind?'

'Surely people understood that?'

'Some did. But many didn't. Any man not in a uniform was a traitor in their eyes.'

'Would you have joined up if it weren't for Sandra?'

He looked at her sideways and gave a dry laugh. 'Are you implying I used her as an excuse?'

'Of course not. I can see you had no choice.'

'I did have a choice actually. I could have left her with my parents in Nova Scotia. But I thought losing her mother was already too much. And someone has to stay behind and look after the people who aren't fighting. So many doctors joined up. Those of us who didn't, had our work cut out for us. I was looking after patients across an area three times as big as my catchment area now. Working round the clock to keep up.'

'Who looked after Sandra then?'

'She was at school – apart from the vacations. Alice Ducroix, I mean Armstrong, Jim's sister-in-law, helped out a lot. She was always happy to take care of Sandra if I was called out in the evenings and during the vacations. And occasionally, if it was the middle of the night, I'd wrap Sandra in a blanket and lay her on the back seat of the car and she'd sleep there while I made the call.'

'Alice helped you?'

'You know her?'

'I met her briefly. I stayed with her in Ottawa overnight on the way here.'

'She's a good woman, is Alice. Although there's a few around here who'd disagree with me. She fell out with her family. There was a lot of gossip.'

'She was pregnant.' Ethel disliked Alice. Talking about her was no more than the woman deserved.

'I'd heard that. Poor girl. She must have been lonely, losing her husband so soon after they were married. I know how that feels.'

Ethel felt ashamed. It was wrong of her to betray this confidence. No matter how much she disliked Alice. She was as bad as the other gossips. 'So do I.' Her voice was small, weak.

Duncan Robinson took her gloved hand and slipped it through his arm. They walked on. Ethel knew she should take her arm back, but she didn't want to. It felt right, comfortable, walking along like this, close to this man, feeling the warmth of his arm through his coat sleeve, watching his breath turn to steam in the cold air.

It was starting to grow dark. Without warning, he drew her aside, underneath a tree, and kissed her. Ethel was stunned. Her first instinct was to push him away, but his lips were warm and soft and his kiss was insistent and she found herself kissing him back. His arms wrapped around her, cocooning her, holding her and she let herself luxuriate in the moment.

When they drew apart, the realisation of what they had done, the threshold they had crossed, struck her and she stiffened and moved away from him.

She looked up the track and saw Sandra Robinson about a hundred yards away, walking towards them with Jimmy at her side. Had she seen them kissing?

Mortification swept over Ethel. What was she thinking? How had she let it happen?

'I'm heading back,' she said, stumbling along the pathway through the fields towards the house.

When she entered the kitchen, there was no sign of the chaos from the enormous meal they had consumed, except for the remains of the turkey, on top of a side cabinet, draped with a cloth. The baby was sleeping in his bassinet and Joan was drinking tea. On the table in front of her was a small pile of wrapped gifts.

'We nearly forgot the presents for the Robinsons. I see you've got one for Sandra. That was thoughtful of you.'

Ethel reached for the gift. 'Maybe it's not such a good idea. I don't want to embarrass her.'

'Nonsense. It's a lovely idea.' Joan moved it away from her cousin's outstretched fingers.

Before she could argue, the door opened, and Dr Robinson came in. 'Are you all right, Ethel?' His face was lined with concern.

Joan looked from one to the other curiously. 'Anyone for a cuppa?' she asked.

'I'll just be five minutes,' Ethel said and rushed from the room.

Upstairs, she sat on the edge of her bed and looked out the window. From the yard below, she could hear the boys and an answering response from Jim, then the sound of the back door opening and closing.

Why had she let him kiss her? Why had she kissed him back? What on earth was she doing? The doctor was obviously a lonely man and she had led him on – pointlessly. In two months she'd be sailing back to Southampton. She got up and took the photograph of Greg out of her book. 'I'm sorry,' she whispered. 'I don't know what came over me.'

Downstairs the thrum of voices was getting louder. She would have to go back and rejoin the party. Pull yourself together, girl. It will soon be over, and they'll be leaving. She picked up her lipstick and went to the mirror to reapply it, conscious, as she ran it over her lips, of how Duncan Robinson's lips had felt against hers. Enough! Get back downstairs.

The company were around the table again, tea and Christmas cake in front of them.

'Here she is!' Joan said. 'We were about to send a search party for you.' She turned to Dr Robinson and his daughter. 'Now, we have a couple of little gifts for you. She handed them each a present. 'From Jim and me.'

Duncan and Sandra opened them to reveal a small box

of cigars for him and some handkerchiefs in a presentation box with a monogrammed S embroidered on them for Sandra.

After thanks were proffered, Joan pushed the gift-wrapped bath cubes to Ethel, her face telegraphing the words 'Go on.'

Ethel turned to Sandra. 'It's just a little thing.'

Sandra frowned. 'I haven't got anything for you.'

'I wouldn't have expected you to. It's only a token.'

Sandra opened the gift, her face impassive.

'I told you. It's only a little thing. Scented.'

Sandra nodded, but said nothing.

It was her father who turned to Ethel and said, 'What a thoughtful gift. Thank you, Miss Underwood.' He was smiling, but his eyes were sad.

Joan got to her feet. 'Now, everyone next door. The boys are going to sing us carols.'

Ethel and Sandra were the last to leave the kitchen. As they got to the doorway, Sandra hissed at her, in a stage whisper, 'I suppose you thought giving me that present would make my father like you. Well, you're wrong. He doesn't. And I don't like you at all.' She pushed ahead into the drawing room, leaving a stunned Ethel to follow in her wake.

---

18

*E*thel woke early the next morning, shivering with cold. She poked her head above the covers and then pulled them back over her. Under her feet the hot water bottle was stone cold, and she pushed it to the bottom of the bed. It was the coldest day since she arrived in Canada. Definitely well below freezing. Stretching her arm out to pull back the curtain she saw there was still no sign of snow. Worst of all possible worlds – perishing cold without the reward of a fairy-tale landscape. Stuffing her arm back under the covers, she curled into a tight ball. It would be best to jump out of bed, get washed and dressed as fast as possible and move into the always warm kitchen. But Ethel didn't want to move. She rubbed her hands up and down her arms and burrowed deeper under the covers.

The memory of kissing Duncan Robinson flooded back and her blood warmed inside her. For a few moments she indulged herself in the recollection of their kiss, remembering how it felt to be held like that, to feel desired. That look in his eyes. His mouth on hers, his body pressed against her, his arms enfolding her. The warmth of his breath. The sound of his breathing. She closed her eyes, drowning in the pleasure of those few brief moments.

The rattle of cutlery rose from the kitchen, the whistle of the boiling kettle, the hammering of Jimmy's feet on the stairs and finally the wailing of Harry in the room next to hers. Reluctantly, Ethel pulled on her dressing gown, shoved her feet in her cold slippers, and went to fetch the baby to bring him down to his mother.

In the kitchen, Joan was frying bacon on the stove, while the boys sat on the rug in front of the Christmas tree playing pick-up sticks.

'I told you, boys, no toys in the kitchen. You've got the whole basement to play in.'

'Too cold.' Sam gave a mock shiver.

'Dad forgot to light the stove down there this morning.'

Jim came in, took off his thick sheepskin-lined jacket and the wool zipped jacket underneath it, jerked his knitted cap off his head and sat down at the table. 'No, I didn't forget. There's no point lighting it 'til later. We're going over to Ma's, aren't we?'

Joan rolled her eyes. 'All right, boys. But no mess. You have to clear up after you. I don't want to be sliding around on those sticks. Morning, Ethel. Sleep well?'

Ethel nodded, though she hadn't.

'You have a choice. You can go with Jim and the kids over to Hollowtree or you can stay here with me. I'm not feeling too marvellous this morning. Spot of indigestion.'

Without hesitation, Ethel said she'd stay.

'You'll miss out on Ma's sweet potato casserole. And her Christmas cake's much better than mine. Secret German recipe!'

'I'm still recovering from yesterday.' Ethel forced a smile, relieved at the prospect of a quiet day.

'Shall we take Harry with us?' said Jim. 'Give you a proper break. And Ma and Pa will want to see him.'

Joan put her arms round his neck and kissed his cheek. 'Really? Thank you, hon. I'll make up a couple of bottles in case he gets tetchy. He should be happy enough with solids. Ask Ma to mash up whatever you're all having.'

After they'd eaten their bacon with maple syrup pancakes, Jim and the children left.

Joan leaned back in her chair. 'What luxury. Total peace!'

Ethel cleared the table and sat down opposite her cousin.

'Let's have another cuppa.' Joan got up and put the kettle on. 'My tea consumption has rocketed since you've been here. I'd been letting the side down!' She sounded wistful. 'It's just like the old days, isn't it? You and me sitting in your mum's back kitchen putting the world to rights.'

Ethel nodded. 'Talking about make-up and boys. Until the war came along and there were no cosmetics for love or money!'

'Well, we can talk about make-up and boys now. As long as the boys aren't under four feet tall with a tendency to talk back and leave their toys on the floor.' She jerked her head in the direction of the Christmas tree where the floor was littered with pick-up sticks. 'What did I tell them? Honestly, Ethel, I despair.'

Ethel poured the tea and took a sip. 'Right, let's talk about make-up then.'

'Well, we can start with Sandra Robinson. I'd love to show her how to put on a bit of lipstick. Maybe some mascara. And get you to give her a shampoo and set.'

Ethel nodded, but said nothing.

'She's actually a pretty girl but it's as if she doesn't want anyone to see it. There's a lot of women like that round here. A bit puritanical. Maybe it's the Mennonite influence.'

'What's that?'

Joan told her about the Mennonites who lived in the area; how they dressed in black garments more suited to the past century, their heads covered with bonnets or scarves. 'There's a mixture of people of all origins round here. From Germans like Helga, French Canadian like Alice's father, Dutch, Scottish. But they all seem quite straight-laced. Sometimes I wish for a good old knees-up in a pub. Hardly anyone drinks either. Even Alice is a bit like that. Never wears make-up. Doesn't drink.'

'You can't compare Sandra to Alice though. Alice dresses well and cares for her hair. And she doesn't need to wear make-up. She's very pretty.'

'I thought you didn't like her?'

'I can still tell she's an attractive woman.'

'But that Sandra. She barely said a word all day. If she cracked a smile once in a while she'd look much better.'

'Do you know her well?'

'Hardly at all. I've seen her in the surgery, but she's never indulged in small talk. I thought she was busy. Or perhaps shy. But yesterday I came to the conclusion she's downright rude and sulky. She didn't even thank you for the Christmas present. I wanted to give her a slap, the miserable cow.'

She giggled, and Ethel found herself joining in.

'I don't think she likes me.'

'What? She hadn't even met you before. She can barely have exchanged five words with you!' Joan paused. 'Ah! I see. It's because of her father.'

Ethel took a sip of tea, unsure whether to tell Joan everything or not.

'I think she may have got the wrong idea about the doctor and me.'

'I doubt it.' Joan was chuckling now. 'I'll bet she's got exactly the right idea. He couldn't take his eyes off you all day.' She waited and when Ethel didn't respond, she said, 'Why did he ask if you were all right when you got back from the walk?'

Ethel let out a protracted sigh. 'I didn't intend it to happen. I'm still not sure how it did. One minute we were walking along and then the next he was kissing me.'

Joan leaned back in her chair and clapped her hands together. 'Yes!' she cried triumphantly. She leaned forward. 'And?'

'And what?'

'Did you kiss him back?'

'For God's sake, Joan, you're relentless. I don't know what came over me, but yes, I kissed him back. I didn't mean to and it won't happen again. I should never have let it happen at all. It was wrong.'

'Why was it wrong? You're two warm-blooded adults with no ties. Why shouldn't you fall in love?'

'Stop!' Ethel raised her hands up, palms forward, alarmed. 'Slow down, Joan. It was a kiss. It shouldn't have happened, but I'd had a glass of wine and it went to my head. It certainly won't happen again.'

'I don't see why it shouldn't. Frankly, if I didn't have Jim, I'd give the good doctor more than a glance or two. He's flipping gorgeous. Those deep brown eyes.'

Ethel groaned. 'Please, Joan. It's not fair.'

'But you do find him attractive, don't you?'

Rubbing her eyes, she said, 'Of course I do. How could I not?'

Joan grinned again. 'Did he ask to see you again?'

'No, he didn't.'

'Well, we'll have to see about that.'

'Jim and he were talking about the four of us going to watch an ice hockey game, but I'll find a way to make my excuses.'

'You certainly won't. I'll be the one making excuses and then Jim can offer to stay home with me and the two of you can go together. Besides I can't leave the boys and they can't stay at Hollowtree while Don's so ill.' A shadow passed over her face.

'Sandra's going to babysit,' said Ethel.

'Really?' Joan looked astonished. 'She offered?'

'No. Dr Robinson suggested it and she had to agree. I don't think she was too happy but she doesn't want to go anyway. Says she hates sport.'

'Right. Well, I'll call off anyway. The thought of cramming myself into a tiny seat with this enormous belly is not a good one. When's the game?'

Ethel shrugged. 'Next week, I think. Or maybe the week after.'

'Either way it's too near my time.' Joan rubbed her hands together. 'So, we have it. A date for you and Duncan.'

'I'm not going. It wouldn't be fair.'

'Why?'

'I'll be going home soon. It wouldn't be right – I'd be leading him on and then having to leave him.'

'You don't have to go back to England, you know. There's no hurry. You can stay here as long as you like. Besides, what do have to go home for? Mum reckons she can easily find a tenant for your house. That would give you some income – or at least pay the bills. And why go back to that hair salon? Vera's never appreciated you. You're a darn good hairdresser and the customers love you. That business will go under without you. Either that, or she'll have to pull her finger out. Serve her right.'

'You're dreaming, Joan.'

'And what's wrong with that? Dreams never did anyone any harm. I can't think of a better dream than you and the doctor falling in love, getting married and staying here in Hollowtree. Perfect!'

'I can't fall in love with him.'

'Why ever not?'

'You know why.'

Joan stretched her hand out and took hold of Ethel's. 'Look, love, you can't keep yourself for a man who's been dead and buried for more than ten years. It isn't natural.'

Ethel started to cry. Silent tears.

Joan moved round to the other side of the table and put her arms around her cousin. 'Go on. Let it all out. The trouble is, Ethel, you didn't do enough crying at the time. You were so determined to be brave. And then with your brother and your mum. And all that time looking out for me.' She stroked Ethel's hair. 'It's time you looked out for yourself, love. It's time you gave yourself permission to be happy.'

'I have nothing left. I gave everything to Greg. I can't possibly love someone else. It would make everything Greg and I had together meaningless.'

Joan shook her head. 'Nothing can ever take away what you had with Greg. It was beautiful. You were beautiful together. It was terrible what happened to him. Shocking. But I know – yes, I am completely certain, without a shadow of a doubt, that if Greg could speak to you now, he'd tell you to let your heart lead you. He'd want you to be happy more than anything else. Oh, Ethel, Greg would *hate* the idea of you cutting yourself off from any possibility of love and happiness because of what you had with him. Please don't do this to yourself, sweetie. Please.' She pulled Ethel closer and Ethel saw that she was crying too.

Next moment, the pair of them dissolved into giggles.

'What are we like?' said Joan.

Ethel wiped her eyes.

'So, you'll see what happens? Go to the hockey game?'

Ethel nodded.

'In that case, I'm going to put the kettle on again. Then we can think about something to eat. How does a turkey sandwich with some pickles sound?'

When they'd finished their simple meal, Ethel told Joan what Sandra had said after she gave her the present.

'The bitch,' said Joan. 'That explains it.'

'Explains what?'

'I found the bath cubes stuffed behind a cushion in the parlour.'

'No!'

'You absolutely have to go for it with Duncan now. Just to spite the little cow.'

Ethel shook her head. 'I feel sorry for her. She lost her mother when she was a baby. She and her father must be very close. I expect she's terrified at the idea of someone coming along and taking him away – not that I'm going to do that.'

'It's no excuse for being rude. She was a guest in my house. How dare she behave like that to you under my roof? I've a good mind to tell that girl her fortune.'

Ethel put her hand on Joan's arm. 'Down, girl! Best we just forget about her. If she feels that strongly, she'll talk to her father and then he'll probably back away. No point in me worrying.'

Joan cleared the plates away. 'Somehow I don't think

Duncan Robinson's going to back away. My money's on you and him!' She grinned at Ethel over her shoulder.

There was a crash against the door and Jimmy and Sam barged into the kitchen, both talking at once, eager to show off the hand-knitted caps their grandmother had made for them for Christmas.

19

*M*r Freeman had been right to be optimistic about the Grant of Probate. In late January he summoned Alice to his office and told her it was now in his possession and work was in hand for the settlement of the estate.

'Once the funds are transferred to your name, my job will be done, er, unless...'

'You want to know if I will continue to retain the services of your firm, Mr Freeman?'

He nodded. Alice realised he actually looked awkward, clearly not relishing being cast in the role of a supplicant.

'You are of course free to retain any legal advisors you choose or – but I would counsel against it – none at all.'

'I intend to continue with you. This firm has served Miss Cooke well for decades and what was good enough for her is certainly good enough for me.'

About a week after probate was granted, there was a knock on the front door. Alice had been about to put on her coat to leave for her daily visit to one of the picture palaces. She opened the door.

Her heart jerked in her chest from fear and shock. Tip Howardson was standing on the threshold, a wide grin on his face.

She started to push the door closed but he had his foot in it.

'Well, well, Alice. As lovely as ever, but maybe lacking in manners.'

'Go away. I've nothing to say to you.'

'That's fine, you can just listen, as I have plenty to say to you. Now, why don't you let me in before all this cold air gets inside your nice warm house.'

'I've told you. I want you to leave, right now.'

Howardson grinned. 'I think you need to hear what I have to say first.'

Alice decided it was better to get it over with. She had nothing to fear from him now. She was immune to him. It was hard to believe she had ever been attracted to him. Opening the door, she let him in and led him into the drawing room.

He sat down, his bulk filling an armchair, his thighs splayed wide, taking possession of the room. Alice stood in front of the fireplace, her nerves twitching. She did have cause for fear. This man had exercised a control over her, exploiting her vulnerability and loneliness after Walt's death.

Looking at him now, she wondered how she could have fallen for his line. He still had that big bull neck, the boxer's broken nose, the narrow lips shaped into a sardonic smile. But his eyes were dangerous. When she'd looked into them all those years ago and seen his naked desire, she had become putty in his hands. Avoiding his gaze, she said, 'Get on with it. I have to go out in ten minutes. You just caught me.'

'I've been doing a lot of thinking, Alice. And I've come to the conclusion that you and I should bury the hatchet and get hitched.'

He got up from the chair and went to stand beside her in front of the fireplace. She moved away. Horrified, she watched as he picked up a framed photograph of Catherine from the mantelpiece.

'She's pretty. Takes after her mom. Does she know about me? What's her name?'

'Put that down. And get out.' Alice went to grab the picture from his hands.

Tip caught her wrist and held it with a grip that made her wince, while he replaced the photograph. Releasing her, he went to sit down again. He leaned back in the chair, spreading his legs out as before. The fabric of his trousers was stretched tight over his solid thighs and she could see the outline of his penis. She felt sick.

'A little girl like that needs her father. When we get married, she'll have one.'

He jerked his head towards the picture of Rose, which stood beside her sister's in a matching frame. 'Maybe I'll adopt the other one too. Walt's girl.' He reached in his coat pocket and pulled out a packet of cigarettes and lit one, drawing the smoke deep into his lungs and exhaling it in Alice's direction. 'Good old Walt. I always liked him. He was like a brother to me.'

Alice batted the smoke away, anger taking over her fear. 'Walt felt sorry for you when you were kids, as you had no friends. Everybody hated you, Tip. Like I do now. In fact, I despise you.'

He laughed. 'You're still a feisty girl, aren't you, Alice Ducroix? Plenty of spunk. I like that in a woman. Someone not afraid to fight her corner.' His mouth curled into a smile.

'And I still reckon, the best fuck I ever had.' He looked her up and down, mentally removing her clothes.

Alice experienced a rising panic. What had possessed her to let him in? How was she going to get rid of him?

Tip seemed to read her mind. He got up and moved towards her. 'I'd like to fuck you right here and now, darling, but I'm not going to. I want to do things properly this time. Make an honest woman of you first. Do the right thing by you and my daughter.'

Alice spluttered in indignation. 'What the hell are you talking about? Coming in here with your filthy talk. And have you forgotten telling me you already have a wife and child?'

He laughed. 'I did tell you that, didn't I? Funny what a fellow will say when he's in a tight spot. But the good news is, Alice my sweet, I made it up. Well, not the wife – but we're divorced. A quickie. She was American. They know how to do these things fast down there. No fuss. No messing about. And the child never existed.' He shrugged.

Alice said nothing. Her heart was hammering against her ribs, her breathing fast and short.

'I know I've been a bad boy in the past. I've had my share of women.' He moved closer to her until he was standing right in front of her. He leaned his forehead against hers. Alice was rigid with fear.

'But there's never been anyone like you, Alice. Reckon I'd never look at another woman again if I'm getting it from you all the time.'

She pushed him away.

He stretched one hand out and cupped her breast. 'Still got those firm titties. I remember how much you liked–'

Alice smacked his hand away. 'Get out of here! Now! Before I call the police.'

He picked up his hat from where he'd slung it on a side table. 'You give it some thought, darling. Maybe you think you don't need a husband, especially now you've come into all this.' He gestured with his hat around the room. 'But that little girl needs a father. And I know better than anyone, how much you need to be fucked. Just bear that in mind.' He gave a dirty laugh.

Alice shoved him towards the front door.

'I'll be seeing you. In the meantime, you think hard, Alice. You don't want that pretty girl growing up as a bastard. Children can be cruel. Word gets around.'

He put on his hat, opened the door and bounded down the steps.

As soon as he'd gone, Alice went back down to the basement kitchen. There was no possibility of watching a film now. Her heart was still racing, and she struggled to breathe. Tip must have found out about Aunt Miriam's death and her inheritance. The obituaries? She went to the cupboard and took down a bottle of Miss Cooke's whisky and poured herself a generous measure. Sipping it, she wrinkled her nose in distaste, then as the warm spirit flooded through her body, she took another sip, and took the glass with her, back to the drawing room.

'*I* want you and Jim to come.' Ethel was sitting at the kitchen table. 'Otherwise I'm not going.

Joan sat down opposite her. 'You've no choice, I'm afraid. Jim dropped by the surgery today and told Sandra she didn't need to sit for us as I wasn't up to going.'

'Noooo!' Ethel put her head in her hands.

'Don't be daft, Ethel. Dr Robinson doesn't bite. You'll have a great time. Ice hockey's good fun. Very violent. They beat the stuffing out of each other. I was shocked the first time I went.'

'You're doing a great job of selling it to me.'

'You'll love it. I do. And you can snuggle up to Duncan and get him to explain what's going on. Men love an opportunity to show their superior knowledge.' She winked. 'Or you can hide your face in his jacket if the violence gets too much!'

'Joan! This is not helping. Can't you tell him I'm feeling unwell?'

'Of course not. You can't have him going on his own.'

'He can go with Jim.'

Joan shook her head and got up. 'Jim's gone over to sit with Don this evening. Helga's got something she wants to go to at the church.' At the sound of gravel crunching, she added, 'Too late now.'

Ethel grabbed her coat and, scowling at Joan, she went out of the kitchen as if she were going to meet her doom.

She was stretching out her hand towards the front passenger door when the rear door popped open and she realised Sandra was sitting in the front. Ethel climbed into the back seat, uncertain whether to be annoyed or relieved that Sandra was evidently going to join them after all.

Dr Robinson had a face like thunder and Ethel could tell from the atmosphere that he and his daughter had exchanged words.

He turned towards Ethel, giving his eyes an almost imperceptible roll in Sandra's direction. 'Sandra's decided to join us this evening.'

'Hello, Sandra. I thought you didn't like sport.' Ethel injected some brightness into her tone.

'One of the patients told me tonight's game was an important one and I shouldn't pass up the chance to come along.'

'You've been passing up chances to come to hockey games for the past ten years or more.' Duncan's tone was impatient.

'I know. But it's only right to give it a chance. I'll probably hate it but at least then I'll know for sure I don't like hockey.' She swivelled in her seat and looked straight at Ethel. 'Anyway, you don't know if you're going to like it either. I'm sure you won't, you being British.' The sneer was evident.

The game was in Kitchener, an interminable hour's drive away. They drove in silence. Ethel stared through the window, even though it was dark and there was nothing to see, silently cursing Joan. Trying to make conversation with Sandra was pointless and she was inhibited in talking to the doctor with his daughter there, like a predatory bird, ready to pounce.

When they reached the stadium, Dr Robinson led the way to their seats. As Ethel was about to follow him into the row, Sandra pushed in front of her and plonked herself in the middle seat. So much for Joan's plan.

The game started, and Ethel hadn't a clue what was going on. When Duncan tried to lean forward to explain something, his daughter bent forward too, so Ethel couldn't hear what he was saying over the roar of the crowd. Despite knowing nothing of the rules, Ethel was soon caught up in the excitement. The home team, The Kitchener-Waterloo Dutchmen, clearly had the upper hand.

Joan was right about it being violent. The inevitable tumbles onto the ice, gashes from pucks, hockey sticks and skate blades, resulted in a plentiful flow of blood. Ethel felt queasy at first, but the doctor told her that even minor lacerations cause copious bleeding and it was nothing to worry about. She was shocked when a scuffle broke out between players when one of them was checked by an opponent. As the punches landed, the crowd roared its approval. Though infringing players were sent for brief exiles into the 'Sin Bin', the game's officials seemed unworried by fighting.

After the game was over and the victory with the local team, they headed back to the car. This time, Duncan Robinson was ready for his daughter. He took the handle of the front passenger door and said, 'Ride up front, Ethel.'

A scowling Sandra got into the back seat and hunched up in the corner. Ethel asked her whether the game had changed her view of sport at all.

'It was just as I expected. Boring.'

'You could call that game a lot of things but boring isn't one of them,' said her father. 'What did you think, Ethel?'

She couldn't help herself. 'I thought it was absolutely thrilling. Joan was right. Ice hockey is very bloodthirsty but very exciting. I loved every minute.' Dr Robinson turned towards her and his hand brushed hers for a moment, before returning to the steering wheel.

They chatted about the highlights of the hockey game, with Duncan elucidating some of the finer points of play, while Sandra sat in petulant silence. When they arrived back at Rivercreek Farm, the doctor got out of the car and escorted Ethel to the door.

'I'm sorry about Sandra. I hope you'll forgive me. I'd like to have a chance to explain. May I see you again?'

Ethel bit her lip. 'I don't think that's a good idea, Dr Robinson.'

'Call me Duncan.' He looked at her intently. 'Please.' They were bathed in moonlight, so she could see the sincerity in his eyes.

'I won't be around for much longer and Sandra–'

'Please. I'll stop by tomorrow after I've finished evening surgery and we can go and have a drink together.' He took her hand.

'I can't tomorrow.' She hoped he wouldn't ask what she was doing.

'Same time next week then?'

She hesitated. How could she possibly have an excuse for that far in advance?

'Right. About eight o'clock. I'll explain then.'

Without waiting for her to contradict him, he squeezed her hand gently and went back to the car. Sandra was still sitting in the back seat and evidently had no intention of moving.

When Ethel walked into the kitchen, Joan and Jim were sitting at the kitchen table. They both looked up expectantly.

'How was it?' asked Joan.

'The Dutchmen won. It was a walkover.'

'I don't mean the hockey! How did you get on with Duncan?'

'You mean Duncan and Sandra.'

Joan gasped. 'You're kidding me!'

Jim snorted.

'Yes. My fears about being alone with him were unfounded. She sat between us during the game. I don't think she even watched it. I could hear her sighing even over the noise of the crowd.'

'What is her problem? And why on earth didn't Duncan tell her where to get off?'

Ethel shrugged. 'I told you, she doesn't like me. And she clearly thinks I have designs on her father.'

'Well, don't you?' Jim winked at her.

Ethel raised an eyebrow, refusing to take the bait.

'She's acting like a child. For heaven's sake the woman's eighteen. You'd think she was a schoolgirl.' Joan raised her hand. 'I told you she needs a good slapping. Anyway, are you going to see him again?'

Ethel nodded. 'I had no choice. He didn't give me a chance to say no. He's picking me up for a drink next Tuesday evening after surgery.'

Joan and Jim grinned at each other.

'He says he wants to explain.'

'He *needs* to explain. I'd like to know why he doesn't stand up to that little madam.' Joan got up and rubbed her back. 'I'm going to bed. There's another little madam who is getting very restless.' She pointed to her stomach. 'I have a feeling it won't be long now.'

'You two go on up,' said Ethel. 'I'm going to make myself some cocoa and fill a hot water bottle.'

After they had said goodnight, Ethel made her cocoa and sat at the table. No matter how hard she tried, she couldn't help feeling drawn to the doctor. Just sitting beside him in the car, there was an invisible current running between them. When he touched her hand, she wanted to hold onto his. She had longed to lean her head against his shoulder. And she was sure that, if they'd been alone, without Sandra slumped in the back seat oozing venom, he would have taken her in his arms and kissed her. And she would have let him.

But Ethel was afraid to feel like that again. If she allowed her feelings to come to the surface, placed her trust in him, she would be tempting fate. When she fell in love with Greg, it ended in tragedy and pain. She couldn't let that happen again. All this time, since his death, she'd been building up her defences, making herself immune to love. How could she let those defences down now – and for a man who lived thousands of miles away from her, and who had a daughter who made it crystal clear that she hated Ethel with a passion?

She would have to tell him. She would have to be strong and not allow herself to be swayed by her attraction for him. Telling him she couldn't possibly see him again was the only solution, the only practical course to follow.

She rinsed out her cocoa cup, picked up the hot water bottle, switched off the light, and went up to bed.

21

The day Ethel was due to see the doctor again, the snow came, covering the fields around Rivercreek Farm in a cotton wool cloud. It was a week into January and Don Armstrong was still clinging on to life.

Joan was standing at the kitchen window, watching the snow falling, when her waters broke.

Ethel looked at the puddle of water on the tiled floor and gave a little cry. Shocked, when a perfectly calm Joan fetched a cloth and began to mop up, Ethel said, 'Let me do that. You need to lie down.'

Joan laughed. 'Lying down is the last thing I want.' She pulled out a chair from the kitchen table, settled into the seat and leaned back, grinning at Ethel. 'This one's not wasting any time. I thought I had another week or two yet.'

Ethel looked at her in alarm. 'You don't mean it's coming right now?'

Joan grimaced. 'I should be so lucky. It'll probably be hours yet. Remember Jimmy. Seventeen hours, he took. But each one's been getting faster.'

'What do I do?'

'Well, I certainly don't want you trying to deliver the baby. You'd probably pass out on the spot. Put some boots on, wrap up and go and find Jim. He's stripping the tractor engine in the barn. Get him to drive over to Hollowtree with you and pick up Ma. You don't mind sitting with Don, do you?' She gasped, and her face creased up in pain. 'Quick as you can, love. I need Ma here soon.'

Ethel did as she was told, swaddling herself in coat, hat and scarf and making her way through the falling snow to find Jim, who wasted no time getting the truck out and driving them across the rough track through the fields over to Hollowtree Farm.

Helga Armstrong was sitting in a chair by the single bed in the corner of the kitchen. Don was propped up against several pillows, his face partly covered by the oxygen mask, a metal tank on a wheeled trolley beside him. Helga was drinking a glass of milk.

'Joan's started?' Helga put the glass down and got to her feet.

Ethel nodded. 'She doesn't think this one's going to hang around.'

'How frequent were the contractions?'

Ethel looked blank.

'Waters broken?'

Ethel nodded.

Helga leaned over her husband's bed and kissed him on the forehead.

He pulled his mask down. 'You get along to Joan. I'll be fine with this lovely lady for company.' He smiled at Ethel and drew the mask back on.

Helga pointed towards the stove. 'There's soup in a pan there and a fresh loaf on the side. Cheese under a cloth in the pantry. Help yourself to anything you need.'

She ran her hand over her husband's hair and kissed him again. And then Helga and Jim were gone.

Ethel looked around the kitchen, wondering what to do. She had met Don Armstrong for only a few minutes and barely knew the man. She offered him a cup of tea which he declined. Making one for herself, she came to sit beside him.

There was a book lying open on the kitchen table. 'Was Mrs Armstrong reading this to you?'

Don nodded.

'Would you like me to carry on where she left off?'

He gave her a watery smile from behind the mask and patted her hand.

The book was called *Sunshine Sketches of a Little Town.* Ethel began to read the humorous study of life in a small Canadian town. She flipped to the front and saw it had been published in 1917 but, apart from the railroad rushing through Mariposa, the fictional town of the book, it might well have been Hollowtree. The time flew by as she read, enjoying the wry, self-deprecating humour and the affection with which the author had painted his home town.

After an hour or so, she was ready for another cup of tea. Putting the book down, she saw that Don had closed his eyes. She went over to the stove and put the kettle on.

'You like Hollowtree?' he asked, making her jump.

'I thought you'd fallen asleep. Yes – it's a nice place. Would you like some tea?'

He shook his head. 'I'll have …a few sips of water.'

Ethel held the glass while he drank.

'That's better. Lived here in Hollowtree all my life…' He made a little gulping noise and raised the mask to his face and took another breath. 'Apart from when… I was in the war…. first one.'

She came back to sit beside him with her cup of tea. 'It's very like the town in the book.'

He put his hand on her arm. 'When I'm done with the book... I want you to have it.

She thanked him. 'I'd like that very much. It will always remind me of Canada and Hollowtree – and you, Mr Armstrong.'

'Call me Don. You not going to stay here?'

'I'll stay until Joan's back on her feet, then I'll be going back to England.'

'You're from Alder... shot?'

Ethel nodded.

'Jim didn't like that place.'

Smiling, she said, 'I suppose it doesn't have a lot going for it. It's basically a military town. Home to the British army.'

Don frowned.

'But it's where I've lived all my life.'

'Your folks all... gone. Nothing for you... there. You're better here.'

Sipping her tea, she wondered why everyone was so intent on persuading her to stay.

Don replaced the mask and kept his eyes fixed on Ethel's face as she finished her tea. Then he pulled the mask aside. 'Hear the doc's sweet on you.'

Her face burned. Did the whole town know? Had Joan been talking to everyone? Ethel seethed with embarrassment.

Don put his thin bony hand on hers. 'He's a good... man.' He began to cough.

She adjusted the pillows behind him, noting how skeletally thin his body was, the bones of his spine and ribcage evident through the fabric of his pyjamas. His skin had a greyish tinge and his eyes were rheumy.

When he'd stopped coughing, he pulled the mask aside again and said, 'You like him?'

Ethel took a deep breath and nodded. She couldn't lie to the man – even if she kept trying to lie to herself.

He grinned at her. 'Thought so.'

'Shall I read some more to you?'

He shook his head and closed his eyes.

While he slept, Ethel washed her teacup and Helga's milk glass and wiped down the table. She looked around for another small task to do. It was almost one o'clock. Lunchtime. Lighting the burner on the stove, she warmed up the soup, cut herself a slice of bread and ate at the table. Don was still fast asleep.

She was desperate to go to the toilet but remembered that here at Hollowtree Farm there were no indoor facilities. She would have to brave the snow and venture outside to the privy – or the biffy as they called it. Pulling on a woollen hat she found on the back of the door, and which looked a lot warmer than her own, she wrapped her coat around her, tugged on her boots and went outside. The wind cut into her, whipping sideways across the yard, driving snow into the gap at the top of her collar. She should have put her scarf on too. Shuddering, she opened the door of the little hut and used the toilet. The wooden seat was as cold as ice and the tiny space was pitch dark. It was only when she opened the door again that she saw the stub of candle and the box of matches on a small shelf.

Back in the warmth of the kitchen she put the kettle on for another cup of tea. At least the kitchen was warm, the stove giving off a heat that filled the whole room – indeed the whole house. She settled herself at the table.

Something was different. She looked over at Don. There was no longer the rise and fall of his chest under the blanket, nor the soft hiss of the oxygen. Ethel moved to the bed. Silence. No more laboured breathing. She slipped her hand under the covers and lifted up his wrist to feel for his pulse. Nothing. Don's eyes were closed, and his skin was cold.

Ethel clutched her hands together, alarmed, uncertain what to do. He looked dead. He was dead. She was sure of that. Should she call Rivercreek? But how could she break the news to Helga, who would be in the midst of delivering Joan's baby? In a panic, she rushed to the telephone, mounted on the wall by the kitchen door. She didn't even know the number. Then she saw a notepad on the windowsill. The word 'Doctor' was written at the top and the number of the surgery. She picked up the receiver and dialled, fear welling up inside her. Was it her fault? Had his oxygen run out? Should she have noticed something sooner?

Sandra Robinson answered on the third ring.

'It's Hollowtree Farm. I think Mr Armstrong may have died. Please send the doctor right away.'

'Who's speaking?'

'It's Ethel Underwood, Sandra. I'm sitting with Mr Armstrong while Mrs Armstrong is at Rivercreek. Joan is having her baby. Please. I don't know what to do.' She struggled for breath.

'Calm down. If he's dead, you can't do anything. I'll send the doctor now. He's just finished surgery. He'll be there in twenty minutes or so.' The line clicked as Sandra hung up.

Ethel paced up and down in the kitchen, walking to the window to watch the track that led to the road for any sign of the doctor. In between, she stood by the bed, hoping against hope that Don Armstrong would open his eyes and tell her he had been in a deep sleep.

He looked calm, peaceful. Ethel had known him for such a short time, yet she'd been relaxed in his company, had enjoyed reading to him. She remembered how Joan had told her he was kind to her when she first arrived in Canada – she'd thought him her only ally at times. She picked up *Sunshine Sketches of a Little Town* from where she'd left it open on the bed. Closing the book, she put it on the kitchen table. Tears rolled down her cheeks, not only for poor Don, but for her mum too.

The door opened, and Duncan Robinson came into the kitchen. Ethel wiped her eyes and got up. The doctor said nothing but went straight to the bedside, while she moved over to stand by the window.

She waited there, looking out at the falling snow, while the doctor checked Don's vital signs, disconnected the oxygen, pulled the blanket up over Don's face and wrote out the death certificate.

Ethel was aware of him coming across the room to her. She turned to face him.

'Was it my fault?' she said. 'Could I have done something?'

He shook his head, his eyes holding hers, his gaze steady. 'Nothing. It could have happened any time. I'm sorry it had to be with you.'

She bit her lip. He pulled her to him, holding her against his chest, his hand cradling her head. She could feel the rise and fall of his breathing, the touch of his hand on her hair.

'Where's Mrs Armstrong?' he asked her eventually.

She explained.

'I'll go over there and break the news. I can check on Joan too. Although she's in good hands.' He thought for a moment. 'Maybe I'll tell Jim first. Let him tell his mother at the right moment. Better to let her bring the new baby into the world before she gets to hear about Don leaving it.'

Ethel nodded. 'You're sure I couldn't have done anything?'

He shook his head. 'Was he unconscious all the time you were here?'

'No.' Ethel was surprised. 'No, I read to him then he was talking a bit. Oh, Doctor, do you think that's what did it? He kept pulling the mask away, so he could talk to me.'

'I've told you, it's Duncan, please. And no. I can't think of a nicer way for him to slip out of this world than having you read to him. And the talking won't have harmed him. If he wanted to talk it was important he did so.'

He picked up the book from the table and examined the title. 'Good choice. He'd have been smiling when you read that.'

'He told me he wanted me to have the book. Do you think...?'

'Take it. Mrs Armstrong's got no time for reading.'

'Only I was enjoying it. Made me think of this little town.'

'Then you must keep it. Anything that makes you see Hollowtree in a good light.' He took her hand. 'We're still going for a drink tonight?'

'Wouldn't that be disrespectful to Don?'

'I think Don would have approved heartily. Now, let's get over there and break the news to Jim.'

They pulled into the yard at Rivercreek Farm just behind Jim's truck. The two boys jumped out and ran into the house.

Jim called out to the doctor. 'It's all over. My new daughter was in a real hurry to come into the world. So I've brought the boys home.' His face was beaming. Then he saw that Ethel was with the doctor and his smile disappeared.

The three of them stood together in the snow. 'He's gone then?'

Ethel nodded. 'I'm so sorry, Jim. He was sleeping and then he wasn't breathing any more. The doctor's number was by the telephone. I didn't know what to do.'

Dr Robinson put an arm on Jim's shoulder. 'I'm sorry, pal. Don was a great guy. But I can promise you it was a very peaceful death.'

Jim sucked his lips into a narrow line, his eyes welling. 'Let's get inside. I need to tell Ma. And there's the under-taker to call.'

Helga Armstrong took the news stoically, with no sign of tears. She just nodded and looked down. Ethel supposed she'd had plenty of time to prepare herself. She wondered what life was going to be like for the woman, all alone at Hollowtree. Would she perhaps move into Rivercreek with Jim and the family? Somehow Ethel doubted it.

Dr Robinson went upstairs to check over Joan and her baby daughter, while Ethel made cheese toasties for the two boys and tea for Helga. Then the boys and Ethel were allowed to go upstairs and pay homage to the new arrival. The novelty of their baby sister lasted only a few minutes before the boys asked if they could go and play.

'Dad's waiting for you in the kitchen. He needs to talk to you first.' Needing no further encouragement, they disap-peared downstairs.

Ethel imagined their small faces, happy at the arrival of their baby sister, dissolving into tears when the news of their Pop's demise was broken to them by Jim.

Joan shook her head, her eyes sad, as she nursed her daughter. 'Don never got to see her, after all.'

Ethel sat on the edge of the bed, tears welling up again. 'What a lovely man. He was so kind today, so sweet. Joanie, I'm terribly sorry.'

'One life ends as another begins.' Joan lowered her head and kissed her baby's. 'I wish he could have hung on for another day or so.' She took Ethel's hand. 'Was it terrible? Being there when he died?'

'No. Not at all. Apart from me thinking I could have done something, but I know I couldn't. He just went to sleep and slipped away. I'd been reading to him. He asked me to have the book when he'd finished with it. Do you think he knew that it was going to be so soon? That he'd never even get to the end of the book?'

Joan squeezed her hand.

'He asked me about Dr Robinson too. Said he'd heard he was sweet on me.'

'Everyone knows that.'

'What'll Helga do now?'

'Jim's asked her to stay here but she won't. She insists on going back to Hollowtree tonight. She wants to say goodbye to him.'

'She wants to be in the house tonight with him... with the body?' Ethel whispered. 'Should I offer to go with her?'

'No. She wants to be alone with him. She's not afraid. Besides, don't you have a date tonight?'

Ethel looked down, plucking at the counterpane with her fingers. 'Do you think I should cancel? You know, under the circumstances?'

'Certainly not.'

The baby began to mewl.

'Get yourself out and have a nice evening with the doctor. We'll all manage fine here. Don would definitely approve of that.'

22

When Alice walked into the schoolyard, only Rose was waiting in the usual place.

'Where's Catherine?'

Rose told her that she'd been to look for Catherine but there was no sign of her.

'Are you sure she isn't still in her classroom?' Alice tried not to show her irritation.

Rose pouted. 'I told you, Mommy, I've already been to look for her. There's no one there.'

'You're supposed to wait here for her. What on earth were you doing?'

Rose looked down. 'I was on blackboard duty. I was wiping the board and putting out fresh chalk for tomorrow. Catherine's supposed to wait there by the gate for me.' Her lip trembled. 'I'm sorry, Mommy.'

Alice grabbed Rose's hand. 'Come on. I need to speak to her teacher. How many times have I told you, Rose. Looking after Catherine is your responsibility until I get here.'

She hauled Rose behind her as she went into the

deserted school building and knocked on the door of the staff room.

A teacher she didn't know appeared.

'Is Miss Pritchard there?'

The woman disappeared back into the room and Miss Pritchard emerged. 'Hello, Mrs Armstrong. I thought you weren't coming today. Mr Armstrong said he'd got off work early and was taking Catherine home.'

Alice's veins turned to ice. 'There is no Mr Armstrong. My husband died in the war.'

'Oh. I'm sorry. I assumed... He said he was Catherine's father. Oh dear.'

'You let a strange man walk off with my five-year-old daughter?' Alice's throat constricted. 'Oh my God. Do you have any idea? You stupid, stupid woman. We need to call the police. My child has been abducted.'

Rose stood, open-mouthed. Miss Pritchard turned pale and looked around her as though Catherine would magically appear.

A voice behind Alice spoke and she wheeled around to see the headmistress, Miss Williams. 'Come to my office please, Mrs Armstrong. Miss Pritchard, take Rose to her classroom and wait with her there.' Miss Williams led a near hysterical Alice along the corridor.

'Sit down and tell me what has happened.'

'Catherine's father has taken her. We aren't married. I haven't seen him in years. He turned up at my house yesterday. He's using Catherine to get at me.' She began to sob. 'He's dangerous. He caused a man's death. He attacked a woman. Twice.'

The headmistress, Miss Williams, handed Alice a handkerchief. 'Calm down, Mrs Armstrong. You say he is Catherine's father. So she and Rose have different fathers?'

Alice nodded. 'I didn't want anyone to know. I made a terrible mistake. But Catherine, my little girl. She's so precious to me.'

'I am sure Catherine will be perfectly all right. If this man is using her to get at you, and he is her father, he won't harm her. Please calm down. I'm going to drive you and Rose home and if Catherine isn't there waiting for you, we'll call the police.' She paused. 'I'm sure you won't want word of this to get around if, as I suspect, Catherine is by now safely back at home.' Her voice was all stern efficiency, but her eyes signalled her sympathy.

When they pulled up outside the house, Alice leapt out of the car and ran up the steps to the front door, which opened before she got there. The housekeeper, Mrs Browning, was standing on the threshold.

'Mrs Armstrong. There you are. I thought you'd forgotten your keys and when I opened the door Catherine was standing here on her own.'

Alice pushed past the astonished woman and ran inside, where she scooped up a bewildered Catherine. 'Thank God, baby. Oh, my darling, I've been so worried. Don't you ever, ever do that again.' She hugged the little girl and covered her face with kisses.

Remembering that Miss Williams and Rose were still outside in the car, Alice went to the door and waved them inside.

'Thank you so much, Miss Williams. Catherine is safe and sound. But please inform Miss Pritchard that if she ever lets either of my children go off with anyone other than me, I will report it to the board of governors and move heaven and earth to see her dismissed.' She grabbed Rose by the hand and took her inside the house without waiting for the headmistress to reply.

Inside, Alice took big gulps of air, until she'd calmed herself. The two girls stared at her, open-mouthed.

'Come in here, girls. We need to have a talk.'

The girls sat side-by-side on the sofa while she lectured them on not going anywhere with strange men.

'But he wasn't a strange man, Mommy. He said he's my daddy.'

'He's not your daddy. Your daddy's in heaven.' Tears rolled down her cheeks as she lied to her child. 'That man is a very bad man and you must never, never speak to him. And you must tell me at once if he comes near you again. Do you understand, Catherine?'

Catherine nodded, sobbing. Alice knelt before her and wrapped her arms around the frightened child. 'I don't mean to be cross with you, angel.' She reached out and took Rose's hand. 'I was frightened something had happened to you. I love you both so much.' She rocked back onto her heels and looked from one child to the other. 'All right? No more going off with strangers. Always wait for Mommy. And if I'm late – which I promise you I won't be – you stay with the teacher.'

The two girls nodded.

Alice couldn't stay in Ottawa now that Tip Howardson knew where she was. He'd managed to find out Catherine's school. Her name. She had to keep her children safe.

Alice had no illusions about Tip's sudden display of fatherly love and desire to marry her. It was entirely down to Miss Cooke's legacy. Were she stupid enough to accede to his wishes, the money would be hers no longer. He would find a way to get his hands on it. That money was Alice's liberation and her children's future. Her mind was made up. She would take the girls home to Hollowtree.

*I*nstead of taking the road towards the town, the doctor turned the car in the opposite direction when they reached the crossroads.

'I thought we'd go to Argyll tonight. It's only about ten miles away. There's a little place there that's not unpleasant.'

Ethel wondered if he was worried about being seen with her. Hollowtree was like being in a goldfish bowl. And maybe he wasn't going to risk Sandra walking in on them and interrupting their evening.

They drove most of the way in silence and Ethel was nervous that she wouldn't know what to say to him. She stole a glance at his profile in the darkened car as he drove: the line of his jaw; the thickness of his hair; once again, noting how nice his hands were. Her stomach flipped and a fizz ran through her body.

Duncan parked outside a small hotel, The Red House Tavern. Argyll seemed a lot like Hollowtree, as far as Ethel could tell in the dark. The snow had stopped falling but lay thick on the rooftops and glinted in the light that spilled out of the hotel front. He held open the door marked Ladies and

Escorts and ushered her inside into the warmth, where he found them a table at the back of the almost empty room. He asked her what she wanted to drink and signalled to the bartender. She looked around the room. A fire was blazing in the grate and candles were ranged along the mantelpiece. The rest of the lighting in the room was muted, coming from dim wall lights. The floor was polished wood and there were stuffed deer trophies and a set of crossed hockey sticks on the wall. The only other clients were another couple seated near the window. She could hear more noise coming from what was evidently the more popular men-only bar.

When the server returned with the drinks, Duncan smiled at her and her stomach flipped again.

'I hope he got that right. You did say half beer, half lemonade?'

She nodded.

'A new one on me. What did you call it?'

'Shandy. You can also have it with ginger beer instead of lemonade.'

Duncan pulled a face and chinked glasses with her. After he'd taken a gulp of his beer, he said, 'I still owe you an apology for the night of the hockey game. I don't know what got into my daughter. What must you think of me?'

'She doesn't like me.'

'It's not personal. Sandra's jealous. She can tell I really like you. It's that obvious.' He looked down into his beer, then up at her. 'I *do* really like you, Ethel.'

Her cheeks burned, and she was grateful for the dimness of the room. Things were going too fast.

'Tell me about yourself, Duncan. I know so little about you.'

'No. Let's talk about you first.'

So, she told him about her work in the salon, the death

of her parents and her brother, and answered his questions about the time since Greg had died.

'And children? Didn't you ever want children?'

She shrugged. 'No. If I'd married Greg it probably would have happened. But no. It's not been a big thing. I suppose I just got used to the idea that I was always going to be on my own. No regrets! And Joan has made up for me.' She gave a little laugh.

'Eleven years is a long time, Ethel. There's really been no one else?' He clearly found that astonishing.

She shook her head. 'No one. What about you? It's been even longer since your wife died.'

'Eighteen years.'

She studied his face, seeing a shadow pass over his eyes.

'How did she die?' She was nervous asking the question. It seemed intrusive, but then he had asked her about Greg.

'Complications when Sandra was born.' He drained his glass. 'Let me order us another drink.' Without waiting for her reply, he waved at the bartender.

When he turned back to her he was smiling again. 'I was explaining about Sandra and her rudeness. I know you and I have barely met, but I feel...' He hesitated. 'I was drawn to you at once. Sandra can see that. She's never known me like this about a woman before.' He looked away briefly. 'There have been one or two girlfriends in the past, but none serious. None lasting. To be honest, I've never had the heart for it. And never had the time. What with the work and bringing Sandra up on my own.' He reached for her hand. 'I never dreamt I could feel like this.'

Ethel squeezed her lips together. She didn't know what to say. Her heart was pounding. What was she getting into? She drew her hand back. 'Duncan, I like you too, but I'll be going back to England soon. You know that.'

He reached for her hand again, lacing his fingers between hers. 'Don't go. At least not yet. Please, Ethel. We have to give this a chance.'

She lifted her eyes to his and her insides melted. 'But how can I? It's not that easy. I have a job. They're expecting me back at the salon. They've kept my job open for me.'

He said nothing, just kept his eyes fixed on hers.

'And Joan and Jim. They won't want me hanging around for much longer.'

She felt the pressure of his fingers.

'You know that's not true,' he said. 'They'd like nothing more than for you to stay. Jim told me that, before you even arrived. Said the only thing Joan didn't like about Hollowtree was that her cousin Ethel wasn't living here too. Now I've met you I can understand exactly how she feels.'

'Did Jim really say that?'

'Yes. And he said they both hoped they might persuade you to stay on here. I'm not making it up. Jim said it before I'd even set eyes on you.' He looked thoughtful. 'What have you got to lose by staying longer?'

'My job?'

He began to smile. He could see she was weakening. 'Tell me more about your job. Tell me everything about you, Ethel.' His finger was stroking the edge of hers and their hands were still locked together.

'I told you. I'm a hairdresser. There's not a lot more to tell than that. It's all I ever wanted to do, since I was a little girl. When I was little I used to do my dolls' hair, then when I was a teenager I started doing my mum's, and Joan's and my Aunty Chris's.'

'Perfect! We don't have a hairdresser in Hollowtree.'

'There's probably a good reason for that. No call for it.'

He grinned. 'You could drive to people's houses.'

'I can't drive.'

'I'll teach you.'

She giggled. 'You're a very persuasive man.'

'So, you'll stay?'

'Don't be daft.'

He looked into her eyes again and there was no doubting his sincerity. 'Please stay. At least a while longer. You must feel it too. I know you do. I swear to God, Ethel, I know there's something special between us. Please give us a chance.'

'Well... maybe until the beginning of March... or 'til Easter.'

He grinned, triumphant. 'I'll settle for that for the moment. That gives me some time to work on you.' He became solemn again as he looked at her, intently. 'I know it's fast, but I think I'm already falling in love with you.'

'Don't. Please don't say that.' She jerked her hand away from his grasp. 'Can you take me home now?' She pushed her chair back. 'I don't want to be out late. Not with the new baby and Don dying and everything. I need to get back.'

She reached for her coat. Duncan helped her into it, his face set hard. They went out to the car and drove in silence.

Ethel felt a mixture of guilt, sorrow, and shame. She knew she'd hurt him. But she was confused. The truth was she was falling in love with him too. Had already fallen, if she were honest with herself. Why had she slapped him down? What was wrong with her? Duncan Robinson might be her only chance for happiness and she was crushing that chance under her foot.

They turned at the junction on to the Rivercreek road. Duncan slammed on the brakes and pulled the car to the side of the road. Before she knew what was happening, she was in his arms and they were kissing with a passion that took her breath away. She luxuriated in the embrace, wanting to stay wrapped in his arms forever, in the warm leather interior of his car, the engine purring and the windscreen steaming up. This time there was no Sandra looming in the distance. His hands cupped her face, his fingers soft against her cheeks.

'I do love you, Ethel. There – I've said it now. There's no point in pretending. It might take you longer to love me back, but I'm not giving up until you do. I'm in love with you.'

'I love you too.' Her voice was barely a whisper. She heard him gasp and then his mouth was on hers again. When they finally surfaced from the kiss, she repeated it, this time louder. 'I love you, Duncan Robinson.

'So, you'll stay? Long enough to make your mind up whether you'll marry me?'

'Is that a proposal, Duncan?'

'It's a statement of intent. You'll get a formal proposal just as soon as I've bought a ring. I'm going to do this properly.'

24

*E*veryone was in bed when Ethel got back to the farm, still trembling after her evening with Duncan. She went upstairs and for the first time since she'd arrived in Canada, fell into a deep and contented sleep.

The next morning, she rose late and had no appetite for breakfast. Drumming her fingers on the table, she nursed a cup of tea with the other hand. The boys were at school and Jim was working. Ethel peered round Joan's bedroom door saw she was still in bed, she and the new baby still asleep, while Harry slept in his cot.

Ethel grabbed paper and pen, left a note and went for a walk across the frozen fields. As soon as she stepped outside the house, the cold hit her. She was glad of her scarf and one of Joan's hats, which had earflaps. The ground was like concrete underfoot, and at least there was no wind today. The sun was bright in a blue winter sky. Being outdoors would help clear her head and allow her to do some thinking.

She and Duncan Robinson were in love. As she repeated the words in her head she could hardly believe them. How was it possible in so little time? Just as with Greg, she had fallen hard and fallen fast. Part of her wanted to sing for joy, but her stomach was churning with a terrible anxiety. It was too quick. They barely knew each other. How could it possibly work out?

And there was still the raw pain of the loss when Greg died. Could she bear to go through all that again, if it didn't work out with Duncan? And what of Duncan? Yes, the mutual attraction was undeniable, electric, chemical, magical. But she didn't *know* him.

Reaching into her coat pocket, she took out a squashed packet and lit a rare cigarette. She'd hardly smoked since arriving in Canada, but she needed the kick of the nicotine and the rush it gave, to help her think straight. She stopped, and, leaning against a fence, surveyed the expanse of empty white fields. It was completely silent, an almost supernatural hush. A splash of colour caught her peripheral vision and she looked up to see a red fox running along on the far side of the field, where it adjoined a copse. She finished her smoke and trudged on, hands deep in her pockets.

At the far side of the field there was a tiny stream that fed into a wider one which then passed through a natural bathing pool. The boys had shown it to her when they gave her a tour of the property. This narrow tributary was frozen. She stretched a foot out experimentally and stood on it – solid – though it couldn't have been very deep. Once winter was gone the water would be flowing freely here, but Ethel couldn't imagine the land ever being warm again, or that the children would be jumping in and out of the pond beyond, shrieking and laughing. How could that rock-solid ice ever be liquid? But she'd thought that about herself too. Just a few brief weeks ago she'd been like that river, her heart frozen inside her, believing that a thaw could never happen, yet here she was, not only thawed but melted, and – last night in Duncan's arms – molten.

But perhaps Dr Robinson was sitting at his desk in the surgery right now, squirming with embarrassment at what had happened between them last night, wondering how he might unsay the things he had said. He had to be having second thoughts. He was a rational man, a widower, in his forties, far too sensible to fling a proposal of marriage out to a woman he'd only met a few times. Far too sensible to behave like a love-struck teenager.

And then there was his daughter. Sandra Robinson had made no attempt to conceal her dislike of Ethel and none to disguise her distaste at her father courting her. While it was none of the girl's business, Ethel didn't want to be the cause of a rift between father and daughter. In the absence of Sandra's mother, Duncan and Sandra appeared to have a strong mutual dependency. She even worked for him. They shared a home. How could Ethel be responsible for driving a wedge between them?

Whichever way she looked at it, it had to be better to end the relationship now. If she stayed on in Canada it would make the inevitable parting from Duncan harder. But wasn't it too hard already?

This miserable contemplation was interrupted by Jim calling out her name, as he walked along the boundary towards her. She waited for him to catch her up.

'How was your evening with the doc?' He moved alongside her and linked arms as they walked on.

'We went to a bar in Argyll. It was nice. Odd though. Women aren't allowed in the bar. They have a separate Ladies and Escorts room.'

'That's the law here. Come on, is that all you're going to say?'

Ethel sighed.

'Bad as that, eh?'

'Oh, Jim. I don't know what to think. I'm so confused.'

'You really like each other, don't you?'

She nodded.

'Well, that's great. What are you worrying about? You know Joan and I would like nothing more than for you to stay here. As long as you like. We love having you around.'

'Thank you. You're both such good friends to me. But I'm scared. It's all moving too quickly.' She hesitated for a moment, but she loved Jim, trusted him, felt safe talking to him. And a male perspective might be what she needed.

'Duncan told me he's in love with me.'

Jim nodded, unsurprised.

She swallowed and took a breath. 'And I told him I felt the same.'

Jim stopped and pulled her into a hug. 'I'm really happy for you, Ethel. Duncan's a great guy. That is the best news. And I'm in need of some good news at the moment with Pa gone.' He squeezed her tightly.

'But it's too fast, isn't it? We barely know each other. We're virtual strangers.'

'Look at me and Joan. We barely knew each other either. And on top of that we had four years without seeing each other at all. It worked out fine for us, didn't it?' He looked towards the horizon, blinking from the glare of sun on snow. 'We only got to know each other once we were married. And yes, as you well know, we've had our ups and downs, but that's what it's about. Getting to know someone properly takes a lifetime. It's a journey with a few bumps in the road but one I want to be on for as long I can. Longer than Ma and Pa were – or my grandparents.' He sucked his lips inwards.

'But you and Duncan, you've known each other about as long as Joan and I did before we tied the knot. Yes, we'd had Jimmy by the time we got married, but that was a happy accident. My one regret is that I missed out on all that. Not being around when Joan was expecting him. Not even knowing I was a father until he was already born.' He grinned. 'Hell, Ethel, Joan and I never even had a date together before we got married. At least not a proper one. All we did was tag along with you and Greg like a couple of stooges. At least you and Duncan have chosen each other from the beginning.' He laughed.

'Do you ever have any regrets?' She was shocked at her own words, but Jim didn't appear bothered.

'Not for a moment. Not anymore. I can honestly say that my feelings for Joan get stronger all the time. Having the kids has made us even closer. I'd love for you to have the kind of happiness we have.'

'I never imagined it being possible for me after Greg. It feels as if I'm betraying him.'

Jim snorted. 'Don't. Greg would hate to know you were thinking like that. He'd want you to be happy, Ethel.' He turned to look at her, his eyes sincere, his hands resting on her shoulders. 'Yeah, of course he'd have preferred it to have been with him. But I'm darned sure he'd have wanted you to marry and have a family rather than spend the rest of your life being lonely.'

'You think so?'

'I *know* so.'

They walked on in companionable silence for a while, then Jim said, 'Duncan must be lonely too although he makes a good show of coping. Has done for years – bringing up his daughter on his own. I could tell the moment he clapped eyes on you he was smitten.'

Ethel grinned. 'Could you really? I was with him too.' Then she remembered Sandra. 'His daughter isn't happy about it. She can't stand the sight of me.'

'You're not going out with his daughter. She's a grown woman with her own life. Sandra will get used to it soon enough. That young woman needs to find someone herself. Maybe then she'll stop going around looking like she's got a wasp stuck in her mouth.'

'Thanks, Jim. You've made me feel so much better.'

'Good.' He looked at his watch. 'Time for me to head over and see how Ma's doing. We're meeting the funeral director at eleven. There's a lot to sort out.'

Ethel gave his arm a squeeze. 'Good luck. Joan says you're calling the baby after Don. Have you told Helga?'

'Joan told her last night. She was pleased.' His smile was rueful. 'Thank God, we're all here for her. The kids are a good distraction. I shudder to think how it might have been if I'd not made it through the war. She'd be all alone now.'

'Well, she's not. So, don't think about it.'

'And you're not either.' He made a fist and tapped her shoulder with it.

When Ethel walked back into the farmhouse she could hear voices upstairs. She walked across the room, undoing her coat as she went, and leaned over the front of the stove, warming herself. The kettle was still hot and there was an aroma of coffee in the air. Hanging up her coat, she noticed an unfamiliar lady's coat already hanging there. She went upstairs.

Joan's bedroom door was open. To Ethel's amazement,

Alice Armstrong was perched on the bed. Her head turned when Ethel appeared in the doorway.

'Surprise!' said Alice, jumping up to give Ethel a hug. 'It's only a flying visit. I'm going back to Ottawa tonight, but I needed to talk to Joan face-to-face. And now I've had the unexpected treat of meeting baby Donna.'

Joan smiled and said, 'I've been trying to persuade Alice to stay a bit longer, but she won't listen.'

'My taxi will be here in less than an hour. I have to get the Kitchener bus from Hollowtree.' Alice looked at Ethel meaningfully. 'Joan and I need to have a little chat. Any chance of some fresh coffee, Ethel?' She beamed at Ethel, who was seething inside but went back down to the kitchen and made the coffee, taking a tray back upstairs, then leaving them to it.

About half an hour later, she heard a scrunch of tyres on gravel and looked out of the window to see the taxi pulling up. Alice appeared and shuffled into her coat.

She went over to Ethel. 'So sorry we haven't had a chance to talk, but I'll be seeing you again soon. Joan will fill you in.'

Ethel stood stiffly as Alice embraced her. 'Ooh, don't you smell nice. Perfume? Very sophisticated.'

Ethel wanted to slap her but said nothing. She stood in the doorway watching as Alice climbed into the waiting taxi and drove away.

When she turned around, Joan was standing in her dressing gown, the sleeping Donna in her arms. 'Harry's asleep in his cot. I'd love a cup of tea. Alice prefers coffee.'

Ethel was still bristling. 'What did she want? Why such a flying visit?'

'Alice doesn't trust the telephone and she wanted some

advice so thought she'd make the trip in person. Crazy. The housekeeper's looking after the girls.'

'She said she'd be back soon. Did I get that right?' Ethel hoped Joan couldn't tell how much she disliked Alice.

'Looks like it. She's going to move back to Hollowtree. She's got some hare-brained plan to open a cinema here using some of her aunt's money.'

'What?'

'I know. Bonkers. But blooming marvellous if she pulls it off. She's fallen in love with going to the pictures and has decided it's her mission to bring them to Hollowtree.'

'Couldn't she have put all that in a letter?'

'Yes, she could. But there's more to it than that. Tip Howardson has appeared in Ottawa out of nowhere. He's found out that she's come into her aunt's money.'

Ethel's stomach clenched at the mention of Howardson.

'It's awful, Ethel. He turned up at the schoolyard and took Catherine. Poor Alice was beside herself. He brought her home again but obviously he intended to scare Alice and it certainly succeeded. She's absolutely terrified.'

'What does he want?' Still reluctant to feel sorry for Alice Armstrong, Ethel thought that any troubles Alice had were brought upon herself – although she wasn't going to say that to Joan.

'He told her he wants to marry her. Fancies playing happy families.'

Ethel snorted in disgust.

'Yep, my reaction too. Alice's as well. She told him to take a hike. But she's petrified he'll turn up again now he knows where to find her.'

'But he'll follow her here, surely? It's his hometown.'

'Alice doesn't think so and she may well be right. There

are plenty of people round here who know exactly what he's like.'

Ethel shuddered. 'He'd better not appear. I'd get Jim's shotgun and blast his brains out.' She realised how silly she sounded and started to laugh.

Joan laughed too, then shook her head. 'Seriously though, Ethel. The man is dangerous.'

'When's Alice moving back?'

'As soon as she can. She wants me to talk to Ma about her and the girls moving back to Hollowtree Farm. Just until she can sort some place out in town.'

'What'll Mrs Armstrong say to that?'

Joan shrugged. 'Ma always loved Alice and of course Rose is her granddaughter. But I don't know how she'll feel about Catherine or about Alice. That's why Alice wants me to talk to her. Sound her out. Warm her up to the idea.'

'What do you think?' Ethel spoke tentatively. She was treading dangerous ground here as she knew how fond Joan was of Alice – even though Ethel had no idea why that should be the case. If it were up to her she'd be delighted if she never had to clap eyes on Alice Armstrong again.

25

*T*he telephone rang soon after Alice left the farm. Joan waved her hand to indicate Ethel should answer the call as she was feeding Donna. Ethel moved towards the ringing instrument nervously. They didn't have a telephone at home and she'd had little cause to use a public telephone box as most of the people she needed to speak to were in the same street. Not even the hair salon had one. It was a neighbourhood place and customers tended to stick their head round the door and book an appointment while out doing the shopping.

She picked up the receiver and said, 'Rivercreek Farm,'

'Ethel. It's Duncan.'

Her knees weakened, and she leaned against the wall. 'Hello,' she said, her voice so faint she could barely hear herself. Across the room she could see Joan looking at her quizzically. She turned her back and, still leaning against the wall, listened as the doctor asked her if she would like to have a hot chocolate in town with him before his evening surgery.

She mumbled that yes, she would, her heart hammering, barely registering when he said he would collect her later. She hung up.

'Dr Dreamboat I presume?' Joan wiggled her eyebrows. 'I thought you were going to slither down that wall onto the floor when you realised it was him. Do you have another date?'

'Just a quick trip to Freddo's. I'll be back in time for supper. I'm going to make a shepherd's pie and put it in the oven before I leave.' She grabbed an apron hanging on a hook near the stove. 'I'd better get the spuds peeled.'

'Let's have a cup of tea and a biscuit first,' said Joan. 'Then I'm going to wash and get some clothes on. I've done enough lying around in bed.' She dipped her head and kissed the thin dark hair of her new baby's head. 'Madam is asleep. But no doubt young Harry will be kicking up a storm before long. Then before I know it, Jimmy and Sam will be home.'

'I don't know how you do it.' Ethel tilted her head back. 'I couldn't cope. But you just take it all in your stride, Joanie.'

'Babies are no bother. But you should hear me sometimes when the other two are playing up.' Joan nibbled her biscuit. 'It could be you before too long.'

Ethel recoiled in horror. 'Me. No. It's too late for that.'

'Don't be daft, duck. You're only thirty-two.'

'I've never seen me as having children.'

'You never saw me as having them either. And look at me now.'

Ethel got up, went to get the potatoes and carried them over to the sink.

'So? Things are getting serious with Duncan then?'

'Let's just say I'm taking each day as it comes.'

'Sounds like a sensible plan.'

The door opened, and Jim came in.

Joan looked up. 'How was Ma?'

'Putting on a brave face. Everything's sorted for the funeral.'

Joan nodded then said, 'Guess who was here this afternoon.'

Jim looked from Joan to Ethel and back again. 'Dr Robinson I presume?'

'No, but close. He's coming to pick Ethel up later. Go on, guess again.'

'I'm hopeless. You know I have no imagination, Joan.'

'That's not true!'

'Come on, put me out of my misery. I haven't a clue.'

'Alice.'

Jim whistled. 'That's a surprise. It must be five years. To what did we owe the visit and where is she now?'

'Already on her way back to Ottawa.' Joan filled him in on Alice's plan and her fears about Howardson.

'If that bastard so much as shows an eyebrow in Hollowtree I'll kick him from here to the other side of Lake Ontario.'

Ethel had never met Tip Howardson, but she hated him with every fibre of her being as the man who caused Greg's death. Nothing she'd heard from Joan and Alice had done anything to moderate that view – in fact the more she knew of him the more he sounded like a thoroughly evil man.

Once she'd got the pie in the oven, Ethel dashed upstairs and readied herself for meeting Duncan. As she spritzed on some perfume she remembered Alice's comment about her scent. What on earth did Joan see in her? As far as Ethel could tell, she was a catty individual. The prospect of her moving back to Hollowtree and living on the farm was not appealing.

Ethel went to the window and saw Duncan's car coming

up the track to the farm. She took a gulp of breath and told herself to stay calm. What had she just said to Joan about taking each day as it came? She needed to keep her nerves under control. Having had a night to sleep on it, the doctor may well be having second thoughts about his spontaneous declaration of love.

She didn't want to greet him with Joan and Jim as her audience, so she said goodbye to them and went straight out to the car. Duncan held the door open for her and gave her a friendly kiss on the cheek. Her heart sank. He *had* had second thoughts.

But as soon as they'd rounded the bend in the drive he stopped the car and pulled her into his arms.

'I've not been able to stop thinking about you all day. I almost prescribed cough medicine for a child with veruccas and I was halfway to visit a patient when I realised I was heading in the wrong direction. What have you done to me, Ethel?' He smiled at her and she thought again that he had the most beautiful eyes.

When they got to Freddo's they chose a table at the back, away from the street and sat with their hot chocolates, knees touching under the table.

'Were you serious when you said you were in love with me?' she said at last, wanting him to say it again so she could wallow in the warm emotion that flooded through her.

He reached over the table and took her hand. 'Honestly, Ethel, I truly believed I would be on my own for the rest of my life. But as soon as I set eyes on you it was as if the piece of my life that had been missing for so long finally slotted into place.' He stroked her hand. 'Does that sound foolish?' He linked his fingers through hers.

She shook her head. 'No. I felt exactly the same way. I

just didn't want to admit it to myself. It was as if a dark cloud had lifted.'

'I *am* going to marry you. You do realise that don't you?'

Ethel nodded. Everything seemed simple. Why had she made it all so complicated in her head? They loved each other. They'd marry. She'd stay in Canada. Everything else could be sorted. It was all just details.

He lifted his hand and pushed a stray curl back from her forehead then leaned in for a kiss, a light brushing of her lips. As they moved apart, Ethel looked up and saw Sandra had walked into the café and was standing beside their table.

'What the hell do you think you're doing, Dad?' Her voice was shrill, strident.

Over at the counter Freddo put down his newspaper and watched what was happening. Two men sitting by the window turned and looked towards them with unconcealed curiosity.

'Can't you see she's been trying to hook you since the moment she saw you? She and Joan Armstrong probably cooked it up together. You can do better than her.' Her eyes fixed on Ethel with a look of pure loathing. 'Just look at her, with her fancy hair-do and her English accent. Hooking a doctor is the top prize for her. I told you. I warned you.'

Sandra stood beside the table, her body shaking, tears rolling down her cheeks, while Ethel gazed at her in horror. Dr Robinson had a face like thunder but said nothing.

'I knew you'd do this to me, Dad. I knew it. She'll push me out. I'll have nowhere to go. I'll be all alone. How could you? Look at her – she's a cheap tart. How could you?'

Ethel could take no more. She slid out of the bench seat, grabbed her coat and heedless of the cold, rushed outside the café and half ran, half staggered, up the main street towards the turning for Rivercreek Farm.

Stumbling along the dark road, anger and humiliation bursting through her, she wanted to scream. And now she had to face the prospect of a long trudge in the freezing cold along an unlit track with no torch.

She heard an engine behind her. Duncan's car pulled ahead of her and he jumped out.

Ethel carried on walking. 'Go away! Just go. It's no good, Duncan. I don't want to hear anything you have to say.'

He tried to hold onto her arm, but she jerked it free. 'Let me go. Don't touch me.'

'Please, Ethel. You have to let me explain about Sandra. She doesn't mean what she's saying. She can't help herself.'

Ethel stopped dead and turned on him, furious. 'You did *nothing*. You just sat there and let her pour her poison over me. She called me a tart, for heaven's sake.' She pushed him away. 'You just let her say it. And you say you love me? Well if that's what you call loving me you can take your fine words and…' She ran out of steam and began to cry.

He wrapped his arms around her and held her as she struggled to break free.

'Stop it, Ethel. Please. You have to listen to me. Come and sit in the car and let me explain.'

'There's nothing to explain. I don't want to see you again. That's it. Over. *Finito*. Done.'

'Get in the car, Ethel. Before you freeze to death.' He held her face between his hands. 'Apart from anything else I need to run you home. Look at the shoes you're wearing.'

Reluctantly acknowledging that she had no choice, Ethel got into the car. She leaned against the door, as far away from him as possible and avoiding his eyes. He turned in his seat to face her.

Duncan spoke quietly. 'My daughter suffers from mood swings which cause occasional emotional instability. Her mother did too, but more severely. I've tried to persuade her to seek psychiatric help, but she refuses. She won't take pills as she is afraid of side-effects. One of the problems of being a doctor's daughter is she has access to the drug literature. Any side-effects are relatively minor and manageable, but she won't even accept that she has a problem. And to be fair, most of the time no one would ever know. Her condition has made her very dependent on me, very reluctant to form friendships and I suppose it's also meant that I too tended to avoid others and have dedicated myself to her. That's why she feels threatened by my feelings for you.'

He stared blindly through the windscreen at the road, illuminated by his car headlights. 'I don't think I've done Sandra a service by allowing things to drift on like this, letting her become reliant on nothing in our life changing, on the two of us muddling along together. Seeing me with you has come as a big shock to her. She realised straight away that there was something different in how I felt about you compared with the one or two girlfriends I had in the past.'

He reached for her hands and held them in his. 'I can't hide how I feel about you, Ethel, and Sandra doesn't understand that loving you doesn't make me love her any less. I think she's frightened about the future. She's very vulnerable.'

'Vulnerable? She's never struck me as that.'

'Part of her way of coping is to put up a hard exterior to the world. She's abrupt, rude even. It's like wearing armour. Hit first, don't wait for the other guy.'

Ethel said nothing, unconvinced, and still reeling from the attack.

'She's wasted working as my receptionist too. She's awkward with the patients, and far too clever to be doing a dull clerical job. She should be doing medical sciences, working in a lab, researching into diseases, something like that. But she's scared. Afraid to leave home.' He put his head in his hands. 'It's my fault. I should never have let it get so bad. I should never have put off seeking help for her.'

Ethel didn't know what to say. Eventually she said, 'You shouldn't have left her back there when she's in such a state.'

'Freddo will see she's all right. She's safe enough for the moment. I'll go back as soon as I've dropped you off.' He stared ahead though the dark beyond the windscreen. 'I can't go on like this, Ethel. I just can't. I need to get her some help. It's beyond my capabilities to manage.'

'It sounds like you're right.' She pulled her hand away from his. 'In the meantime, it's better we don't see each other. I don't want to be responsible for your daughter having a nervous breakdown.'

'No, Ethel. Please. Let me talk to her. Given some time, she'll accept the situation. She'll come to be fond of you. How couldn't she be?'

'Did you hear what she said to me? Weren't you listening?' Ethel was shaking. 'It was horrible. Nasty. Poison. Maybe you're right and she can't help it, but I'm not going through that again.' She swallowed. 'I don't want to see you again, Duncan. And yes, you need to get your daughter some help before she does any more damage. Now take me home, please.'

After Duncan had driven away, Ethel hurried inside and went straight up to her room, closing the door and flinging herself on the bed.

She had gone from the heights of happiness to the

depths of despair. Sandra Robinson had been vicious, malicious, cruel. Ethel was cut to the quick. After that she didn't want anything more to do with the woman – and that meant she could have nothing more to do with Duncan. While his explanations were plausible – understandable even – nothing excused the fact that he had not risen to her defence.

But as she lay there, gazing blindly at the ceiling, she had to admit that Duncan was probably as shocked as she had been. And after all, he had chosen to go after her rather than stay and comfort his daughter.

Ethel turned on her side and thumped the pillow. It wasn't fair. Just as she had let her guard down and opened her heart, life had done it to her again. Happiness had been dangled in front of her, within her grasp, then just as she reached for it, jerked away, leaving her alone again.

26

*J*oan waited until she was alone with Helga
before raising the question of Alice returning.
They were in the kitchen at Hollowtree Farm,
choosing hymns for Don's funeral.

'Alice came to see me yesterday. It was just a flying visit.
She's back in Ottawa now.'

'Alice?' Helga's voice was sharp. She looked up from the
battered hymnal she was holding.

'She's coming back to Hollowtree.'

'What's brought that on? She's been gone five years.'

'It didn't take Tip Howardson long to find out she'd
come into her aunt's money. He turned up on the doorstep,
asked her to marry him and when she sent him packing he
took Catherine from the schoolyard, without permission.
Alice was frantic. Fortunately, he dropped her home. It was
all designed to frighten Alice.'

Helga turned her attention back to the hymnal, but was
evidently curious because after a few minutes, she asked,
'Does the child know he's her father?'

'She didn't but he told her he was – told the teacher too and the damn fool woman let him take her. Alice told Catherine it was untrue, but she's petrified he'll take her again. Catherine has to find out eventually that she's illegitimate, but Alice doesn't want her to know Tip's the father. Doesn't want him anywhere near her girls. Or herself, for that matter.'

'She should have thought of that years ago, instead of opening her legs to that thug.'

'Please, Ma. Don't talk like that. If Alice could wind back the clock she would, but that would mean not having Catherine – and she loves her. So does Rose. The poor child can't help who her father is.'

Helga sniffed. She went back to studying the hymnal, but after a while said, 'I thought Howardson was already married. Some woman in America.'

'Divorced.'

Helga curled her lip.

'And the story he told Alice about having a child was made up. He's a complete and utter lowlife. Poor Alice was well and truly suckered by him.'

Helga gazed out of the window. 'Mind you, Tip could be charming when he chose to be. He was a sweet kid when he was small, until the bullying started at school. Maybe that's what turned him bad. Walt was the only classmate who gave him the time of day.'

'Really? He's the biggest bully himself.'

'It's often the way. A bullied kid can turn into a bullying adult – especially when he gets a bit of power.'

They lapsed into silence, for a few moments, until Helga asked, 'So where's she planning on living when she comes back?'

'She mentioned buying a place in town, close to the school. But in the meantime–'

'She wants to move back here.' Helga jerked her head in the direction of the barn.

Walt Armstrong had built a makeshift home next to it when he and Alice had married. Alice and Rose had lived there until they went to Ottawa.

'I can't stop her anyway,' said Helga. 'She owns that place. Even if it is on our land.'

Joan placed her hand on her mother-in-law's arm and squeezed. 'She's family, Ma. Walt's wife and the mother of his daughter.'

'When's she coming?'

'As soon as she can make the arrangements and sort out the girls' schooling. She wants to be here for Don's funeral but doesn't think that's going to be possible. She was devastated when I told her about him. Rose will be too. It's such a pity they can't be here.'

Helga's lip curled with contempt. 'I'll be happy enough to have Rose around again.' She got up from the table. 'But don't expect me to roll out the red carpet for Alice – or her bastard daughter.'

'Ma! Stop that right now.' It was rare that Joan had to confront her mother-in-law these days, but she remembered only too well what it was like to be on the wrong side of Helga Armstrong. 'Think of Don. Think of Walt. Neither of them would have wanted Alice and her daughter to be treated this way. Walt loved Alice and you know this whole thing with Howardson would never have happened if he'd been alive. All these years later, she's still not over Walt. What happened with Tip was hard to excuse, but she was lonely. In fact, she still is. Coming home to Hollowtree is probably the best thing she can do.'

Helga sat down again, arms folded, a sour expression on her face.

'Look, Ma. You're a church-going woman and one of the kindest people in this town. Can't you spare a little kindness and forgiveness for Alice? For Walt's sake?'

Helga pursed her lips. 'I'll do my best.'

Joan jumped up and hugged her. 'Thanks, Ma. You won't regret it.'

Back in Ottawa, Alice was in the advanced stages of packing. She was only taking clothes at the moment, as the furniture from Miss Cooke's town house wouldn't fit in the modest dwelling Walt had built for them – either in style or available space. There were also the vast quantities of her aunt's papers that she had yet to find time to go through. She intended to put the house on the market eventually but couldn't face doing it yet. The real estate agent advised waiting until spring.

She decided to retain Mrs Browning, her housekeeper, and give her instructions that if Howardson should call at the house, she was to say Alice had gone on an extended trip to Europe with her daughters. She wasn't sure it would convince him – she'd never previously shown any signs of wanderlust. But Walt was buried there; she told Mrs Browning to mention that they were going to visit his grave. If she could delay his knowledge of her return to Hollowtree, it would buy her some time. It was unlikely he'd ever go back there, but she didn't want to take the risk. If Tip sniffed money he would chase after it – even if it meant returning to a town where he was unwelcome.

Mr Freeman was proving to be a rock to Alice. He agreed

to liaise between her broker, property manager and any other business interests and report to her on a regular basis.

'There is another matter, Mr Freeman,' she said one morning, when they were sitting in his office discussing her plans. 'It's rather delicate.'

He assured her of his complete discretion.

'My younger daughter, Catherine...' She swallowed, suddenly nervous. 'She was born out of wedlock. An ill-advised liaison.'

The lawyer gave a little cough of surprise but nodded his head discreetly.

'Her father recently turned up out of the blue. He took Catherine from the schoolyard. He's made threats.'

'Threats?'

'Well, not exactly threats. Not to hurt her or anything. But he must have got wind of my inheritance as he asked me to marry him. Talked of adopting Rose too.'

'And would that be so terrible?'

'It would be disastrous.' She closed her eyes for a moment. It was awful sitting here, laying bare her dirty linen. 'He's a violent man. He was dishonourably discharged from the army during the war. I won't go into the details, but he's dangerous. I don't want him near me and I certainly don't want him near my daughters.'

'I see.'

'Is there a way I can prevent him from contacting us?'

'Mm. He has made no actual threats you say? And he's the child's father. It's unlikely a court would grant you an injunction in such circumstances.'

Alice twisted her lip. 'I'll just have to hope he buys the story I've told my housekeeper to tell him – that we're in England on an extended educational trip, visiting my late husband's last resting place.'

'You could instruct her to direct any enquiries here. I suspect I may be a little more adept at handling misinformation than your housekeeper is. Particularly if, as you say, he has a threatening manner. I will be more than happy to deal with him and keep him at bay.'

27

The mildness of the winter meant that there was no delay in Don's funeral. The service was in the Catholic church in the town, which was packed to capacity – evidence of Don Armstrong's stature and popularity. Afterwards, the interment was attended only by the family and a small group of close friends.

The Armstrong family plot was in a small area at the edge of the cemetery, close to the boundary fence beside a copse of trees. A quiet and shady spot away from the more recent regimented areas of the burial ground. There were two other graves there, neatly tended. Although the metal crosses were rusted, the names carved on the memorial stones were still clearly visible: Nathan Armstrong 1850-1927 and Margaret Armstrong 1861-1894.

Ethel did the mental calculation. While Don's father had lived to seventy-seven, his mother had died at only thirty-three. Her own age. She wondered what had been the cause of such an untimely demise, but back at the turn of the century people died of all manner of causes that could be easily treated these days. And life on an isolated farm then would have been tough. Ethel wasn't even sure much of Hollowtree town would have existed – certainly not as much as was there now, little though it was. Then it dawned on her: Margaret must have died around the time Don was born – possibly when giving birth to him.

Looking at the coffin, tears stung her eyes. She'd known Don Armstrong for such a brief time. She remembered what Joan had said about him being the father she never had. Joan was weeping freely, but beyond her Helga Armstrong stood, shrouded in a black coat and hat, stoical as always, standing as tall as her small frame permitted, ramrod straight beside her son.

A small hand slipped into her own and, looking down, Ethel saw Jimmy next to her, lip trembling as he kept his eyes fixed on the wooden coffin. She squeezed his hand gently, her heart filling with sadness for the whole family.

The priest finished his prayers and shook a metal stick with what Ethel presumed was 'holy water' over the coffin. Helga moved forward and placed a small posy of snowdrops on top of the coffin, then two men took up the ropes and gently lowered it into the ground.

Each person in turn dropped their handful of soil into the grave, then the priest led the procession away from the plot.

As they moved off, the two men began to fill in the hole. It was only at the sound of the first shovelful of earth hitting the wooden coffin, that Helga Armstrong finally broke. Her wailing was searing, primal and raw with grief and Ethel found herself crying as she witnessed it.

～

A few days after the funeral Ethel was walking along a pathway towards the natural bathing pool behind Hollowtree Farm. She liked to walk around the fields and surrounding woodland most days, relishing the quiet and the peace away from the hubbub of the farmhouse. It was a chance to think. She'd been doing a lot of thinking since she'd been in Canada. Mostly, these days, about Duncan Robinson and how much she was missing him. In the distance she saw Helga crossing the Hollowtree farmyard. On a whim she decided to call on her and turned onto the track that led towards the house.

She found Helga in the barn, collecting eggs. She looked up in surprise but greeted Ethel warmly.

'I hope I'm not disturbing you, Mrs Armstrong?'

'I've told you before, Ethel, call me Helga. I was about to brew up some coffee. You want to join me?' She sighed. 'I can use the company. It's very quiet round here these days. But I suppose I should make the most of it before Alice and Rose move back here.'

Ethel noted the omission of Catherine's name but made no comment.

When they were settled on either side of the table, tin mugs of steaming coffee in front of them, Helga took a deep breath. 'I wanted to thank you, Ethel, for being with my Don in his final moments. I never dreamt it would happen so suddenly.'

Ethel looked down into her mug. 'It was like that with my mum. The night she died I'd just sent her sister, Joan's mum, home. I'd no idea it would be that night. When someone's been ill for such a long time it's hard to believe that they'll ever finally let go.'

'That's it exactly. The doc warned me, but I thought I'd

have known when it was about to happen. I'd never have left him otherwise.'

Ethel looked across at her. 'You must miss him dreadfully. How long were you married?'

'Forty-one years. And other than when he was fighting in Europe, never a day apart.'

'I was looking at the dates on his parents' graves. They must have had a very short marriage.'

Helga nodded. 'No time at all. His mother died in childbirth. She'd already lost three babies and never lived to enjoy Don, poor soul. And he never had the love of his mother.'

'That must have been hard for him. And for his father – losing his wife so young? How did he manage? I'm surprised he didn't marry again. Running a farm and raising a child, alone. That can't have been easy.'

Helga looked at her, as if weighing up her answer, then said, 'He wasn't alone. He had a woman, but they were never married. She took care of Don and cooked and cleaned for the old man.' She snorted. 'More than that if you know what I mean.'

'Why didn't they marry?'

'She was a native Indian.'

Ethel tried not to look surprised. 'Oh, I see.'

'People would have talked. That kind of intermarrying wasn't looked well on. Still isn't, to be honest.'

'What happened to her?'

'When Don was fifteen she disappeared. Near broke his heart.'

'She walked out?'

Helga put down her mug. 'I think she'd had enough. Nathan Armstrong was a difficult man. Not the kind to appreciate what other people did for him. When Don and I married, his father led me a merry dance. Made my life hell. It nearly broke our marriage. Then one day, Don had had enough. He put the old bastard in his place. Never a squeak from him after that.' She didn't elucidate further, and Ethel didn't like to ask. 'He died when Jim and Walt were in their early teens and, God forgive me, I didn't shed a tear.'

'Maybe he never got over losing his wife?'

'Maybe. Though I find it hard to imagine the old goat ever grieving for anyone.' She got up and fetched the pot of coffee and refilled their mugs. 'So, tell me about you and the doctor. Joan says you've had a falling out. I'm very sorry to hear that, Ethel. I think you make a lovely couple.'

Ethel's face turned crimson at the sudden change in the conversation. She stuttered, 'I – I didn't know you knew we'd been seeing each other.'

Helga made a soft snorting noise. 'This is a small town, my darling. Everyone knows everything. I'd have thought you'd realise that by now.'

'We decided to stop seeing each other. His daughter didn't like it. I probably shouldn't be telling you this, but she has some nervous problems. I thought it was better we put everything on hold until he's managed to persuade her to get treatment.'

Helga nodded. 'Not sure I understand why that should stop you seeing the doctor though.'

'Our relationship was causing her distress. She flew off the handle when she saw us together one afternoon in Freddo's. She was hysterical. She said some terrible things. It was very unpleasant.'

Helga shook her head. 'Can't say I'm fond of the girl. A cold fish. Not at all like her father. She barely gives anyone the time of day. Miserable thing, she is.'

Ethel was relieved she wasn't the only one who was not enamoured of Sandra.

'You don't want to let that girl stand in your way, Ethel. The doc's a good man. My Don became very attached to him.' She huffed. 'Funny really, as he refused to see him when he first came to town.' She leaned forward. 'The doc didn't serve in the war and Don took against him for that, without even having met him. It was Joan that finally persuaded him to see him about his cough.'

Helga looked across at Ethel and added, 'It wasn't because the doc didn't want to serve, mind you. He had his daughter to take care of. She was a small child when the war began.'

Ethel felt a sudden sadness. It seemed hopeless. She loved Duncan, but everything was so complicated.

As if reading her thoughts, Helga put her hand on hers and said, 'Life's so short, Ethel, my dear. One moment I was walking down the aisle and all the years after that went by in a flash until I was watching them put my husband in the ground. What is it they say? Make hay while the sun shines. Don't let a good man get away. You're a lovely girl and you deserve to be happy. And so does Dr Robinson.'

Walking back to Rivercreek, Ethel mulled Helga's advice over and over in her head. But she knew she wouldn't act on it. Duncan had to make the decision for himself. She wasn't going to come between father and daughter.

28

*I*t was a Saturday afternoon in early February when Sandra Robinson appeared at Rivercreek Farm. She was alone. Joan was washing nappies and dried her hands quickly and went to the door.

'Is Miss Underwood here?'

'She's out in the barn. Helping my husband repaint the barn doors. Come in, sit down and I'll give her a shout, Sandra.'

'I'd like to speak to her in private.'

Joan, surprised, said. 'All right. Keep your ears open in case the baby starts crying. She's upstairs asleep and should be fine. Harry's in his playpen over there.' She nodded towards the corner of the room, where Harry was chuntering to himself and playing with some wooden bricks. 'I'll take over the painting from Ethel and she can talk to you in here.'

Sandra nodded but said nothing and Joan thought what an unlikeable woman she was.

She went across to the barn and told Ethel.

'What on earth does she want? I don't think I want to

talk to her. Not after her outburst in Freddo's. I've never been so humiliated in all my life.'

'I imagine she's come to apologise.'

Ethel looked dubious but shrugged. 'Oh well, I'd better get it over with then.'

Ethel, dressed in an overlarge pair of Jim's overalls and with a cotton scarf on her head, walked into the kitchen. Sandra was sitting cross-legged on the rug beside Harry's playpen, watching him playing.

She looked up and said, 'I like babies. He's sweet.'

Surprised by the softness in her voice, Ethel waited for the explanation for her visit.

Sandra got to her feet. She looked uncharacteristically bashful. 'I came to say sorry. I shouldn't have said what I said. It was wrong of me. It's made Dad very unhappy.'

Ethel stared at her, open-mouthed, but said nothing.

'It's just... Dad and I are close, and he's never had a serious girlfriend before. It's taken me a while to get used to the idea. I was upset. I was afraid actually...' She nibbled at a fingernail and Ethel noticed all her nails were gnawed to the quick. 'I was worried that he'd be out with you all the time and I'd be left alone. Selfish, I know.'

Ethel hesitated, 'I'm going to make a pot of tea,' she said, and moved over to the stove.

Sandra came to stand beside her as she prepared the tea. Ethel tensed, uncomfortable.

When the tea was made, Ethel sat at the table and signalled to Sandra to sit down opposite. The young woman was painfully thin. Her dark hair was scraped back in a ponytail and her eyes were like sad dark pools. She'd undone her coat and removed her hat and gloves, but she kept the coat on and continued to nibble at her nails. Ethel, hoping to get her to stop, offered her a biscuit, but she declined.

'Look. Dad says you won't see him. Says you won't go out with him anymore and it's all because of what I said. It's making him sad. When he's sad that makes me sad too.' She looked down at the tabletop. 'He wants me to see a psychiatrist. But I don't need to see one. I'll be all right now. I've got used to the idea of him dating you. I don't mind. Please say you'll go out with him again. If you don't, he'll force me to see the psychiatrist in Kitchener and I don't want to. I don't need to. Please, Miss Underwood.'

Ethel was stunned. She didn't know what to say. This was as surprising as the attack in Freddo's had been.

'So, will you? He really likes you.'

'I like him too.'

'Then say yes. Please.' The big saucer eyes fixed on her. 'There's something else I want to ask you.'

'Yes?'

'Will you do my hair for me? Dad says you're a hairdresser. Maybe you can show me how to put on some cosmetics as well.'

Ethel nearly fell off her chair with surprise. 'I'm not sure,' she said tentatively.

'I'll pay you of course.'

'You don't need to pay me.'

'I want to. Then I'll feel able to ask you again, which I won't if you do it for free.'

Still astonished, Ethel found herself saying, 'All right then. When?'

'I was thinking Tuesday. You can do it at our house while Dad's doing his house calls and then you can have supper with us.'

Ethel hesitated. 'Does your dad know you're asking me this?'

'Yes. It was his idea you come to supper. But he said *I* had to ask you. Please.' Sandra bit her lip. 'It's important. I have a date on Wednesday. I want to look nice.'

'A date?' Ethel was curious. This might be just what Sandra needed to break free of her father – and allow him to break free of her.

'I've just met him. He's a rep from one of the drugs companies. He doesn't live in Hollowtree. He's going to take me skating at the ice rink in Kitchener.' Sandra's eyes were lit up.

'That's nice, Sandra. What's he like?'

For a moment, Ethel thought Sandra was going to tell her to mind her own business – she looked annoyed. But her face cracked into a smile and she said, 'Very sure of himself. Older than me. But don't tell Dad that. He doesn't know. I'm rather hoping you'll go out with Dad on Wednesday evening, so I don't have to tell him I'm on a date. I'd like to wait to introduce them until I've got to know him better.' She gave Ethel a shy smile. 'I'm scared Dad might not approve, and I don't want to have an argument about it unless I'm sure Steve's worth fighting over. Do you know what I mean?'

Ethel nodded. 'His name's Steve?'

'Steve Johnson.' She gave a little giggle. He's twenty-six, but he looks a bit older.'

'Well, that's terrific, Sandra. If he's a medical rep how come your dad hasn't met him?'

'He dropped by the surgery with some leaflets, but Dad was seeing patients. Steve was going to make an appointment to meet with him another time, but then we got talking and he asked me out and I realised afterwards we hadn't actually booked the meeting.'

'He clearly had his mind on you.'

'Gosh, I hope so. I've never had a boyfriend before.'

Her face was suffused with colour. But she had dropped her usual frown and Ethel realised as Sandra's face relaxed that she was a pretty woman hiding behind an austere expression and hairstyle. One of those women who concealed themselves behind unadorned faces and drab clothes – Ethel had known many who, when transformed at the salon, emerged like butterflies from the chrysalis.

'Right then. Tuesday it is. We'll have you looking like a film star for your date. I'll show you how to fix your make-up, so you can do it yourself before you go out on Wednesday.'

Donna's high-pitched cries filtered down from above.

Sandra got up. 'I'd better be going.' She crossed the room and leaned over the playpen. 'Bye bye, Harry.' Buttoning up the coat that she had refused to remove, she called to Ethel. 'See you on Tuesday.'

Ethel went upstairs to pick up Donna. As she rocked the baby in her arms, she struggled to understand what had just happened. It was as if the woman today who was so open and eager to confide in Ethel was a completely different person from the one who had subjected her to that angry and hurtful tirade in Freddo's.

*M*r Freeman handed Alice his fountain pen and watched while she signed the series of documents with shaking hands.

'All done,' he said, as she returned the pen. 'The money's yours and I have Power of Attorney to administer it until you choose to revoke that power. Any time you wish to increase your monthly income let me know. And the capital sum to fund your business project is waiting in the bank for you.'

'You're absolutely sure Howardson can't get his hands on any of it?'

'Not even over my dead body.' He leaned back in his chair, arms folded – a posture less lawyerly than usual.

'Well that's a relief, to be honest. Killing someone wouldn't be something he'd have too many qualms about.'

'He sounds a particularly nasty individual. Might I venture to ask–'

'You want to know how I managed to get mixed up with him?'

The lawyer tilted his head to one side, with the slightest

lift of his eyebrows. 'I don't want to intrude, but yes, I'm curious.'

'I ask myself that question every day of my life, Mr Freeman. Let's just say it was ill-judged – although it's nearer the truth that I'd lost my mind. But I wouldn't want to be without Catherine for anything.' Alice's eyes were fierce.

'We won't divulge your whereabouts, should he approach us here.' Mr Freeman picked up a manila folder from the desk. 'Now to the other matter you asked me to handle. There is only one site in Hollowtree that offers the potential for the development you propose. It's a former storage facility. Hasn't been used in a decade but it's sound enough. The agent has sent some photographs.' He handed the folder to Alice.

She flipped through the file, which contained a few images, a plan and a short factsheet. 'I know it. It's just down past the library. It will be perfect.'

'There's a lot of work needed, but the agent, a gentleman named Mallory, is able to assist, should you decide to go ahead with the venture.'

A thrill surged through her. She was really going to make this happen. She was going to give Hollowtree its movie theatre. Nothing was going to stop her now.

～

Two weeks later, Alice and her daughters left for Hollowtree. She was surprised to feel a wrench at leaving Ottawa and the big draughty house. While she'd had no chance to make any mark of her own on the place, it had been a sanctuary and she had happy memories of her time there with her aunt.

As the train ate up the miles, she asked herself whether

she was doing the right thing in going back home. But Rose and Catherine ought to know their extended family and be a part of it. She wanted the girls to feel secure and part of a bigger entity. On the other hand, she had left Hollowtree Farm under a cloud, having argued with her mother-in-law over her affair with Howardson. And her own mother had told her she never wanted to see her again. Both Ada Ducroix and Helga Armstrong came from a generation that believed having a child out of wedlock was a terrible sin and a source of lasting shame. Alice wanted them to welcome and accept Catherine – but was filled with dread that they might not. That would have devastating consequences for the child.

As the train lumbered on, she mulled the issue over and over in her head, while Catherine played with her dolls and Rose read a book.

At last they reached Kitchener and the local bus to Hollowtree. She would have to buy a car if she were going to stay out at the farm. The girls would get the school bus, but she didn't want to be beholden to Helga by asking to use the old farm truck. As soon as the cinema was up and running she'd think about moving into town, buying one of those big houses near the lake. It was the right thing to do by the girls – though Alice knew she'd feel a wrench, leaving, again, the humble little home Walt had built for her.

.

he afternoon Ethel was to give Sandra her makeover, Joan offered her a lift, claiming to have cabin fever after the birth of the baby and wanting a trip into town.

'If you need to be collected later tonight, which I doubt, here's our number. Jim or I will come and fetch you. But I've no doubt the good doctor will oblige.' She raised her eyebrows at Ethel.

Ethel gave Joan a smile, desperately trying to look relaxed about what lay ahead, but feeling anything but. Sandra's sudden change of attitude made her nervous. After what had happened in Freddo's, how could she trust her? But more than anything she was terrified about seeing Duncan again. Terrified and excited. She had missed him so much – but was she making a mistake?

Dr Robinson's surgery consisted of two rooms on the ground floor of his house. He and Sandra lived upstairs, which had been converted into an apartment. The house fronted the street, about half a mile from the centre of town, its rear overlooking the park and lake. A brick-built villa, and quite imposing, it was on the side of the town that Ethel knew least, on the edges, where there were half a dozen similar houses, each standing apart in its own grounds. This was the more affluent end of town, the houses built by men of standing, about a century ago.

As Ethel approached, two people were leaving, presumably patients departing after a consultation. She pushed open the front door and found herself in a lobby that led into a waiting room. It was empty except for Sandra, sitting behind a desk. She looked up as Ethel entered. The younger woman didn't smile. Ethel wished she hadn't come. Anxiety coursed through her. What had she let herself in for? What had possessed her to agree?

'I've just sent the last patient in, so I can pack up here now. Dad will be going straight out to do his calls when he's finished.'

Not even a greeting. Ethel offered her own which earned only a nod from Sandra. Ethel wanted to turn on her heel and leave.

Clutching a vanity case, containing her hair-styling equipment, as well as a selection of cosmetics and a pot of cold cream, she followed Sandra up the wide stairway.

As they left the surgery and entered the private part of the building, Sandra's demeanour changed.

'The kitchen and dining room are downstairs behind the surgery, but everything else is up here. We can wash my hair in the bathroom and then you can do what you need to do to me in my bedroom.'

It sounded as though Sandra was viewing the makeover as an ordeal. 'What you need to do to me' was hardly the way to refer to a pleasurable experience. Realising that

Sandra was as nervous as she was, Ethel relaxed a little and followed Sandra towards the bathroom.

'Just a minute. Aren't we going to cut it? It's very long.' She looked at the young woman, whose hair was scraped back into her usual ponytail. 'I was thinking it might be nice to take some of this length off, then set it, to give you some height and volume. If you like it, I can always give you a permanent wave another time.'

Sandra looked sceptical.

'I brought a magazine. Have a look. I was thinking something on these lines.' Ethel flipped through the pages until she found a double spread of photographs. 'Like this. Soft waves at the top and more curl and body down here.' She cupped her hands at chin level.

'That's very short.' Sandra sounded wary.

'Not really. This will give you more body. Soft and smooth up here, fuller and softer here.'

Sandra responded with a shrug.

'And it will be easy to maintain. I'll show you what to do each night – just a few rollers before you go to bed. If you don't want a perm, I can give you a shampoo and set each week if you like. See what you think when it's done.'

'Let's get on with it then.'

Ethel explained she would need a sheet for the floor to catch the hair. 'We'll cut it in here. Then I can style it and do your face in your bedroom.'

Setting about her task, Ethel washed and cut the young woman's hair. Released from the constraints of the severe ponytail, Sandra had plentiful manageable hair with a slight wave, reminiscent of Duncan's. Ethel gathered up the sheet and they went into Sandra's bedroom. The house was quiet. Dr Robinson must be out on his calls by now.

'Are you excited about your date tomorrow?'

'Nervous.' For the first time, Sandra ventured a hint of a smile. 'I've never been on a date before.'

'And you said he's taking you skating?'

'No. Change of plan. He called this morning to say we we'd go for a drink in Hartley. That's about ten miles away.'

'He's picking you up?'

Sandra blushed. 'He doesn't have a car.'

'He doesn't have a car?' Ethel, astonished, echoed her words. 'How can a drugs rep get by without a car?'

'It's being serviced at the moment, so I said I'd drive over there to meet him.'

'I see.' Ethel curled a strand of hair around a roller and secured it. 'Does your father know?'

'No – and I told you, Ethel. I don't want him to find out. Not yet. Promise me, Ethel, you won't say anything.'

Reluctantly, Ethel agreed. After all, at eighteen, Sandra wasn't a child, even if she lacked maturity.

Ethel pulled a plastic hood with a tube out of her bag and attached it to the end of the hairdryer. 'A present from Joan for Christmas,' she said. 'The latest thing! It makes sure the hot air gets all around your head. Otherwise it means waiting for hours for your hair to dry and you probably don't want to be eating your dinner in rollers.'

Sandra looked dubious. 'I usually just let my hair dry naturally.'

Ethel swallowed the temptation to tell her that was obvious. 'It takes a while for the setting lotion to work and the heat helps. Tell me if it gets too hot.'

Returning to the subject of Sandra's prospective boyfriend, Ethel asked, 'So this fellow lives in Hartley?'

'I think so. I'll have a chance to find out all about him tomorrow night.'

'And you say he's new in the job?'

'No. I think he's been doing the repping for a while. He's just new to this area. It was his first call at the practice.'

'He must like you a lot to ask you on a date the first time he meets you.'

'I do hope so.'

'I'm pleased for you, Sandra.'

Sandra was actually blushing.

'Tell me more about him.'

'I don't know much yet. Just that he was in the army in the war. Served in the Pacific.'

'A war hero too!' Ethel gave a whistle.

Sandra giggled in response. She was younger than her years and clearly lacking experience, but her excitement was infectious and Ethel for the first time saw another side to Duncan's daughter.

There was some self-interest of course – if Sandra had a boyfriend she would be less likely to repeat the antagonism she had shown to Ethel. Switching on the hairdryer, Ethel told herself that Sandra's odd behaviour was probably down to loneliness and the lack of a mother.

Sandra's hair stowed inside the plastic helmet, Ethel began doing the young woman's make-up, explaining each step as she went. Deciding to keep it simple, she used only a light dusting of powder, and a soft sweep of shadow on her eyelids, to tone with the blue of her eyes.

'Now for the mascara. It works better with spit than water. I've brought you this one as a gift.'

Sandra spun round in the chair. 'Really? Thank you.'

Ethel showed her how to apply it, instructing her to spit a little onto the cake and use the brush to mix it.

When she'd finished, Sandra spoke, her voice quiet. 'I'm sorry, Ethel. About stuffing your Christmas gift down the back of the chair. I suppose you found it and knew what I'd done.'

Surprised, Ethel nodded.

'It was mean. I don't know what came over me. I'm really sorry.'

'Forget it. It was probably a bit overwhelming, being with the Armstrong clan when you're used to it being just you and your dad. I know I find that at times. Don't get me wrong – I adore them all, but sometimes I have to be on my own for a bit of peace and quiet.'

'It wasn't that. I was jealous.' Sandra's lips tightened. 'Of you and Dad. I wanted to hurt you. It was a horrible thing to do. I'm sorry.'

Ethel squeezed her shoulder. 'Forget it. I already have.'

As she was applying the finishing touches to Sandra's make-up, they heard footsteps on the stairs.

'Don't come in,' Sandra screeched. 'You can't see me yet.'

'I was just going to say that supper will be ready in half an hour. It's been in a slow oven,' said Dr Robinson from the other side of the closed door.

He and Ethel exchanged greetings through the door, over the sound of the hairdryer.

After his footsteps had receded, Ethel asked, 'Your father's cooked the supper?'

'He does a lot of the cooking. He likes it. I don't. He had to start when my mum died. We've always had a house-keeper as he's so busy with the practice but it's her day off today.' She tilted her head at Ethel and gave an uncharacter-istic smile. 'Anyway, he probably wants to impress you.'

As Ethel removed the dryer hood and began to unroll the curlers from Sandra's hair, the sound of piano music began.

'Is that a gramophone?'

'No, it's Dad. He loves to play the piano. I told you he was trying to impress you.'

'Well, it's certainly working!' Ethel grinned. 'The music is beautiful.'

'It's Chopin. A Nocturne.'

'Do you play too?'

'No. I had some lessons when I was a kid, but I never really took to it. It's Dad's thing.'

Ethel listened to the music as she brushed through Sandra's hair. A succession of little trills, sweeping from high to low notes, one moment soft and lyrical, the next more urgent. She wanted to be in the other room, watching his hands moving across the notes, seeing the expression on his face as he coaxed the music from the keys.

'It's so beautiful,' she murmured. 'Haunting.'

The sound wrapped around her, swaddling her in a warm glow. The notes, tender and plaintive, rose and fell. Captivated, Ethel moved across the bedroom and opened the door wide, so she could hear better.

Although she was abandoning Sandra, she couldn't stop herself, and went across the landing, drawn by the irresistible pull of the music. In the doorway of the drawing room, she stood, watching him. He was absorbed in his playing, oblivious to her presence, his back turned to her. His head dipped down then moved back up. His arms moved sideways as his hands glided over the keys at a speed and accuracy that looked effortless. The music was now rising to a crescendo as his fingers raced up and down. How was it possible to conjure forth such sounds?

Conscious that Sandra was waiting for her in the bedroom, Ethel reluctantly withdrew and returned to finish brushing out her hair. She completed the task without talking further, wanting only to hear the piano, caught up in the beauty of the music Duncan was playing.

When the hairstyling was done, and the music had stopped, she allowed Sandra to look at last in the mirror.

Sandra gave a little gasp. 'Is that really me? I can't recognise myself.'

A voice came from the doorway. 'You look beautiful, Sandra. Absolutely stunning.' Dr Robinson came into the room. 'Ethel, you've turned my daughter into a movie star.'

'All I did was highlight her natural beauty.' Ethel glanced at him shyly. 'Your piano playing was wonderful.' Her voice sounded gushing to her, but the doctor's face reflected pleasure at the compliment.

'It's the way I relax. I love to play.'

'It was very impressive. Like listening to a concert pianist.'

'Have you heard a lot of concert pianists?'

'No. None.' She grinned.

'I thought not!'

'I can't believe they'd be any better than you. You play so fluently. It was magical. I was transported to another place. I'm not used to listening to that sort of music, but I could listen to you all day.'

Their eyes met, and Ethel's stomach flipped – as it always did when she saw him. He held out his hand and took hers. 'Come on. The meal's ready. I've made something called a goulash. One of my patients is Hungarian and gave me the recipe.'

Holding her hand, he led her downstairs to the dining room.

The goulash was the most delicious meal Ethel had ever eaten. With Sandra at the table with them, neither of them mentioned their previous quarrel, nor Ethel's stated intention not to see him again.

Over the course of the meal the conversation moved to the subject of medical care. To Ethel's surprise it appeared to be a topic of great interest to Sandra – if a source of contention between her and her father.

'I can't seem to convince Dad that a national health care system is a good thing.' She gave a brittle laugh. 'He seems to believe it will open the doors to socialism.'

'Really?' Ethel looked at Duncan.

'Doctors like being our own bosses. None of us want to become servants of the state – glorified government employees. I've no wish to become a civil servant.'

'We've had the National Health Service for a few years now in Britain and I can tell you it makes such a difference. My mum died recently and had to have the doctor round constantly. In the old days it would have cost us a small fortune. And poor people couldn't afford medical care at all.'

'Exactly.' Sandra's voice was triumphant, and she flashed a grin at Ethel. 'You tell him.'

'No one gets turned away from treatment by me when they can't afford to pay. Most people have insurance anyway. It all works fine. Why rock the boat?'

Ethel said, 'I don't really understand politics, but I can say that no one back home has a bad word to say about the health service. Well, until this year when the government introduced a charge of a shilling for a prescription. There was an outcry. In just a few years everyone's got used to medicine being completely free.'

'But it isn't free. Even in Britain. You pay higher taxes for it.'

'We're paying a fortune in tax anyway because of all the debt from the war. We all happen to think the health service is worth it. And it makes for a fairer system. Those who earn more, pay more.'

'See? Socialism.' Duncan's mouth turned up into a smile directed at his daughter.

'I see nothing wrong with that.' Sandra leaned back in her chair.

'Socialism's a slippery slope to communism.'

'Hardly,' Ethel protested. In England we've got a Conservative government again – and they've kept all the welfare reforms the socialists brought in – apart from adding the prescription charges. You couldn't get further from communism than the Tories–' She stopped, suddenly embarrassed. 'But as I said, I don't really understand politics.'

Sandra grinned at her across the table. 'I think you're talking complete sense. Maybe you can drum some into Dad's thick skull.'

'My daughter is an idealist. Especially where medicine is concerned. I keep telling her she's wasted working as my receptionist. She should go to university and study to be a research scientist. It's what she cares about most, isn't it?'

Sandra turned to address Ethel. 'I'm perfectly happy working here for Dad. I keep hoping that I'll win him round on health care in the end.'

'Why don't you want to go to university?'

Ignoring the question, Sandra pushed her chair back from the table, made her excuses and disappeared upstairs to her bedroom, leaving them alone.

'University is a bone of contention between us.' His face was grave. 'I don't know why she's so obstinate about it. You'd think she'd jump at the chance to get away from Hollowtree. There's nothing here for her. She's a smart kid and could do well in an academic environment.'

'Maybe she doesn't want to leave you.' As she said the words Ethel knew she didn't want to leave him either.

He made no comment, so she helped him clear the table and wash the dishes. The domesticity and companionship of this shared task gave her a joyful feeling. As they stood side-by-side at the kitchen sink, she was highly conscious of his proximity and knew without a shadow of a doubt that he would soon kiss her. The anticipation made her tingle.

Sure enough, as soon as he unplugged the sink and wiped his hands dry, he took the tea towel from her hands and drew her into his arms.

His hands cupped her face after the kiss finally ended.

'I've missed you so much, Ethel. I know it's only been a few weeks, but I thought I was losing my mind. You've no idea how many times I turned the car in the direction of Rivercreek.'

'I've missed you too.'

Duncan gave a gasp of joy.

'And Sandra's like a different person.'

He pulled his mouth into a tight mirthless smile. 'Only partly. She's taking her medication but won't agree to seeing a psychiatrist. The pills seem to have calmed her. I still want her to see a specialist but it's hard to push it since she's become more cheerful lately. Unusually so. It's as if something's changed in her life.'

For a moment Ethel was tempted to tell him about Sandra's upcoming date with the medical rep but knew she mustn't betray the confidence. 'Maybe it has.'

They went into the drawing room, where Ethel prevailed upon him to play the piano again. She leaned against the instrument, rapt, watching his fingers move up and down the keys, captivated by his ability to wring emotion from the music. Her eyes filled with tears, and she was uncertain whether the music was making her sad or happy.

All too soon the evening came to an end. The doctor had early morning calls and Ethel didn't want to come back to the farm too late, conscious that she was a guest there and Joan's nights were anyway disturbed by the new baby. He dropped her off, kissing her slowly and lovingly.

31

*A*bout a week after her dinner at the Robinsons', Ethel walked into the kitchen at Rivercreek and found Alice at the table with Joan.

Alice jumped up when she walked in. 'Hey! Ethel! I'm back! The girls and I have moved back to Hollowtree Farm.' She rushed over and wrapped her arms around Ethel as though they were the best of friends.

'Good to see you, Alice.' Ethel tried to sound as if she meant it.

Joan beamed at her cousin. 'We were just chatting about you. Alice has come up with a brilliant idea. Absolutely the tops!'

Ethel pulled out a chair and sat down, uneasy.

'As you know, Ethel, my great-aunt left me a stack of money. Most of it's invested but I'm using some of it to start some business enterprises – just as Aunty Miriam did herself when she inherited from her parents. I want to build up something concrete that I can hand on to my girls. If my aunt could do it, then I can. These days people are more accepting of women getting involved in businesses.'

Ethel was puzzled. 'So?'

Behind Alice, Joan, who was making tea, pulled a face at Ethel, as if to tell her not to be rude.

Alice appeared to be oblivious to any resistance on Ethel's part. 'You probably know the first bit of my plan is opening a movie theatre here in Hollowtree – but there are other things this town can benefit from and I want to be the one to provide them.'

Ethel asked her to go on.

'A hairdressing salon!' Alice clasped her hands together. 'And who better to run it than you!'

'What?'

'There are two ways we could do it.' Alice looked at Joan, apparently seeking reassurance in the face of Ethel's lack of unbridled enthusiasm. 'Either I own the business and pay you a salary to run it, which may suit you if you don't want the responsibility. And I will pay generously. Or, I can buy the premises and kit the place out with all the equipment you'll need, and you can rent it from me, but the business will be yours. That would give me an income stream, and, assuming you are willing, I could retain a stake, a shareholding, say ten or twenty per cent. But you would have the final say and the controlling vote of course.' She hesitated, seeming less self-assured. 'I'd be like a sleeping partner.'

'Sounds like you already have it all worked out.' Ethel's tone was frosty.

Joan pushed a cup of tea towards her cousin. 'It's a brilliant idea. Tell her about the flat, Alice.'

Alice stirred her coffee. 'I've found the perfect spot for a salon. Bang in the middle of town, a few doors down from Freddo's. It's got an apartment upstairs – just a bedroom with a kitchenette and a bathroom.'

Joan rushed in. 'Of course, Jim and I would prefer you to

stay on here, but I know you want your independence and it would be so convenient for you. And the door here will always be open to you.'

'Please say yes, Ethel.' Alice looked at her intently, her eyes pleading. 'I know you'll make it a huge success.' She waved her hand at Joan. 'You've made Joan look absolutely gorgeous and she says you've completely transformed the doctor's daughter. And that must have taken some doing as she's such a frump.'

Ethel bristled on Sandra's behalf. She felt cornered. Taking a sip of her tea, she put the cup down, splashing tea into the saucer. 'Can I sleep on it? It would be a big commitment. I need time to think.'

'Of course,' said Alice. 'But don't take too long. We don't want someone else to come along and snap the place up.'

The barn was dark when Joan walked in. She blinked and adjusted her focus before she could make out Jim in the corner, standing by his workbench, sharpening tools. He looked up at her approach surprised and pleased. Joan leaned against the bench, watching him work.

'Donna sleeping?'

She nodded. 'Harry too. Ethel's home though. She'll hear them if they wake.'

'She made up her mind yet about Alice's offer?'

Joan picked up a spanner from the bench, running a finger around its edge. 'She's pondering. I know she wants to do it, but she's still got a problem with Alice. Doesn't trust her. Doesn't even like her.'

Jim leaned his head on one side. 'Alice is an acquired taste, I suppose. You didn't like her at first. Ethel will come round – especially once she starts working with her. I'm sure of it.'

'I'm not. Alice doesn't exactly help herself where Ethel's concerned. If I were in Ethel's shoes, I'd be wary too. Sometimes I don't get what goes on in Alice's head.'

He shrugged and grinned. 'Trouble with Alice is she opens her mouth before she switches on her brain. Her heart's in the right place, but her mouth's often in the wrong one.'

Joan laughed, resisting the temptation to add that it wasn't just her mouth she opened before using her head. She pulled herself up to sit on the bench, legs swinging under her. 'You're dead right about that, hon.'

He winked at her. 'I am about most things.'

She swatted at him with her hand.

Jim continued. 'Seriously though, Ethel would struggle to find a better offer. And being in town would help her get to know more folks. Not to mention the doc. Only thing against it is how you'll manage without her being on hand here to help you out.'

'That's not a problem. I can cope. Ma's just a short walk away. Alice too – although she's preoccupied with getting her cinema up and running – and she's looking out for a place to buy in town herself.'

'She getting along with Ma?'

'Still a bit frosty, I gather. But Ma seems to have got over her aversion towards Catherine. Not surprising – that kid is cute as a button. Impossible to believe who her father was.'

Jim frowned, evidently not wanting to think about Howardson. 'You reckon her movie theatre is going to work?'

'It's what Hollowtree needs. They just don't know it yet.'

Jim put down the grinding stone and wiped the blade of

the knife he'd been working on. 'You didn't come out here to chat about Ethel and Alice, did you?'

Joan swung her legs back and forth again. 'I've been doing the farm accounts. Maybe I've made a mistake, but it looks like we've missed several instalments on the insurance payments. I've been over the bank statements two or three times.'

Jim looked sheepish. 'I was hoping you wouldn't spot that. I reckoned it would help ease our cash flow if we took a few months' holiday from the premiums – so I let them lapse and delayed the annual renewal. I'll reinstate it in spring.' He looked down at his hands. 'Only with the new hoppers for the beans and those tractor parts I hadn't budgeted for, things have been a bit tight. We'll get back on track in spring with all the orders for maple syrup. And I'm optimistic about winning the contract with Winterforth for the apples. This year all our investment in the orchards should pay off. Especially if they take our complete tonnage.'

Joan leaned back on her hands. 'And just exactly when did you intend to tell me this?'

'You've enough on your plate, Joanie, with the baby and Harry.'

'Thanks for the vote of confidence. I'm only the missus. Popping out babies must have addled my brain.'

He looked abashed. 'I'm sorry. I should have told you, but–'

'But you knew I wouldn't agree with what you've done. And I don't.' She folded her arms.

'It's just for a couple more months.'

'And what happens if we get a crop failure? A flood? A plague of bloody locusts? That's what insurance is for. You pay it month after month for nothing – until one day you find you need it for something. And that could be a whole lot of something.'

'I know. I know.'

'So, you'll reinstate it?'

'Yes.'

'Right away?'

Jim rolled his eyes. 'Right away.'

'Now, give me a kiss.' She curled one leg around his waist and drew him towards her.

It took a lot of persuasion from Joan and Jim before Ethel agreed to go and look at the prospective hairdressing salon premises. In the event, Duncan accompanied her, and it was he who finally convinced her to give the salon a go.

The space was bright and cheerful – a vast improvement on Vera's tatty premises in Aldershot. It was flexible too. Small enough not to intimidate her – her fear was she might not find enough clients. Big enough that there was room to expand if it did take off. And it was slap in the middle of the main street, where there would plenty of passing trade.

Duncan watched her as she paced around, weighing it up, thinking. She knew it was perfect but still she hesitated.

Eventually he spoke. 'You know how I feel about you, Ethel. Anything that keeps you here in this town is all right by me. But more than that, I want you to have a chance to fulfil your dreams. You love hairdressing, and this is a golden opportunity to be your own boss.'

'I'm not sure about Alice Armstrong.'

'She's only putting up the cash and she'll just be a sleeping partner. Alice knows nothing about hairdressing. All she'll care about is that the business is a success.'

Ethel nodded. 'You're right. I know. But it doesn't make me feel any easier about taking Alice's charity.'

Duncan laughed. 'You're not taking her charity. She's making an investment. A smart one too. Alice knows exactly what this town needs and she intends to be the one to provide it. Hollowtree is growing. The more facilities there are here, the more the town will prosper. She's got a sound business brain and a list of ideas. Didn't you say she's also thinking about opening a dress shop?'

Ethel pursed her lips and nodded. 'Yes. I know. I know. I'm being irrational. But I've never been comfortable around Alice.'

'You won't be around her. All you have to ask yourself, Ethel, is do you want to carry on hairdressing?'

Ethel jumped in. 'Yes, yes! I love hairdressing. I don't want to do anything else.'

'Well, all I want is for you to be happy. And when you're ready, I want us to marry. You know that. I'm not one of those old-fashioned guys who thinks a woman should quit working as soon as she's married.' He grinned at her. 'Unless she wants to, of course.'

'Oh no. I'd hate not to work.'

'So that's settled then?'

She grinned. 'I suppose it is.'

He bent down and kissed her. 'Right, let's go and tell Alice the good news. She's set up her office on a table in Freddo's. Then, I'm taking you for a celebratory shandy.'

32

*A*lice was a bag of nerves. Terrified of seeing her own mother. How had it come to this? They'd always been so close. Alice's father's drinking had brought them even closer – two women united against Jack Ducroix' violent outbursts. And Mrs Ducroix had adored Rose – still did – but, as soon as Alice had confided in her mother about her pregnancy and her ill-fated affair with Tip Howardson Ada Ducroix wanted nothing more to do with her daughter.

Mrs Ducroix was a devout Catholic and a staunch member of the St Vincent De Paul Society. But her sympathy towards the poor and unfortunate evidently did not extend as far as her own daughter. Alice, while not as committed as her mother, was a regular churchgoer and had brought up both her daughters as Catholics, but she didn't want the first time she saw her mother in five years to be across a crowded church, on a Sunday morning, with both girls present. While she could face being snubbed herself, she couldn't bear that to happen to Catherine. The only solution was to call on her mother at home and try to win her round. All her letters had been ignored – even the one informing her of Miriam Cooke's death. Mrs Ducroix had even written her aunt out of her life once she knew she had taken Alice into her home.

Alice chose a time when the girls were at school and her father would be unlikely to be around. His abusive and unpredictable behaviour would guarantee the visit would end in a row. If her mother was alone, there was at least a possibility she might be able to get her to see reason.

The house was a single-storey timber dwelling on the outskirts of Hollowtree, where the town met the woods. When Alice had last been there, the place had been run-down, testifying to her father's neglect and his lack of employment. She was shocked as she walked towards it today. The garden, once her mother's pride and joy, was a tangled jungle and the short stone path to the front door was cracked and riddled with weeds. What had been a pretty, late nineteenth century cottage when Alice was a child, now looked like a dilapidated hovel. The paintwork was blistered and cracked. The windows were unwashed and dark with grime. Guttering hung loose from the roof and one of the downpipes was leaning perilously away from the wall. How had her house-proud mother allowed this to happen?

Alice made her way round to the rear of the building, following the flattened grass where there had once been a clearly demarcated pathway. She took a deep breath and pushed open the door to the kitchen, noticing a crack in the glass panel.

There was no sign of her mother. Alice moved through the house from room to room, calling for her, but there was no one there.

Back in the kitchen, the sink was piled with unwashed plates and pans. Alice slipped off her coat and set a pan of water to boil on the stove to wash the dishes. Why had her mother let things go? It was so out of character.

She was drying the last plate when the door opened.

'What do you think you're doing?'

'Mom! I thought I'd tidy up a bit while I was waiting for you to come home.'

'Well, you've no business doing that.' She grabbed the tea towel from Alice's hands. 'Why are you here?'

'I've come back to Hollowtree.' She was met with a stony stare. 'I want the girls to grow up here. Where their family is. And now that Aunty Miriam's died–'

Her mother tutted at the mention of Miss Cooke. 'You needn't think of bringing your brat here. Rose, yes, but that other one will never cross this threshold.'

Alice ground her teeth together. 'I'm not sure I want either of them to cross this threshold, now you mention it. The place is unsanitary. What the hell's going on, Mom?' She swept her arm out to indicate the messy kitchen.

Her mother said nothing, but Alice realised she was wheezing.

'Are you all right, Mom? Sit down.'

Scowling, Ada Ducroix sank into the rocking chair in the corner of the room. 'It's my heart. And there's no money for doctors and medicine now.'

Alice moved towards her. 'That's terrible, Mom. You have to see the doctor. You can't just leave it. I'll take care of the bills.' She hesitated a moment. 'Aunty Miriam left me all her money. I have lots of plans. But top of the list must be getting you well. And fixing this place up.'

'I don't want your money. I won't accept a cent from a tramp who opens her legs for a man like Tip Howardson.'

Alice was cut to the quick. Her own mother. Where was

this vitriol from? How could she be so cruel to her own daughter?

'Please, don't say that. You don't mean it.'

'Of course I mean it. I'm ashamed of you. You've brought disgrace on this family and I want nothing to do with you or your bastard child. You made us the talk of the parish. I haven't been able to hold my head up since word got around about you and that man. I always said he was bad, but I thought better of you. I didn't bring you up to behave like that.'

'If I could undo what I did, don't you think I would? I don't know what possessed me. All I can say is I was lonely. Missing Walt.'

Her mother snarled in derision. 'Funny way to show how much you missed him. Going with another man. Fouling his memory. Walt Armstrong will be spinning in his grave.'

Alice started to cry – more from anger than sorrow. 'Walt loved me and he would forgive me. He was the only person in the world who truly understood me. How dare you say that? I love him still. And yes, I wish I hadn't let Tip have his way – but something good came out of it and that was Catherine. My lovely little girl. I will never regret having her.'

'The apple never falls far from the tree. She may be an angel now, but the devil will out in her. Mark my words.' Ada started to wheeze again. When she had regained her breath, she said, 'I don't want to see her. And I don't want to see you either.' She paused, her eyes narrowed. 'Helga Armstrong hasn't taken you in again, has she? And don't even think about living here.'

'Yes, I'm living back at Hollowtree Farm. Not that she's 'taken me in' as you put it. Walt built that place next to the barn. It's mine and I have every right to be there. And Ma is happy to have us there. She's a more charitable woman than you are. But as it happens I'll be buying a place in town soon. I have a lot of plans.'

Again, the sneer.

'I'll be going then.'

'Rose enrolled in the school?'

'*Both* girls are.'

'She can come here for her tea then. Wednesdays are good.'

Alice put her hands on her hips and stared at her mother. 'Oh no. Rose won't be coming for her tea this or any other Wednesday. I don't want my daughter being poisoned by your filthy talk and your filthy home. And where Rose goes, so does Catherine. They're *sisters*.' She grabbed her coat and shrugged it on. 'My offer stands about the medicine, Mom. I'll get the doctor to make a call and sort you out.'

She opened the back door and left the house, her heart pounding. If that's how her mother wanted it, then so be it. Alice had got by without her for the past five years; she could do so now.

33

_As_ the time passed, Ethel grew increasingly comfortable in the doctor's presence and was slowly building a relationship with his daughter. She was now visiting the house once a week to set Sandra's hair and join them for supper.

One evening, about a month after her first visit, Ethel and Sandra were setting the table for supper while Duncan was out on his house calls.

'I'd like to bring Steve to have supper with us,' Sandra said, looking sheepish. 'I still haven't told Dad about him and was wondering if you might raise the subject, prepare the ground for me. I think it's about time they met.'

'So, it's serious then?' Ethel grinned – it was a big moment for Sandra. 'I'm so pleased. As you haven't mentioned him since your first date, I presumed it had fizzled out.'

'No! I really like him.'

'Hasn't your father run into him at the surgery yet?'

The younger woman shook her head. 'Steve was moved to another district. He hasn't called on us since that first visit.' She grinned. 'To be honest, I was relieved. I was nervous about them meeting before Dad got to know what the score is. He's always impatient with the medical reps. Calls them snake-oil pedlars. I didn't want him saying something bad about Steve and then having to take it back!' She gave a little giggle.

'You like him a lot then?'

Sandra nodded.

Ethel was pleased at the way Sandra was increasingly willing to take her into her confidence. The absence of a mother in her life must have left a big void. They had come a long way since that horrible outburst at Freddo's. Her showing interest in the blossoming relationship with Steve was no doubt helping.

'Where does he take you when you go out?'

'Mostly we just sit in my car and talk. Neither of us likes dancing. Sometimes he takes me to a tavern. But he doesn't have a lot of money as he's saving up for a new car.'

'I thought you said his car was being repaired?'

Sandra nodded. 'It was beyond repair. The engine packed up. It was ancient. That's why he's saving up.'

'Gosh. How does he manage to do his job without transport? Isn't a car essential to his work?'

Sandra shrugged. 'To be honest, I've never asked. Perhaps he gets a lift with another rep.' She blinked her eyes and giggled again.

'I'll talk to your dad as soon as I get an opportunity. Maybe when he runs me home tonight.'

'Thanks, Ethel. That's sweet of you.'

As they finished laying the table, Duncan stuck his head round the door. 'Sorry, my darlings. I'm going to have to miss supper. Leave a plate in the oven for me, Sandra, and I'll grab it before I drop Ethel home. I have to go and see the

Holloway lad. Apparently, there's a problem with his stitches.'

Ethel and Sandra ate their supper. Sandra was never much of a conversationalist, leaving Ethel to do most of the talking. But tonight, as they cleared the plates away, Sandra said, 'Ethel, can I ask you something? I bumped into a friend in town the other day and she asked me a question I wasn't sure how to answer.'

'Of course.'

'When you kiss someone and stuff, are you meant to like it?'

Ethel was taken aback. 'Yes. If you have feelings for the other person, kissing is very pleasurable. Don't you have feelings for Steve?'

Sandra's face was scarlet, her expression indignant. 'I just told you – I wasn't talking about Steve. It was one of the girls I was at school with. She said she dreaded having to do it every time she saw her boyfriend.'

Ethel put down the last piece of cutlery. 'That's such a pity. Kissing someone you feel a lot for is the most wonderful thing.'

'I know that. That's how it is with Steve. But I'm not experienced enough to know if what happened to her is unusual. You're the only person I can ask, Ethel. And my friend has no one either.'

'What did she tell you?'

'She says she gets scared that he might not stop. That he might make her go all the way.'

'Make her? Are you saying he forces himself on her?'

Sandra shook her head. 'No. She said, so far, she's always got him to stop before... you know... going all the way. But he laughs at her and calls her frigid.'

'Frigid? That's ridiculous. Every woman has a right to

say how far she wants to go before she's married.' She paused and turned to look at Sandra. 'Steve isn't like that is he? He isn't trying to push you too far?'

'No! I told you I was talking about a friend... I didn't believe her when she told me because Steve's not at all like that – that's why I asked you. Forget I even mentioned it. I probably shouldn't have told you.'

Ethel put the pile of cutlery she was holding in the sink and turned on the taps. 'I'm very glad you told me. And please tell your friend she might want to think about breaking up with this chap. A decent fellow never forces himself on a woman. Never.'

In the car on the way home, Ethel mentioned Sandra's boyfriend to him.

'A boyfriend? Sandra? You're sure?'

'Of course I'm sure, darling. Aren't you pleased?'

'Yes, I suppose so.' He was frowning. 'But why didn't she tell me herself? How long has she been seeing him?'

'Only a month or so.'

'You've known all that time?'

Ethel nodded, uncomfortable. This was exactly what she'd hoped to avoid. 'I suppose she was embarrassed and found it easier to confide in another woman.' She stroked his arm.

'What? I'm her father. I have a right to know.' He slammed his fist on the steering wheel.

'That's precisely why she didn't want to tell you. She knew you'd react like that.'

Duncan sighed. Then he turned to look at her. 'I'm sorry, Ethel. I'm delighted that Sandra's chosen to confide in you, rather than me. It's fantastic news and shows that at last she can see what a wonderful woman you are.' He gave her a rueful smile. 'Just takes a bit of getting used to. She doesn't need me anymore, at least not in the same way.'

'She's a grown woman, Duncan. It doesn't mean she loves you any less. And having a boyfriend is probably just what she needs.'

Duncan's expression was one of resignation. 'You're right. I have to get used to that she's an adult.'

Ethel could see his hands were gripping the wheel tightly. 'But she's so naive. Sandra may be academically bright but when it comes to human relationships, she's still a child.'

'This Steve fellow sounds like a decent man. It could be the best thing for Sandra. I have the feeling she's quite lonely.'

Duncan looked at her. 'You're right. She is. I don't think I've been the model parent. I've let her become too dependent on me. She's always struggled to form friendships. I was more concerned about her mood swings. But maybe the two things are connected.' His lips stretched into a sad smile. 'Poor Sandra missed out on having a mother. I've never been able to substitute for that.'

Ethel moved towards him. 'Don't be too hard on yourself. All parents struggle bringing up children and doing it on your own can't have been easy. You've done a great job. Sandra's just going through the inevitable phase of moving from childhood to womanhood. And I'm sure there'll be other boyfriends after this one before she finds the right person.'

Duncan pulled her into his arms. 'And now Sandra's got you too. Thank you. I'm sorry I've been so grumpy. It's taken me most of my life to find the right person. But I'm certain I've found her now.'

Later, when the doctor dropped Ethel off at Rivercreek, he kissed her and then put his hands on her shoulders. 'I've had an idea. Instead of this Steve coming for supper, what if it were Sunday lunch and you and the Armstrongs come too? Sandra and I still owe them for their generous hospitality at Christmas. And that way Steve won't feel so much in the spotlight. Do you think Helga would be up for looking after the children?'

Ethel said she'd ask. 'Joan will have to bring Donna as she's breastfeeding. But it will be good for her to have a break and get out for a while.'

'I hope they can make it.'

'Won't she prefer it to be just the three of you?'

'I'll ask her. It'll make the whole thing more casual and less about parading the new boyfriend for inspection.'

'That's a super idea.' Ethel leaned in for another kiss.

34

When Ethel arrived with Joan and Jim at the doctor's house the following Sunday, they were greeted by the delicious aroma of roast beef. Duncan opened the door and told them Sandra had gone to collect her boyfriend in the car and they would be joining them shortly.

As their host made the final preparations for the meal, they sat around the kitchen table, chatting, speculating as to what the mysterious Steve would be like.

'So, what does this fellow do?' asked Jim.

'He's a rep for one of the drugs companies.'

Jim tilted his head. 'Good secure job then.'

'So, you've met him?' asked Joan.

'No. He manages a different territory. He made one call here, but I was out on my rounds. But he made a big impression on my daughter.' He laughed, but Ethel could see he looked nervous.

'Definitely a good job though – with prospects,' said Joan. 'It sounds like they're getting serious if she's bringing him home to meet you.'

'Looks that way.' Duncan had a forced smile on his face, but Ethel could see he was as nervous as Sandra must be.

Several times, Duncan glanced at his watch. 'She's taking her time. I expected them twenty minutes ago.'

Joan laughed. 'I expect they've taken the scenic route. Plenty of stops for kisses.'

They all laughed, then turned their heads at the sound of the front door opening. 'We're back here in the kitchen,' the doctor called.

The smile of greeting froze on Ethel's face when she heard the gasps from the Armstrongs, as Sandra and Steve entered the room. Jim looked furious and there was a mixture of loathing and fear in Joan's face.

Steve Johnson was tall, broad and bull-necked with a nose that looked like it had been broken. Much older than Ethel had expected, or Sandra had indicated. Probably the same age or even older than Ethel was. There was a coldness about his features: his narrow eyes and thin-lipped mouth. His hair was cropped short and he clearly hadn't shaved that morning. Hardly the way to prepare for meeting his girlfriend's father for the first time. His mean-looking mouth formed a smile as he stood in the doorway, surveying the occupants of the room, evidently enjoying the reaction his appearance had provoked. He began to laugh. It was a hollow sound, ill-willed, nasty, cruel.

'Well, well, well. Fancy seeing you two here,' the man said. 'When Sandy mentioned some neighbours were joining us I never expected it to be you two. How's it going, Joanie?' His lip curled. Gesturing towards Donna in Joan's arms, he said, 'I see you've squeezed out another brat? Old Jim Boy can't keep his paws off you, eh? Can't say I blame him.'

Jim started to rise, but Duncan, who was standing with a

ladle in his hand and his mouth open, grabbed Jim's arm restraining him. Sandra, meanwhile, had eyes wide like a startled animal.

Jim spoke first. 'What the hell are you playing at, Howardson? What in God's name are you doing back in Hollowtree?' He called out to Sandra. 'This man isn't who you think he is.'

Duncan moved towards his daughter. 'Come here, Sandra.' His face showed disbelief at what was happening, as well as concern for his daughter.

Howardson stepped in front, his hand gripping Sandra's arm. 'Stay right where you are, honey.'

'Sandra, this man's name is Tip Howardson. And he's been feeding you lies,' Joan said. The baby, evidently sensing her mother's anger and fear, began to cry.

Duncan looked to his daughter, stretching out his hand to her. 'If he's Tip Howardson, he's a bad man. He's done bad things.'

Ethel thought her heart was going to stop. She looked at Joan, whose face was flushed, her eyes full of anger, the baby twisting around in her arms. Before she could stop herself, Ethel pitched herself across the room and was hammering her fists into Howardson's chest. 'You killed Greg. You killed my fiancé. You filthy, dirty bastard.'

Howardon's chest was like granite. He dropped Sandra's arm and grabbed at Ethel's wrists, jerking her away from him, holding her in a grip like handcuffs.

He whistled. 'Aren't you the looker? So, you're the Grasshopper's woman? I have to hand it to old Hooper – he had good taste.' He looked towards the doctor. 'You too, Doc.' His tongue flicked out and ran over his lips. Ethel wanted to throw up.

Meanwhile, Sandra had started to cry. Big jerky tears.

Shoulders shaking. She looked at Ethel with hatred. 'Why have you ruined everything? I hate you all! You're all liars.' She backed away from the door and ran up the stairs. They heard her bedroom door crash shut.

'Sounds like the little lady's lost her appetite. Shame, as that beef smells delicious.' Tip leaned against the doorframe. 'It's a real pity I won't be able to stay and enjoy it. But I can tell when I'm not wanted.'

'If you know what's good for you, Howardson, you'll get the hell away from Hollowtree,' said Jim. 'Because so help me, if I clap eyes on you in this town again, I'll kick the living daylights out of you.'

Duncan moved towards him. 'And that goes for my daughter too. Keep away from her.'

Tip Howardson raised his hands in front of him and pretended to quake with fear. 'Oh, I'm so frightened.' Then he laughed sardonically. 'Don't worry, Doc. I've no interest in your frigid little daughter. She's not worth the effort it would take to get her to put out. I've other fish to fry.'

He looked at Jim. 'Hasn't Alice told you? She and I are getting together again. That little girl of ours needs her daddy.' He pushed himself off the doorframe and went out of the house.

A moment later they heard a car engine starting up.

'God dammit. That's Sandra's car.' Duncan lurched towards the doorway.

Jim caught his arm. 'Let it go, Duncan. Call the police and let them deal with it. Right now, the sooner he gets the hell out of Hollowtree the better.

Joan looked at Jim. 'We're going to have to warn Alice. She was convinced he wouldn't come here. She thought he'd believe the story that she and the girls had gone to England.'

Sandra's car was found abandoned and burnt-out on a back road near to the main highway towards Kitchener. Confronted with this further evidence of Tip Howardson's bad character, Sandra was mute, shell-shocked. The realisation that her boyfriend was not who he had claimed to be and was guilty of theft and arson, as well as impersonation, attempted rape and violent behaviour, sent the young woman into seclusion. She performed her duties in the surgery, but otherwise remained in her bedroom, refusing to discuss what had happened with her father. Desperate to break the deadlock, Duncan asked Ethel to mediate but it made matters worse. When Ethel announced her presence through the locked bedroom door she was greeted with the sound of shoes being hurled against it as Sandra screamed at her to go away.

The local police advised Duncan that in the absence of solid evidence that Howardson was responsible for the theft of the car, there was little they could do. They searched a wide arc around Hollowtree and Hartley and alerted neighbouring police forces, but Howardson had vanished. Duncan hoped it was for good.

A couple of evenings after the confrontation with Howardson, Duncan and Ethel were sitting in the Ladies and Escorts room in the hotel in Argyll that had become a regular haunt.

Duncan reached for her hand and wove his fingers through hers. 'I tried talking to Sandra again this morning. She wouldn't answer. Apart from dealing with the necessary business of the practice she hasn't spoken a word to me since the disaster with Howardson. She's acting like a deaf mute.'

'Surely she doesn't blame you for what happened?'

'I don't know what she thinks.' His eyes were sad.

'If I'd had any idea who he was... I would have talked to you about him.'

'It's not your fault. If I'd been more approachable, Sandra would have told me herself about him. What kind of father am I?'

'A good one. The kind who cares, who shows infinite patience, who supports and loves her.'

Duncan took a long draught of his beer. 'I keep asking myself why? Why her? What's he playing at?'

Ethel shrugged. 'Maybe it was chance. Or perhaps he knew about you and me. Who knows what goes on in that sick head of his? Who cares? Just as long as he keeps away from Hollowtree now he's been exposed.'

35

'Mr Freeman, I need your help.' Alice spoke quietly into the telephone. Helga was in town visiting a sick friend, but Alice was nervous that she might return without warning. 'The man I told you about – he's turned up here in Hollowtree.' She told the lawyer about Howardson's appearance at the doctor's lunch, explained that, no, she hadn't seen him herself yet, but that she was terrified he would approach Catherine.

'He told my friends that he came back to Hollowtree to marry me, so our plan to convince him I'd left the country didn't work.'

'I'm sorry, Mrs Armstrong, but I've told you before, there's little I can do in the absence of him making a threat or abducting the child.'

'He already did abduct her. He took her from school.'

Mr Freeman looked puzzled. 'I'm sorry, but you told me he returned her safely home within an hour and he had the consent of Catherine's teacher.'

'That woman had no right to give him consent. And he lied to her.'

'He told her he was the child's father. You've already told me he is. There's no lie there I'm afraid. Look, Mrs Armstrong, you have all my sympathy and I share your frustration, but we are going to have to wait until he makes some kind of move. Once we have something more substantial I will immediately apply to the courts for an injunction preventing him making any contact with you or your daughters.'

'Look, I can't afford to wait until he makes a move,' Alice snapped at him in frustration. 'This is my five-year-old child we're talking about.' An idea formed in her head. 'I'll pay him to go away. That's all he wants. Money. So, let's give him some and buy him off.' She leaned against the kitchen wall twisting the telephone cord through her fingers.

'I don't recommend doing that, Mrs Armstrong. If you pay him now, he'll be back for more – and he'll keep on coming back until he's bled you dry. I know his type.'

Alice sighed. 'You're right. He will. He doesn't want me and he doesn't want Catherine. It's just the money. What am I going to do?' Her tone was desperate.

'Let me look into it. A man like him, if he's done half the things you've told me about, he's bound to have a criminal record here or in the United States. I'm going to have someone do some looking. An investigator.'

'Hurry, Mr Freeman, please hurry. I'm living in constant fear right now.'

Alice had plastered the town with posters to announce the opening night of the movie theatre. After mulling over numerous options for naming the place, she had settled on *The Rose*, in honour of her daughter. From her days working in the Hollowtree Library, she remembered that there had been a popular Elizabethan theatre with that name. She thought it classy – different from the usual names for movie houses, derived from ancient Greek. Those grandiose names were suitable for the giant pre-war picture palaces of the big cities, but The Rose was perfect for a modest place in a small country town.

Some members of the community had been expressing disapproval of the project, saying it would cheapen the town and bring in undesirables. She brushed the objections aside, when the chief librarian mentioned them to her. 'Some folk look for anything to complain about. If they don't like it, they can stay away.'

When Alice attended Mass the week the posters went up, the parish priest approached her after the service. 'Alice, I chose not to speak of the movie theatre from the pulpit today, but I hope you'll be taking your responsibilities as a Catholic seriously and not showing any dirty pictures.'

Alice's mouth dropped open, as she bristled at his words. 'It's not that kind of place. What do you take me for, Father? I have two young daughters. I'm not going to do anything that would bring shame on them.'

The priest studied her, then shook his head. 'If I were being uncharitable I might say you already have – the little one being born outside marriage. But God is merciful, and I have prayed to the Blessed Virgin to intercede on your behalf. Has the child been baptised into the holy church?'

'Of course. In Ottawa.'

'Good. Good. Now hear what I say. We don't want to be having any of those filthy immoral films, with women showing their bosoms and committing adultery.'

Alice glared at him. 'Why do you assume it's the women

committing the adultery? Come on, Father, even you have to admit it takes a man too.'

He pursed his lips. 'Ah, yes, but it's the women who tempt them into it. Ever since the Garden of Eden. Leading men astray.'

She turned away and strode down the path to where her daughters were waiting for her. Shaking with anger, she took a couple of deep breaths and put on a smile, not wanting to upset the girls. While she was closely tied to her religion and had found it some comfort when Walt died, it was impossible not to feel resentment at the way the church appeared to see women as the source of all evil. What did the priest know about life? He hadn't fought in a war, known a woman, brought up children, suffered from money troubles. He was cocooned in the protective shield of the Catholic hierarchy, with no real perception of what life is like in the wider world. How dare he speak to her that way? Where was his compassion? Why did he see women as shameful creatures? That's it, she decided. *They can excommunicate me if they like. I know exactly which film I'm going to go with on opening night. Plenty of bosom and adultery. I just have to convince the distributor to let me show it.*

Later that afternoon she walked across the fields to Rivercreek, still burning with indignation at what the priest had said. She unburdened herself to Joan. 'Can you believe the man? And it sounds like he actually contemplated denouncing me from the pulpit.'

Joan shook her head. 'I'm sorry, Alice, it doesn't sound very Christian to me. But what would I know? I've never been one for religion. Weddings, funerals and Christmas. That's about it. And my family were Church of England, so I don't get the whole Catholic thing. Did you talk to Ma about it?'

Alice snorted. 'Ma's a pillar of the Catholic community. She'd probably agree with Father Connolly.'

'How are you two getting along?'

'Well enough, I suppose. Which is exactly why I don't want to raise it with her.'

'And have you decided what the opening night film will be?'

Alice tapped the side of her nose and grinned. 'Yes, but it's a secret and I intend to keep it that way until the last minute. Build up the curiosity. Besides I still have to convince the distributor.'

'Whatever it is, I can't wait. Jim's going to stay home with the kids, so I get a night out.'

36

*I*t was not until the day before the opening of The Rose that the name of the first film was revealed. Alice had chosen *Niagara* and won her battle to get to show it. It had taken all her powers of persuasion to convince the distributor to let her have the print – ahead of other larger towns. She had calculated that choosing a film that featured such a world famous Canadian landmark, and the equally famous Marilyn Monroe, would be a massive draw. The chance to see Monroe in what was already a box office sensation in the United States should certainly prove to be a winner in Hollowtree. The movie poster featured the starring actress, half-naked, and promised 'a raging torrent of emotion that even nature can't control'. Alice wondered how the parish priest would react, then realised she no longer cared.

The audience on opening night was at full capacity – larger than Alice had anticipated. It seemed that every resident of Hollowtree, and many from beyond, had turned up for the grand opening. She didn't know whether it was a genuine desire to watch a movie, to see Marilyn Monroe and all the glory of her décolletage, or the promise of free food and drink after the show. She had prevailed on Helga Armstrong to bake several batches of her butter pies. Alice knew her mother-in-law's willingness was less out of generosity or support for her enterprise than down to the fact that Helga couldn't resist an opportunity to showcase her baking prowess.

The decision to do an initial children-only launch, on the Saturday afternoon, gave Alice the chance to iron out any glitches before the more critical adults showed up that night for the official opening. A free showing of a double bill of *Lassie Come Home* and *Cinderella* ensured that every child in town was grinning from ear to ear when they left The Rose. Appetites whetted, she knew she'd get a full house for the future Saturday morning kids' shows she planned to screen every week.

The movie theatre's origins as a storage facility were no longer in evidence – the walls were swathed in draped fabric and Alice had invested in upholstered seating – an acquisition from a theatre in Kitchener which was being refurbished.

Ethel and Duncan took their seats near the front of the house, with Joan on Ethel's left. Duncan's efforts to persuade Sandra to join them had been in vain. The young woman was still refusing to leave the house, let alone have anything to do with Ethel. She was equally determined not to attend an appointment her father had made for her to see a psychiatric specialist. Instead she continued to shut herself away in her bedroom when not working. Ethel was uncertain whether it was distress at the discovery of her erstwhile boyfriend's past and character – or humiliation that it had been exposed so publicly. Duncan's insistence that she have nothing more to do with him proved unnecessary as

Howardson appeared to have unceremoniously dumped her.

Ethel had opened the doors of the new salon. Within a few days of opening it was proving a success. She had expected the place to operate as a walk-in until the business became more established, but the constant stream of clients meant that already she was booked solid and was forced to turn away anyone who hadn't made an appointment.

She hadn't moved into the rooms upstairs yet, preferring to remain at the farm to help Joan out until the baby was a little older.

Alice was delighted and effusive over the salon's early results, beaming at Ethel and clapping her hands with glee. 'We've got ourselves a goldmine here, Ethel. If it keeps up like this, you're going to need to take on more staff. You shouldn't be having to sweep the floor and manage the bookings yourself.'

'But can we afford to pay someone else?'

'Your decision. You're the boss, Ethel. But my dime's worth is that it's a sensible investment.'

'It would be a huge help to have a junior to do some of the basic tasks – and I could train her to become a stylist.'

Alice clapped her hands. 'Now you're talking! Why don't I speak to the school and find out if there's a recent leaver who wants to learn the trade.'

Ethel grinned. 'It would take some of the pressure off me.'

'Done! If The Rose is even half as successful as this place is turning out to be, I'll be a happy woman, Ethel.'

She flung her arms around Ethel, who was embarrassed by the sudden display of affection. Although her hostility towards Alice had softened, she wasn't ready to count her as a friend. She doubted she ever would. But as a business partner, she was proving exemplary.

The evening of the grand premiere at The Rose, Alice, stood vigil in the tiny foyer, welcoming the patrons. Her hair coiffed by Ethel, she was wearing a pearl pendant that Walt had given her when they married, and an elegant gown bought for the opening,

Along with Ethel's salon junior, Alice had recruited a young woman, newly graduated from the local high school, to operate the box office, but she wanted to be on hand herself in case of any problems. Looking around her, Alice felt a surge of pride. She'd done it. Despite the naysayers, the scepticism of the cinema manager in Ottawa, and the reaction of Mr Freeman to her plan, she had pulled it off.

She smoothed her hand down her figure-hugging taffeta dress – people in Hollowtree were used to seeing her in work clothes or cotton frocks. Maybe being dressed up wasn't such a bad thing – when you could afford fancy clothes why not wear them? And she had to admit she enjoyed the appreciative looks she got from the men and the sour ones from some of the women. It traced to envy and that felt good.

Her only disappointment was that her own mother had failed to turn up. While Alice had not spoken to Mrs Ducroix since the day she had called on her, she had sent her an invitation to the opening and hoped and prayed that her mother would attend – even if driven by curiosity rather than pride in her daughter's achievement. At Alice's request, Dr Robinson had called on her mother and prescribed medication for her heart failure but warned Alice that the prognosis wasn't good. She hated the thought that her mother might go to her death still nurturing anger and disgust at her only child.

Brushing aside the threat of tears, she took a deep breath and was about to move inside to take her own seat when the glass doors swung open and Tip Howardson strolled in and approached the ticket booth. Alice stepped in front of him.

'We already have a full house.' She turned to the woman selling the tickets. 'Put the sign up, Susan.'

The woman pulled a cardboard notice out and covered the ticket window.

Howardson stood in front of Alice, grinning at her. 'There must be room for one more, especially since I'm part of the family.'

'You're nothing to do with my family. Leave now. I don't want any trouble.'

Howardson grabbed at her arm. 'You're looking good tonight, Alice. Now why don't we go inside and watch the picture? I came here specially to celebrate your success. Then afterwards we can have our own private celebration.' He ran a finger over her skin where her breasts met the neckline of her gown.

She jerked away. 'Susan, run inside and ask Constable Mitcham to step out here. Dick Henderson, Freddo and Dr Robinson too. Be discreet. Tell them we have an unwanted guest who's threatening trouble.'

The ticket seller disappeared. Howardson jerked Alice's arm behind her back, wrenching it. 'You'll regret this, Alice. I'm not done with you. All I want is my rights.'

'Rights? What rights? You have no rights over me.'

'Maybe not, but I have rights over my daughter. I've seen a lawyer.'

Heart hammering, Alice hissed at him, 'Then take me to court and we'll see what happens. But I can save you a heap of money – no court's going to let a brute like you anywhere near that little girl. And you have no proof she's your daughter. You have no claim on me, so shove off, you creep.'

The local constable appeared through the door, the doctor close behind him.

Howardson released his grip but pointed his finger at Alice. 'You've not heard the last of this, Alice. I know my rights.' Then he turned away and was gone.

'You all right, Mrs Armstrong?' The constable stared after Howardson.

'What was that lowlife doing here? Was he threatening you?' The doctor moved across towards the doors. 'Do you want us to go after him?'

'Thank you, gentlemen, but all's well now. He's gone, and good riddance. Now let's all go inside and watch the movie.'

The Hollowtree audience lapped up every minute of *Niagara*. Whether it was a taste for thrillers, pride in seeing the spectacle of Niagara Falls in glorious Technicolor, or appreciation of the wonder that was Miss Monroe, Alice didn't know, but as the credits came up at the end of the movie, they burst into spontaneous applause and Alice breathed a sigh of relief.

37

*W*hen the film show was over, the food and drink consumed, and Alice congratulated on the undoubted success of her new venture, Duncan drove Joan and Ethel back to Rivercreek Farm. Alice was staying in town, sleeping in the still-vacant flat above the hair salon as she wanted to be on hand to oversee the post-party clear-up the following day.

As they drove towards the farm, Ethel peered through the windscreen. 'Look at the sky! Isn't it a bit late for a sunset?'

'Oh my God,' Joan gasped. It's a fire! It's Hollowtree!'

Dr Robinson pressed the accelerator and the car hurtled forward, turning off the road to Rivercreek and down the bumpy track towards Hollowtree Farm.

'Who's there tonight? Is Mrs Armstrong on her own?' he asked.

'Alice's girls are with her. Please hurry!' Joan begged. 'For heaven's sake, hurry! Oh God! Let them be safe!'

They screeched round a bend in the road to the top of the hill above the farm. Below them they could see the big

Dutch barn was alight. Orange and yellow flames leapt skywards, vivid against the dark of the sky, and a black pall of smoke billowed out above the flames. The distorting effect of heat gave the whole scene a blurred, out-of-focus appearance. An inferno. Out of control.

Joan shrieked, 'Rose and Catherine are in there. That's where they sleep. Alice's place is right behind the barn.'

The car roared along the unmade track, skidding and swerving as Duncan whipped the vehicle along the rough surface of the road. As they rounded the last corner into the farmyard, a collective sigh of relief rose up between them when they saw Helga Armstrong standing on the doorstep with the two little girls in their nightgowns beside her.

Joan threw herself out of the car. 'Thank God. You're all safe!' She swept the two girls into her arms. 'Oh, Ma!'

'We're all fine,' said Helga. 'The girls were sleeping over here with me. Jim's on his way and he's called the fire volunteers. The fire's taken hold so fast. It's piled high with hay in there. Dry as a bone, like tinder.'

'Livestock?'

'A couple of cows and the old billy goat. The rest are in the pasture, thank God.' As she spoke, a line of trucks appeared over the brow of the hill, the ladder truck in front, the water pumps following and a series of smaller trucks bringing up the rear.

Jim's truck pulled into the yard from the opposite direction. Joan ran over to meet him. The baby was in a Moses basket on the back seat, beside Harry, who was swathed in a blanket and supported by Jimmy, while Sam sat in the front seat. Donna was crying, and her screams were mingled with the excited barking of Olive Oyl – also in the back.

Joan scooped up the baby and called out to Ethel. 'Can

you take Harry inside?' She bit her lip. 'No use trying to get the boys away. Firemen are their heroes.'

'Don't worry, Joan,' Helga called out. 'I'll keep the boys close to me.'

Joan stood, open-mouthed, framed by the kitchen door, Donna in her arms, watching helplessly as the fire consumed the wooden structure, acrid smoke catching the back of her throat. Behind her, Ethel was standing at the kitchen window. Without warning, the back wall of the barn blew apart and a deafening explosion split the air. Wood and debris flew upwards like rockets and landed in the field and the yard in front of them.

Jim had been with the fire crew, directing them to the pond behind the barn where they could set up the water pumps. He ran back towards his wife. 'You all right, Joan?'

Helga threw up her hands as if in supplication. 'Holy Mother of God, save us, what was that? Was it gasoline?'

Jim clapped his hand to his head. 'The new tractor is in there. I moved it there this morning. I hadn't got around to taking the last of Pa's gas bottles back. Liquid oxygen. No wonder they popped. It's a blessing the explosion didn't take the farmhouse with it.'

The fire chief ordered everyone back inside the house. 'If anything else like that blows, there could be shrapnel flying everywhere.'

They all knew saving the barn or anything in it was impossible. It took more than three hours to bring the fire under control, leaving just the concrete foundations, some twisted ironwork and a few charred uprights.

Once most of the fire trucks had driven out of the farm-yard, Joan emerged from the house to stand beside Jim, looking at what was left of the once magnificent structure. The air was thick with the stench of smoke and the ground underfoot was sodden with the water from the hoses. The fire chief and one or two of the volunteers were still there, trying to establish what had caused the fire. Underneath the smell of burning was the unmistakeable aroma of barbe-cued meat and Joan gagged as she thought of the two dead cows, the goat and the chickens that failed to make their exit in time. Two of the surviving hens were now pecking around in the rubble.

Tears pricked Joan's eyes. It wasn't just the loss of the barn, it was also the many memories she associated with it – along with the kitchen, it had been the living heart of Hollowtree Farm. Jimmy as a five-year-old boy, clutching his grandmother's hand the day he met her, when she took him into the barn to watch her churning butter and inspect a new family of kittens. Joan herself sitting in its cool interior on a hot day, watching as Jim worked on mending the tractor.

These days, the barn had only been used to shelter the few animals they still kept, more for sentimental reasons than financial, and to store hay – the Rivercreek barn being larger, more modern and more convenient. Joan leaned against her husband and he stretched an arm around her shoulders, drawing her closer.

'Alice will be devastated,' she said. 'There's not a stick left of her place.'

'She's buying a house in town anyway. She wasn't going to be here much longer.'

'It was her only link to Walt. The home he built for her.'

Jim's face was grim at the mention of his brother. He closed his eyes.

'The only photograph of her and Walt will have gone up in flames too. On their honeymoon in Toronto.' Joan made a little choking sound.

'My grandfather built that barn. With the help of his neighbours. Must have been about seventy years ago.'

'The biffy's burned too. Maybe Ma will finally let you put a bathroom inside the house. The older she gets the less fun it's going to be, traipsing across the yard every time she needs the toilet.'

'I doubt she'll agree to that. You know what she's like about change. Besides, it's only the roof that's gone. The rest of it is intact. I can fix it soon enough.'

'More's the pity!' Joan remembered her horror at venturing out to use the toilet there when she first arrived at Hollowtree Farm. Trudging through snow with a full bladder on cold mornings had not been a happy experience.

Smoke still hung in the air. Joan sensed a movement behind them and saw Ethel and Dr Robinson approaching, carrying mugs of tea. The four of them stood together in the yard, sipping tea and staring at the blackened skeleton of the barn.

'The kids are asleep,' said Ethel. 'All piled in together, topping and tailing.'

'And Ma?' asked Joan.

'Sleeping too. The babies are in with her. She's exhausted.'

'How's she taking it?' asked Jim.

'She must be shocked, but she isn't showing it. She has the Blitz spirit,' Ethel said.

'That's Ma. This is the last thing she needs though. And it means Alice and the girls will have to move into the house with her. Not sure how that's going to work.'

'It'll only be for a few weeks. Alice is planning to make an offer on one of those big houses near you, Doc,' said Joan. 'And at least Ma seems to have accepted Catherine – even if it isn't with open arms.'

'It'll take her some time but Catherine's a sweet kid and Ma's not a monster.'

'Where is Alice?' Jim looked around.

'Sleeping over at the salon. She wanted to stay in town to be on hand to clear-up after the party today. And I imagine she would have been late getting to bed.'

A voice behind them said, 'No. She's right here. I've been here all night.'

They turned in surprise. Alice was still wearing the dress she had worn to the premiere – the cream silk taffeta now filthy from the smoke.

'Where've you been?'

She pointed to a copse on the far side of where the barn had once been. 'I wanted to be on my own. Once I knew the girls were safe. Didn't want to talk to anyone.'

'When did you get here?' Joan asked.

'With the crew. I hitched a ride with Hank Rogers in his truck. As soon as the fire bell went off I had a bad feeling. When I heard it was here I had to come. I had to watch.' She brushed her hair away from her eyes, leaving a dirty streak across her forehead. 'I had to witness the last I had of Walt disappearing. Now I have nothing. Only what's in my head. That can't ever go.' She began to sob.

Ethel, who was standing nearest to her, put an arm around her and drew her close. 'I'm so sorry, Alice.'

Alice leaned into Ethel, evidently grateful for the comfort – then pulled away. 'You all know this was no accident, don't you?'

'What?' Jim's face was grim.

'This was Tip's doing.'

'Tip?' Joan and Jim spoke as one.

'He turned up at The Rose tonight. Talking of marriage. Making threats. I threw the bastard out. He's trying to frighten me.' She looked at the astonished faces in front of her. 'You were there, Dr Robinson. You helped get rid of him.'

Duncan nodded.

Joan didn't want to believe it but knew it was exactly the sort of thing that bastard was capable of. She looked at Jim. 'It's almost dawn. Why don't we go over to Rivercreek and I'll cook us a big breakfast? We can talk about it there. You too, Doc.'

'Thanks, Joan,' said Alice, 'but I'll stay here. I need to talk to the girls when they wake up.'

'You need to get some sleep.'

'I'll sleep in with Ma.'

'Then I'll go and fetch the babies. We can leave the boys here. They're in with Rose and Catherine – so they've probably been awake talking all night. They'll all sleep late this morning. Thank goodness it's Sunday.' Joan gave her head a little shake.

Jim followed Joan upstairs. He took the sleeping Harry and Joan picked up Donna, also fast asleep in her straw bassinet. As they lifted up their children, Helga stirred and opened her eyes. Alice was standing in the doorway behind them, hesitant. Helga sat up and opened her arms and with a little gasp, Alice moved across to the bed and into her mother-in-law's embrace.

They were finishing breakfast when the telephone rang. Jim got up to answer it, while Joan, Ethel and Duncan stopped talking and waited.

'You're sure? How do you know?'

Jim was frowning as he held the receiver to his ear. 'So,

what happens next?' His expression was inscrutable as he listened to the response. 'Thanks, Ron. I'll drop by in about an hour. And thanks to you and all the guys for everything you did.'

He hung up and came back to sit down, his face creased with worry.

'Well?' Joan demanded. 'Was that the fire chief? What did he want?'

'Alice was right. The fire was started deliberately.'

There was a collective intake of breath around the table.

'They found two empty cans of gasoline. Lids off. Whoever was responsible had flung them into the pig sty.'

Jim swept his hair back from his brow, his face tired. 'I have to go into town and talk to Jeff and the police. They need to rule me out.'

'Rule you out? That's preposterous! Why on earth would you fire your own barn?' Joan was indignant.

The doctor interjected. 'They probably want to rule out insurance fraud.'

Joan paled. 'Insurance,' she whispered then looked up at Jim, her eyes questioning.

Jim dropped his gaze. Elbows on the table, he put his head in his hands.

Ethel turned to look at Duncan, wondering if he was any the wiser than she was, but he gave a little shake of the head.

Joan's voice was icy as she said, 'Well they can rule that out quickly, as the barn wasn't even insured. Was it, Jim?' She got up from the table, knocking her chair over. 'I'm going to check on Donna.' She half ran out of the room.

The doctor bent down and righted the chair. 'You okay, Jim? Anything I can do?' Met with silence, he turned to Ethel, his eyebrows raised meaningfully. 'I need to get back to town. I'll pick you up later, Ethel. Try and get some sleep now.' He dropped a kiss onto her head and left the house.

'Are you going to tell me what's going on, Jim?' Ethel asked.

Jim expelled the air from his lungs loudly. 'I've messed up badly, Ethel. I took a vacation from paying the insurance premiums – just for a couple of months. Joan found out and went berserk. I promised to reinstate them but–'

'But you hadn't got around to it?'

He nodded.

'How much was the barn worth?'

'Enough. Enough to set us back several years. Oh, God, Ethel. I've been a fool. I was going to sort it out, but things have been hectic lately. I kept telling myself I'd do it tomorrow.'

'How long's this been going on?'

'I promised to sort it out back in March.'

'Oh, Jim. It's already May now.'

'She'll never forgive me.'

'Of course she will. Joan knows you're under a lot of pressure. However hard it is, you'll both get through this. Together.'

'I need to go into town and see the police and the fire chief. At least I can clear up any suspicion that I set the fire myself.'

'No one in their right mind would think that of you, Jim.'

'They have to follow every possibility.'

'You need to tell them it was Tip Howardson.' Ethel shook her head. 'He needs to be locked up. What a vindictive, evil man. He knew Alice and the girls were staying there. Catherine's his daughter, for pity's sake.'

'But the girls were safe in the farmhouse,' said Jim. 'He would have known that Ma wouldn't have left them alone in

Alice's place. It would have been easy enough for him to start the fire and get away before Ma even knew what was happening.'

'I suppose that makes sense,' said Ethel.

Jim got up from the table and moved towards the door. 'Oh, and the chief said it looks like the fire began in Alice's place and spread from there to the barn. Howardson was definitely getting at Alice. The son of a bitch.'

38

*D*uncan picked Ethel up that evening from the farm. They were going to a piano recital in Kitchener. Both exhausted after being up all night, Ethel had at least managed to get some sleep in the morning, but the doctor had to face a normal day's work. She'd tried to convince him to give the concert a miss, but he wouldn't hear of it.

'We won't get another chance in who knows how long to hear this guy playing.'

As they drove, Ethel told him about the fire chief confirming the source of the fire was Alice's house not the barn. 'That means it must be Howardson.'

'How do we know?' The doctor's face was grave.

'Jim's got no proof, but who else round here is going to torch Alice's place?'

'He was angry enough when he left the movie theatre. And angry at Alice. But how could he be really sure those kids weren't there? And one of them is his own daughter.'

'Jim says he knows Alice wouldn't have left them on their own. He'd have realised they were with Mrs Armstrong in the farmhouse. And he probably went in and had a look around.'

'If the wind had been in the other direction the whole place could have gone up including the farmhouse.' He shook his head, his fingers white where he gripped the steering wheel. 'And to think that madman has been hanging around my daughter.'

Ethel put her hand on his arm. 'Not any more though. You can be sure of that.'

'How can I be sure? Sandra's barely speaking to me. She locks herself away in her room. And I can't watch her all the time. Tonight for example – how do I know she hasn't arranged to see him?'

'Surely not. Not now that she knows what he's capable of.'

'Jim warned Alice about him but that didn't stop her seeing him. Having a child with him!' He banged his palm against the steering wheel. 'He's clearly a persuasive man when he wants to be. He had Sandra completely under his spell.'

Ethel tightened her fingers into fists. 'There's something else. Something Sandra told me about a girl she knows. She was adamant she wasn't talking about herself but about a former school friend. She said this friend had a boyfriend who was always pushing her to go further than she wanted.'

Duncan turned the steering wheel, spinning the car around, almost throwing Ethel out of her seat. 'Why didn't you tell me this before? Sandra has no friends.' His expression was grim, and he drove so fast that Ethel had to cling onto the edge of the seat. 'How can I sit in a concert hall when that maniac might be with my daughter?'

They drove on in silence, Ethel squirming in shame that she hadn't told him of her fears before. How had she been so stupid? She prayed that when they got back to town they'd find Sandra at home.

But when they reached the doctor's house, there was no one there.

~

They eventually found Sandra in Freddo's. She was sitting alone at the back of the café, slumped over the table, her head on her elbows, an untouched hot chocolate in front of her.

'She's been here for an hour,' said Freddo, nodding towards the back of the room. 'I was about to close up but she's showing no sign of wanting to go home. I didn't want to throw her out.'

Duncan reached for Ethel's hand and they moved together towards the table. Sandra was in one of the booths that lined the rear wall and they slid onto the banquette opposite her. She lifted her head and they saw she'd been crying. Her eyes were red-rimmed, and her face was blotchy with black streaks under her eyes where her mascara had run. Ethel noticed that she was wearing lipstick, and eyeshadow too.

'Steve said he'd meet me here. But he hasn't come.' She began to sob again. Big jerky sobs.

Duncan exchanged a look with Ethel then moved to the other side of the table and put his arms around his daughter.

Sandra raised her eyes. 'I thought you were going to a concert.'

'It was cancelled,' he said, quickly, glancing again at Ethel.

Ethel rummaged in her handbag and found a clean

handkerchief. She passed it over the table to Sandra who scrubbed at her eyes with it.

'Oh, Dad, he hasn't shown up.' She wiped her nose, then looked at Ethel, hatred in her eyes. 'You turned him against me. All that stuff you and Mrs Armstrong said. It wasn't true. He told me it wasn't.'

'When did you see him?'

'Last week. You were on your calls. He came by the house.'

Duncan sucked air into his lungs and Ethel could see he was trying to control his temper. 'He came to the house?'

Sandra nodded. 'He told me he knew Jim Armstrong from years ago when they were in the army in the war. He said Mr Armstrong resented him because he was his superior officer, even though Steve's younger than him. Mr Armstrong's got a real grudge against Steve. All that stuff about Steve attacking Mrs Armstrong was untrue. She'd been coming on to him and didn't want her husband to find out.'

Ethel could stand it no longer. 'That's utter rubbish, Sandra. Joan's never looked at another man since she met Jim. Don't you dare try and blacken her name.'

'Calm down. Both of you.' Duncan turned and called over his shoulder to Freddo, who was patiently but unnecessarily polishing the chrome taps of the soda fountain, 'Sorry, Freddo, but we need three coffees over here.'

Freddo brought a tray of drinks over, removing Sandra's congealed chocolate.

'We won't keep you too long, Freddo.'

'Don't you worry about that, Doc. You can stay all night if you need to. I hate to see Sandra so sad.'

Duncan took his daughter's hand. 'Sandra, you may not want to believe all these things about Tip Howardson, but you need to understand, he's a bad man. And it's not just everything you heard from the Armstrongs and Ethel here, he stole your car–'

'He didn't steal it. I gave him the keys. He always drove it when we went out. Said it wasn't right for a woman to drive a man about. He's considerate like that.'

Ethel could tell Duncan was struggling to control his rage.

'He set your car alight and abandoned it in the middle of nowhere.'

'That wasn't him. He stopped to get gas and, while he was paying, someone stole the car.'

Duncan expelled his breath impatiently. He grabbed Sandra's hands and turned her to look at him. 'That's not all. The barn over at Hollowtree burned down last night.'

'I know. I heard the fire trucks.'

'It was deliberate. Arson. They found empty cans of petrol.'

'Oh, no, no, no! No, you don't. Don't you dare try and put the blame on Steve.'

'His name's not Steve, for Christ's sake, Sandra. And yes, it was Howardson. The police are searching for him now.'

Duncan looked at Ethel, his expression a mixture of anger and helplessness in the face of his daughter's intransigence and delusion.

Ethel said, 'Your dad's right. I know it's hard for you to accept this about the man you trust. I know you care for him, Sandra.' The words were sticking in her throat, but she forced herself to continue. 'When we care for someone, we can often be blind to their faults. The Steve you know and... felt for... well, he's like a different person from the Tip Howardson we're talking about. But they are the same person.'

Sandra was looking at her now.

'It may take you some time to see that good Steve and bad Howardson are one and the same person.' She paused. 'It happened to Alice Armstrong too–'

Sandra jerked away from her father and glared at Ethel across the Formica table. 'That's not true.'

Ethel looked at Duncan, who nodded. She chose her words carefully. 'Howardson's the father of Alice's younger daughter. He made Alice pregnant then refused to marry her. Just last night he turned up at the new cinema.' She paused again, watching Sandra intently. 'He asked Alice to marry him, then, when she threw him out, he went over to Hollowtree and set fire to her place.'

'He would never have asked her to marry him. It's not true. He wants to marry me.' She began to sob again.

'Maybe he does,' Ethel said, trying to humour her. 'But he knows Alice is a wealthy woman and he wants a part of that.'

Sandra turned towards her father, her eyes wild. 'Is she telling the truth, Dad?'

He nodded, and Sandra's tears flowed again. She buried her face in his jacket and he held her tightly as she wept. She jerked back her head. 'Take me home, Dad. I want to go home.'

39

*I*t was the middle of the afternoon when Jim walked into the kitchen. Joan had been cold-shouldering him since breakfast the previous day when he'd admitted he'd failed to reinstate the farm's insurance. She'd served his meals in silence, talking only to the boys. When he'd tried to put his arms around her in bed she turned away from him and moved to the edge of the mattress.

Now she was sitting at the scrubbed pine table, sewing name tapes into Jimmy's school sports clothes. Jim scraped back the chair opposite her and sat down. 'We need to talk.'

Joan continued to sew, not even looking up.

'I mean, *I* need to apologise.' Silence greeted him. 'I'm sorry, Joan. It wasn't that I deliberately didn't renew the insurance – just that I hadn't got round to it, what with getting in the main crop potatoes and mending the broken fences round the Hollowtree pasture.'

Joan looked up at him. 'I don't want to hear your excuses. You told me you were going to sort it out right away. You lied to me.'

'I didn't lie to you.'

'So, telling me you were going to pay it right away and then deciding it wasn't important enough, isn't lying to me?'

Jim looked down. 'I told you. I meant to do it. Come on, Joan, don't be like that.'

'Like what? A pain in the arse? A nag? Is that what you think I am?'

'I never said that.'

'But that's what you meant, isn't it?'

'For Pete's sake, stop putting my words in my mouth.'

'It's about trust. And we've been here before. I left you and went back to England when I believed I couldn't trust you before. You convinced me to give you a second chance and now you've betrayed my trust again. Not once but twice.' She bit through the cotton thread with her teeth, rethreaded her needle and picked up a pair of shorts. 'First, by stopping the premiums without telling me and then by promising me you'd reinstate them right away. How do you think that makes me feel?'

He tried to take her hand, but she jerked it away.

'I'm sorry. It was stupid. But it wasn't deliberate. I just kept thinking I'd do it later. I never dreamt that bastard Howardson would burn the damn barn down.'

Joan bowed her head over her sewing, trying to control her anger. Tears of frustration and disappointment stung the back of her eyes. 'We talked about it. What did I say? Insurance only seems like a waste of money until you need to make a claim.'

'I've certainly learned that lesson.'

'I'm your wife. How many times do I have to get it through that skull of yours that marriage is all about trust? If you were too darned busy, you could have got me to do it.'

'You have Donna and Harry to think about. And everything else.'

She flung the pair of shorts down. 'I've told you before. Having children hasn't addled my brain. For heaven's sake, Jim, it would have been a ten-minute job.'

Jim filled his lungs with air and let it out slowly. 'I am truly sorry. I've messed up badly. On so many counts.'

She looked at him, her gaze steady. 'What are we going to do?'

'We'll have to delay the investment in the sugar house in order to pay to rebuild the barn. And then there's the loss of the livestock and the hay. Not to mention all the tools and kit in there – including the corn picker and the new tractor.'

Joan closed her eyes, struggling to control her anger. 'How much has this put us back?'

'A couple of years. Maybe three.'

She gasped. 'We were relying on that sugar plant. You reckoned it was going to boost our income by about twenty per cent.'

'I know. If only I could turn the clock back. I've been a damned fool.'

Joan picked up her sewing again. 'What if you delayed rebuilding the barn? Or even not rebuild it at all.'

'I can't not rebuild it. What about Ma? The cows. The butter.'

'You were saying only a couple of months ago that the livestock's more trouble than it's worth. And the tiny amount of cream and butter your mother makes isn't economical. It's only enough for the family and for making her precious butter pies.'

'Come on, Joan. That's a low blow! We can't. That would be like cutting off Ma's legs. And anyway...' His voice tailed off and he looked away.

'And anyway what? You haven't told her about the insurance, have you?'

Jim's expression was sheepish. 'You know what Ma's like.'

'Well, you can damn well get over there and break the news to her. Because we have to start rethinking our priorities to get this farm back on an even track – and building a new barn for your mother to keep a couple of cows and a goat isn't one of them.'

'Joanie–'

'Don't Joanie me. Are you going to tell her, or will I?' She started to get up from the table.

'I'll go and see her now.'

When Jim returned a couple of hours later, he was grinning. Joan was getting the boys their supper. Jimmy and Sam seemed more intent on bickering than washing their hands as their mother had asked. Seeing Jim's cheerful demeanour irritated her, and she yelled at the boys. 'I won't ask you again. Get your hands washed then you can come back here and set the table.'

Once the two boys had left the room, dragging their feet and muttering at each other, Jim put his hands on Joan's shoulders, still smiling. 'That wasn't so bad.'

'She agreed?' Joan was stunned. It was unlike Helga Armstrong to give way so easily, particularly on anything that involved change and to what she regarded as her personal domain within the farm.

'Better than that. Alice was there. She's offered to lend us the money to rebuild and to replace everything we lost. Interest-free.'

'What?' Joan shrugged his hands from her shoulders

and stepped back. 'I hope you told her that's not going to happen.'

'Why ever not? It's the answer to our prayers.'

'We're not taking charity from Alice.' Joan folded her arms.

'It's not charity. It's a loan. Alice is family and she has money coming out of her ears. She's pleased to help.'

'Out of the question. We're not going to be dependent on Alice for the future of this farm. It's too important. If we can't do it ourselves, we don't do it at all.'

'Have you lost your mind, Joan? We have four kids to support. We can't just refuse Alice's kindness because of your pride.'

Joan turned on him, furious. 'My pride? This is nothing to do with my pride. It's entirely down to your negligence.'

'How many times do I have to tell you? I'm sorry. But now this is about running the farm and that's down to me, not you. And I'm going to take Alice's money whether you like it or not.' He left the kitchen, slamming the door behind him.

Ethel was driving into the farmyard as Jim left the house. Duncan was in the passenger seat, giving her a driving lesson. Seeing Jim storming off towards the Rivercreek barn, his face like thunder, she hastily kissed Duncan goodbye and went into the house.

Joan was standing by the stove, crying. Ethel rushed over and put her arms around her. 'What's wrong, love? Have you two had a row? Is it about the insurance?'

'He told you then?'

'Yesterday. After breakfast when you shot out of the

room.'

'Alice has offered to lend us the money to rebuild the barn and replace the tractor and any other equipment. Thousands of dollars.'

'That's good of her.'

'I won't have us being beholden to Alice.' Joan pulled away.

'Why not? She's family, isn't she?'

'You sound just like Jim. And anyway, since when have you changed your tune about Alice?' She wiped the back of her hand over her eyes.

'Since you persuaded me to accept her help in setting up the hair salon. You were happy enough for *me* to be beholden to her.'

'That was different. She was making an investment in you. She's offering us an interest-free loan.'

Ethel went over to the sink to fill the kettle. 'Let's have a nice cup of tea and talk about it.' She looked back over her shoulder. 'You could always make it an investment for her. Offer her a share in the profits.'

'Jim would never agree to that.'

When the tea was made, they went with it into the sitting room rather than sitting as usual across the kitchen table.

'What kind of a marriage do we have when we can't trust each other?'

'You have the best marriage I've ever seen. Look, Joan, everyone makes mistakes. Even Jim.'

'I can't trust him. He went behind my back to cancel those premiums and then when I found out he promised to reinstate them immediately but, more than a month later, he still hadn't.'

'He's got a lot on his mind, what with his father dying,

the new baby, all the responsibilities of the farm.'

'That's just it. Exactly! The responsibilities of the farm – and making sure he insures it, so we don't go under, is right at the top of that list.'

'I'm sure he had a good reason–'

'If he'd had a good reason he should have told me. But no, the only reason he claims is that he just didn't get round to it.'

'A very human reason.'

Joan snorted.

'An honest one.'

Joan still said nothing.

'I know Jim is mortified. He feels terrible. I just saw him storming off looking as angry as I've ever seen him. And you and I know that anger is directed at himself, not at you.'

Lifting her eyes, Joan looked at her cousin then dropped her gaze.

'What you and Jim have is too precious to fall out over something like this. You love each other. You love your kids. Don't let anger and resentment ruin that, Joanie. Please. Jim is a wonderful chap, but you sometimes hold him to impossible standards. He made a mistake, and one we all know he'll never make again. But he *is* human.'

Joan gave a little sob and pushed her tea away. 'Can you give the boys their supper? Stew's on the stove.' She left the room and went to find her husband.

Jim was sitting on a hay bale with his head in his hands.

'Room for one more on there?'

He looked up and she saw the hope in his eyes. Joan perched on his knees and put her arms round his neck and her head on his shoulder. 'We'll get through this,' she said. 'We'll get through it together.'

'I'm truly sorry, Joan.'

'I know you are. I'm sorry too that I was so angry with you. Ethel's made me see sense. Nothing matters as long as we're together. The only thing I couldn't cope with is being without you.'

'I'll tell Alice we'll find a way to do without her money.'

'No. If Alice wants to help we should let her. Something Ethel said gave me an idea. If we take her money for the barn and the kit we can still make the investment in the sugar house as planned?'

He nodded.

'In that case, why don't we pay for our losses ourselves and use her money to fund the sugar house? We could treat it as her investment in the maple syrup production and give her a stake and a share of the profits. We operate it and she's the sleeping partner. Just like Ethel's hair salon.'

Jim thought for a moment. 'That's not such a bad idea.'

'And I know she'll want to. She's looking for business ideas.'

He nodded slowly, still thinking. 'I think Alice blames herself for Howardson coming back to Hollowtree.'

'Everyone in Hollowtree is a bit too handy with pouring blame on their own heads. That man is insane. Destroying the barn and everything in it is down to him and him alone, and the sooner he's behind bars the better. Now, I don't want to talk about him, or Alice, or your ma. Ethel's going to give the kids their supper. We have some making up to do and only an hour before Donna needs her feed.'

Jim's face broke into a grin as he jumped off the bale, pulling her behind him and led her by the hand to the back of the barn.

hree days after the fire, Alice bought a house. It wasn't pretentious – just a comfortable family home, a few streets away from the main street in Hollowtree. There was a garden with a lawn and a tree from which the previous owners had suspended a pair of swings – perfect for Rose and Catherine. There was enough room for Helga to move in, if she ever chose to – but Alice knew it would take a lot to convince her mother-in-law to leave the farm. And as to her own mother? She was a lost cause.

Her pleasure in having a place she could truly call her own was tinged with regret. Walt would never see it and the home he had built her – little more than a glorified shack – was now just a pile of charcoal and ash. Even though she had not intended to live there longer term, it was painful knowing it was gone, and everything that had belonged to Walt with it. But Alice was determined not to brood. Life must go on. And this new house would be a wonderful family home.

When the deal was done and the keys to her new home in her pocket, she walked back into town, intending to drop by the salon to call in on Ethel, and then onto the movie theatre. She now kept an office there, having outgrown the table at Freddo's.

Alice was excited about the future. Her aunt had not only set her free financially, she had opened new doors for her.

And Mr Freeman had written with some good news about his investigations into Tip Howardson. Apparently, he was wanted in the United States for racketeering and possible involvement in the death of his former wife, whose charred remains were found in the burnt-out ruins of her home in Chicago. Mr Freeman had contacted the Mounted Police and alerted them to Howardson's presence in Canada and the goings-on in Hollowtree. Alice was optimistic. It was only a matter of time before he would be brought to justice – and not a moment too soon.

She strode along, mulling over what her next project would be. Mr Freeman had cautioned her not to overstretch herself and to allow her two business ventures to bed-in before embarking on another, but Alice had the bug for it now. She loved the idea of businesses that she could finance without actually running them herself. Jim's suggestion for her funding his maple syrup plant was perfect. What next? A bookshop? A farm produce store? A beauty parlour next to the hair salon?

But folk round here preferred to use the library rather than buying books – and those who read were anyway a minority. Farm produce would compete with the general store and it might be better not to take them on so early in the game. And it was hard to picture farmers' wives, hands calloused from hard work, nails chipped and dirty from planting, queuing up to have a manicure. Maybe she should ask people what they wanted. But Alice had been borrowing business books from the library and read that people never knew what they wanted until you gave it to them, because they lacked imagination. It was Henry Ford, wasn't it? What was it he'd said about the Model T automobile? Something about if he'd asked people what they wanted they'd have said a faster horse.

She weighed up the possibility of a dress shop. Now that Ethel was ministering to their coiffures it would surely make sense for local women to have somewhere in town other than the general store with its poor selection of dressmaking fabric and a few tired blouses. No wonder most people relied on ordering from the Eaton's Catalogue.

Yes, a place where women could relax, try on garments and get expert advice. That would really be something! Alice herself would be of no use in that regard – while her interest in clothes was growing, her knowledge was limited. No – she would do as she had done with Ethel and Jim and invest behind someone with the requisite expertise.

She was so caught up in thinking that she didn't see Tip Howardson until she was almost upon him. He was leaning against the trunk of a tree, smoking as usual, a motorbike propped up on its stand at the edge of the road.

'Well, if it isn't my future wife. I was planning on heading over to Hollowtree Farm today to call on you. And to see our little girl, of course.'

Alice stared at him. 'Why do you hate us so much?' she said, at last.

'I don't hate you, Alice. I love you. I'm going to marry you.'

She ignored the comment. 'Why do you hate Jim? Why do you keep picking on him? You know Hollowtree belongs to him.'

Howardson face expressed surprise – undoubtedly feigned. 'Of course, I know that. What's the news in that?'

'I mean that you burnt down my home and Jim's barn. That's what I mean.'

'There's been a fire?' He whistled. 'That's bad. No rain for a week. I guess things get dry. All it takes is a small spark.'

'Don't give me that, Tip. I know it was you. Now answer my question. Why do you hate Jim?'

'I had nothing to do with a barn burning and I have an alibi to prove it.'

She snarled at him, triumphant. 'How can you have an alibi if you don't even know when the fire happened?'

He laughed sardonically. 'It was the night your fancy picture palace opened. I heard the sirens and the bells. Just didn't know it was Hollowtree Farm.'

'Well, you're going to need that alibi because the police are looking for you. And that's not the only alibi you're going to need. Now answer me. Why do you hate Jim so much?'

He crushed the butt of his cigarette beneath his heel and immediately lit another one. He exhaled a series of smoke rings and said, 'Because he always gets what he wants, starting with you when we were in school.'

Alice shook her head in disbelief. 'That was years ago. We were kids, for goodness' sake.'

'Then again in Aldershot. He was a cocky son of a bitch. Popular with all the guys. They hated me.'

'You're breaking my heart, Tip. Maybe you should try being nice to people for a change.'

He laughed. 'Always happy to be nice to you, Alice.' He reached out and grabbed her arm, jerking her towards him.

'In fact, let's take a walk in those woods over there and I'll show you how nice I can be.'

She pulled her arm free. 'Torching those buildings up at Hollowtree hasn't harmed me. I've already got somewhere else to live.'

'Oh yeah?' His interest was piqued.

'But you won't be darkening the door. I'm calling my lawyer today to seek a legal injunction against you. But as it happens, it probably won't be needed. Once the police get their hands on you they're going to lock you away for years. You seem to make a habit of arson.' She was about to mention the dead ex-wife in the Chicago house fire but decided not to alert him that his past was catching up with him. 'There's also the car you stole and set fire to. The doc's daughter. Why the hell did you pick on her?'

'Why not? I've always enjoyed corrupting the innocent and I'm a sucker for a pretty face.'

'She's eighteen, for pity's sake!'

'Someone's going to fuck her someday. Might as well be me. I like a challenge. It's time that girl had her cherry popped. Especially since you're being such a stuck-up bitch at the moment.'

'Leave the kid alone. You're sick. It was the same with Joan. When she wasn't interested, you tried to rape her. Twice.'

'Ah, Joan. I always had a soft spot for her.' He reached out for Alice again, but she side-stepped him. 'But you, Alice, there's no one like you. I've told you before, you're the best fuck I ever had.'

'Why do you always have to be so crude. Wash your filthy mouth out.'

'You bring that out in me.'

'Well, enjoy the memories, Tip, because you won't be

getting near me again. And stay away from the Robinson girl.'

She started to walk off but turned back to face him. 'And whatever happens, Tip Howardson, I will *never* marry you and you will *never* see my daughter again.'

She heard the roar of ignition and the revs from the oversized engine as he raced his bike away in the opposite direction.

41

*T*he sun shimmered on the surface of the lake, causing the light to refract into a series of tiny rainbows. It was a warm day yet, as it was school term time, the park was almost deserted. Ethel and Duncan walked hand-in-hand beside the water's edge. This had become a custom for them since the weather had improved, meeting when the hairdressing salon and surgery were closed at lunchtime. They would eat sandwiches, drink homemade lemonade and talk.

Business at the salon was still brisk and word of Ethel's skill had spread around Hollowtree and the surrounding district. The women of the town were already questioning how they had managed for so long without an Ethel. And now that The Rose was the fulcrum of the town's night life, the farmers' wives had a reason for having their hair set, putting on their Sunday best, and coming into town to watch a movie.

Ethel and Duncan sat down on a bench beside the lake, watching geese and ducks swimming across the smooth surface. The sun was warm on Ethel's skin and she felt happy as she always did when she was with Duncan. She leaned against him, relishing the proximity of his body and the feel of it against her own.

'I'm going to move into town next month,' she said. 'Joan's coping really well with the baby and I think it's time I moved on. Give them some more room. It will be so much more convenient living above the salon. Alice has decorated it really nicely. I'm coming to the conclusion she's not so bad after all.'

Duncan put his drink down on the bench beside him and twisted round to look at her. 'Don't move in there. Come and live with me. Marry me, Ethel, please. I can't bear to wait any longer.' He squeezed her hand and his eyes locked on hers. 'Let's do it as soon as possible. I love you and I want to be with you all the time. I'm sick of saying goodnight and going home to an empty bed. I want to hold you all night long.' He fished in his pocket and pulled out a small box. 'Here – open it. I've been carrying it around in my pocket for weeks, waiting for the right moment. I didn't want to rush you.' He slid off the bench and bent down on one knee in front of her. 'Will you be my wife, Ethel Underwood?'

Ethel's heart hammered. He hadn't brought up the subject of marriage since Sandra's first emotional outburst. 'But what about Sandra?'

'What do you mean?'

'What does she think about us getting married?'

'I haven't told her.'

'Don't you think you should ask her first?'

'Hell, Ethel, I'm not asking my daughter's permission to marry you! Now, please answer me before I get cramp down here.'

'Of course I'll marry you, Duncan. I want nothing more than that. I love you.'

He jumped to his feet and flung his arms around her, knocking the lemonade bottle onto the ground.

When they finally broke apart from the kiss, Ethel said, 'Let's do it as soon as possible.'

His face broke into a grin. 'I'm going back right now to sort out a locum – I haven't had a break from work for years. And I'm taking you away on a honeymoon. Once I've sorted the date can you close the salon for a few days while we're away?'

Ethel looked up at him. 'Yes, yes, yes. Where will we go?'

'I'll have a think about that.'

'Can I make a request?'

'Your wish is my command.'

'I'd like to go to Niagara Falls. It looked so beautiful in that film.'

'Niagara Falls it is then.' He kissed her again.

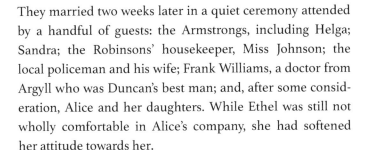

They married two weeks later in a quiet ceremony attended by a handful of guests: the Armstrongs, including Helga; Sandra; the Robinsons' housekeeper, Miss Johnson; the local policeman and his wife; Frank Williams, a doctor from Argyll who was Duncan's best man; and, after some consideration, Alice and her daughters. While Ethel was still not wholly comfortable in Alice's company, she had softened her attitude towards her.

The wedding breakfast was in a small hotel on the road between Hollowtree and Hartley. After waving the happy couple's car off on their honeymoon to Niagara, the children played in the garden while the adults lingered around the table, talking. Inevitably, they discussed the continuing war in Korea, now in a protracted stalemate while peace negotiations stuttered on.

Evidently bored by the conversation and the company, Sandra got up from the table. 'I'm going to head back home. You want a ride, Miss Johnson? I have my new car with me.'

Miss Johnson scrambled to her feet and the two women left.

As soon as they were gone, Joan said, 'I hate to be mean, but that girl's like a wet weekend in July.'

Alice shrugged. 'Poor kid's probably unhappy about her dad getting married. It's inevitable – another woman entering her domain.'

'I do feel sorry for the kid,' Joan replied. 'She's obviously lonely. And getting mixed up with You Know Who. Have you heard any news of him?'

'Thankfully not,' Alice said with a shudder. 'I talked to my lawyer about getting an injunction to protect us if he does turn up, but the law moves slowly. He's confident the police are going to find him. Honestly, Joan, he's got a list of crimes as long as your arm. But I tell you this, if I so much as lay eyes on Howardson again, I'll go out and buy myself a shotgun!'

Constable Mitcham looked over at the two women. 'Did I hear you mention Tip Howardson?'

Jim leaned forward, interested.

'The police force is still investigating that car theft and the fire you had up at Hollowtree Farm, but apparently the FBI are also making enquiries, as he's wanted for arson and the possible murder of his wife down in Chicago. There's a nationwide manhunt for him.'

'Well, I for one can't wait for that evil bastard to be behind bars,' Joan said.

'I'm pretty sure it won't be long now. He's run himself out

of road.' Mitcham snorted. 'He was a horrible snivelling little shit when we were at school, eh Jim? Never liked him. Rotten to the core.'

'I hope you're right and they catch him soon.' Alice looked pensive. 'I'm not a fan of the Robinson girl, but I'd hate for that swine to come near her again. I wouldn't wish Tip Howardson on my worst enemy.'

42

NIAGARA FALLS

*E*thel and Duncan arrived at Niagara Falls as dusk settled. After checking into their hotel and leaving the luggage with the porter, the newly-weds walked hand-in-hand towards the Falls, which were lit up in a spectacular display of light, a rainbow of colours. Ethel murmured that she'd never seen anything so beautiful.

'Neither have I. But I'm looking in your direction, Ethel.' Duncan moved closer, locking his eyes onto hers. 'I've never been so happy. *Never*.' She pressed her body against his.

She knew he was thinking of his first wife and, for a moment, she thought of Greg. With absolute certainty, she replied, 'Me neither. Never.'

'Let's go to bed,' he said, his voice husky.

They turned away from the bright lights of the Falls and hurried towards the hotel, holding hands and turning to look at each other as they walked. Ethel felt a combination of excitement and nerves. She wanted him so much.

When she emerged from the bathroom, wearing the nightdress Joan had given her as a wedding gift, Duncan gasped and moved towards her. 'You are so beautiful, my dearest darling girl. I have to keep telling myself that this isn't a dream.' He drew her into his arms. 'But you're shaking. What's wrong?'

'Just nervous. I've never done this before.' She looked up at him. 'Not even with my fiancé. We spent the night together in a hotel in London with single beds. We just kissed and held hands across the gap. He said he wanted to wait until we were married.' She hesitated, wondering whether it was right to be talking about another man when her husband was about to make love to her on their wedding night. But she didn't want any secrets between her and Duncan. 'I was grateful that he respected me. That he wanted to wait until we were married. There were so many stories about Canadians and American GIs having their way with English women, so I was glad he was different. But when he died, I wished so much that I'd told him I didn't want to wait.' She looked up at him shyly. 'But now I'm so glad.'

Duncan bent to kiss her urgently, then lifted her into his arms and carried her over to the bed. Ethel's nerves disappeared as she was swept up in desire for him. She relished the touch of his hands upon her skin and, overcoming her nerves, began to explore his body too. He broke off for a moment and turned on his side and she heard the rustle of something. As she was about to ask what he was doing, he rolled back and eased himself on top of her. She cried out when he entered her, clutching him tightly, arching her back as he moved in her, the pain giving way to waves of pleasure.

When it was over, and they lay back, side-by-side, spent and gasping, Duncan turned away from her again, fiddling under the covers and she realised he was removing a condom.

A wave of revulsion swept over her. 'What are you doing?' she asked. 'Why did you wear one of those things? Have you got a disease?' Then a worse thought came over her. 'You don't think I have, do you? I told you I've never been with anyone before.'

Duncan turned to look at her face. 'Where on earth did you get that idea? What are you talking about? Of course I don't think you have a disease – and nor do I.'

'In the war. When I worked in a munitions factory. They showed us a film. All about venereal diseases and said if you went with a man – especially a soldier – you should get him to wear a French Letter as it stopped you getting the clap, as the girls called it.'

He started to laugh. 'Oh, my darling girl, condoms certainly do that, but the main reason for using them is as contraception. Stopping pregnancy. If you don't like it – and I'd certainly rather not have to wear one – there are other methods we can use. It didn't seem appropriate to talk about such things before we were actually married so I thought I'd take responsibility for now.' He stroked her hair. 'But you could get fitted with a diaphragm. Or we could use the safe period – though it's not as reliable and involves a lot of abstinence.' He looked at her smiling apologetically. 'I don't like the thought of abstinence. Or we could use a mixture of both.'

'Why do we need any of it?' Ethel looked at him askance. 'We're *married*.'

'But you could get pregnant.'

'So?' She could feel her stomach sinking. Where was this going? Why did she have a bad feeling?

He gave an awkward laugh. 'You don't want that to happen, Ethel. Neither of us want that.'

Ethel drew her legs up in front of her and sat upright. 'Who says? I never said that.'

Duncan looked shocked. 'But we talked about it. You said you didn't want to have children.'

'I never did.' She was indignant.

'You did. When we went to Argyll for a drink. Our first date. I asked if you wanted children and you said you didn't.'

She gazed at him, open-mouthed, then said, 'I said I hadn't *missed* having children. Not the same thing at all.'

Duncan stared at her, his face anguished, words deserting him.

'I love you, Duncan. And things are different when you love someone and get married.' She looked down at him where he lay on the bed beside her. He rolled onto his back, eyes closed.

'Having a baby with you is different from whether or not I wanted to have a baby when I was on my own. I didn't feel a child was missing. Only love was missing. But now I have love, and if a baby happens then that's a completely different story. If it doesn't, we'll still have each other. But if it does–'

He interrupted, his voice quiet but firm. 'I don't want us to have a baby.'

It was a punch in the stomach. Shocked, she whispered, 'You don't want it? You don't want us to be a family?'

'We *are* a family. I just don't want to have more children.'

She gasped, anger now flooding into her. '*More* children? I don't have *any* children. What on earth are you saying?'

Duncan reached up and tried to pull her down onto the mattress beside him. Ethel pushed his hands away. She started to cry. It wasn't meant to be like this. Her honeymoon was supposed to be magical. And until now it had been. But at this moment her world was rocking off its axis.

Duncan sat up and put his arms around her. She shrugged him off and got out of the bed. Grabbing her negligee and pulling it on, she sat opposite him in the chair, fear and anger running through her. 'What's all this about, Duncan? Why are you saying these things? And why now? Why not before?'

'You mean if I'd said it before, you wouldn't have married me? Is that what you're saying? That you'd only have married me if we could have children?' His voice was cold. The love and warmth of their lovemaking seemed a distant past. A chasm had opened up between them, as deep as the waterfalls they had just seen.

'I didn't say that at all. You're twisting my words.'

'I genuinely believed you didn't want to have children, Ethel. I thought you felt as I do – that all we need is each other. *You* are enough for me. As far as I'm concerned, we're complete already.'

Ethel stared at him, realising she didn't know him at all. She had made a terrible mistake, allowing herself to rush headlong into marriage after only a matter of months with a man who was little more than a stranger. She started to cry. Duncan didn't really love her. If he did, he would want her to have his children – or at least he wouldn't want to actively prevent that possibility.

'Please don't cry, my darling. I hate to see you unhappy, to see I've hurt you. I love you and the last thing I want to do is upset you. Don't you understand it's because I love you so much, Ethel? You are enough for me. I thought I was enough for you.'

'You are. If children don't happen, it wouldn't change how I feel about you.' Her words mingled with her sobbing. 'But that's very different from taking steps to prevent the possibility. To do what you're doing is to show you don't want to have a baby with me, that the very idea is...' She struggled for the right word then decided it was pointless. How could she convey the depths of her hurt? It was a rejection. A terrible loneliness swamped her; desolation, like a dark fog.

Duncan was watching her intently, his face contorted with anxiety. 'I love you, Ethel. Completely, madly, more than I can find the words to express. Not wanting a baby is not a rejection of you. It's the opposite.'

She stared at him, uncomprehending.

'You're all I need.'

'You've made me feel cheap. You want to have sex with me but not to have children with me. Do you have any idea how hurtful that is?'

Duncan closed his eyes and leaned back against the headboard. Eventually he spoke. 'My late wife... I told you she died of complications when Sandra was born. Well, it wasn't strictly true. Helen had suffered with her nerves ever since we moved to Sioux Lookout. She hated the isolation up there. She hated the months of snow. But after Sandra was born she disappeared into a black hole. I can't begin to tell you how terrible it was. How distressing for me to watch her. She didn't want anything to do with the baby.' He buried his head in his hands. 'It was the worst time of my life. Each day was worse than the one before. I began to believe this was how it would be for ever. I had to get a local woman to come to the house to care for Sandra as Helen wouldn't go near her. Then, one day, she woke up and seemed different. Happier. She got up. Got dressed – she'd spent weeks wearing only her dressing gown. I thought we'd turned the corner at last. It was a huge relief. I went to work. I said I'd be back as usual at lunchtime.'

His head was in his hands and Ethel suddenly felt

afraid. He dropped his hands and looked up at her. She fixed her eyes on his face, reading the pain which radiated from him.

'When I came home I heard the baby crying. I went into the bedroom and Sandra was soaking wet in her cot in a soiled nappy. There was no sign of Helen. No sign either of Mrs Foster, the home help.'

He twisted his hands together. 'I cleaned the baby up and searched the house for Helen. Nothing. Not even a note. We lived in an isolated spot at the end of a long road. The nearest neighbours were about five hundred yards away. I settled Sandra down in her cot to sleep and went outside to look for Helen. There were no footprints in the snow, but there'd been a fresh fall that morning. I found her body in the boat-shed by the lake at the bottom of our property. She'd hanged herself from a beam.'

Ethel stared at Duncan in horror, her hand clamped over her mouth.

'I later discovered she'd sent the home help away. As she'd appeared so unusually rational, Mrs Foster accepted what she was saying. Thought she must be back to normal. When she heard what Helen had done, she was wracked with guilt, poor woman. But Helen would have done it anyway. She'd have found the moment. If not that day it would have been another.'

Ethel moved to the bed, climbed up and knelt beside him, wrapping her arms around him.

'I'll never forget finding her. Dangling on a piece of rope. She'd pushed an upturned rowing boat under the ceiling beam, slung the rope over the rafter, climbed on top and pushed herself off.'

Ethel kissed the top of his head, her hands stroking his hair.

'There needs to be more research into the way childbirth can affect women. In Helen's case I'm certain if she hadn't had Sandra it wouldn't have happened.'

'But you said she had nervous problems anyway – she didn't like where you were living.'

'It was nothing in comparison. Before the baby, she was like Sandra is now – she had mood swings. But not that darkness, that descent into total passivity and blankness. She stopped speaking, stopped caring about anything. She was in a place where I couldn't reach her – locked away inside herself. Lost.' He looked up at Ethel. 'Don't you see? I can't let that happen to you. I've never forgiven myself for what Helen did and I won't risk that happening to you.'

Tears pricked at Ethel's eyes. 'It won't. I'm not Helen. Not all women suffer that way. You said she had difficulty coping with life anyway and having a baby made it worse. But you're a doctor. You know how rare that is. Most women are like Joan – they have babies and take joy in them. I know if I had your baby I would be so very happy. Don't you see that?'

He groaned and shook his head. 'I know. It's not logical. It goes deeper than logic.' He looked up at her, his eyes full of love and fear. 'I can't risk it. I can't let it happen to you, Ethel. I just can't. Please try to understand.' He grabbed for her hand. 'Sandra doesn't know her mother killed herself.'

'You haven't told her? Doesn't she have a right to know?'

'How could I possibly tell her? How would she feel knowing that her mother killed herself because she didn't want her?'

'You wouldn't say that. You'd tell her she was mentally disturbed. Not of sound mind.'

He shook his head. 'It would still feel to her that her mother had rejected her. That she'd preferred to kill herself rather than care for her and see her grow up. I can't do that to Sandra.'

Ethel wrapped her arms around him, her heart full of love for him, but her head full of misery. Had she made a terrible mistake? What had she let herself in for?

When she woke next morning, Ethel felt no better. Lying in the hotel bed, while Duncan was still sleeping beside her, she nursed her grievance. She rolled onto her side and studied his face. He looked calm and untroubled and she seethed with resentment towards him. So much for things feeling different in the morning – his words from the previous night stung her afresh in the harsh light of day. In spite of his protestations, his declared reluctance to have a child was, to Ethel, a rejection of her as his wife and an indication that he simply didn't love her enough.

Surely that was what marriage was all about – loving someone enough to want to have a child together? In refusing to contemplate becoming a father again, Duncan was regarding Ethel as unworthy of his love. His attitude was selfish. She couldn't find any justification for it. He had Sandra but was denying Ethel the opportunity to have her own child. Before meeting Duncan, she had not experienced any compulsion towards motherhood. She had never gazed into other women's prams, never for a moment envied Joan her children – much as she loved them. But now that it was being denied her – like a heavy door slamming shut in her face – she was bereft, wounded, damaged.

Duncan stirred in his sleep but settled again. She continued to watch his face, the steady pattern of his breathing, the slight flaring of his nostrils. His sleeping so peacefully while she lay here in turmoil made her pulse with indignation. And she didn't buy the excuse about his first wife's problems being entirely down to having a baby. Yes, what happened to her was shocking. Horrible. Ethel shuddered at the thought of a woman so young – a mother – being so desperate as to take her own life. But no one – particularly a medical man – could possibly think that what happened to Helen and what she had done was in any way commonplace for a new mother.

Ethel twisted her new wedding ring around her finger. Her legs were restless, twitchy. She thought about everything Duncan had said to her the night before. He must be using his late wife as an excuse. It boiled down to not wanting the disruption of becoming a father again in his forties, when he already had a grown-up child. While she couldn't blame him for feeling that way, she was angry that he'd waited until they were married before dropping that bombshell.

She slipped out of the bed, shivering as her bare feet hit the floor, and went into the bathroom, grateful that it was attached to their bedroom and she didn't have to pad along a draughty corridor to a bleak shared facility.

As she washed, she grew increasingly indignant. Duncan was selfish, unfair, and had married her under false pretences. He'd tricked her into saying that she hadn't missed having children. While it was true – she hadn't – it was not at all the same thing as *choosing* not to have them. And why, why, why hadn't he talked to her about it?

She shuddered, remembering the furtive scrambling to put on the condom, the crackle of the wrapper, the fiddling about as he put it on – underhand, shameful, awkward, embarrassing. Ethel felt cheap – dirty. What Duncan had done wasn't the kind of thing a man did with a wife he loved. It was tawdry, smutty, like a music hall joke. Jim Armstrong would never do anything like that. Look at him and Joan – four children and each one greeted with joy. While Ethel wouldn't blame her cousin if she and Jim decided not to have any more children, she was certain that such a decision would be taken jointly.

The towel was rough, but she rubbed it hard against her skin, uncaring of the redness it caused to her arms and legs. It was as if she were trying to scrub off the tracks of Duncan's touch. How could it have come to this? She loved him. Didn't she?

She sagged against the vanity unit. The mirror above the wash basin was steamed up and she rubbed at it with the towel. She looked awful: red-rimmed eyes from lack of sleep, hair tousled and flattened from tossing and turning all night. Yesterday had been the happiest day of her life. How could everything change so rapidly? Was she being unreasonable?

Ethel asked herself what her mother would have said had she been around to advise. Staring at her face in the mirror she tried to summon up her mother's counsel. Violet Underwood would have been unequivocal – why throw away her only chance at happiness? Her mum would have shaken her head and told her that compromise was the key to a happy marriage. The choice facing Ethel was clear – either accept Duncan's terms or destroy her marriage before it even started.

Through the door she could hear Duncan moving about the bedroom. Ethel hesitated, then, unwilling to roll over completely, she decided to appeal to Duncan's reason again.

He looked up at her warily as she came into the room. He was sitting on the end of the bed.

They started to speak at the same time, then each paused, only to crash into each other again. Ethel gave way.

'I'm sorry we argued last night, Ethel. I love you with all my heart and soul.'

Ethel squeezed her lips together. His eyes were sincere, and she felt a rush of love for him. It was going to be all right.

'That's why I don't want anything to come between us. You and I are all we need. We're already complete. We don't want to spoil that.'

Her heart sank. 'What are you saying?'

'That we don't need to have children to prove our love for each other. You are enough for me and I hope and pray that I'm enough for you.'

'Please don't say that. I never said you weren't enough for me.'

'Then you agree? And as I told you last night, we don't have to use prophylactics. There are other methods. Much less intrusive.'

'It's not about what method to use. It's about you not wanting to have a child with me.' Ethel could feel her heart pounding in her chest. Where was this going to end up?

'Are you saying that you *want* to have a baby?'

'Yes. I suppose I am.' Ethel was suddenly certain. 'Yes, I do want a child.'

'So that's the reason you married me, is it?' He frowned, his eyes cold.

'Don't be ridiculous.'

'What else can I assume? If this was such a big thing for you, why didn't you tell me?'

'Because we were getting married. That's what happens when people who love each other get married. They have babies.'

'Not when they're in their mid-forties.'

Ethel stared at her husband. She knew him so little. This was a stranger before her now, saying these things. How could she have been so deluded? 'I'm not even in my mid-thirties yet.'

Duncan bent forward, head in his hands. 'That's why I don't want to take the risk. You and I have a wonderful future ahead of us. Why should we jeopardise it? I couldn't go on if anything were to happen to you, Ethel.'

'You're being stupid.' Anger was rising inside her. 'You're using what happened to your wife as an excuse. Why don't you just come out and say it? Tell me you don't want to have a child with me.'

He said nothing.

Ethel grabbed her cardigan. 'I'm going for a walk.'

He started to get up.

'Alone.'

She banged the bedroom door behind her.

She made her way from the hotel towards the Falls, a short distance away, hoping walking would help clear her thinking.

At the rim of the waterfalls, she stared down at the spectacle in front of her. The water was emerald green, merging into jade beneath the clear early morning sky. Under the cascade it was a churning mass of white crashing foam. Birds circled and wheeled above the water, swooping and diving as if daring each other to get as close as possible to the turbulence. It was a majestic and terrifying sight, a cauldron of violent water, smashing into the rocks.

Ethel leaned on the railing. She could feel the vibration

from water hitting rock. It was elemental, primeval, powerful. An information sign told her that the water flowed at seven hundred and fifty gallons a second. She didn't know how to relate to that. Nor did she care. Duncan should be standing here beside her now, holding her hand, drinking in the beauty and power of the scene. Instead, she had never been lonelier.

Why was this coming between them? Ethel had a terrible choice facing her – either lose the chance of having a family or lose him. Why did she have to make this choice? It should never have come to that. Having a baby had been the last thing on her mind until this happened. Was she wrong now to let it come between them? Besides, what choice did she have? If she left Duncan she would be childless anyway, so why not stay and at least she would have him? Round and round her head the thoughts churned, a febrile mass of tangled emotions.

But whichever way she looked at the situation, something had been destroyed between them. Their love and trust had been shattered and had broken up like a boat going over the top of the falls, crushed on the rocks of Duncan's intransigence.

As she looked at the panorama in front of her, she made her mind up to go back to Hollowtree. She needed time to work out whether she would stay in Canada or return to England. But whatever she decided, she wasn't going to stay with Duncan. Suddenly she was certain. She didn't want to argue any more. Going back to that hotel room was unthinkable. Ethel walked towards the railway station and waited for the train.

Twenty minutes later she was in an almost empty carriage, blind to the passing scenery and the presence of the other passengers.

Returning to England was the obvious course of action. Staying in Hollowtree with Duncan just down the road was unthinkable. It had to be a clean break. But as those two words shaped themselves in Ethel's head, her heart raced and struggled to breathe. How would that be possible? How could she let him go? He was her husband. The love of her life.

Why not give in, swallow her pride and accept his condition? But doing that would be to betray herself.

The life Joan had was denied to her – Ethel could have the loving husband but no house full of children. Did she really want that for herself though? While Joan was blissfully happy, Ethel hated the thought of living entirely through her husband and family. Hairdressing was part of her life too. Duncan hadn't asked her to give that up. Was it so terrible to forgo the possibility of children when she didn't even know how she'd feel about a baby if she had one?

Or Ethel could take a leaf out of Alice's book and throw herself wholeheartedly into her work. Alice appeared to do well enough without a man around. But she had Rose and Catherine. Ethel would have no one. Just herself in that apartment over the salon.

To choose Duncan would mean she had her work and also him. She closed her eyes and, in her head, heard the rustle of the French letter wrapper. Sordid. Unnatural. Calculating.

She squeezed her hands into fists, feeling her fingernails bite into her palms. Why couldn't she have it all? It would be so easy. All Duncan had to do was say yes. And his fears were so stupid. Irrational.

But words and arguments were as nothing in the face of Ethel's feelings. The pain of losing Duncan cut through her, laying her bare, flaying her. Raw, empty, alone, miserable. She was back to where she'd been before she'd left England. No. Worse. Back then she'd been secure in the knowledge that Greg had loved her. Now Duncan had rejected her. His actions proved that he saw her as not good enough to be the mother of his children.

The tavern was deserted when Jim walked in. He blinked in the gloom and saw there was someone sitting in the shadows at the back, shoulders hunched, and arms slumped over the table.

Duncan Robinson got up as Jim approached. 'Thanks for coming, Jim. I ordered you a beer.'

Jim took a seat at the table and waited while the waiter brought over their beers. Something was seriously amiss. It seemed sneaky, going behind Ethel's back and coming here to Argyll, but Duncan had sounded desperate. And Joan had urged him to come.

They each took a gulp of beer then Duncan said, 'I've screwed up mightily, Jim. Ethel's left me.' His face was gaunt, his eyes wretched, and he hadn't shaved.

Jim was astonished it was as bad as that. 'But you were on your honeymoon. Where's Ethel gone? She's not with us. You do know that, don't you?'

Duncan nodded. 'We argued. She walked out of the hotel. Must have taken a train home. She didn't even come back to the room to collect her luggage. I think she's staying in the salon. But she won't see me. Won't answer the door. Hung the phone up on me. She doesn't want to see anyone. I'm terrified she's thinking of going back to England.' He groaned, rubbing his forehead.

Jim raised his eyebrows. 'Joan knows nothing of this. Ethel hasn't been in touch.'

'We argued on the first night of our honeymoon. Things were still bad between us in the morning, then she went out for a walk and didn't come back. I thought she was just clearing her head. I waited in the room. I wanted to go looking for her, but I kept thinking she'd be back any second and if I went out we might miss each other. When it was more than an hour I went all over Niagara Falls searching for her. It was hours before it dawned on me she must have taken herself back to Hollowtree.' He looked at Jim, his face abject.

'Look, Duncan, I don't really feel comfortable talking about this kind of thing. What happens in the bedroom should be kept between a man and his wife, so I'll say only this. You may need to give Ethel some time.' He looked away, embarrassed. 'Ethel's always been a bit of an innocent. Perhaps I can get Joan to have a word with her. Reassure her. You know what I mean...'

'No.' Duncan looked mortified. 'It's not that at all. Everything's fine in that department. More than fine. I told her I don't want us to have children and she flipped.'

Jim stared at him, stupefied. 'I'm not surprised, pal. That's quite a thing to drop into the conversation on your wedding night. Why the hell don't you want kids?'

'Look, I don't want to go into the details behind my reasons, but it's precisely because I care for Ethel so much... but she can't seem to understand that.'

'Sorry, Duncan, but I don't blame her. That must have

been a body blow to the poor girl.' He shook his head and took another mouthful of beer. 'Why didn't you clear this up with her before you asked her to marry you?'

'I thought I had. But it seems I misinterpreted what she said. I'm such a blessed fool.'

Jim looked at his friend, trying to read him, puzzled by what he was saying. 'So, let's just suppose you'd asked her fairly and squarely and she'd said she *did* want children. What would you have done? Walked away?'

'No!' Duncan's response was bullet-fast. 'I can't be without her.'

'Well, there's your answer. Go and tell her that.'

'But–'

'No buts. If you'd asked me if I wanted to have kids, before Joan had Jimmy, I'd have run a mile. Specially after what I saw in the war – bringing children into such a world was the last thing I wanted to do. But I love my kids now I've got them. I couldn't be without them.'

Duncan stared down at the table. 'I don't want to risk anything happening to Ethel. If she were to die...'

Jim paused, taken aback by the direction of the conversation. 'I'm not going to pry into what happened with your first wife, but whatever it was, Ethel's a different person. Hell, man, you're a doctor, you know the odds. All around the world women are having children every second and the vast majority do fine.'

Duncan gazed into his beer glass.

There was a long silence, then Jim decided bluntness was the best option. 'Look at it this way, Duncan. It sounds to me that unless you make it up with Ethel, you're going to lose her anyway. And you may be worrying pointlessly – she may not even get in the family way.' He looked thoughtful for a moment. 'But if it does happen, I can promise you, it's one of life's greatest blessings. Having kids has brought Joan and me closer together.' He drained his glass and beckoned the bartender. 'Let's have another beer.'

After sipping his fresh beer, Duncan said, 'Logically, I know you're right, Jim. But I'm scared.' He looked ashamed. 'It's hard to admit this, but you're the only real friend I have. I couldn't talk like this to anyone else – even my best man.' He lifted his glass then put it down again. 'Without going into the details, I feel responsible for my first wife's death. It haunts me.'

He pushed the beer glass away and looked Jim in the face. 'I feel guilty about the war too. The fact that I didn't serve. My brother was shot down over Germany on a bombing raid. I was back here bringing up Sandra. I never did my bit. What kind of man does that make me?'

Jim shook his head. 'Don't go there, pal. You had no choice with a small child. Don't beat yourself up about that. If I'd been in your shoes I wouldn't have joined up either.'

'I could have left Sandra with my folks. It might even have been better for her.'

'Duncan, you can't waste your life on what-ifs and might-have-beens. Anyway – you did your part back here. People in Hollowtree still needed a doctor.'

Duncan said nothing.

Jim looked at him, remembering how he had also suffered from guilt in the early days of his marriage. Guilt over what he had seen and done in the war. Over what he had not done. And most of all that he had come home and his brother, Walt, had not.

He took a slug of beer. 'Guilt's poison. It eats away at you. Believe me, I wrote the book about it. If I hadn't joined up, my brother wouldn't have done either, and he'd have still been here. He'd only been married a few weeks. I can't help thinking about that whenever I look at Alice and Rose – or even at my mother. Ma mourns the loss of Walt every day of her life. How am I supposed to live with that? But I do.'

'I didn't know. I mean I knew he'd been killed but I didn't know he only joined up because you did. How can you be sure he wouldn't have done it anyway? The pressure to serve was pretty strong. I certainly felt it.'

'Because I knew Walt. Going to war was the last thing he wanted. But he always believed he was in my shadow and wanted to measure up. If I'd stayed here, so would he. Pa might even have been alive today. Running Hollowtree on his own was more than he could manage.'

'Well, here's where I step in and tell you that's crazy.' The doctor shook his head. 'Your father's condition wasn't caused by hard work. Quite the contrary. It probably helped him at first. Kept him fit. So you've no need to feel bad about that.'

Duncan took another swig of beer. 'How did Walt die?'

'In the Dieppe raid. It was all over for him a year before I even got started.' Jim swigged some more beer and wiped his mouth with the back of his hand. 'Ironic, considering I joined up before he did. I was on the quayside at Newhaven doing the body count as they unloaded the dead from the ships. I didn't expect one of them to be my own brother.' Jim leaned back in his chair. 'So, yes, I do know all about guilt and I know it's corrosive. It nearly came between me and Joan. Don't let it get a hold, Duncan. You have everything going for you. Don't throw it away.'

Jim knocked back the rest of his beer. 'Ethel's a great girl. You're a lucky man to have her and I can tell you she's never been happier than she is with you. If she wants to have a baby, don't let it come between you. I promise you, pal, if it happens, it will be a wonderful thing. If it doesn't, you'll still have each other. But don't let Ethel walk out of your life.' He stretched out his hand and gave Duncan's arm a squeeze, withdrawing it quickly. 'Now get your beer down you, as I need to head home.'

Duncan slugged the rest of his drink back and stretched his mouth into a smile. 'Thanks, Jim. You're a good friend.'

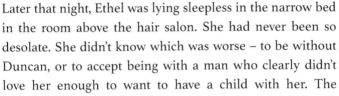

Later that night, Ethel was lying sleepless in the narrow bed in the room above the hair salon. She had never been so desolate. She didn't know which was worse – to be without Duncan, or to accept being with a man who clearly didn't love her enough to want to have a child with her. The thought of life without him was unbearable, unthinkable, but to accept marriage on his terms was anathema. How could she possibly agree to deny herself the possibility of motherhood, to have a child with the man she had believed to be the love of her life? But most of all she was hurt, cut to the core, rejected. How could he really love her and behave like that?

She would have to go back to England. Living here in Hollowtree and seeing Duncan all the time without being with him would be impossible. But she shuddered at the prospect of returning to Aldershot, to an empty house, to that miserable salon and bossy Vera, to a life without love. A life without Duncan.

Ethel knew she'd have to go and talk to Joan about what happened. She'd been putting it off, hiding out behind the closed doors of the salon, fearful of the humiliation of telling Joan that Duncan didn't want to have children with her. She cringed at the thought. Why, why, why? Duncan was behaving irrationally. It was crazy to think what had happened to Sandra's mother would happen to her. And to put it down to love for her? Where was the sense in that? When he knew the alternative was to lose her anyway.

Then it dawned on her. Duncan hadn't thought he was going to lose her. His twisted male logic had assumed that she would come round to his way of thinking; that she would give way and agree to a childless union rather than walk away from the marriage. Well, she wouldn't. She couldn't. It would be acknowledging that he didn't love her enough. Her sorrow turned to anger.

From below in the salon, she could hear someone hammering on the door. It could only be one person. She pulled the covers over her head and tried to ignore Duncan's frantic knocking. But he wasn't going to go away – the banging got louder. Afraid of waking the neighbours, Ethel scuttled downstairs and opened the door.

Duncan came in and leaned against the wall staring at her. Ethel's heart pounded as she waited for him to speak. She could smell the hops and yeast of beer. The despair in his eyes spoke louder than words.

'I'm sorry, Ethel,' he whispered eventually. 'Please come back to me. Please forgive me. I was wrong. If you want us to have a family, then I want that too.' He looked into her eyes. 'I can't promise I won't be afraid. But if it happens, and we have children together, I will love them because I love you.'

The ground swayed underneath Ethel. 'Nothing's going to happen to me, Duncan. I promise you.' Then she was in his arms.

When they paused in their kissing, he said, 'I've missed you, my beautiful girl.'

'I've missed you too, Duncan.'

Their lovemaking that night, on the carpeted floor of the tiny bedsit above the shop, was passionate yet tender. The packet of unused condoms lay in the trash bin. Ethel clung to him, holding onto him as though if she let go she would be washed away. She tousled his thick silky hair through her fingers and locked her eyes onto his.

'I love you, Duncan Robinson, with my whole heart and soul.'

44

The following morning, Ethel and Duncan woke at first light.

'Good morning, Mrs Robinson,' he said. 'It's time we went home. I want to carry you over the threshold then make love to you all over again in a big comfortable bed. I'm going to make things up to you for our lousy honeymoon.'

'It wasn't a completely lousy honeymoon. It started off rather well.'

'Until I screwed everything up.'

'Please, Duncan. Let's pretend it never happened.'

'We could always go back to Niagara. We have the rest of the week off. The salon's closed and the locum's covering for me. And Sandra's still at my folks' in Halifax.'

'No,' she said. 'I don't want to go back there. Maybe one day. But not now. Right now, I want you to take me home.'

～

As soon as he set Ethel down after carrying her over the threshold, they both sensed something was wrong. Even though it was Sunday and the surgery closed, the place didn't feel empty. Through the silence, they heard a faint noise from upstairs. They exchanged looks.

'Maybe Sandra decided to stay home?' Ethel said.

'Or has delayed leaving.'

They walked up the wide wooden staircase, Ethel feeling nervous and, if she were honest, annoyed. She hadn't expected to see her new stepdaughter yet and wasn't keen on spending these first days of married life with Sandra around the house.

They found her lying on the landing.

She was slumped against the bathroom door, her clothing torn, one of her breasts exposed and a bruise across her right cheek. Her stockings were laddered and there was a bloody streak across her forehead. Though her eyes were open, her expression was blank.

Ethel gave a little cry as Duncan rushed to his daughter and scooped her up off the floor.

Wordlessly, he carried her into her bedroom, Ethel following. Inside, the room was chaos. Broken glass littered the floor. A scent bottle had been swept off the dressing table and lay amid a pile of cosmetics and clothing. The bed looked like a crime scene, blood soaking the pillow, presumably from the blow to Sandra's head. There was also blood on the sheets. Ethel's foot caught something, and an empty beer bottle rolled across the wooden floor.

Sandra began to whimper.

'We can't put her there. Take her into the other room,' said Ethel.

Duncan, his face transfigured with anger, carried his daughter across the landing and laid her on the bed in his room.

'Get some hot water and towels. But pass me my bag

first.' He jerked his head in the direction of his black doctor's bag on a chair in the corner of the room.

Sandra's eyes were wild and frightened. She was twisting about on top of the bed, making little moaning noises. Ethel stood helpless, watching as her husband cleaned the wound on his daughter's face and applied a dressing. He opened his bag and took out a syringe then injected her in the arm. 'Just a mild sedative.' He turned to Ethel. 'I don't need to spell out to you what's happened.'

She shook her head.

'Can you call Colin Mitcham? Tell him to get over here right away. The number for the police station is on the wall by the telephone in the surgery.'

Ethel ran downstairs. When she returned, Sandra was sleeping.

'I'm going to move her into the spare room.' He fixed his eyes on Ethel. 'You know who was responsible for this, don't you?'

She nodded.

'I'll have to stay with her. Constable Mitcham will alert the provincial police but, on the basis of their failure to track the bastard down so far, I'm not going to rely on them.'

'He said they're all already looking for him. The FBI too – he's wanted in the States as well.'

'Since none of them have managed to find him so far...' He reached for her hand, leaving the sentence unsaid. 'Can you get over to Rivercreek and let Jim know what's happened? Ask him to get a bunch of guys together to try and track Howardson down. It can't have happened long ago. He must still be in the area. I'll put Colin in the picture when he gets here.'

'Don't you think we should wait for him? Howardson's dangerous. Surely it's better to leave it to the police.'

'They've been useless up to now. Jim and the locals will do a better job. They'll know where to look.' Seeing her still hesitating he said, 'Just do as I ask, Ethel. Please. Jim will know what to do.' He threw her the car keys.

Without waiting further, she ran out of the house, fired up the car and drove towards the farm.

The Armstrongs were having a late breakfast. Helga, Alice, Rose and Catherine had come over after church and were also seated at the table when Ethel burst in. They all looked up, shocked at her sudden appearance. She stumbled out an explanation, choosing her words carefully because of the children.

'Kids – go and play next door,' said Joan, ushering the four children into the sitting room.

Jim was on his feet and moving towards the telephone. 'I'll get up a search party.' He made a series of calls, barking instructions into the receiver. When he'd finished, he said, 'We're meeting in town and we'll divide into groups. Don't worry, Ethel. We'll find that son of a bitch.' Then he was gone, the door slamming behind him and the truck bursting into life outside in the yard.

The four women looked at each other. 'How is Sandra?' asked Joan. 'Did he hurt her badly?'

'She's in a terrible state. Mentally more than physically, I suspect. Her face is badly bruised and cut. A lot of blood.' She looked around the table at them. 'And not just from her face,' she said meaningfully. 'She must have put up quite a fight and it appears he was very rough with her.'

Helga crossed herself. 'Holy Mother of God. That man is the devil himself.'

'Duncan's sedated her. She was terrified, traumatised. The poor girl. I've never seen anyone in such a state before.'

Alice scraped her chair back and got up. 'Joan, Ma, I'm leaving the girls with you. I'm going to find that pig. I know exactly where to find him.'

'No!' Joan grabbed Alice's arm. He's dangerous. Stay here, Alice. Leave it to the men.'

'He'll never touch me. I'll be fine. Safer than they will. And he might just listen to me.'

'He'll listen to no one.'

Ethel looked at Alice. 'I'll come with you.'

'Please, no!' Joan sounded desperate. 'He might be armed. Stay here, Ethel. You don't know what he's capable of.'

'If anyone knows what that man is capable of, it's me. He killed my fiancé and now he's raped and beaten up my step-daughter.' Her face was defiant. 'Just try and stop me, Joan!' She grabbed Alice's sleeve. 'Come on then. What are we waiting for? Car's outside.'

As Ethel gunned the car down the road, her usual car-driving nerves replaced by anger and adrenaline, Alice gave her directions. They were heading to the former Howardson farm, which was about ten miles north of the town – around fifteen miles from Rivercreek. After the death of Tip's brothers during the war, his parents had given up trying to work their farm unaided, Tip having shown no interest in anything close to hard work. Wanting only to have his share of the profits, he had bled the coffers dry until his parents had moved out and gone to live in the north of the province. Since then it had been untenanted.

'But surely it would have been the first place the police looked for him?'

Alice nodded. 'They've searched it dozens of times.

That's why he'll be there. He's always one step ahead. The police are sick of looking in the same places and finding nothing.'

'You've seen him, haven't you, Alice? Since that time he turned up at Duncan's, pretending to be Sandra's boyfriend? And since the night he burned down the barn.'

Alice nodded.

'So why didn't you tell the police?'

'I did tell them. I also told them he'd all but confessed to setting the fire. I ran into him on the outskirts of town. He was riding a powerful motorbike.'

'But why didn't you tell them to check his farm?'

'I did tell them, but he wasn't there. They convinced themselves he'd gone back over the border.' Her voice was full of irritation. 'Turn left here. The Howardson place is just past that stand of trees.'

Ethel swung the car round the bend and there it was. There were signs of neglect about the house and outbuildings, some of which were near derelict. Weeds clogged the pathways and farmyard as well as growing out of roofs and walls. There was no sign of human habitation. No smoking chimneys. No car. No motorcycle.

'Now what?' Ethel drummed her fingers on the steering wheel.

'Now you wait.' Alice opened the car door. 'Stay here. Don't move. Lock the doors. I'll be back soon. Trust me.'

Ethel's initial hostility towards Alice returned. The woman was so difficult. Ethel wished she hadn't agreed to come. She didn't trust her. How could she be sure Alice wasn't here to warn Tip, to help him escape? After all, she'd had a child with the man.

She looked at her watch. Five minutes. That's all she was giving her.

Looking around she saw the house must once have been a fine place, bigger than Hollowtree – bigger even than Rivercreek. A weather-beaten sign hung askew from a post – Thistledown Farm. A romantic name. A pretty name. Not at all what she'd have expected for the former home of a rotten crook.

One man. How many lives had he ruined or tried to ruin? Greg, Alice, Joan, Jim, Sandra – possibly Catherine, the poor child having to face the stigma of her parentage. His former American wife – the woman he was believed to have killed too. And who knew who else? Ethel wondered what it was that could make a man turn so thoroughly bad. Jim had told her that, while never popular as a kid, Howardson had shown no signs of the evil that was so evident in him now. The rest of his family had been well-liked and respected and the loss of his elder brothers in the war mourned by many.

Glancing at the wristwatch Duncan had given her as a wedding present, Ethel got out of the car. She walked in the direction she had seen Alice heading, towards a more modern aluminium-sided building – some sort of grain storage facility.

It was dark inside when she opened the door, and Ethel realised she was standing in the narrow inspection area of a grain elevator. A metal ladder rose up the side of the structure to the top of the vast vat that presumably was once used to hold grain. Her heart pounding, she called out Alice's name. Her voice echoed inside the metal building but was met with silence. She'd have a quick look inside the silo before returning to the car. At least she'd be able to see if it had been used as a hideout. It was unlikely he'd be there now but there might be something to indicate that he had been there.

Her eyes were gradually adjusting to the gloom, helped by a narrow crack in the sidings where daylight filtered though. She put her step on the bottom rung, took a big lungful of air, and legs trembling, began to climb up the ladder. It took a couple of minutes to reach the top. When at last she heaved herself up above the rim of the silo she saw it wasn't empty. The huge tank was about two-thirds full. A musty, yeasty smell rose up to her and she gagged. Glancing behind her when she heard a creaking noise, she saw the flare of a match striking. It lit up Tip Howardson's face, as he stood with one foot on the bottom of the ladder. Wordlessly, he put the cigarette to his lips and pulled the door closed behind him, pushing a metal barrel in front of it to block anyone else coming in. He began to climb after her.

Ethel's heart clenched in terror. If he was coming up here after her, there could only be one reason. Desperate, she struggled to see in the gloom, conscious of him moving closer, taking his time and pausing every couple of rungs to savour his cigarette. The ladder went down inside the silo and there was a corresponding one on the other side of the metal tank. It was her only hope. If she could get down there onto the top of the grain, get across it and climb up the other side she might be able to get out before he caught her.

She scrambled over the top, her last sight before she flung herself down the ladder inside, was Howardson tossing his butt down to the ground and moving up the ladder more rapidly. Her legs sank into the grain up to her calves and she struggled with every step, powered on only by her desire to stay alive and the adrenaline surging through her body.

The sound of someone rattling the door. Alice. But she'd never be able to open it with the metal barrel there. Ethel had to keep going.

She was halfway across when she felt the grain shift under her. Turning to look back she saw Howardson jump from the top of the ladder. He was only a few feet away from her. In the gloom she saw the flash of his teeth as he grinned at her. His arm went out to grab her and with an effort of will she lurched forward, hauling her feet out of the grain which clung to her and sucked at her legs like quick sand.

'Over here, Ethel!' Alice's voice pierced through the heavy air of the silo and, through the thick clouds of dust rising as she and Howardson disturbed the grain husks, she could sense Alice, invisible, at the top of the ladder on the other side of the tank. There must be another entrance.

Ethel started to move towards Alice's voice, then her heart jumped in her chest as Howardson's hand grabbed hers. His grip was a vice, cutting off her circulation, dragging at her, pulling her towards him. Stumbling, lungs bursting, she tried to break free, but the grain was slithering under her like molten ash, sucking her downwards, inescapable. Either Howardson would kill her, or the grain would pull her under, drawing her deep into the heart of the silo, suffocating the life out of her. With a superhuman effort, she jerked her hand away and pitched herself forward. Alice's fingers grasped at hers, the tips touching but too far for her to get a firm grip. Panic rose as the slippery grain drew her deeper downwards towards its core.

A terrible cry rose up and a chasm opened in the grain behind her. Where Howardson had been standing there was a vast cavity in the grain pile. She could see the top of his head and one hand in the air opening and closing as he desperately sought for something to hang onto. Ethel started to slide down the slope towards him, then her own hand was caught, and she was held back.

'Hold on. Don't let go.'

Ethel tried to push herself upwards, but the grain was rushing past her, sliding down towards the void that had swallowed Tip Howardson.

'Keep still or you'll make it worse. Don't struggle. Keep your head above the surface.'

Ethel's arm felt as though it was being torn from its socket. Behind her, Howardson's waving hand had disappeared under the grain.

Alice's voice again, from above. 'I'm going to throw you a rope.'

Ethel pitched forward again. It was like a different world, one without gravity, without air, without solid ground. Without all the things she had taken for granted. She resigned herself to her fate – to sliding down that giant pile of corn grains and letting it carry her away. She stopped struggling and closed her eyes.

The rope hit the side of her face and then rose back again. 'Catch it, Ethel. I'll try again.'

'It's no good. I'm sinking. I can't stop it.'

'You damn well will stop it, Ethel Robinson. I'm damned if I'm going to see you sharing a grave with that heap of shit. Now grab the goddam rope.'

Maybe it was Alice calling her by her new married name, her unaccustomed swearing, or the prospect of sharing her last moments on earth with Tip Howardson, but something took over Ethel so she found the strength to free her arm and grab hold of the rope next time it swung towards her. She twisted round and put her other hand on the rope.

'Slowly. Hand over hand. Pull yourself towards me.'

With a creaking noise the grain underneath Ethel collapsed, falling into what must have been a hollow space underneath it and the bottom of the silo. Ethel was pulled downwards but clung onto the rope. The grain tumbled past her, freeing her legs and leaving her clutching the rope and hanging in space. She almost lost her grip when the sudden disappearance of the grain sent her swinging back to crash into the wall, her bones smashing into the hard metal of the ladder.

'You're okay now, Ethel. Grab onto the ladder. It's about ten feet to the top. You're safe now.'

Summoning her last vestiges of strength and willpower, Ethel dragged herself up the metal ladder to the top of the silo. Alice helped her over the top onto the small wooden parapet which ran around the perimeter. Alice flung her arms round her and both women sobbed with relief. It was over.

They reached the firm ground at the bottom of the ladder, to hear the sound of a car engine and emerged in time to see Jim drive into the yard in his truck, with another man Ethel didn't recognise in the seat beside him.

Jim jumped down and ran towards them. 'What the hell are you doing here? You're taking a stupid risk. Howardson's probably armed and he knows how to use a gun.'

'It's all right, Jim.' Alice laid a hand on his arm. 'Tip's dead. His body is under a couple of tons of grain.'

'What happened?' Jim's eyes darted between the two women.

'He followed Ethel into the elevator. She's one brave strong woman. There must have been a bridge in the grain and when he stepped on it, it collapsed and took him with it. Almost took Ethel too.'

Ethel, still shaking, added, 'I'd have been sucked under if it hadn't been for Alice. She saved my life.' She turned to the woman she'd always mistrusted and flung her arms around her again. 'And I haven't even thanked you yet, Alice.'

Jim shook his head. 'Christ, Ethel, it's a miracle she was able to grab you. Once that grain gets a grip of someone it sucks them right under.'

Alice released herself from Ethel's embrace. 'There must have been another air pocket and that collapsed under Ethel but she was holding onto the rope so the train left the station without her.'

Jim grinned. 'And you managed to hold onto her?' His face was full of admiration. 'I always used to say you had the best biceps in the county.'

Alice swatted at him. 'Nothing to do with me. The rope was fixed to the wall behind me. All I did was pitch it. Ethel's the one who caught it and held on.'

The other man, who had gone into the elevator while they were talking, returned and said, 'Must be five tons in there. Looks like it's been lying there for years.'

It took over two hours for the elevator to be emptied and Tip Howardson's body recovered. Ethel and Alice stood side-by-side, watching while the grain was sucked out of the store and onto trucks using an auger and conveyor belt. Tip Howardson was lying on his back on the concrete floor, his mouth and nostrils filled with grain and his eyes open, staring in disbelief.

As the last grain truck and the ambulance pulled out of the Thistledown yard, bearing the body, Ethel began shaking and shuddering, despite the warmth of the afternoon.

Alice said, 'We need to get you home. I'll drive.'

Alice found a rug on the back seat of the car and wrapped it round Ethel's shoulders. Ethel turned to her. 'Thanks again, Alice. I owe you my life.'

Alice gave her a grim smile. 'I wasn't going to let him take you with him. And now at last I'll be telling the truth when I tell Catherine her daddy's dead.'

45

The months passed since Tip's attack, but Sandra refused to resume her duties at the surgery, telling her father she didn't want people to see her. Instead she spent most days closeted in her room and never crossed the threshold of the house, remaining upstairs until surgery was closed each day.

Nothing either Duncan or Ethel could say would change her mind. Shame enveloped her, and it was impossible to convince her that what happened was not her fault. She stayed inside the house, behind the closed door of the guest room she continued to occupy, still unable to enter her own bedroom. Usually she came downstairs for meals but was silent and ate little, picking at her food, head down.

Sandra's silent presence in the house was causing additional strain between Ethel and Duncan. Ethel was anxious anyway, it being six months since their marriage and she had not yet conceived. Whenever she voiced her worry, Duncan tried to reassure her that it was perfectly normal, but she had started to doubt that she would ever have a child.

Sometimes she asked herself how things had come to this.

Had she bitten off more than she could chew marrying a man with a grownup daughter beset with problems? After her reconciliation with Duncan, she had expected that marriage would bring her joy. Instead Duncan was morose and anxious about his daughter and Ethel felt like a failure every time her monthly period arrived. Sandra's gloomy presence didn't help matters. Only the salon and her growing friendship with Alice kept Ethel positive.

Mealtimes were tense, with Sandra barely speaking and Ethel feeling constrained by her stepdaughter's presence. Sandra's eyes were cold, dead pools, revealing no emotion, no expression.

'I don't know what to do,' Duncan said one evening, his face twisted with concern and worry. Sandra had left the table and returned to her room. 'She refuses to see a specialist. She's afraid they'll shut her up in a mental hospital and, to be honest, Ethel, she's probably right. There are new drugs in the offing but the standard response to any mental disorder is electroconvulsive therapy. How can I let them do that to Sandra?'

'But if it works? And it must work, or they wouldn't keep doing it?'

'I'm no expert in psychiatric medicine – just a journeyman quack – but I have serious doubts about the merits of that kind of treatment and no doubts whatsoever about the brutality of it. When I was doing my medical training, I had a few weeks working in a psychiatric hospital and I'll never forget what I saw there – people who had become withdrawn from the world, silent, locked inside themselves. And as for the treatments... The scientist in me tried to convince myself they were helping these poor unfortunates, but the human being struggled to believe it.'

'What did they do?'

'They strapped them down, gave them rubber mouth guards to bite on so they wouldn't bite off their own tongues, then attached metal discs to their heads and sent electric current through them.'

Ethel gasped.

'Watching them buck and twist as the shocks went through them. Brutal.'

'Did it work?'

'It appeared to. But I can't let them do that to Sandra. I just can't.'

He was bent forward, head in hands, his plate of food barely touched.

'What about medicines? You said there were new drugs?'

'I've been reading the journals – there are promising signs particularly for something called chlorpromazine but it's still being tested in Europe. Here it's electric shocks or nothing.' He raised his eyes to hers and Ethel saw the pain in them. 'Even if it works I can't put her through that. Not after everything else she's been through. After the trauma she experienced anyone would be suffering, regardless of their previous state of mind.'

Ethel moved over to stand behind Duncan and dropped a kiss on his head. 'We have to give her time. I know it sounds corny but it's true that time is the best healer. Sandra has been through a terrible experience, but things will improve for her. I know they will. We have to be patient.'

'I suppose at least we must be thankful that the bastard didn't make her pregnant. I couldn't have borne her having to face that.'

Ethel winced at this reminder of her own infertility.

That morning her period had arrived like clockwork to flout her hopes. She had sat in the bathroom, weeping.

She blurted out, 'My period came.'

Duncan's expression was sympathetic, but Ethel didn't want sympathy.

'Joan got pregnant with Jimmy the first time they ever did it.' Her lip trembled. 'And since then she's had no trouble at all – she even started with Donna while she was still breast-feeding Harry.'

'Everyone's different, Ethel. Don't compare yourself with Joan.'

'It's not just Joan. What about Alice? There must be something wrong with me.'

'There's nothing wrong with you. Apart from a complete lack of patience. Besides, it gives us plenty of excuse to keep trying.' He sat down and pulled her onto his knee.

'I know,' she said. 'But I feel like a failure.'

'How can you possibly be a failure, my love? You are never going to be a failure. If we don't have a child I will love you just as much.'

Ethel pushed him away and sprang to her feet. 'Oh yes, you would be happy. You never wanted me to have a baby in the first place.'

'Please, Ethel, don't dredge all that up again.' He reached for her hand. 'When I held Sandra in my arms for the first time it was one of the best moments of my life, so how could I not want to experience that feeling again? Especially with you, the love of my life.'

Ethel knew he was telling the truth. She could see the sincerity in his eyes. But she couldn't help the way she felt. It was a gnawing hollow inside her. Each month was like a bereavement – a loss of hope. Sex had become a means to an end for her – an end that never arrived. Instead of the pleasure and passion she had enjoyed with Duncan at the beginning, now she imagined that, each time, it would lead to a baby, and willed her body to make it happen. Making love had become a source of disappointed hopes and fading dreams. While she tried to disguise how she felt, she knew that Duncan must sense it. She was hurting him, but she couldn't help herself.

～

One afternoon, just as Ethel was applying the finishing touches to the last client of the day, the salon door jangled and Helga Armstrong walked in.

'You got time for one more?'

Ethel struggled to hide her astonishment. Helga, like many women of her age and background, kept her long greying hair in an untidy bun. Until now she had never shown any interest in hair styles or fashion.

'Of course.' She showed her to a chair. 'I'll be with you in just a few minutes.' She handed Helga a small pile of copies of *Chatelaine* and *The Canadian Home Journal* while she dealt with the departing client.

When Ethel was ready, Helga pointed at a photograph in *Chatelaine*. 'That's what I want. A permanent wave. Cut all this off.' She tugged at the pins holding her hair in place and let it cascade onto her shoulders.

Ethel, taken aback, said, 'It's rather late. A permanent wave takes a lot of time. How about I cut it and give you a shampoo and set? The set will last about a week. If you like the style, you can come in earlier one afternoon and I'll give you a perm. And if you don't like it we can try another style.'

Helga nodded. 'Can you make it look like that?' She prodded her finger at the page.

Ethel lifted a few strands of hair. It was heavy and would take a wave well. 'I'll do my best. As long as you're sure – last chance to change your mind before I get the scissors to it.'

'My mind was made up before I set foot in here.'

Ethel washed the woman's hair then set about cutting through the thick locks that reached almost to Helga's waist.

'Don wouldn't let me cut it.' She gave a dry chuckle. 'In his eyes, it was still the way it was when I was the girl who married him. I don't think he noticed it's been getting greyer every year for the past ten years.' She looked into the distance. 'He used to get me to unpin it at night. Drove me mad. He liked to see it spread all over the pillow.' She gave a little snort. 'I want it short. Something that's easy to manage and doesn't take a whole day to dry when I wash it.'

Ethel moved her hands over Helga's head, snipping and combing, as long thick strands of grey hair fell around them onto the floor of the salon.

As she began to curl the hair in the rollers, she saw Helga watching her in the mirror.

'You don't seem very cheery these days, Ethel. You look sad. Hope you don't mind me saying so.'

Ethel tried to craft her face into a smile. 'Oh, I'm fine.'

'Fine, fiddlesticks. If you don't want to talk about it, that's all right by me. It's none of my business, but I've always said, a trouble shared is a trouble halved – and maybe this old broiler hen might have some advice for you.' She looked at Ethel intently in the mirror.

'Maybe you're right. I was going to talk to Joan but every time I try something stops me.' She shook her head. 'I usually tell her everything. We've never had secrets before.'

Helga narrowed her eyes. 'Could that be anything to do with Joan being a human baby machine? Every time my son hangs his trousers over the end of the bed she gets in the family way.'

Ethel was shocked, then, unable to stop herself, began to giggle. 'I do feel rather inadequate in comparison. I keep hoping and praying, but it hasn't happened. I'm starting to think it never will. I hate to feel envious of Joan, but I can't help myself.'

'If you had a newborn, another still crawling and two boisterous boys, you might feel less inclined to envy her. Poor Joan's a slave to those kids.' Helga waved her arm around the salon. 'And you'd have to say goodbye to all this.'

'Not for ever. Just while the baby was small.'

'Babies are demanding creatures. You can't turn them on and off. And one has a tendency to follow another – before you know it, you've said goodbye to everything but being a mother.'

Ethel gulped. 'I can't stop thinking that Duncan is pleased I haven't managed to get pregnant. We fell out about it when we were on honeymoon. Now he says he does want a child but somehow I can't believe it.' As she spoke she felt guilty – it was a betrayal of Duncan. She wanted to take the words back. Why had she confessed all that? And to Helga Armstrong too, when she barely knew the woman.

Helga pursed her lips and studied Ethel in the mirror. 'It's causing tension between you, I'll bet?'

Ethel nodded, wordlessly.

'Don't tell the doc this, since he's a medical man, but I reckon the worst thing a couple can do when they want to have a baby is think about it too much. My mother used to say that getting all het up and bothered was the best way to make sure a baby didn't take. Getting anxious takes all the fun out of it and makes it harder. You've a better chance of getting a baby if you're relaxed.' She tapped Ethel's arm.

'Now don't you going telling your husband I said that. He'll tell you it's old wives' tales.' She winked at Ethel in the mirror. 'But old wives have been around in the world a lot longer than doctors have.'

'You mean you think me worrying about getting pregnant is making matters worse?'

The older woman nodded sagely. 'Forget about babies. You'll have more than enough time to think about them when they do come along. Just have fun and enjoy yourself.'

Ethel was blushing.

Helga narrowed her eyes and lowered her voice. 'You do have fun with the doc, I presume? Only you don't strike me as one of those prim and proper women who believe all pleasure is the work of the devil.'

Ethel could see in the mirror that her face was the colour of the Brylcreem advert on the page of the magazine in Helga's lap.

'I thought not,' Helga raised one eyebrow. 'I may not approve of those women who grant their favours too lightly, but when it comes to folk who are married, that's a different story. Some of the happiest times I've ever known have been spent in bed.'

Changing the subject, Helga pointed to her head where Ethel had now finished fixing the rollers. 'Now what?'

'Under the dryer.' Ethel pointed towards the pair of chromium dryer hoods on the opposite wall.

'Heavens preserve us. You don't expect me to sit under that thing, do you?'

'Afraid so. It won't take long and it's completely painless.'

'Don't you dare electrocute me, Ethel Robinson!'

Ethel grinned. 'I promise. I won't.'

Later, as Ethel was removing the rollers from Helga's dry hair, ready to brush out, Helga said, 'I haven't seen the doctor's daughter for a while. Joan told me what happened to the poor girl. God forgive me, but I hope Tip Howardson is burning in hell. Is the girl all right?'

Ethel nodded. 'She's a lot better than she was, but she won't go back to work. Duncan had to get someone else in to take care of the surgery. For weeks she shut herself in her room hardly eating or speaking.'

'I'm sorry to hear that. Can't say I knew the girl well, but I wouldn't wish what happened on anyone.'

'Things are getting a little better though. She joins us for meals and is making a real effort. She started to go out for walks and the exercise and being outdoors seems to be doing her good. I just wish she'd agree to go to university and make something of her life. It's so awful to think that because of Tip Howardson she's been reduced to this. And Duncan is worried sick about her.

That night, Ethel looked at her husband across the table as they ate dinner. Sandra had finished her meal, made her excuses and retired upstairs. Ethel noticed the deepened lines on Duncan's forehead, as she studied his face – the brown eyes that had exuded warmth now showed only pain.

He was avoiding her gaze. It dawned on her that this had become the norm between them. Once, they had locked eyes and seemed to drown in each other's. Now they avoided eye contact – as if they had each become like Sandra, focused inward, closed off from each other.

As these thoughts formed in her head, she remembered Helga's words: 'Have fun and enjoy yourself.' There hadn't been much joy in their marriage lately. Ethel remembered how she'd felt when her mother died. How lonely, how lost she had been. Frozen. Locked inside herself. Duncan had rescued her, loved her, thawed her, breathed life back into her. Loving Duncan had helped Ethel to like herself again. It had given her purpose in a world that, until then, had been bleak and full of pain and loss.

She put down her knife and fork. She wasn't going to let herself live that way again. She stood up. Duncan raised his eyes, surprised. Ethel went to the other side of the table and pulled him to his feet. He looked at her, and her stomach flipped over. Their eyes locked. Ethel twisted her fingers through his hair. 'Let's go to bed, Duncan,' she said.

He looked puzzled, glancing at the calendar on the kitchen wall. 'It's not an optimal day.'

'Every day is an optimal day.' She plucked the calendar off the wall and flung it on the fire. 'I love you, Duncan Robinson.'

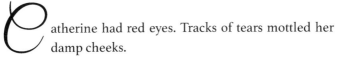

atherine had red eyes. Tracks of tears mottled her damp cheeks.

Alice dropped to her knees in front of her daughter and gathered her into her arms, cupping her head in her hand. 'What's wrong, baby? Tell Mommy what happened.'

The little girl began to shake, and Alice held her tight against her breast, fear, anger, and a desire to make everything better, coursing through her. She looked over Catherine's shoulder at Rose, who was leaning against the door, shamefaced and ashen.

'Rose? What happened? What's upset Catherine? Did someone hurt her?'

Catherine jerked her little body away and looked up at her mother, eyes anxious, afraid. 'I'm fine, Mommy. I just hurt myself falling over.'

Alice looked at Catherine, instinct telling her she was lying. She checked her daughter over and found no sign of any physical injury. Turning her attention to Rose, she said, 'Tell me right now, Rose. Why is Catherine crying?'

Rose scuffed her shoe against the floor. 'Some of the older girls were talking to her.'

A shard of ice ripped through Alice's insides. Her little girl was being bullied. And she could guess why.

'What did they say, baby? You can tell Mommy.'

'They said my daddy was a bad man and he's died and gone to hell.' Catherine began to sob. 'They said I'll be going to hell too.'

Alice lifted her eyes to Rose, who nodded, then began to cry herself.

For the first time in her life Alice had absolutely no idea what to do or what to say. She held Catherine against her, the little girl's tears dampening her blouse. She stroked her hair, desperately trying to think how to answer, how to make everything all right again.

Eventually, she picked her daughter up and carried her over to the settee, where she sat down with the child on her knee. She signalled to Rose to join them. Anger at the cruelty of those girls mingled with sorrow at the plight of Catherine, who was sniffing, lip quivering, nose running. Alice took a handkerchief from her pocket and wiped the little girl's eyes and nose. She took a deep breath and sent up a silent prayer for help.

'Sometimes when a good person makes bad choices they can turn into a bad person. When your daddy was young, he was a good boy, but somewhere along the way he made some choices that weren't the best ones. I didn't know that when I met him again when he was a grown-up.' She swallowed. This was coming out all wrong.

'But you said my daddy was already in heaven.'

Alice pushed her hair back from her eyes. Sometimes it was so hard being a husbandless mother. 'I said that because I didn't want you to be upset like you are now. I'm sorry, baby, I was only trying to protect you.'

She tried a different tack. 'I love you with all my heart and so does your sister, don't you, Rose?' Rose nodded but her face was closed, and Alice couldn't read it. The older girl was sitting as close to the edge of the sofa as she could go without slipping off.

Catherine gave a sob, then said, 'They told me my name isn't really Armstrong. They said it was something else. I can't remember what the name was, but I don't want it to be that, Mommy. I want to be the same as you and Rose.' Her voice was coming out in between sniffles and sobs and her little body was shaking. 'They said cos my daddy was bad that makes me bad too.'

'That's not true, Catherine.' Alice's voice was fierce – anger at those senseless girls rose up inside her until she could taste it in her mouth. 'Having a father who did bad things doesn't make you bad.' She sucked more air into her mouth then exhaled it slowly. 'My daddy, your grandfather, did a lot of bad things too but that doesn't make *me* bad, does it?' She looked into Catherine's teary eyes. 'Does it? You don't think Mommy's bad, do you, honey?'

'No.' Catherine's voice was hesitant.

'The man who was your father came from a good family. His mom and pop were good people and his brothers too. Every person is different, and nobody can be blamed for what their mommies and daddies did. It's all about making good choices not bad ones.' She gently pushed back a strand of hair from her daughter's face. 'You understand that, Catherine?'

The child nodded.

'And Mommy and Rose love you. And we'll always love

you, no matter what. And your name is Armstrong. Don't let anyone tell you otherwise.'

'But I want my daddy to be the same as Rose's.'

'Rose's daddy is in heaven, but I promise you, baby, if he were alive he'd love you just as much as I do, and he'd want to be your daddy too.' As she spoke, her own tears coursed down her cheeks.

Rose moved closer, then the three of them were hugging each other.

'We don't need daddies. We've got each other to look out for us, haven't we, girls?' Alice stroked Catherine's hair, feeling its fine silkiness under her fingers. 'Now you hold your head up high, Catherine Armstrong. You've got nothing to be ashamed of. Those girls are stupid and ignorant, and they'll soon wish they'd never said such bad things to you. What are their names, Rose?'

Rose told her.

'Right. Mrs Sanders at the school is going to hear about this and they're going to wish they'd never said anything.'

'No, Mommy.' Both girls spoke in unison.

'Please don't go to the school,' Rose added.

Alice thought for a moment. 'Those girls are always at the Saturday morning picture show. But not anymore. They won't be seeing any more *Lassie* films until they've apologised to Catherine. That'll teach them. They won't mess with the Armstrongs again!'

Before either girl could reply, there was a hammering at the door. When Alice opened it, Dr Robinson was standing there with his daughter beside him.

'Alice. I have some bad news for you. Your mother's in the hospital. I went to call on her this afternoon to check her blood pressure and found her collapsed on the kitchen floor. She's asked to see you.'

Alice made a little choking sound and turned to look towards the girls who were still sitting on the settee.

The doctor had his hand on his daughter's shoulder. 'It's Ethel's late night at the salon but Sandra will stay with the girls 'til you get back.'

Sandra nodded in confirmation but said nothing. She went over and sat between the two girls on the settee.

'Let me get my coat.' Alice returned and gave her daughters a hug, then, telling them to be good for Sandra, followed the doctor out of the house.

47

*A*lice was shocked by the sight of her mother. Ada Ducroix seemed to have shrunk in upon herself, her body taking up little space in the bed and the skin on her face and neck hanging loose, where the once plump flesh had melted away. The outline of her legs under the blankets showed that her ankles were severely swollen. Her eyes were shut but as Alice approached the bed she opened them.

'You came then.'

'Of course I came, Mom. The doc told me you're very poorly.' She stretched her hand out to touch her mother's and saw her mother was about to pull hers away but changed her mind. As Alice stroked her hand, Mrs Ducroix closed her eyes.

She opened them again, narrowing them as she looked at her daughter. 'You been paying that doctor?'

Alice nodded.

'Thank you for that. I can't afford to pay the hospital bill. That no-good father of yours has drunk all the money I had.'

'I know, Mom. You don't need to worry. I'm taking care of all that.'

Her mother pursed her lips but said nothing.

'I hear Tip Howardson got what was coming to him.'

Alice nodded again.

'Like your father.'

Alice was puzzled.

'I mean bad, not dead. Your father's still alive, more's the pity.'

'Has he been to see you here?'

Her mother gave a snort. 'What do you think?' She paused, gathering her breath. 'I was lying on that kitchen floor for more than a day 'til the doctor found me. Lord knows where your father is. Probably drunk in a ditch or a haystack somewhere.'

Alice continued to stroke her mother's hand. The skin was almost translucent and cold to the touch. A saline drip stood on the far side of the bed, the tube attached to the other arm. There was an oxygen cylinder behind it, connected to a mask which lay waiting, unused, on the bedcovers.

On the way to the hospital Dr Robinson had told Alice that her mother was severely dehydrated, and her blood pressure was dangerously high.

Alice said to her mother, 'The doctor says you haven't been taking the pills he gave you.'

'Pills?' She snorted derisively. 'Don't believe in pills.'

'You know better than the doctor then?'

Her mother shrugged. 'Everyone's time comes in the end.'

'Yes, Mom, but you're not done yet. The doctor says you'll be fine in a week or so. As long as you start taking the medication.'

'He would say that, wouldn't he? He gets paid for it.'

'Don't be cynical, Mom. The doctor brought me here and his daughter is at my place right now looking after the girls. He and his wife are good friends of mine. He cares.'

Ada pursed her lips but said nothing.

For about fifteen minutes they were silent, Alice stroking the back of her mother's hand as Ada Ducroix lay, eyes closed, apparently sleeping. It was not so long ago – only five years – that Alice and Rose would visit her mother regularly, enjoying picnics in the park and family trips to Freddo's for ice cream. Ada Ducroix had put a brave face on then, despite the drunkenness and occasional bouts of temper meted out by her husband. Looking at her mother now, Alice found it hard to credit that she was the same woman.

Her reverie was interrupted by her mother's voice. 'I hear that movie theatre is a big success.'

Alice sat upright, surprised. 'Better than I ever dreamed. A full house almost every night.'

'I should have come to see that film when you asked me. Missed my chance now.'

'There'll be other times, Mom. You're always welcome.'

Her mother studied Alice's face as though disbelieving her daughter. 'Anyways, I want you to know I'm proud of you, Alice. Proud of how you've managed since Walt died. Bringing up two daughters on your own. And making that place so popular.' She struggled for breath and Alice reached for the oxygen mask, but her mother brushed it away. 'Doc says you opened a hairdressing shop too. A real business woman.'

Tears stung Alice's eyes.

Her mother looked at her. 'I'd like to see the little one. Maybe you can bring the two of them to see me? I shouldn't have been so hasty saying what I did.' She paused to take more air into her lungs. 'I saw her, you know. I watched them coming out of school. Pretty little thing – Rose looks like Walt, but that little Catherine looks just like you. Made me remember when you were that age. Always bright as a button. Bring her to see me tomorrow. Both of them.'

'Oh yes, Mom. I'd like that. Very much.' She leaned forward and kissed her mother, noticing that her face was cold like her hands, yet her forehead was clammy.

Her mother grasped Alice's hand. 'Good. I was wrong to condemn you. I was bothered about what they'd say at church. That people would blame me. And then there was your father, too. He may be a drunk but he's a self-righteous drunk. He was angry you had a child out of wedlock.' Exhausted by the effort of speech, her mother closed her eyes again and drifted off to sleep.

Alice sat by the bedside holding her mother's hand, offering silent prayers of thanks that they were at last reconciled.

That night, Alice sat up late, drinking whisky with Sandra Robinson. When she had eventually returned home, she found Sandra had given the girls their supper and put them to bed. After checking her daughters were asleep and dropping a kiss on their foreheads, she went downstairs and found Sandra had made her a sandwich.

'Thank you. That was thoughtful. But I can't face food. I'm going to have a drink instead. Will you join me?'

'I don't drink.'

'Neither do I. Only under extreme circumstances but I can understand now how my late aunt got so fond of this stuff. It certainly helps to relax you.' She held up the bottle of whisky, before pouring herself an inch.

'How was your mother, Mrs Armstrong?'

'Call me Alice.' She swirled the amber liquor around in the glass and sipped it appreciatively. 'For years my mom didn't want anything to do with me. But we've reconciled.' She breathed out audibly. 'She looked so ill tonight I thought she was dying, but they say she'll make a full recovery. Funny how, even though I'd only seen her once in the past five and half years, losing her now would be a terrible loss. I suppose that's true of all mothers and daughters.'

Sandra made a strange sound and Alice looked up.

'Oh, I'm sorry, Sandra. Me putting my big foot in it as usual. I'd forgotten you lost your mother when you were a girl.'

'I was a baby. New born. And I didn't lose her. She killed herself.'

Alice gasped. She hadn't expected that.

'Dad doesn't think I know. He pretended she died giving birth to me. But I never believed that. Then I found out. She hanged herself.'

Alice was out of her depth. This was the first time she'd had any more than a brief exchange of words with Sandra Robinson – when she'd registered herself and the girls with the doctor. And she had no idea about what the young woman was telling her now, or even whether it was true or not. 'Are you sure you haven't got the wrong end of the stick?'

'I'm not an idiot.'

'Sorry, I didn't mean–'

'I overheard my grandparents talking about it when I was sixteen. Then I found the death certificate in the back of

Dad's sock drawer with a report on the inquest from the local newspaper.'

'Did you talk to your dad about it?'

Sandra shook her head rapidly, as if the very idea was anathema. 'No. He obviously didn't want me to know – and I didn't want him to find out I'd been snooping around.' She looked down, examining her bitten fingernails.

'It must have been a terrible shock to you.'

'Yes, it was.' Sandra's voice was flat, bland, expressionless, conveying none of the pain that must have beset her. 'Your little girl told me she was called names today at school. Because of *him*. That man.'

Alice nodded. Where was this leading?

'You got any lemonade?'

'Yes, you want some? Sorry, I should have offered.'

'I'd like to try some whisky with lemonade in it.'

Alice fixed the drink, liberal with the lemonade, thrifty with the scotch, and handed it to Sandra, who sipped it slowly.

'It's quite nice. Warms you up inside.'

'Look, Sandra, Ethel told me what happened to you with Tip Howardson, and I'm very, very sorry.'

'Stop saying you're sorry all the time. That's the fourth time.' Sandra laughed drily. 'Did he do that to you too? Did he hurt you?'

Alice shook her head. 'No, he didn't hurt me. But that was because I was willing. He did try to hurt Joan. Twice. He was a violent man.'

'It was the worst thing that ever happened to me. Worse than finding out what my mother did. I thought of doing what she did and killing myself. But I was too scared.' She sipped her whisky. 'I'm glad he died. Dad told me he was killed falling into a grain silo. He said you and Ethel were there.'

Mute, Alice nodded.

'I hope it was a horrible death. I hope he suffered. Today's the first time I've felt better since it happened. It's thanks to your little girl, Catherine. She told me she wasn't going to believe what those girls said about her being bad just because her father's bad. She made me realise I'm not going to be crazy just because my mother was. And I'm not going to let what that man did to me ruin my life. Not anymore.'

Alice gave Sandra's arm a little squeeze.

Sandra's voice was barely a whisper. 'I thought he loved me, you know. He said he wanted to marry me. But Dad said he wanted to marry you for your money.'

Alice winced. 'That's true. He certainly didn't feel anything for me. Ever.'

'But you had Catherine with him. Why?'

'I didn't plan to. It was a mistake. Tip could be very persuasive. And I was lonely.' She paused. 'A mistake but one I can't really regret because Catherine came out of it. And I'd do it all over again to have Catherine.'

Sandra was studying her face. 'Did you like what he did to you? Didn't he hurt you?'

'Sex is very different when you do it from choice, Sandra. He forced himself on you. That must have been horrible.'

'It was. I will never ever let a man come near me again.'

Alice winced. She tried to find the right words, but before she could answer, Sandra spoke again.

'Don't worry. I don't care about getting married. You manage well enough without a husband.' She swirled her drink around the tumbler and took a gulp to empty the glass. 'Can I have another please?'

Alice remembered how she used to feel about her late aunt's overindulgence with the whisky bottle, but then relented. They had both been through a lot. Sandra may be on the brink of breaking through her self-enforced withdrawal from life. She poured the whisky, refreshed her own glass, then settled down to continue the conversation.

After the weeks of silence, the floodgates had opened, and Sandra wanted to keep talking. Alice settled back and listened as the young woman spoke about her feelings of both loss and resentment towards the mother she had never known, her discomfort about sharing her home with her father and Ethel. 'Not that Ethel's done anything wrong – I can see how much she and Dad love each other. And I like her. But I feel awkward. They don't need me around. So, I'm going to go.'

'Where?'

'I don't know. I suppose to university.' Her voice betrayed her lack of enthusiasm. 'Dad always wanted me to study medical sciences. I used to be scared at the idea of going away. Of being with a lot of strangers. But now it's different. Nothing can ever be as bad as what's already happened to me.'

'But do you *want* to go to university?'

'Not really. But I can't stay here. Not with everyone knowing what he did to me.'

'Look, Sandra, Hollowtree's your home. You don't have to go away if you don't want to.' Alice clasped her hands together. 'Tip Howardson caused me to run away from here, but I decided I was going to come back. I thought everyone was talking about me, so I thought I'd give them something else to talk about. Now they talk about what a great thing

The Rose is. I really believed everyone had forgotten about Catherine being illegitimate, until today. But you've helped her, Sandra. I'm grateful for that and I'm not running away any more. My girls and I are going to keep our heads high in Hollowtree and I defy anyone to whisper about us. The same goes for you.'

Sandra huffed. 'I don't have a movie theatre and a hair salon to keep people happy. Or a lot of money in the bank.'

Alice swallowed – Sandra didn't hesitate to say what she thought. 'Maybe not. But you've done nothing wrong. *Nothing*. People will only feel sympathy for what happened to you.'

'I don't want their sympathy. Or their pity.'

'Then show them you don't need it. Just like I did.'

Sandra shrugged, her face doubtful.

'Look, I have an idea. You've plenty of experience running your father's surgery–'

'I'm not going back to that. Anyway, he's got someone else now. I'd be doing her out of a job.'

'Come and work for me.' Alice was excited. 'I need someone to handle all the administration. It's getting too much for me – and I want to start some new businesses – a dress shop – and I'm investing in Jim Armstrong's new maple syrup production – so I need help to keep on top of things. My lawyer is marvellous, but I need someone on the spot. Someone here in Hollowtree.' She took another sip of her scotch. 'And I think we'd get on well, Sandra. We have a lot in common.'

'I don't know... I want to get away from Dad and Ethel.'

'I can help you with that too. There's the apartment over the hair salon. It's empty and you could move in right away.'

Sandra looked uncertain. 'But–'

Alice thumped the arm of her chair. 'Even better! You

can move in here with us. The girls like you. They must do if they told you what happened today – and you got them settled in bed, which is quite a feat.'

'I get on better with children than adults. I don't feel they're judging me.'

'And I could do with the company too. What do you think?'

'You mean it? You're not just being polite?'

'I'm never just being polite – as you'll learn soon enough if you do come to live here.'

'Then, yes!' Sandra grinned, and Alice realised it was the first time all evening the girl had cracked a smile.

Alice leaned forward and chinked glasses. 'It's a deal then! You want to move in tomorrow?'

48

The annual Hollowtree barn dance at the Lonsdale place, the largest and most prosperous farm in the district, was an event almost the whole town attended. Four years ago, the Lonsdale family switched the date to early September to coincide with the peak harvest period, instead of November before the snow came.

Ethel had never been to a barn dance before and knew it would be packed. The thought of being stuck all evening in a crowded noisy space made her queasy, but she'd promised Joan and Alice that she'd be there.

Across the landing, she could hear Duncan playing the piano. It was a gentle and lyrical piece that made her think nostalgically of England before the war. He'd told her it was called 'To a Wild Rose' and was by an American composer. As she listened, she tried to imagine how her life would have been had she stayed in Aldershot – stuck in the salon listening to *Music While You Work* or eating a solitary Sunday dinner with *Educating Archie* on the wireless.

Her dress was laid out on the bed. Before long she wouldn't be able to fit into it. She stepped into it and pulled it up over her shoulders, then went into the other room. 'Can you zip me up, darling?'

Duncan spun round on the piano stool. 'Wow! Just wow!' he said. 'You sure you wouldn't rather stay home?' He was smiling broadly.

Tempting as the prospect of an evening alone with her husband was, Ethel twisted round so he could zip the dress up. He planted a kiss on the back of her neck and then took a step back to look at her. 'There'll be a lot of men with their eyes on stalks tonight when you walk into that barn.' He pulled her into his arms and kissed her gently, his eyes fixed on hers. 'I'm glad I'm the one that gets to go home with you.'

'I love you, Dr Robinson,' she said. 'Thank you for marrying me.'

'Once I'd set eyes on you, Ethel, no one was ever going to stop me. I'm the luckiest man in the world.'

Alice had reluctantly suspended the picture show at The Rose that night, knowing few people would turn up. For a while she'd toyed with the idea of screening an unmissable film for one night only to compete with the barn dance. She'd established a strong relationship with the distributors and was confident that she could secure a special one-night-only screening of *White Christmas*, the current big box office draw. But she'd gain more goodwill from the townspeople by avoiding them having to choose between the tradition of the local dance and the excitement of the latest top billing movie.

All the same, Alice was ambivalent about going to the barn dance. Her last Lonsdale dance had triggered her decision to leave for Ottawa, when Tip Howardson refused to marry her after she told him she was pregnant with Catherine. At an earlier barn dance, fourteen long years ago, Alice's husband, Walt, had broken the news to her that he was joining the army and following his brother Jim to Europe. No, the annual dance was not a source of happy memories for Alice. But she'd promised Joan and Ethel to go along and wouldn't let down her friends.

Catherine and Rose came into her bedroom, eager to see what their mother would wear, before she drove them over to Joan's place where Helga was going to babysit. Last time, in the early stages of pregnancy, she'd struggled to squeeze into her old yellow dress at Rose's insistence and had felt frumpy in comparison with Joan. Tonight, she had no such problems. Her dress shop meant that she was never in short supply of something to wear, and Alice had developed a love for fine clothing.

'Wear the red one, Mommy!' Catherine was bouncing up and down on the bed.

Rose ran her fingers over a blue silk taffeta gown – a full skirt with a cinched waist. 'I like this one best.'

'I'll try them both on.'

As she slipped on the blue gown, she knew she looked good, the dark blue setting off her blonde hair.

Rose bent over Alice's jewellery box and produced a gold necklace with a single pearl droplet. 'Wear this. The one Daddy gave you.' She knelt on the bed as Alice sat down so she could fasten it round her mother's neck.

If only Walt were still around to see her. She could imagine his long whistle of appreciation, but Alice had to settle for her daughters telling her that she looked as beautiful as a movie star.

~

The barn was buzzing when Joan and Jim arrived with Alice. A band of musicians – a guitarist, a double bass player, a drummer, a banjoist and a couple of fiddlers – were playing fast and furious, and the dance floor was packed. Freddo from the café was calling the steps and the room was a whirl of sweeping skirts and whoops of delight. While many of the men were dressed in farm overalls or blue jeans, most of their wives and girlfriends had taken advantage of Ethel's hairdressing services, and Alice's dress shop must have been doing a brisk trade. Joan had never seen such a well-turned-out group of women in Hollowtree.

She remembered her first barn dance when she had stuck out from an under-dressed crowd, wearing her red polka dot dress – now turned into cushion covers as, three more babies later, she was no longer able to squeeze herself into it. Tonight, she was wearing a pair of slacks and a checked blouse with a scarf tied loosely round her throat – these days comfort was her ruling influence.

That first dance was not a happy memory for Joan. She tried not to think about Howardson attempting to rape her in the stable and Jim attacking him with a frenzied violence that had terrified her. Shuddering, she pushed the recollection from her head. Howardson would never harm anyone again and Jim's terrible wartime experiences no longer troubled and disturbed him.

Alice had disappeared into the crowds, so Joan leaned back against a hay bale and watched the proceedings, reflecting how much impact Alice had made on the town in such a brief time, Ethel too. Thank goodness she'd finally persuaded her to come to Canada. Joan winced to think of what Ethel would be doing had she stayed in Aldershot, lonely and slaving away for buttons in Vera's scruffy old hair salon, instead of being happily married to Duncan and running her own business.

The war had been a grim time and had destroyed so much and so many, but Joan had to admit it had brought only good things to her. Without it she would never have met Jim, neither she nor Ethel would have come to Canada, and her children would never have been born.

She looked up and saw Ethel and Duncan entering the barn. Her cousin looked stunning in a sizzling pink dress and was drawing appreciative glances from all the men in the room as she made her way, smiling, towards Joan. Duncan said something to her, kissed her quickly and moved over to the drinks table where Jim and a number of other men were gathered.

'Where's Alice?' Ethel asked after giving Joan a hug.

'Somewhere around. She came with us.'

Jim and Duncan arrived, bearing glasses of fruit punch for the women, then retreated to the makeshift bar to resume the pressing business of discussing the latest results in the ice hockey league.

Alice appeared. 'How come the handsome doc isn't giving you a spin round the dance floor, Ethel?' Alice nudged her in the ribs.

'I'm not in the mood for dancing tonight.'

'For goodness' sake, Ethel. Enjoy yourself. It's great fun and Freddo's calling all the steps out. You'll pick it up right away.' Joan sipped her drink. 'Not like you to be a wallflower.'

Ethel blushed. 'I told you – I'm not in the mood at the moment.' Then, before either woman could press her further, she turned to Alice. 'How's it working out with you and Sandra? Must be six months now?'

'Eight. And we're getting along just fine. The girls adore

her, I enjoy her company – and she's doing a great job for the business. My lawyer is impressed with her bookkeeping and organisation skills – and that's saying something.'

'I'm so glad,' said Ethel. 'There was a point when we thought she'd never get over what happened to her.'

'Sandra's a strong woman. Much more resilient than she appears. And she and I have discovered we have quite a lot in common.' Alice pointed across the room. 'She's over there.'

Ethel and Joan turned to look. Sandra was standing by the refreshment table, deep in conversation with a young bespectacled man.

'The new librarian,' said Alice. 'I wondered why Sandra was reading so many books lately. Looks like there may be a blossoming romance there.'

'Gosh, I hope so,' said Ethel.

'If anyone deserves to be happy it's that kid. She's not an easy person to like though.'

'She's a bit like whisky. She improves with acquaintance,' said Alice and laughed. 'Never thought I'd develop a fondness for hard liquor. But unlike my dear old aunty, I save it for moments of severe need and fortunately I haven't had any of those lately.'

The music was getting louder, competing with the noise of the crowd.

'Let's go outside for a while so we can hear ourselves speak,' Joan suggested.

The three women sat down on the edge of an old wooden cart that stood just across the barnyard. The sky was tinged with pink and the evening still warm. They sat in a companionable silence, watching as the sun went down, the sky darkened, and the stars came out.

Ethel's voice broke the quiet. 'I wasn't going to say

anything yet, but I want the two of you to be the first to hear our news.'

Joan gasped. 'No!'

'Yes!'

'Oh, my goodness. You're expecting a baby, Ethel?' Alice grabbed at Ethel's arm.

'Next spring. March. I'd given up hoping and thought it would never happen.' She gave them a wide grin. 'It must have been our anniversary trip in June to Muskoka. Maybe because we were both relaxed and having such a wonderful time. Helga once told me it was fatal to worry too much about not getting pregnant. Looks like she was right.'

'She usually is.' Joan and Alice spoke in unison then both flung their arms around their friend.

'Ease off, girls. You're squeezing me to death,' Ethel said with a laugh.

'That's the best news I've heard in a long time.' Joan beamed at her.

Ethel, in the middle, linked arms with her friends. 'I'll be looking for tips from the pair of you. Frankly, now that it's happening, I'm scared to death.'

'How does Duncan feel about becoming a father again?' Joan asked.

'He's thrilled. Nervous. But excited. It's going to be a big change for both of us.' She turned to Alice. 'Don't worry about the salon, Alice. The new girl has come on in leaps and bounds since she started and she's handling her own clients already. She'll keep the ship afloat while I'm off. And I'm going to take on a new junior to train next week.'

'You're surely not intending to go back to work after you've had the baby?' Joan looked aghast.

'Why not?'

'Rather you than me!' Joan pulled a face.

'That's rich coming from you, Joanie. When has a day gone by that you haven't worked? And you have four of them!'

'I defy anyone to work as hard as you do, Joan,' Alice put in. 'You were out in the fields helping plant the spring barley when Sam was just three months old. Not to mention doing your share of the maple syrup with Ma.'

Joan shrugged. 'Well, I do know that trying to stop Ethel doing hair is like trying to stop the tide coming in. Ever since she was tiny and doing her dolls' hair, it's been impossible to prise a comb out of her hands.'

Alice laughed.

Ethel wondered how she'd ever disliked her. Alice was often tactless, sometimes thoughtless, but always with a big heart. And since that day when she'd thrown her a rope to save her life, Alice could do no wrong as far as Ethel was concerned. 'All we need now is for *you* to meet someone nice, Alice,' she said.

'Yes. We need you to find happiness too,' said Joan.

'I *have* found happiness. Life is good. I'm happy with my girls. I love my work. I'll always miss Walt but I'm not looking for anyone else. I don't need a man to define my happiness for me. That's one thing I've realised about myself. And I have my Aunt Miriam to thank for that.'

Alice jumped to her feet. 'If neither of you are going to dance, I'm going to steal one – or maybe both – of your husbands to help me strip the willow.' She winked at them and headed back into the barn.

Joan reached for Ethel's hand. 'We've come a long way haven't we, cuz? Remember that night in the snug at the Stag when I first met Jim and you met Greg? It feels as if we were completely differently people then.'

Ethel laughed. 'Our lives were measured out in bitter

shandies and the occasional port and lemon. We *were* different people. You were in uniform for a start. And I was slaving away in that horrible munitions factory.'

Joan laughed. 'And Aunty Vi used to insist on you being home by eleven.'

'The horrors of waiting for the last bus in the blackout.' Ethel looked thoughtful. 'I did love Greg, but you're right, I was a different person then. It's hard to imagine how that person felt, when I'm so happy now.'

'No regrets about me insisting on you coming to Canada?'

Ethel looked up at the full harvest moon. 'Oh, Joanie, how could I? You changed my life – no – you saved my life – just as much as Alice did.'

The cousins sat, side-by-side, reflecting on their past, grateful for the present and looking forward to the future.

THE END

A word from Clare Flynn

These days, everyone from the barista serving your coffee to the plumber mending a leaking pipe asks for a review. And it can get wearisome!

Authors are no different – but after months or years of research and writing and providing hours of reading pleasure for readers, I hope you'll understand why we ask.

Reviews help readers to discover good books. They also influence retailers and promoters to feature the book if it has garnered a good quantity of reviews.

No need to write a lot – a rating and a few words to say why you liked it (or not) on the retailer site where you bought the book – or on GoodReads– is all that's required! And it is hugely appreciated by me (and by any author!).

If you're a book blogger, send me a link to your review and I'll share it on social media.

Many thanks and happy reading

Clare Flynn

GET A FREE EBOOK FROM CLARE

If you enjoyed *The Frozen River* why not sign up for my monthly newsletter? I'll keep you posted about progress on upcoming books, share exclusive offers, prizes, cover reveals, location reports, information about upcoming price promotions, special news etc.

As a thank you, you'll get a free download of my short story collection, *A Fine Pair of Shoes and Other Stories.*

To sign up and get your free book click here or go my website clareflynn.co.uk

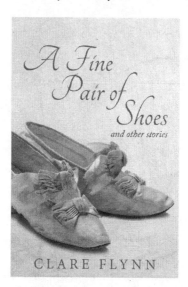

A Tapestry of True Tales from Then and Now

ACKNOWLEDGMENTS

My thanks to my wonderful editor, Debi Alper, who never stints in pushing me to do the best I can. To the talented Jane Dixon-Smith who has dreamed up another beautiful cover design for me and to Helen Baggott, my proofreader.

I am so lucky to have found my posse of Canadian former librarians, Peter Monahan, Janine Harris-Wheatley and Adelaide Campbell. All of them live in Ontario and have been a fantastic source of information and always ready to answer my questions about anything from ice hockey to licensing laws and Christmas menus. Thanks especially to Peter for reading the draft – any errors are mine not his. And to Hilary Bruffel for introducing me online to these amazing people!

To Clare O'Brien, Susanna Sewell and Debbie Marmor for your great comments and insights on the first draft. Thanks also to Jessica Nye for her insights into mental health. To my Eastbourne critique group – Margaret Kaine, Maureen Allingham, Jill Rutherford and Jay Dixon.

I'd also like to acknowledge the growing number of

readers who keep on reading and enjoying my books. I love getting your emails, hearing about your lives and reading your reviews. You are why I love my life as a writer! Thank you.

ALSO BY CLARE FLYNN

The Chalky Sea - The Canadians I

The first novel in The Canadians trilogy is the story of Englishwoman, Gwen, on the Home Front in a seaside town, under siege from the Luftwaffe. And of Jim, a Canadian soldier, who volunteered to fight so he could escape from a traumatic experience – only to get caught up in worse ones.

The Alien Corn - The Canadians II

Set in Canada, where Joan, a war bride, struggles to adapt to a new way of life, an unwelcoming mother-in-law and a husband still haunted by his terrible wartime experiences on the Italian front.

The Gamekeeper's Wife

A gripping story of love, duty, sacrifice and determination in the aftermath of the First World War. Two people from different classes and different worlds were never meant to fall in love...

The Green Ribbons

Hephzibah Wildman's life is dramatically changed when her parents die in a tragic accident. Homeless and penniless, she must now face the challenge of finding her way alone in the world as a governess.

Letters from a Patchwork Quilt

Two young lovers in late Victorian England are torn apart by fate and the Catholic Church. Each copes with what faces them in a very different way. "A heartbreaking and moving tale" *Readers' Favorite*

Kurinji Flowers

Marriage to a man she barely knows. Exile to a country she doesn't know at all

An emotional love story set in the last days of colonial India

A Greater World (Across the Seas Book 1)

"A dramatic story of finding yourself and the one you love". Two people forced to flee home and country to build a new life on the other side of the world in Australia.

Also in Audiobook

Storms Gather Between Us (Across the Seas Book 2)

A compelling story of love, strife and the power of determination. "Great writing, well drawn characters, enough action and description to keep the reader turning the pages" Sally Stackhouse

Also in Audiobook

Sisters at War (Across the Seas Book 3)

1940 Liverpool. The pressures of war threaten to tear apart two sisters traumatised by their mother's murder by their father.

With her new husband **Will**, a merchant seaman, deployed on dangerous Atlantic convoy missions, **Hannah** needs her younger sister **Judith** more than ever. But when Mussolini declares war on Britain, Judith's Italian sweetheart, **Paolo** is imprisoned as an enemy alien, and Judith's loyalties are divided.

Each sister wants only to be with the man she loves but, as the war progresses, tensions between them boil over, and they face an impossible decision.

A heart-wrenching page-turner about the everyday bravery of ordinary people during wartime. From heavily blitzed Liverpool to the terrors of the North Atlantic and the scorched plains of Australia, Sisters at War will bring tears to your eyes and joy to your heart.

COMING SOON AS AN AUDIOBOOK

The Pearl of Penang

Winner of the 2020 BookBrunch Selfies Award for Adult Fiction;

Discovering Diamonds Book of the Month

"Following the death of my wife, I am in need of support and companionship. I am prepared to make you an offer of marriage."

Flynn's tenth novel explores love, marriage, the impact of war and the challenges of displacement – this time in a tropical paradise as the threat of the Japanese empire looms closer.

ALSO AVAILABLE AS AN AUDIOBOOK narrated by Victoria Riley

A Prisoner from Penang

After Penang is attacked by the Japanese at the end of 1941, Mary Helston believes Singapore will be a safe haven. But within weeks the supposedly invincible British stronghold is on the brink of collapse to the advancing enemy.

Mary and her mother are captured at sea as they try to escape and are interned on the islands of Sumatra. Imprisoned with them is Veronica Leighton, the one person on the planet Mary has reason to loathe with a passion.

As the motley band of women struggle to adapt to captivity, relationships and friendships are tested. When starvation, lack of medication and the spread of disease worsen, each woman must draw on every ounce of strength in their battle for survival.

A vivid and moving story of sacrifice, hope and humanity.

"In this testament to the strength of female friendship and endurance under the harshest of conditions, Flynn has imagined the unimaginable - a dazzling achievement." Linda Gillard, Author of *The Memory Tree* and *House of Silence*

ALSO AVAILABLE AS AN AUDIOBOOK narrated by Victoria Riley

A Painter in Penang

Sixteen-year-old Jasmine Barrington hates everything about living in Kenya and longs to return to the island of Penang in British colonial Malaya where she was born. Expulsion from her Nairobi convent school offers a welcome escape – the chance to stay with her parents' friends, Mary and Reggie Hyde-Underwood on their Penang rubber estate.

But this is 1948 and communist insurgents are embarking on a reign of terror in what becomes the Malayan Emergency. Jasmine goes through testing experiences – confronting heartache, a shocking past secret and danger. Throughout it all, the one constant in her life is her passion for painting.

A dramatic coming of age story, set against the backdrop of a tropical paradise torn apart by civil war.

"A moving, poignant, involving read." Author Lorna Fergusson

"If you like well-researched historical sagas with depth, you will enjoy this." Deborah Swift, Author of *The Occupation*

"The PENANG trilogy is a testament to human endurance, the triumph of the spirit, but above all, to the love of family and friends." Amazon reviewer

ALSO AVAILABLE AS AN AUDIOBOOK narrated by Victoria Riley

ALL THREE PENANG NOVELS also available as a 3-book digital collection at all retailers and as an audiobook collection.

ABOUT THE AUTHOR

Clare Flynn is the author of nine historical novels and a collection of short stories. After a career in marketing and strategic consulting that took her all over the world, she now lives by the sea in Sussex. When not writing she loves to paint and play the piano – as well as quilt – but increasingly struggles to find time for any of these pursuits!

If you would like to know more about Clare and her books get in touch with her via any of these – she loves to hear from readers.

facebook.com/authorclareflynn

twitter.com/clarefly

instagram.com/clarefly

bookbub.com/authors/clare-flynn

Made in the USA
Columbia, SC
16 August 2024